THE HOUSE OF DEATH

THE HOUSE OF DEATH

Peter Tremayne

**SEVERN
HOUSE**

First US edition published in the USA in 2021
by Severn House, an imprint of Canongate Books Ltd,
14 High Street, Edinburgh EH1 1TE.

Trade paperback edition first published in the USA in 2022
by Severn House, an imprint of Canongate Books Ltd.

severnhouse.com

British Library Cataloguing-in-Publication Data
A CIP catalogue record for this title is available from the British Library.

ISBN-13: 978-0-7278-8965-2 (cased)
ISBN-13: 978-1-4483-0568-1 (trade paper)
ISBN-13: 978-1-4483-0567-4 (e-book)

All Severn House titles are printed on acid-free paper.

MIX
Paper from
responsible sources
FSC® C013056

Typeset by Palimpsest Book Production Ltd.,
Falkirk, Stirlingshire, Scotland.
Printed and bound in Great Britain by
TJ Books, Padstow, Cornwall.

For Susanna Kleeman
Welcome to the crazy world of authorship.

A Findias tucadh claidhim Nuadad; ní thernadh nech uadha;
o dobertha as a intig bodba, ní gebtha frís.

From Findias was brought the sword of Nuada; no one would escape from it; when it was drawn from its battle-scabbard, there was no resisting it.

Lebor Gabála Érenn, twelfth century

PRINCIPAL CHARACTERS

Sister Fidelma of Cashel, a *dálaigh* or advocate of the law courts of 7th-century Ireland
Brother Eadulf of Seaxmund's Ham, in the land of the South Folk, her companion

At Cashel
Colgú, King of Muman and brother to Fidelma
Finguine, Prince of Glendamnach, *rodamna* or heir apparent
Dar Luga, *airnbertach* or housekeeper of the royal palace
Fíthel, Chief Brehon of Muman
Abbot Cuán, of the Abbey of Imleach, and Bishop of Cashel
Brother Conchobhar, an apothecary
Brother Laig, a physician
Brother Fidach, a chaplain
Brother Dáire, a librarian
Cainder, a kitchen maid
Sister Ernmas

Warriors of the Nasc Niadh or Golden Collar
Gormán, reappointed commander of a *catha,* or battalion, of Colgú's warriors
Enda, commander of the *lucht-tighe*, or household guard
Luan, a warrior
Dego, a warrior

In Cashel township
Rumann, a tavern owner
Della, Fidelma's friend and mother of Gormán
Aibell, Gormán's wife
Gobán, a smith

Princes and guests at Cashel
Elódach, Prince of the Eóganacht Áine

Congal, Prince of the Eóganacht Loch Léin
Furudrán, Prince of the Eóganacht Airthir Chliach
Moncha, his wife
Selbach, Prince of the Eóganacht Ráithlinn
Blinne, his wife
Esnad, companion to Blinne
Donennach, Prince of the Uí Fidgente
Céit, son of Conmael, his bodyguard
Conrí, warlord of the Uí Fidgente

At Ráth na Drínne
Ferloga, the tavern-keeper
Lassar, his wife
Echdae, a wagoneer from Dairinis

At Cluain Meala
Arard, *bo-aire* or magistrate

Also mentioned
Prince Cummasach of the Déisi

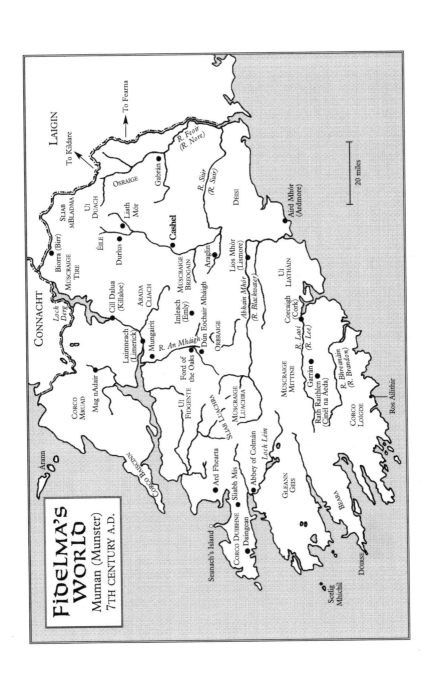

FIDELMA'S WORLD
Muman (Munster)
7TH CENTURY A.D.

LAIGIN

To Kildare

To Fearna

CONNACHT

OSRAIGE

R. Feoir
(R. Nore)

Gabrán

SLIAB
MBLADMA

UÍ
DUACH

R. Siúr
(R. Suir)

DEISI

Biorra (Birr)

Liath
Mór

MUSCRAIGE
TÍRE

Cashel

Aird Mhór
(Ardmore)

Loch
Derg

Durlus

ÉLE

Araglin

Lios Mhór (Lismore)

Cill Dalua
(Killaloe)

ARADA
CLIACH

Imleach
(Emly)

MUSCRAIGE
BREOGAIN

Dún Eochair Mháigh

Abhain Mhór
(R. Blackwater)

UÍ
LIATHÁIN

Corcaigh
(Cork)

Mag nAdair

Luimneach
(Limerick)

Mungairit

R. An Mháigh

ORBRAIGE

R. Laoi
(R. Lee)

CORCO
MRUAD

UÍ
FIDGENTE

Ford of
the Oaks

MUSCRAIGE
LUACHRA

MUSCRAIGE
MITTINE

Garrán

Arann

SLIAB LUACHRA

R. Bhreanáin
(R. Brandon)

Ráth Raithlen
(Cinél na Aeda)

CORCO BAISCINN

Ard Fhearta

Sliabh Mis

Abbey of Colmán

Loch Léin

CORCO
LOIGDE

Ros Ailithir

Seanach's Island

Corco Duibhne

Daingean

GLEANN
GEIS

BEARA

20 miles

DOIRSE

Scelig
Mhichil

AUTHOR'S NOTE

This story takes place in the latter days of the month known in ancient Ireland as *Giblean*, the month of the geese flying north. In the modern calendar, this would be April. The year is AD 672. The following month of *Cét Samhain* (May), the first month of summer, is fast approaching. That was when the Feast of Beltaine, the Fires of Bel, was celebrated throughout each of the five kingdoms of Éireann. It was a mystical time when certain rituals from the ancient pagan past were still performed. This was the festival marking the end of the dark half of the year, a time when all fires had to be extinguished and then ritually rekindled from the rays of the sun. It had been a Druidic festival that the new Christian Faith could never suppress and so it was incorporated in accordance with Pope Gregory the Great's advice to Bishop Mellitus when he set out as a missionary to Britain in AD 601. May Day still remains a day of celebration.

For the kingdom of Muman (today's Irish province of Munster) it was a time when King Colgú's *ceithirfine*, consisting of the seven leading Eóganacht princes, met in council to voice any criticism of the King's leadership. If his decisions were approved, the council culminated with the handing of the sacred sword of the old god Nuada to the King, who raised it to verify he was a just and rightful ruler. The seven Eóganacht princes listed in the earliest genealogies are discussed in Professor Francis J. Byrne's seminal work *Irish Kings and High-Kings* (1973). These were Eóganacht Chaisil (Cashel), Eóganacht Áine, Eóganacht Loch Léin, Eóganacht Glendamnach, Eóganacht Árann, Eóganacht Ráithlinn and Eóganacht Aithir Chliach. I have followed the argument that the Eóganacht Ruis Argait were added much later when they moved from Osraige and eventually disappeared from history.

Professor Byrne presents the argument that the Déisi and Uí Liatháin were considered unconnected with the Eóganacht but related to the Uí Fidgente. However, in an eighth-century text, popularly known as 'The Expulsion of the Déisi', the scribe makes the claim that they had a common descent with the Eóganacht but the rejection of this claim by the Eóganacht princes was a factor in the animosity between them.

Chronologically, this story follows on from the events in *The Shapeshifter's Lair*, after Fidelma and her companions have returned to the royal fortress of Muman following the rescue of the Princess Gelgéis so that she could then marry Fidelma's brother, King Colgú.

It has never been my practice to instruct readers on Irish pronunciation, especially the Irish of Fidelma's period, known as Old (Classical) Irish. On the website of The International Sister Fidelma Society is a brief guide to pronunciation based on English phonetics. In this case, and because it does not follow usual rules, I give the pronunciation in English phonetics for the name of the apothecary Brother Conchobhar – *kru-húr*.

The adventure in which Fidelma recovered the sword of the High King Sechnussach mac Blathmaic (AD 665–671) is recounted in the short story 'The High King's Sword' in *Hemlock at Vespers* (1999). My thanks to David R. Wooten for advice on the practical aspects of the sacred sword of Nuada.

ONE

Fidelma halted her grey-white Gaulish pony on top of a slight rise along the broad track. The track led across the low, level plain, which stretched south like a green carpet towards the imposing limestone thrust that dominated the area. No matter how many times she approached her brother's fortress, rising on that towering rock, she found that she had to pause a moment to take in its awesome beauty. Each time she felt an empathy with her ancestor, Conall Corc, who, centuries before, had decided to make it the capital of his kingdom of Muman. Muman was now the largest and most south-westerly of the five kingdoms of Éireann.

Fidelma leant forward and patted the neck of her pony. She had named him Aonbhárr, after the magical horse of the ocean god, Manannán Mac Lir; the mystical beast that could gallop over land and sea. She stretched back in the saddle and drew in a deep breath. Spring was in the air and she was filled with contentment; a gratification at just being alive.

It was not yet midday but the sun was already high in the cloudless sky, throwing shadows westward across the plain. The grasslands surrounding the great rock had been converted to cereal crops centuries before, making these plains rich and fertile. The bright green carpet was created by the stubble of the newly emerging crops of barley, oats and wheat. They had been dug in only weeks before, this being the time of the early spring planting. A few months from now these cereals would rise to a metre tall and turn golden, ready for harvesting. There was little movement across the planted areas because the crops were in that halfway stage when birds had ceased to be interested in them as seedlings, yet they had not matured sufficiently to be revisited for their own seeds.

Thankfully, the sky was fairly clear, although Fidelma noticed, across the fields to her right, a number of wood pigeons in display flight as they climbed steeply with clapping wings

before turning into their unmistakable glide. These, the largest
of the pigeons, were the mortal enemies of cereal crop planters:
when the grains were ready, whole flocks could descend and
devastate the fields. Fidelma mentally rebuked herself for
feeling sorrow for the small sparrow-like birds perched in a
nearby bush who ceased their jingling warble for a moment
until she passed by. She knew well that these dunnocks were
as much a potential enemy of the crops as the wood pigeons.

Fidelma closed her eyes and turned her face towards the
morning sun, inhaling as if she could breathe in its warmth.
Of course, there was little warmth in the springtime sun as
yet. However, she breathed contentedly for a moment before
gently urging her pony to continue along the track towards
the great, grey fortress.

That morning, her fancy for her morning ride had taken her
northwards along the broad road in the direction of Dúrlus
Éile. She had meant to ride only a few kilometres through the
flat countryside before turning back. It was a calm day with
hardly a cloud in the pale blue sky and a warm westerly breeze
that portended the arrival of the summer months. So she had
halted and dismounted for a while on the bank of a small
stream, leaning back against the trunk of a yew tree and
listening to the chattering music of the waters. It was soporific
and she felt she could have stayed there for ever.

It was good to be riding in isolation after the recent days
in the crowded fortress. Now was a busy time, with the
approach of the annual Feast of Beltaine with its great fair.
However, more important than the markets and entertainment
was the annual gathering of the seven princes of the Eóganacht,
the council of the *ceithirfine*, cousins of the fourth circle of
kingship. It was an important council for Fidelma's brother,
Colgú, who ruled Muman, this being the meeting at which
the King had to give his annual account of his governance of
the kingdom and submit himself for the approval of the princes.
The annual Fires of Bel, with its days of feasting and celebration, was an ancient pagan festival sacred to Bel, the bringer
of light. The day heralded the start of summer and the light
half of the ancient year. Not even the New Faith could abolish
it, so it continued with the blessing of the abbots and bishops.

Pope Gregory the Great had authorised that if such pagan rites and rituals could not be suppressed, they should be blessed and incorporated into the new Christian faith.

Several of the seven princes and their wives and escorts had already arrived. Most of their escorts or bodyguards had gone to stay at Ráth na Drínne as guests of the fortress. This was the main location of the fair, just to the south. Soon the remaining princes and prelates would be crowding the fortress. Among them would be Abbot Cuán of Imleach, as Chief Bishop of the kingdom. He would later be performing the marriage of Fidelma's brother to the Princess Gelgéis of Dúrlus Éile, which had been postponed because of her recent kidnapping, and subsequent rescue by Fidelma.

The only uncomfortable aspect of Fidelma's solitude that morning was a feeling of guilt because she was enjoying her time away from Eadulf and their small son, Alchú. Eadulf had seized the opportunity to take the boy to the Abbey of Imleach Iubhair, the abbey of the Borderland of Yew-Trees, which had been founded by the Blessed Ailbe, who had been the first to bring the New Faith to Muman.

As Fidelma drew closer to the fortress, she could see more people pursuing their various daily tasks. From the north, the rock on which the fortress was built appeared a forbidding place, stern and friendless. The single entrance to the fortress lay on the southern side and it was on this side that the little township had grown up under the protective shadow of the great citadel of its kings, which rose over sixty metres above. Fidelma had to circle the great rock and then approach the tall oak gates at the top of the steep sloping road. She had noticed several members of the *lucht-tighe*, the household guard, in a larger group than usual at the entrance. The guards often took the opportunity to pause and gossip with one another but they seemed unusually animated as she approached.

What caused Fidelma disquiet was the expression on the face of Enda, the commander of the household guard, as he hastened forward across the flagstone courtyard to meet her. As she drew rein she saw also that his whole body seemed to exude anxiety to match.

He halted, oddly short of breath, which she quickly realised was not from exertion but from an uncharacteristic emotion. His features were taut and pale.

'Lady,' he gasped, 'lady, I must take you to the King at once.'

An icy fear stabbed at her.

'Colgú? Has something happened to my brother?' Her voice rose almost to a shout as she slid from her horse and tossed the reins to a stable lad who had emerged to take charge of them.

The young warrior shook his head before turning to lead her across the courtyard.

'No, lady. Not to the King. But you must come quickly.'

'Has something happened to my husband, Eadulf? To my son, Alchú?'

Enda turned back with something like a beseeching gaze on her.

'Lady, so far as I know Eadulf and your son are both fine. But the King is waiting impatiently. Please come to him.'

'It is not a message from Imleach then?' she pressed, reluctant to move. 'Are you sure all is well with my son and his father?'

Enda was now sensitive to her uncertainty, and especially to the fear in her eyes.

'There has been no message from Imleach, lady. I tell you that Eadulf and your son are well. Please come with me.'

He almost broke into a trot as he hurried across the courtyard to the entrance to the main building that housed the King's private chambers. A guard outside stiffened in a partial salute in recognition of the King's sister before he turned to the bronzed handles to pull open the great oak doors and swing them back to allow Fidelma and Enda to pass inside. She followed him hurriedly down the familiar passageway to the King's chambers. Another guard, observing their coming, turned, rapped on the door behind him and then swung it open before standing aside. Enda stood back to allow Fidelma to move into her brother's private reception chamber, then swung the door shut behind her, leaving her with her brother.

Colgú paused in apparently restless pacing before the fire and hurried across the room to greet her, arms outstretched.

Any observer would have found it easy to see their relationship: the same red hair, the same blue-green eyes and facial features. His anxiety was clear on his face as he reached forward, both hands held out to greet his sister.

'Fidelma, there is bad news . . .' he began, and then hesitated.

'Bad news? I have been told it is not you, Eadulf or Alchú that . . .' She paused, realising she had forgotten one important person and cursed herself for her selfish neglect. Her eyes widened slightly. 'News from Gelgéis . . .?' She hesitated. 'I thought it was just a minor domestic matter that she had to attend to that drew her back to Dúrlus Éile. Is something amiss with her?'

She knew how much her brother cared for the princess, who had also become her close friend. It had only been little more than a week since Fidelma had rescued Gelgéis from an attempt to kidnap and hold her prisoner in the forbidding mountains of Cualann, in the neighbouring kingdom of Laigin. But Colgú was already shaking his head, his grim expression not altering.

'Gelgéis is well,' he replied flatly. 'It is Brother Conchobhar who is dead.'

For a moment Fidelma's mind did not comprehend the news. A feeling of remorse registered in her mind when she realised that she had felt a moment of relief at the news that her relatives were safe. Then the shock and sadness hit her for she had known the old apothecary all her life.

Brother Conchobhar was not only the aged apothecary of the fortress but he had been the closest to a father that she had. When King Failbe Flann had died, his three children, Fidelma and her elder brothers, Colgú and Fogartach, had been left without protection. Several distant cousins followed Failbe Flann into the kingship; all except one wanted nothing to do with the children. Each of the three had taken a different path. Colgú had trained as a warrior, Fogartach had left to seek his fortune elsewhere, and Fidelma, under the mentoring of Brother Conchobhar, had gone to study law and seek security among the religious at Cill Dara. Only when another cousin, Cathal Cú-cen-Máthair of Glendamnach, had become King did Colgú find himself elevated to the position of *rodamna*, his heir apparent. Thereafter matters improved for the children of Failbe. When Cathal died of the Yellow Plague and Colgú had become King, Fidelma returned to Cashel as his legal adviser.

During those difficult years of childhood, old Brother Conchobhar had always been there, guiding and advising as best and where he could. Now Fidelma felt a growing guilt at her moment of relief that the bad news was unconnected with her immediate family. Brother Conchobhar had, in many ways, been more than their family. He had been a guide, teacher and friend to both her and Colgú. Yet in some ways she now felt a curious detachment from him. Old people die. That was a fact of life. Her brother, however, seemed strangely distraught, which was unusual, for he had had companions, friends and relatives killed in battle, or who had died from pestilence before old age was upon them, and he had been accepting of their fate.

'I saw Brother Conchobhar this morning,' Fidelma reflected. 'He waved to me as I was leaving the fortress just after first light. His death must have been sudden and maybe we should be grateful for it rather than that he suffered infirmity and helplessness.'

She saw a momentary expression of anger begin and fade on her brother's features and wondered why.

'I am filled with sorrow to hear this news, brother,' she continued. 'His counsel will be a tremendous loss to us. However, he led a long and a good life, and death always comes at the end of it. He looked happy when he waved to me, and in that much we must be happy for him. Was it not said that Brother Conchobhar was born in the time of Fergus Scandal? That would make his life span about—'

Colgú's voice was sharp as he interrupted. 'Brother Conchobhar has been murdered.'

TWO

Fidelma stared at her brother nonplussed. Suddenly she sat down on the nearest chair. She was rigid for a moment before she shook her head slowly as if in denial of his words. Then she tried to clear her throat, which had tightened with the shock of the news.

'How was he murdered? I left the fortress just after first light this morning. I saw him as I rode through the main gate. He was on the far side of the courtyard when he waved to me. I think he was about to enter his apothecary.'

'It does not alter the fact that he was found dead a short while ago,' returned her brother shortly 'His skull was smashed.'

'Is it known who was responsible?'

Colgú made an impatient motion with his hand. 'It is not known yet. The initial signs are that he was attacked and robbed when in his apothecary.'

Fidelma's eyes widened. 'Robbed? Who would want to rob an apothecary? It makes no sense. Herbs and plants are free for anyone to gather.'

'There might be other things he kept that could have attracted a thief,' her brother said hesitantly.

'Other things?'

'You know the rituals of this household at Beltaine. Brother Conchobhar was the Keeper of the Sword and some of the sacred ritual impedimenta with which kingship is conferred during the ceremonies.'

'Why would thieves be so stupid as to dare to attempt to take such well-known artefacts, and from the King's fortress? Surely they could not sell them?'

'Unless to an enemy of this kingdom,' Colgú replied grimly.

'You mean the King of Laigin?' Fidelma said at once.

'He does come immediately to mind. The symbolic value of those items in his hands would be very damaging to us.'

Fidelma had to admit that she had little use for icons and their symbolism. After her father died she had spent most of her childhood and youth pursuing her education and had seldom witnessed such ceremonies.

'The fact is, some priceless ceremonial items have been removed from his apothecary,' her brother explained. 'I think you will understand when you see where he was killed.'

Fidelma frowned. 'Are you asking me to officially investigate this matter?'

'Who else can I turn to?' Colgú declared. 'Fíthel, the Chief Brehon, has gone to hear a case with Prince Finguine of Glendamnach, in his territory.'

For a moment or so, Fidelma did not say anything. Then she said briskly: 'I accept. Who discovered the murder?'

'Enda!'

Fidelma relaxed a little. She knew Enda was trustworthy; he had shared many adventures with Eadulf and herself. 'Let's call him in. Time is usually essential in such matters.'

Colgú called Enda's name and the young warrior entered immediately.

'I want you to assist my sister in the matter of Brother Conchobhar's murder. She will be in charge of the investigation.'

Enda inclined his head slightly to Fidelma. 'I am at your service, lady.'

'Explain how you found the body of Brother Conchobhar,' she asked immediately.

The young warrior squared his shoulders, his features clearly showing he was facing an unpleasant task. He, too, had known and liked the old apothecary.

'This morning I had occasion to go to the apothecary. I wanted to see if Brother Conchobhar had some *barrlus* for our cook.' It was clear that Enda meant the cook in the barracks of the household guard.

'Surely your cook could find his own supply of leeks,' Fidelma observed pedantically.

'He had run short,' Enda replied, 'and I remembered Brother Conchobhar kept a good selection of such plants, growing them in his little garden at the back of the apothecary.'

'Go on,' Colgú snapped irritably. It was well known that the apothecary prided himself on his herb and vegetable garden. 'Go on with the story.'

'I went to the apothecary and entered. There was no one about, which is not unusual, but I noticed the door to the back room was wide open. It's the place where Brother Conchobhar did his autopsies and, if needed, where he dressed corpses prior to their being interred. He also stored a lot of medicines there.'

Fidelma knew the apothecary well, having made much use of it and of Brother Conchobhar's knowledge since her return to Cashel. She made an impatient motion with her hand as if to press him to move on.

'Some instinct made me move inside. At the back of this room I saw that a heavy chest had been moved aside to reveal a trap door. This trap door was closed but I noticed the bolts were not drawn and there was no other means of locking it. This made me curious as it was unlike Brother Conchobhar to leave anything open when he was away from the apothecary. All I had to do was reach down and pull open the trap. I did so and saw a ladder led down, but the area below was in darkness. I leant in and called his name several times. There was no answer.'

Fidelma waited impatiently while it seemed the young warrior was gathering his thoughts.

'I decided to light a lamp and go down,' he continued just as she was about to prompt him. 'I suddenly thought the old man might have fallen and not been able to reascend the ladder.'

'So you went down?' Fidelma pressed, pre-empting another pause.

'I did so, lady.'

'What did you find?'

'The ladder descended to a depth of three or four metres into what was a small circular chamber, hewn into the rock. Almost in the centre of this was the huddled form of Brother Conchobhar. It was easy to see from the way the body lay that he was dead. I have seen too many dead to question death. I went nearer with the lamp and saw the back of the head was covered in blood and a bloody rock lay nearby the body. There was nothing else in the chamber; nothing except the rock and the corpse. However, as I peered round I suddenly noticed a small opening to one side. I nearly missed it because of the uneven rocky surface of the walls, which cast shadows, and the fact it was a black opening that was only large enough for one person, turned sideways, to push through.'

'To push through?' Fidelma was astonished. 'You could pass through this narrow opening? Where did it go to?'

'As I squeezed into the aperture, I could feel the ground began to decline but it was not long . . . not long before I came into another circular chamber. It was only just big enough for a tall man to stand up in. I could feel the roof with the top of my head. In the centre of this chamber was a rectangular oak table. It looked solid. There were carvings on its sides while on the top was an oak wooden fitment for something to rest on. It was almost like an altar that I have seen in the ceremonies of the New Faith.'

Colgú interrupted: 'When Enda described it to me, I was astonished. I thought I knew this fortress well but I had never seen nor heard of these chambers carved into the rock itself. When he reported it, I asked Enda to take me there and show me.'

'So you have already been to see this and to view the body of Brother Conchobhar?'

'Nothing was touched,' her brother assured her. 'We left it all as it was.'

'I also have never heard of chambers or caves in this place,' Fidelma observed thoughtfully, 'yet I have spent many hours in the apothecary.'

'You will see for yourself when Enda takes you there.'

'But what did you deduce from these chambers?'

'When I saw the second chamber, I realised that this was where Brother Conchobhar must have stored some of the ritual impedimenta; the priceless relics of our dynasty.'

Fidelma turned back to Enda. 'You said that there was nothing else in this chamber? So what did you do?'

'I returned to the other chamber where Brother Conchobhar's body was. There was nothing more to do and so I climbed back up the ladder into the apothecary.'

'This was the only way in or out of those chambers below?'

'Yes.'

'What then?'

'I replaced the trap door and moved the chest back on top of it in case someone else came in and was prompted with the same curiosity as I had when seeing the trap door. Then I came straight away to inform the King. We returned there together.'

'I confirm this,' Fidelma's brother agreed. 'There is little else to say.'

'The priceless relics, the ritual impedimenta Brother Conchobhar stored – what sort of things would they be?'

'I suppose the most well known would be the sword of Nuada. Also, other items used on certain occasions at feasts. When not on display, old Brother Conchobhar must have kept them in these chambers. They were beyond price.'

Abruptly, Colgú stopped speaking and his face whitened. His features assumed a look of horror. He sprang up without warning and rushed from his chamber. Even Fidelma was taken aback. She exchanged quick glances with Enda, who shrugged, rose and followed, Fidelma close behind.

Colgú had not gone far. He had entered the great hall of the citadel where the King's official feastings were always held. Here he hosted not only the princes and nobles of the kingdom but visitors from the other kingdoms as well. Even the High King had been entertained here. It was a long room of red yew panelling, about twice as long as it was wide. At one end was a dais on which the King usually sat in an ancient carved oak chair of office. On either side were less imposing chairs for his advisers and members of his household. When the hall was used for feasting, long wooden tables and benches would be brought in and each guest seated in order of precedence, the shields and banners bearing their family emblems displayed behind them. Now the hall was empty.

Colgú had stopped just inside the door, his eyes focused on one thing. Behind his chair of office, covering most of the wall, hung a great tapestry coloured a bright deep blue on which was an image of a stag rampant picked out in golden thread. It was the symbol of the Eóganacht, the ruling dynasty of Muman. High on the wall in its scabbard, hanging over the great tapestry in a symbolically dominant position, was a sword. The scabbard was intricately worked with precious stones, as was the hilt, the only part of the sword visible. Gold, silver and jewels had not been spared in enhancing the decorations of the scabbard.

Colgú looked at it for a moment and then gave a long sigh, which welled from the depth of his being.

Fidelma had seen the naked blade raised on the few occasions she had attended the ceremony of Beltaine.

'Well, if robbery were the motive, it was not to steal that,' she said. Then she hesitated as a thought struck her. 'Why is it hanging up there?' she asked. 'Usually it is not placed there until the council is ready to meet. Since we are considering the matter of theft, are we sure that this sword is genuine?'

Colgú reluctantly drew his gaze away from the sword.

'What do you mean?'

'I don't know much about these rituals but I recall Brother Conchobhar only brought out the sword and hung it in place when the council met at Beltaine.'

Anxiety abruptly changed her brother's features. He turned to Enda. 'Fetch a ladder.'

Enda left and quickly returned with a ladder. He climbed up and removed the sword with its scabbard.

Colgú took it from his hand. Fidelma and Enda waited while he released the sword from the scabbard and examined the area around the hilt. The pommel, secured in a silver mesh, was of white quartz, the *grianchloch* or sunstone emblem of the gods. The crossbar guard was curious, for it was of finely worked bronze, terminating with clenched fists at either end. The fists were turned towards the very pointed end of the blade. At the wrist of the fists on one side was inset a green emerald while on the opposite fist was a red ruby. Colgú peered at the hilt briefly, smiled and handed it back to Enda.

'You can put it back. That is the sacred sword of Nuada, right enough. That is *Frecraid* – The Answerer – the symbol of our dynasty. Thankfully, it was hanging safely here and not in Brother Conchobhar's secret chambers when the attack took place.'

Fidelma was frowning at her brother. 'Why, when you say that the artefacts were missing, did you not check on this before?'

'I've only just recalled that Brother Conchobhar asked me yesterday if he could hang the sword in the great hall earlier than usual. There were other things on my mind.'

'Did he give you a reason? Surely that was unusual?'

'He did say something about the princes arriving, and that it would impress them to see the sword.'

'So when was it hung there?'

'Last evening.'

'Everyone can see it hanging there.'

'If you are worried about its safety now, I could have a warrior placed here as security,' Enda offered.

'I would be happier if it were so,' Colgú agreed.

'That would be wise,' Fidelma agreed, 'until we have a better understanding of why Brother Conchobhar was killed.'

'If they wanted to steal the sword, they had only to come in here and take it,' Enda pointed out.

'If Brother Conchobhar's chamber was broken into for the sacred relics then the thieves did not realise it was here,' Fidelma pointed out softly. 'But you are saying all the other relics were taken from the apothecary's hidden chambers?'

'Yes. Perhaps it was just for their monetary value that the thieves stole the relics,' Colgú muttered. 'Perhaps they were satisfied with the items they took.'

'Anyway, you'd best arrange a guard in the meantime,' Fidelma reminded him.

'Very well. I hope the thieves' motive was financial gain. But the symbolic worth of the sword is infinitely more valuable. Do not forget that Brother Conchobhar was the Keeper of the Sword and many people believe in its sacred symbolism.'

'Well, the sword is safe enough now. What other artefacts do we know he kept?' Fidelma asked.

'All I know is from the story about the old gods and goddesses,' Colgú said. 'It is from the same story that we all grew up with about Nuada of the Silver Arm handing the sword, *Frecraid*, The Answerer, to our ancestor, Eógan Mór, symbolising the sovereignty. You'll recall that Eógan Mór

afterwards declared himself to be the "Servant of Nuada". We
need to solve the crime of Brother Conchobhar's murder as
soon as possible. I hardly need to remind you that the council
is due to meet in a few days . . . to witness the ceremony in
which the Keeper of the Sword hands it to me to affirm that
I am a just and righteous King.'

Fidelma hesitated a moment. 'Presumably no one else has
been told of Brother Conchobhar's death?'

'No one so far,' Colgú assured her immediately.

'But the guards have been alerted to watch people leaving
the fortress,' Enda pointed out. 'I have not told them any
details, but I have asked them to tell me if there are any suspicious movements of people out of the fortress.'

'Rumours will spread quickly,' Fidelma pointed out. 'If
robbery was a reason the apothecary was killed I would have
no doubt that those involved would have left the fortress
immediately. Has there been any movement at all?'

'No one of consequence has left the fortress this morning,'
Colgú told her. 'The guests that were here last evening are
still here. Only a few merchants and traders have entered and
left.'

She looked at him curiously. 'Do you suspect that it was only
a person of consequence who did this? Why would that be?'

'Who else would want to steal such things? Only someone
who knew the value. An ordinary thief would know he would
draw attention to himself if he stole them just to sell them?'

Fidelma hesitated but then realised that her brother was
correct in part.

'I will need a physician to examine the body. It's a pity
Eadulf is absent at Imleach. Who is next qualified as a physician here?'

'I don't think a physician's opinion is necessary, lady,' interrupted Enda. 'It is clear that the apothecary was killed by
having his skull smashed in from behind by someone wielding
a rock.'

'I would like to make up my own mind,' Fidelma replied
sharply. 'Also, the law requires a proper examination in
a case of murder. Now, you were about to tell me about a
physician.'

'There is a physician that came from Imleach. Dar Luga knows all about him.'

Dar Luga was the *airnbertach*, or housekeeper, of the royal household and was now considered almost as steward. Colgú had not appointed anyone else to the post since his last steward had been discovered in a conspiracy against him. Fidelma had always thought that Dar Luga deserved the more prestigious title as well as the practical role.

'Is this physician someone trustworthy?'

'Who is to say? He has not been here long. He is Brother Laig, who serves as part of the religious community under Abbot Cuán,' replied Colgú. 'I can send for Dar Luga and ask her opinion, if you like. I shall have to let her know about Brother Conchobhar's death sooner or later. It will be her task to organise the obsequies anyway.'

Fidelma saw no objection and so she agreed. It was Enda who went to the door and summoned a guard to ask Dar Luga to join them. A few moments passed before the plump house-keeper arrived.

'I am told you know the new physician?' Fidelma began without preamble.

'Brother Laig? I do so, lady.'

Only Fidelma noticed the corner of the elderly woman's mouth turned down for a second in disapproval.

'Is he trustworthy?' Fidelma pressed.

Dar Luga stared at her for a moment. 'That is not for me to say, lady. I could only give an opinion of him as a man, but not on his ability as a physician. He came on the instruc-tion of Abbot Cuán with the new religious.'

'I am told he is now the only physician in the fortress.'

'I have met him a few times. I have no great opinion of him and if his manners match his abilities, then I would seek other advice if I wanted a physician's aid. He is arrogant.'

'But if he was recommended by Abbot Cuán then he must have found some favour with him as a physician.'

'A physician's ability is not a mark on the *fé* but how the worth of his character – good or ill – can be measured. A physician is a man like any other.'

Fidelma frowned for moment, wondering if she was reading

an insult into the old woman's choice of the word *fé*, or the rod used for measuring a man's grave.

'Very well, you have no liking for the man but we are immediately in need of a physician. Can you find him and ask him to report to me at Brother Conchobhar's apothecary at once?'

Dar Luga hesitated and looked anxious. 'At Brother Conchobhar's apothecary? Is a physician needed? Brother Conchobhar has knowledge enough and will not approve. I don't think there is any friendship between them, lady.' Then she caught sight of Fidelma's expression. 'Is something wrong?'

There was a pause as Fidelma glanced at her brother. He made a grimace. 'You will know soon enough,' he said. 'I am afraid Brother Conchobhar is dead.'

Dar Luga glanced from one to another as if failing to understand. Then she let out a sobbing gasp and took a step backwards as if she was about to fall. Enda moved forward and grabbed a chair with one hand and the woman's arm with the other, helping to lower her into the seat.

Fidelma turned in annoyance to her brother but he had already taken a mug and filled it with water, handing it to his sister. She put it into Dar Luga's trembling hand. The plump housekeeper took several swallows, before handing it back.

'I am sorry,' Fidelma said, glancing reprovingly at her brother. 'I am afraid my brother does not have a natural gift for tact.'

'It is a shock, lady,' the plump woman replied. 'I have known Brother Conchobhar for many long years.'

'We are all sad at this news, Dar Luga. It is a great shock to all of us. We must remember that he was old and that death must come to us all.'

'But he was so alive and active last time I saw him.'

'When was that?'

'Yesterday, in the evening. He was coming from the apothecary with a sack and the sacred sword of Nuada to place it ready for the Feast of Beltaine.'

'You actually saw him coming from the apothecary carrying the sacred sword?' Fidelma pressed.

'The sword of Nuada – *Frecraid* – The Answerer,' Dar Luga confirmed.

'Was he carrying the sword open or in a scabbard or some other covering?'

Dar Luga thought for a few moments. 'Not in its scabbard. He carried it wrapped in a piece of sacking. But I saw the distinctive hilt. He said he was going to hang it in the great hall ready for the council meeting. He was also carrying a heavy box and asked me if I would look after it until he could pick it up this morning. I said I would keep it in my small room next to the kitchens.'

'But as to the sword – did anyone else see him or what he was carrying?'

'There was no one else about.'

'And that was the last time you saw him – yesterday evening?'

'It was. But Cainder reported him well this morning. I sent Cainder to him to collect something for me.'

'Cainder?' Fidelma demanded, puzzled. 'Who is Cainder?'

'She helps me in the kitchens. I was preparing the *primchutig*, the first meal of the day, when I sent Cainder to fetch something from the apothecary.'

'Why?'

'You know well that Brother Conchobhar has a *lóbgort*, a herb garden of which I am most envious. I needed some *cno-mes*, hazelnuts, for my dish.'

'So this girl saw Brother Conchobhar this morning? When was this? Can you be precise?'

'Not long after first light. It was early and the sun was just rising behind the eastern hills.'

'She saw him at that time and was all well with him?'

'So she told me. Anyway, she brought back the nuts I needed.'

Fidelma compressed her lips for a moment in thought. 'She must have seen him about the same time that I left the fort. I will have a word with her later. Do not tell anyone this news until the King announces it. For now, just send this physician to meet me and Enda at the apothecary.' She hesitated. 'Did you say that Brother Conchobhar carried a box? Did he come back for it?'

'No. As I said, he asked me to take care of it until this morning as it was too cumbersome to carry while he attended to positioning the sword. It was just a metal box. One of those shrine boxes that religious often use. I still have it.'

'I will want to see it later.'

Dar Luga rose and glanced at the King. 'Should the rest of the household attendants know that Brother Conchobhar is dead? They all knew and loved him.'

'We will follow my sister's orders,' Colgú told her, trying to adopt a sympathetic tone. 'After Fidelma has made her examination, I shall summon the guests and their attendants and announce the news. Then the death bell can be rung. You will be wanted to make all the arrangements that are necessary. I shall leave the matter of the obsequies in your hands.'

The housekeeper inclined her head in acknowledgement, turned and left the chamber.

'And now, Enda,' Fidelma said, 'I think it is finally time to show me the scene of poor Brother Conchobhar's death.'

THREE

Enda's description of the state of things in Brother Conchobhar's apothecary had been very precise. He led Fidelma through rooms already familiar to her, with their claustrophobic and almost choking odours of herbs and musty spices. In the back room, where she knew the apothecary would examine and prepare corpses for burial, there was a chest, which Enda moved aside to reveal a trap door in the floor. Apart from the bolts there was a metal handle that had been carefully inset so that it lay flush with the surrounding boards. Enda bent and quickly lifted the trap to reveal a ladder leading into the semi-gloom below.

'I'll go first,' Enda said. 'When I brought your brother to see . . .' He hesitated, and then continued, 'We left a lantern alight below.'

Fidelma followed him silently down the ladder. She thought she knew every *céim*, or metre, of the great fortress; every corner to a *bas*, the width of a man's palm. Now, standing in this small limestone cave, sunk into the great rock on which Conall Corc had built his royal stronghold three centuries ago, she realised there were strange and hidden places that she did not know. She paused, looking around in surprise at the interior domed roof. The walls and dome itself were not exactly smooth and had clearly been chiselled out with great patience. They were dry, which surprised her. Despite the rains that often beset the rock above, it seemed that no water or dampness permeated this small chamber. The only objects in this chamber were the prone body of Brother Conchobhar and, beside it, a piece of bloody jagged rock.

Fidelma moved forward to kneel and examine her former mentor. He lay face down with his right arm outstretched, his left arm slightly behind him. It was clear he had fallen forwards. She wrinkled her nose in distaste as she saw the mangled flesh and bone on the back of the head and the heavy piece of

limestone rock, with its bloody traces, lying by the corpse. It
appeared exactly as Enda had described it. There was little
she could do. She tightened her expression and rose to her
feet.

'There is nothing I can learn from this until the physician
comes,' Fidelma told Enda. 'Meanwhile, where is this second
chamber you spoke of?' She peered round curiously, trying
to identify the entrance.

'It is a narrow entrance, lady,' he replied, pointing to a
corner.

She raised an eyebrow. 'I can't see anything.'

Enda went to a particularly odd-shaped piece of rock and
pointed to it. When she approached, Fidelma realised the
curious shadows of the rocky surface, helped by the flickering
light of the lantern, caused a distortion that effectively hid the
entrance. From the new angle, she could see a dark space
which, if a person turned sideways, was just big enough to
squeeze through.

'The other chamber is through there, lady. I would say the
tunnel is no more than two or three metres in length but it has
a sharp angle turn in it.'

Fidelma was curious. 'How did you find this concealed
passage?'

Enda shrugged. 'It was as I was examining the walls that I
saw the shadow of the entrance.'

'You took a chance in entering it,' she commented. 'What
if it had led nowhere and what if you had become caught and
unable to exit from it?'

The warrior shrugged. 'One cannot learn by being timid and
not taking chances. Since I did enter the second chamber
and have safely returned the question is somewhat irrelevant.'

Fidelma felt a moment of irritation because she prided
herself on logic. It was the sort of remark she would have
made.

'Did you also show my brother into this inner chamber?'

'I showed him what I had found. He was surprised because
he did not know of the existence of these chambers.'

Fidelma hesitated a moment. So why had old Brother
Conchobhar kept such a secret to himself? She sighed. 'Let

me see this second chamber. You go first and show me the way.'

The narrow connecting entrance was a tight squeeze even for Fidelma to negotiate. It was, however, too short to really be called a passage. Just beyond the entrance, the way suddenly turned at a right angle, which was a means of obscuring the second chamber. It meant that the light from one chamber was effectively hidden from the other. With some twisting, she emerged behind Enda, who had taken the lantern with him. He stood holding it up to illuminate the chamber. She halted and gazed around, even more surprised than she had been by the first chamber.

This chamber was actually panelled in wood. It was as if they had stepped from a cave into a conventional room. The panelling had a reddish reflection in the lantern light. A gauge of the height was that Enda had to duck now and then so as not to bump his head. Looking at the panelling, Fidelma thought it must be of red yew, a wood commonly used for such purpose. The first question that sprang into her mind was how the wood could have been brought through that tight entrance to construct the interior of this chamber.

As she gazed at the panels the answer to her question became apparent. None of the pieces of wood, if disassembled, was too big to have been negotiated individually through the curious entrance. It would have meant painstaking and time-consuming labour but it had evidently been done.

In the centre of the chamber was a rectangular altar-like table, also of red yew wood. On this was a long cushion of some blue silk covering, and she saw an indentation in it about a metre in length. There was no question from the shape of the indentation that a sword had once lain there.

'We presumed that was where the ceremonial sword was kept when it was not hanging in the council chamber for the special occasions,' Enda offered. 'As you see, to the side of the altar there is a chest, but we found it open and empty. The King, your brother, believes that is where the sacred icons were stored and so he deduced the theft.'

Fidelma moved to the chest and lifted the lid. It was certainly empty.

'What sort of things would you expect to find here?' she asked.

'I would expect the sacred *cath*, the battle emblem of the warriors,' Enda replied.

Fidelma recalled that the battle emblem, a silver image of a stag rampant, the emblem of the Eóganacht, was carried into battle and had to be paraded *deisol,* or sun-wise, three times around the army before the battle began. Fidelma had only heard stories about this; she had never witnessed a full-scale battle. As a young girl she remembered hearing how an ascetic religious named Finch of Bra Govan had also carried his *cenn-cathach,* a crozier of the Blessed Ailbe, at the head of the army of Muman. Before a battle he had marched three times around the army in a ritual that went back to the time before time. Christianity had to accept these emblems and amend them to fit the New Religion. Also, she recalled, the chalice used by Muman's first great teacher of the New Faith, Ailbe of Imleach, was regularly displayed on certain days. These items were now missing.

'Brother Conchobhar would have kept the war banners here, too,' Enda pointed out. 'The war banners of the seven princes. See the fixtures there to place the flagpoles where they should stand? But there is nothing here. That is why we realised it was a robbery, lady.'

Fidelma returned her attention to the altar.

On each of the four red yew side panels of this altar-like table were carvings. The central motif was a stag rampant, the symbol of the Eóganacht. The wood seemed to be lovingly tended. She ran a finger over it where she could feel the polish and then raised the finger to her nostril. It smelt as if it had been regularly rubbed with beeswax. She stood back, asking Enda to bring the lantern nearer, the better to see the panels and their carvings.

'As you see, lady, there is nothing else in here. I have checked,' Enda said a little defensively.

Fidelma made a fist and knocked on the panels. The sound came back hollow. Then she frowned as a thought struck her. She knelt and began to knock on the panels, listening to the echoes.

'You think it is hollow, lady?' ventured Enda.

'It was worth checking,' she replied evenly. 'Did you do so?'

The warrior shook his head. 'I did not want to desecrate this altar, a revered construction on which the sacred sword was placed.'

'Well, it is hollow right enough, but is there a means of opening it?' Fidelma pointed to one end of the rectangular altar. 'Have you noticed this?'

Enda peered forward. 'I see only a wooden carving of a stag rampant. What of it?'

'It stands slightly proud from the wood panel.'

'Of course, as a carving that is natural.'

'You do not remark on it being slightly worn and it has scratch marks on it?'

Enda smiled grimly in the flickering half-light. 'It might be loose. I have not touched it.'

Fidelma knelt down and pushed tentatively at it. Nothing happened. It did not move. She looked at it carefully and then pushed in the other direction. This time it gave a fraction and there was a click. Immediately Fidelma bent forward, instructing Enda to hold the lamp nearer.

The carving had definitely moved. She reached out a hand to the antlers, for that allowed her a better hold on the raised wood. She pushed again. Her efforts were rewarded by another click and the panel seemed to move sideways. This gave her a space to get a purchase and the lower half of the front panel slid along to reveal two long shelves running the length of the altar-like construction.

'Empty!' she commented tightly.

'There *is* something inside.' Enda, peering over her shoulder, pointed to a dark corner. 'Oh, it's only a piece of parchment.' He sounded disappointed.

Fidelma did not answer but stretched in as far as she could. It was difficult to reach. Had it not been for the way Enda held the light, the object would have been easily overlooked.

It took several attempts before her outstretched fingers grasped it. It was a fragment that looked like parchment with some writing on it.

'Not parchment but *palimpsestos*,' she said pedantically as she examined it.

Enda frowned. 'It looks like parchment to me,' he said.

'It is stretched goat's skin but scraped. The original writing has been taken off so that it can be written on again.'

Enda stretched his arm into the dark space, examining the interior with his fingertips.

'Nothing else there, lady,' he grunted in disappointment.

Fidelma held up the torn scrap of paper-like material. The few marks looked like the ancient script Ogham. As she tried to decipher it they heard a voice calling.

'Is anyone down there?' The voice sounded far away.

It was Enda who responded quickly. 'It must be the physician that you sent for, lady.'

Fidelma took the scrap of papyrus and thrust it into her comb-bag, which she always carried at her waist. For some reason she felt she wanted no one else to see this curious sanctum. She closed the panel before giving a nod to Enda to move back through the narrow passage into the first chamber. She followed quickly. It seemed that the physician had not descended the ladder and still stood in the apothecary above them.

'Don't mention this second chamber,' she whispered quickly to Enda before she turned to the ladder and quickly scrambled up, pausing with her head and shoulders just above the level of the apothecary floor. A male figure in religious garments stood in the room above.

'We are in a cellar below,' she said sharply, causing the man to start at her unexpected appearance. 'Come down.'

She descended quickly. They waited until the man followed and turned to face them.

Brother Laig was one of those handsome young men that Fidelma found herself disliking at first sight. He was not tall but had a well-proportioned athletic body. His copper hair, to her surprise, was worn long without any form of tonsure. His blue eyes shone quizzically in well-balanced features. There was nothing to dislike about his physiognomy except some deep expression of vanity in the features; something about the slight lifting of the corner of the lips and the regard of the eyes that gave an expression of superiority and contempt for others. It was also clear that he took great pains with his personal appearance. As she surveyed the arrogant features Fidelma silently rebuked herself for her prejudgement. The words of Herodes Atticus sprang to mind. '*Barba non facit philosophum*' – 'A beard does not make a philosopher'.

'Are you Brother Laig, the physician?' she asked as he stood staring at his surroundings.

The young man returned her gazed disdainfully. 'I do not carry this for exercise,' he replied shortly, holding up a *lés,* in his right hand. The *lés* was the medical bag of the type Eadulf often carried. Although he had left his studies years ago, and before qualifying, he found it useful to carry it during their investigations. His knowledge had often been of value in finding solutions to the mysteries they encountered.

Someone more familiar with Fidelma would have noticed the tightening at the corner of her mouth and the slight brightening of colour in her blue-green eyes at the man's sarcastic response.

'I did not ask you why you carried a medical bag,' she replied coldly. 'I asked whether you were Brother Laig and thereby a physician.'

The young man was not in the least bit disconcerted.

'Is it not obvious?'

'Since I do not know you, it is not obvious,' Fidelma responded without changing tone. 'I am told that a Brother Laig is a physician recently appointed to my brother's court. I summoned him to this apothecary to give me his knowledge in my role as *dálaigh* and as legal adviser to my brother, the King. So now I ask again for your identity.'

The young man hesitated a moment and then he shrugged. His body had not lost its arrogant stance but his tone was less conceited than before.

'I am Laig, son of Intat, and I hold the degree of *druimclí* in the healing arts.'

'And you have studied . . . where?'

'I was a student of Callanáin of the Uí Cairbre.'

'Then come look here, Laig, son of Intat, and give us the benefit of your learning.' She did not disguise the ironic tone

in her voice as she pointed to the body of the old apothecary.
Enda stood back with the lantern, ready when the young physician would need it.

'I am told this is the body of Brother Conchobhar,' the
physician commented.

'You have not been wrongly informed,' Fidelma agreed
gravely. 'You have just passed through his apothecary above us.'

'And this cave is part of it?' Brother Laig asked as he looked
around enquiringly. He seemed more fascinated by the chamber
than the corpse.

'His main apothecary is above us,' Fidelma repeated, stubbornly denying the man further information.

'Interesting. So what did the old man use this space for?'

'We might presume it was a storage place.'

'He didn't store much, then?'

Fidelma began to be irritated. 'You were asked here to
examine a corpse. There is the body for you to examine.' A
thought occurred to her. 'Do I understand that you did not
know Brother Conchobhar? I thought you had met.'

Brother Laig sniffed dismissively. 'I am but recently come
here and had little cause to meet him, although I saw him
once or twice and exchanged a few words.'

'Well, now you meet him in death and we await your opinion
of how he came by that death.'

Without another word, Brother Laig crossed to the body
and bent down. Enda moved forward, still holding the lantern
high.

The young physician put down his bag and began to examine
the body, looking at it from several angles. Fidelma could not
fault the young man's thoroughness. This took a little time before
he turned the body, repeating the examination on the right side,
which had not been exposed before. Then he examined the back
of the head closely. He did not speak a word during this time
and Fidelma stood by, trying to conceal her impatience.

Finally she said: 'I think the cause of death is probably
obvious.'

'You think so?' Brother Laig responded dryly.

Fidelma suppressed the angry retort that sprang to her lips,
then rephrased what had come into her mind. 'I would say

that the killer struck him from behind and smashed in the back of his skull.'

'Indeed, that much would seem obvious,' was the dry response.

'You will have noticed that rock lying by the corpse?'

'I have. Do you find it of significance?' asked the physician in an irritating tone.

Fidelma frowned. 'I presume it is the weapon that was used since there are no other weapons nearby that would inflict the injury.'

A smile played on Brother Laig's lips. 'And because the rock is there and nothing else, then logically it must be the weapon?' He asked the question in a mild tone that was mocking.

Fidelma compressed her lips tightly a moment before replying. 'There is, of course, blood on the rock. But I presume you have another theory?'

'Oh, it's blood right enough, but a few tiny smears. Look at the wound where the skull was smashed. Look closely and tell me what you see?'

Fidelma reluctantly leant down and examined the wound. It was not as large as she had thought it was when she made her first cursory examination. Even though she could see the bone was fragmented in a small area, there had been considerable bleeding. She now realised that the wound was too small to have been made by a large rock surface.

Brother Laig stood with a superior smile on his features.

'So, you are telling me that this was not the weapon?' Fidelma asked shortly.

'Obviously not,' he replied in his patronising tone. 'In the first place, the wound bled more profusely than the small amount that has adhered itself to that rock. In the second place, by observing this chamber I would say that it was something small and round and even smooth; something akin to a hard stone or metal ball. It struck with such force against the skull that the old man's cranium fragmented around the impact. I would say that the injury immediately caused unconsciousness and subsequent death.'

'Subsequent death? Are you saying that he was not killed instantly?'

'I would not say so. But whether he recovered consciousness at any time after the blow, I would not take oath upon
it. But I think he might well have done so.'

Fidelma glanced moodily around. 'You see how empty this
chamber is? There is no other weapon here. Certainly there
is not one that looks like a round ball.'

'Nevertheless, I can only tell you what I observe.'

'Why leave a jagged rock smeared with blood by the body
as if to mislead us that it was the weapon?' she pressed.

'That is not up to me to say but for you to find out. You
tell me that you are the *dálaigh*.' The young man smiled
annoyingly. 'You merely asked me for my opinion of the
body's wounds and cause of death. As a physician I am happy
to confine myself to the knowledge that you ask for, although
I could make a few observations.'

Fidelma stared in annoyance at the arrogant young man.

'What observations?'

'You tell me that this is part of Brother Conchobhar's apothecary. An empty chamber hewn in the rock below his actual
apothecary? Why did he keep it clean but with nothing in it?
As I examine him I see he was elderly, frail, and certainly not
sprightly in his movements. My examination,' he gestured to
the body, 'confirms that estimation.'

'What is your point?'

'Two points. First, this chamber is empty. I wonder why he
used it. It is plain that he did not store any of the herbs and
potions down here. It seems superfluous to his needs and yet
it has been kept spotlessly clean. Why? Why would an old
man, with some difficulty in movement, keep so clean this
chamber, which was so difficult for him to access by means
of trap door and ladder?'

He paused, perhaps expecting an answer, but Fidelma
quickly made the decision not to supply it for the moment.

'You mentioned two points?' she prompted.

'Whatever the reason for the first point, I would say that
Brother Conchobhar knew his killer well enough to be confident to bring them down into this chamber. The purpose raises
a question but, moreover, he was confident enough to stand
with his back to the killer and be struck by him. Also, the

weapon must have been raised high to attain the force needed to smash the skull.'

'Are you saying that the blow needed the strength of a tall, strong man?'

'Strength? Yes. But the old man could have been kneeling when attacked.' Brother Laig smiled cynically at Fidelma. 'He could have been pushed to the ground before the blow was struck. Needless to say, I speak in possibilities, for one cannot speak in certainties. It might be a young man or it might be a tall young woman, but this person was able to lift the weapon and smashed it down on the back of the skull with some force.'

Fidelma was thoughtful. 'And you also say that, judging from the wound, it was definitely a small smooth ball of stone or of metal?'

'That is how I see the wound. A ball that is small enough to be held in the hollow of a person's hand.'

Fidelma suddenly noticed that Enda, who had stood by quietly while Brother Laig was making his examination, was looking very uncomfortable.

'Do you have anything to add?' she asked. He swiftly shook his head but she had the impression that he did not want to say anything in front of the young man.

She turned back to the physician. 'I am grateful for your observations, Brother Laig.'

'I did not wish, as a physician, to intrude into your role as a *dálaigh*.' The conceit in his voice was obvious. When Fidelma made no response to his provocation, for that was clearly the challenge to Fidelma's ability, he continued: 'Do you wish me to arrange with Dar Luga for women to come and dress the corpse for the obsequies and burial? No more can be learnt from it and it should be buried at midnight tonight. I presume the members of the royal household will wish to hold a *cro-lige,* the feast of the deathbed, and prepare the requisite time for *aire,* the watching of the corpse?'

'The rituals will be observed,' Fidelma responded tersely. 'Tell Dar Luga that I shall speak with her shortly.'

'Very well.' He was still hesitant. 'I presume you have no objections to the *clog-estechtae*, the death bell, now being rung? That would be the usual form.'

'Not yet. My brother wants to make an official announcement after I have discussed this matter with him. As this is
murder, it requires certain legal procedures.'

Brother Laig appeared as if he did not want to be dismissed.

'I suppose you will need to question all those who saw
Brother Conchobhar earlier this morning.' He glanced at the
corpse. 'I now realise that I saw him this morning.'

Enda's eyes narrowed. 'You said that you did not know
him?'

'I said I had seen him and even conversed briefly. There is
a difference. It was early morning and I was crossing the
courtyard. I saw this old man waving. I turned and saw you
leaving through the gates on horseback,' he added to Fidelma.
'You returned his wave.'

'That is true. You saw only that?'

'He turned into the apothecary. But I did see that there was
a young woman waiting for him at the door and they went
inside together.'

'A young woman? Ah, one of the kitchen maids.' Fidelma
remembered what Dar Luga had told her about sending
Cainder, a maid, on a mission to get some hazelnuts from
Brother Conchobhar.

'She did not look like a kitchen maid. I have seen her among
the King's guests.'

Fidelma tried to disguise her surprise.

'Among the guests? There are few guests here at the moment
and these, some of the princes and their wives and attendants.
Are you sure it was not one of the female attendants?'

'She was a tall woman with hair the colour of golden wheat
during days of Lughnasa. She was well dressed and had a
bracelet of silver with some colourful stones inset in it.'

Fidelma recognised the description he gave. 'You have
quite a poetic turn of phrase,' she observed dryly. 'There is
one of the guests who would fit that description. You say
that they went inside the apothecary together? And what did
you do?'

'I went about my business.'

'Which was?'

'I had to see Dar Luga. One of her attendants had burnt

themselves on the kitchen stove. I needed to check that the burn was healing.'

'Very well,' Fidelma sighed with a gesture of dismissal. 'You may go with my thanks for your help. I have to demand that you do not speak of what you have seen and especially where you have seen it.'

'I will say nothing, as you require, but I do not think you have the right to command me to do so.'

'I have the authority to do so,' she assured him. A *dálaigh* had the authority to place such a prohibition upon a person as an injunction to forbid any actions of that person regarding certain matters. Those who broke it lost all honour and often rights.

The physician gazed at her resolute expression for a moment and then shrugged.

'I will say nothing.'

'Especially about this underground chamber,' she pressed. 'You accept my injunction?'

'I do, since it is imposed under the law,' He turned with a further half-shrug and left them. They stood in silence, watching as he climbed the ladder into the apothecary above.

Once she heard the apothecary door close, Fidelma turned immediately to Enda. 'We need to make a special search in both chambers. Let us try to find the small round ball, the real murder weapon.'

It was some time before Fidelma had to admit that there was no sign of it. It had occurred to her that the murderer might have taken it away, especially as they had laid a false clue with the piece of rock.

Finally she said: 'I don't want anyone else to come to these chambers so I am afraid, Enda, you will have to carry poor Brother Conchobhar up into the apothecary as best you can. I don't think I can be helpful in that respect.'

'I will have no difficulty, for poor Brother Conchobhar was a frail old man. I can carry him on my shoulder.'

'That is good. We don't want too many people viewing this chamber nor finding the special second chamber,' she explained.

'So you are not going to tell people about that chamber?' Enda was puzzled.

'Not at this moment. While you take the body up, I will make a final search. When we leave here, we'll swing the chest back over the trap door to cover it. I'll ask Dar Luga to see what can be arranged to prepare the body. You can put the body on the table that Brother Conchobhar usually used for that purpose in his apothecary. Be careful about getting blood on your clothing,' she added.

The same worried expression crossed Enda's face that she had noticed previously.

'What is it?' she demanded. 'Brother Laig has gone so you can speak freely.'

Enda was hesitant. Then he shrugged. 'Something occurred to me.'

'Which is?'

'I have heard stories that this place was once thought to be one of the entrances to the Otherworld. Its ancient name meant the Ridge of the Otherworld people.'

'Well?' She was impatient. She knew Enda was not one to discount superstitions entirely.

'These chambers were unknown even to you and your brother. If old Brother Conchobhar was the Keeper of Sword, the sacred sword of Nuada, supposed to have been made by the gods in the Otherworld, then we should bear the stories in mind.'

'The sword's origin is a tale told by the bards.' Fidelma could not help smiling.

Enda was serious. 'When I was young I was told of the killing of a king by means of a small ball, which was hurled at him and lodged in his brain. It became known as the brain ball. It was launched at him by a warrior called Céit, son of Mágad. The ball stuck in the king's skull and his physicians were unable to remove it. One day an anger rose in him. His brain became swollen in fury and because the ball was lodged there, his head exploded.'

Fidelma was shaking her head in disapproval. 'You like gruesome tales. Anyway, what has that to do with us?'

Enda grimaced worriedly. 'I have just recalled his name. The king's name was Conchobhar.'

Fidelma suppressed a tired sigh. 'And you find that

significant? I have an even more pertinent comment. Why would the assassin kill the victim with this ball or rounded object and then bring a rock into this chamber and smear it with blood? We can both see that there are no loose rocks to hand here. The walls of this chamber are of limestone and there is no sign of anything being cut from them. Why go to that trouble? Was it to mislead us as to the murder weapon or is there another reason?'

FOUR

The solemn tolling of the *clog-estechtae*, the death bell, from the fortress's chapel, had ceased to sound when Fidelma, accompanied by Enda, entered the great hall. Once Fidelma had made her initial report to Colgú, the task of announcing the death of Brother Conchobhar, who had surely been the oldest living inhabitant of the royal household, had been left to Brother Fidach, the senior religious of the chapel. In normal circumstances the task would have been that of Abbot Cuán, whose role as Abbot of Imleach also encompassed the title of Bishop of Cashel. Among the insular churches, the abbots were always senior to bishops. But Abbot Cuán was at Imleach. After Brother Fidach had made the formal proclamation, the death bell, which announced the departure of the soul, was sounded. Those hearing it knew the cadence of its notes and their solemn meaning.

The guests already in Cashel had been summoned to the great hall with their attendants. As she entered the hall, Fidelma was aware of rising whispers of curiosity from the gathering. Colgú was seated in his ornate carved oak chair of office. Standing immediately behind him was Enda, as commander of the household guard. In the absence of Fíthel, the Chief Brehon of Muman, Fidelma took her seat immediately to the right of her brother for, as his personal legal adviser, she would assume the Chief Brehon's role. Seated near the King were those other members of the household that sat in advisory capacities.

Next to Fidelma sat Dar Luga, the housekeeper of the royal household – in practice, the steward – looking uncomfortable and sad. She had known Brother Conchobhar for such a long time.

On the left hand of the King was another comparative newcomer to the fortress, Brother Dáire, who seemed to Fidelma too young for the role of librarian. He had a special seat with a table because his task was now to note down any decisions that were made. Next to him was Brother Fidach, a thin-looking man of middle years, a recent arrival but who was now the senior religious in the fortress. There was a saturnine quality about him with his jet-coloured hair contrasting with pale blue eyes and, while not unpleasant-looking, his features seemed to have an aggressive quality highlighted by a pugnacious jaw and a pudgy nose that did not seem to fit his slim build.

Fidelma glanced round in search of the physician, Brother Laig, and found him standing to one side with a few other members of the religious whom she did not know. Even as she spotted him, she saw Luan, the second in command of the household guards, take him by the arm, pointing out that he should take his official place with the members of the King's advisers, such as the *echaire* or stable master, the chief blacksmith and the *bruigad,* the keeper of the guest quarters.

She now turned her attention to the guests, who had been allowed to seat themselves opposite the King.

Prince Furudrán, a mild-looking man, was Prince of the Airthir Chliach. Next to him was his wife, Moncha. They wore expressions of curiosity on their faces. Fidelma knew little of them except that Moncha had a reputation as a poet and a scholar. With them was Congal, Prince of Loch Léin, whom Fidelma always found rather diffident, preferring to keep himself to himself.

To his left, slightly isolated from any group, was a melancholy-looking, dark-haired man with a bristling black beard. Fidelma recognised him as Prince Elódach of the Eóganacht Áine, another of the seven senior princes. His territory was to the north-west of Cashel, where it bordered the Uí Fidgente lands to the west and the Airthir Chliach to the north-east. She had heard that he had fought at the great battle on Cnoc Áine in that memorable year that her brother became King. She knew that Elódach had only recently succeeded his brother as ruler of the territory. The brother had been killed in a hunting accident, struck by an arrow while in pursuit of a stag. Scandal had it that there were questions as to who had loosed the arrow, since the brothers were known to have disliked one another. Elódach seemed to be permanently sunk in melancholy, his expression thoughtful and sombre.

Slightly forward of the rest was Selbach, Prince of Eóganacht Ráithlinn, a senior Eóganacht prince from the south-west, who always looked to Fidelma as if he were the worse for a night of drinking and feasting. She had discovered that he was someone much given to mood swings; a strange, bitter man. He preferred to use an island called Raerainn, in one of the great south-western inlets, as his main fortress. Next to him sat his wife, Blinne, a young, attractive woman, but wearing an expression of disapproval, though of what, Fidelma could not tell. Standing behind her was a tall, fair-haired woman who seemed to be her personal attendant, with an attractive silver bracelet on her wrist. Fidelma frowned: this was the woman who had immediately come to her mind when Brother Laig had described seeing a woman speaking with Brother Conchobhar earlier.

Slightly apart from the other princes and their attendants and bodyguards was Donennach, Prince of the Uí Fidgente, one-time enemy of the Eóganacht and now in peace and alliance with Colgú. That peace had come about through the efforts of Fidelma only a year before and had yet to be approved by the council of the seven Eóganacht princes. That approval was one of the major items for the council to decide. Behind Donennach was his bodyguard, Céit, and standing alongside him was Conrí, the former warlord of the Uí Fidgente, who had been a friend of Fidelma in spite of the former conflicts.

The general atmosphere was one of puzzlement and nervousness.

Colgú leant forward to Fidelma.

'All is as you required,' he told her in a low voice. 'Dar Luga has given instructions for the washing and dressing of the body of Brother Conchobhar, and Brother Fidach made the official proclamation in the chapel. As soon as arrangements for the burial service this evening are finalised, they will be announced.'

'Who has been told that the death was caused by murder?' she asked.

'I have left it to you to impart as much or as little as you feel necessary.'

'I will make the announcement then,' she said, before turning. The gathering fell silent as she raised her voice slightly.

'As you have probably deduced by the ringing of the bell, someone is dead. Those who went to hear Brother Fidach's announcement in the chapel will have learnt the news. Brother Conchobhar, the apothecary, who has served us here for longer than we can remember, has been murdered.'

There was a slight murmuring, which died away almost immediately when she raised her hand.

'The basic facts are that he was found dead in his apothecary this morning, having had the back of his skull smashed. In the absence of Fíthel, the Chief Brehon, I shall be conducting the investigation into this murder. At the moment, the motive seems to be theft; theft of several ritual impedimenta. The nature of the murder means that I shall be questioning anyone who saw Brother Conchobhar or who had conversation with him either last night or this morning. Death came to him in the early hours. Until I have finished my investigation I will have to request that you all remain within the grounds of the fortress. Of course, the funeral, for those attending, will take place before midnight in the usual form.'

She paused and Brother Fidach called out: 'Many of you will know that the *relig na rí*, the burial ground, is outside the walls of this fortress. I suppose those who wish to follow the bier will have to seek permission to quit the fortress?'

Fidelma felt herself scowling at the man.

'I thought that this would be obvious,' she replied in a heavy tone. 'If not, then logic should have made it clear. The details will be confirmed later. As custom dictates, at midnight, when doubtless Brother Fidach will hold a service, we will all follow the *fuat*, the bier, as it is borne to the grave. Everyone may attend the graveyard.'

Dar Luga rose from her chair. 'Lady, I shall be overseeing the washing of the body and its wrapping in the *recholl*, the winding sheet. I shall do that in the apothecary just as Brother Conchobhar used to do it. But is there to be a period for the *aire,* the watching, to be allowed? Is there to be a *fled cro-lige*, a funeral feast?'

'Those who want to do so may conduct the *aire* and, if I had a choice, I would have liked a full traditional period to be allowed with the funeral feast. But a foul murder has been done and to one whom my brother and I honoured greatly. My first service to his spirit must be to catch his murderer and there must be no distractions.'

'So no days of lamentation?' It was Brother Fidach who raised his mocking voice again, referring to the traditional ceremony of *laitihi na canti*, when mourners gathered round and raised their voices in wailings and clapping of hands to express sorrow.

'There is no prohibition. Those who want to carry out such ritual may do so as individuals. I wonder why you need ask?' Fidelma snapped back. 'With the usual ceremonies, such as the *nuall-guba*, the obsequies will go ahead and I am sure my brother will deliver the eulogy.'

Colgú leant forward, with a censorious frown at Brother Fidach.

'I can assure everyone that all will be done in the proper form to honour Brother Conchobhar. He has a special place in the hearts of my sister and me. Of that fact you may be certain. He came to Cashel as a member of our father's retinue when my father, Failbe Flann, became king. For over ten years he served my father well. When our father died, he became mentor to me, to my sister and to our brother, Fogartach. Indeed, he will not go unmarked to his grave.'

There was a few moments' silence before Fidelma spoke again.

'The best tribute to our friend and guide will be to discover who killed him. That is my immediate task. I will need to ask some of you questions so that I may have a clear picture of events this morning. For that purpose, and if she has no objections, I will make use of the small chamber that Dar Luga uses for administering the affairs of the royal household.'

Dar Luga immediately agreed. 'The chamber is your own for as long as you need it, lady.'

'Then we shall go there first. Enda will continue to assist me to liaise with anyone that I feel the need to listen to. He will act with my authority. I think that is all that can be told at this stage.'

She turned and gave a quick glance to her brother to see if he had anything further to add. He replied with a look that implied the matter was now entirely in her hands.

'In that case when there is more positive news, it shall be shared with you.'

There were murmurings of surprise when Colgú then dismissed the gathering.

Fidelma gestured to Enda to follow her as she made her way to the door. There she paused by the patronising figure of Brother Laig.

'You mentioned seeing a lady with Brother Conchobhar early this morning. Can you identify her in this room?' she asked in a low voice.

Fidelma had already deduced from his description that this was the woman attending Prince Selbach's wife. However, she wanted a formal identification from the physician.

Brother Laig gave a quick glance round, staring over her shoulder. Then he shook his head.

Fidelma tried not to show her surprise. She turned and examined the woman with the golden hair.

'Are you sure she is not here? I speak of the woman you so vividly described.'

'I do not see her,' confirmed the physician stubbornly.

Fidelma glanced again at the woman who had fitted his early description. She was still in plain view, talking in a small group. Fidelma turned back to the physician just as he was making to leave the hall.

'Stay a moment,' she instructed sharply.

'I hope this will not take long,' he replied in a bored tone.

'What do you hope will not take long?' she asked as if puzzled. However, the irony in her voice was clear.

There was just a slight flicker of confusion in his eyes.

'These interrogations that you have said you are going to do.' It was plain that he had to think about a reason. 'I have a busy schedule to fulfil and—'

'Then I suggest you go and fulfil it,' she replied tersely. 'I have no need to question you further at the moment.'

The arrogant young man's jaw dropped a little as she made to move on.

'I had presumed that you would need my services to help you interrogate others,' he replied. This time there was a little uncertainty in his tone.

'Why should you presume so? You gave me your opinion about the body and cause of death. That is all I require from you. As you have remarked before, you are the physician and I am the *dálaigh*.'

She moved on, leaving the young man with reddening cheeks and a look mirroring a conflict between bewilderment and anger.

The little chamber in which Dar Luga ran the affairs of the household was warm and comfortable. A modest fire was burning, for it was chill in spite of the approach of the first of the summer months. Enda stood to one side as Fidelma seated herself at the small table and motioned the plump housekeeper, who had conducted them to the chamber, to do likewise. Fidelma gave the anxious woman a quick smile of encouragement. She had known Dar Luga for several years now. The steward or *rechtaire*, Beccan, had been murdered by his own fellow conspirators a year or so ago, when he was no longer trusted by them. He had not been replaced but Dar Luga, as *airnbertach,* or housekeeper of the royal palace, seemed to fill the post naturally. Fidelma had often remarked to her brother that he should make her appointment an official one, even though it was unprecedented that the steward of an Eóganacht king should be female. Fidelma was disparaging of this fact as females fulfilled practically all official roles in society now. In some ways, her brother was very conservative.

'I'll not keep you long, Dar Luga,' she smiled. 'I want to get clear in my mind the events of the morning.'

'I can only tell what I know, lady.'

'That is all I want. First, about that metal box you told me about.'

Dar Luga turned to a cupboard and immediately drew forth an ornate square object of various metals and studded with semi-precious stones. Fidelma had seen reliquary shrines in which many abbeys kept the bones of their venerated founders, but this was somehow different.

'It looks valuable, lady,' Dar Luga said.

'Valuable to the right person,' Fidelma replied. 'It is not an ossuary, reliquary box, but it is a *cumdach*.'

'Your pardon, lady?'

'It is a book shrine,' Fidelma explained. 'It is a fashion

among certain librarians or prelates to have some of the books of the New Faith put into elaborately ornamented metal boxes for safety. Boxes like this one. The boxes are made from precious metals and encrusted with jewels to honour the value of the work and enhance its worth.'

It was certainly a beautiful work of art.

'What book is contained in it? I thought I knew most of the symbols used at the ceremonies here but the symbols on the box seem different.'

Fidelma saw the catch on the book shrine cover and pressed to open it. It did not work.

'Your pardon, lady,' Dar Luga said, 'but I think Brother Conchobhar had mislaid the key because, when he asked me to look after it last evening, he was muttering about the key and that the key was crucial to everything.'

'There seems to be a tiny lock there,' Enda interrupted, pointing.

'But no key. You say Brother Conchobhar had mislaid it?'

Dar Luga shrugged. 'I think that was what he meant.'

'It is a strange way of putting it – "the key was crucial to everything"? Well, if you have mislaid a key and can't open a box, I suppose it would be crucial. Very well. In the circumstances, I'll take it with me,' Fidelma said. 'Tell me, since poor Brother Conchobhar is dead, who remains in the fortress who is expert enough to open such shrines?'

Dar Luga frowned. 'You say it is like a religious reliquary? Then I suppose Brother Fidach himself must know something about book shrines.'

'I know book shrines are often used among the religious so you are right: he might be versed in such things.' Fidelma paused for a moment before continuing, 'Now, you told me that you sent one of your attendants to Brother Conchobhar's apothecary this morning?'

'I wanted some hazelnuts for the meal I was making. As I said, I sent young Cainder to get them.'

'Tell me something of her before I see her. Is she trustworthy?'

'She shows promise as a cook but is perhaps a little too forward in manner.'

'Forward?'

The plump woman grimaced. 'With men, if you know what I mean, lady.'

'Very well. I am wondering how long she had been in service here. The name is unfamiliar.'

'She has not been here long. It was a few days before the Feast of Brígit, the feast of the goddess of . . .' The woman caught herself. 'The feast of . . . of the fertility . . . er . . .'

Fidelma regarded her sympathetically. 'It's all right, Dar Luga. We all know that Brigit was the daughter of The Dagda and goddess of cattle, fertility, crops and poetry before the coming of the New Faith. The old feast day is still so well kept that there is a proposal among the abbots that it should be thought of as a feast day for the Blessed Brigit of Cill Dara who, of course, was named after the goddess. Anyway, it is well known that her father was Dubhtach, a Druid. So never be afraid of recognising our ancient beliefs and culture.'

Dar Luga was still nervous 'I am not sure I understand, lady. Sometimes I am confused. We are told that we walked in darkness before the coming of the New Faith and that we should therefore turn to accept it otherwise we will remain in darkness. Brother Fidach is very harsh if we refer to the ancient beliefs and . . .'

Fidelma sighed. 'I have only seen him from a distance and only exchanged words in the great hall, like just now. I will say this: you cannot change a way of living that has lasted from the time beyond time in the space of one lifetime. So let us get down to Cainder. You say that she has been here for only two months?'

'About that time, lady.'

'She is from – where?'

'A farm not too far away but her uncle is Rumann.'

'Rumann, the tavern-keeper, in the township below?'

Fidelma knew Rumann well enough for he kept the *bruden*, the tavern, in the central square of the township that had arisen under the walls of the fortress rock on which the royal palace stood.

'Indeed, lady.'

'If her people kept a farm, why did she feel best suited to come to serve here? Why not serve in her uncle's tavern?'

'It was her choice, lady. Even Rumann suggested in my hearing that he had proposed that she could help out at his tavern but she was not interested. She was determined to seek a place in the royal household. She wanted to learn to be a cook. And—'

'Well, most people know there is probably no greater teacher than yourself,' Enda interrupted for the first time. Dar Luga had a reputation for her presentation of the dishes at the feastings given by Colgú.

Fidelma ignored his interruption. 'Very well. I want a word with this girl. Would you ask her to come here?'

The housekeeper rose with a quick bow of her head and left.

Enda was silent for a moment and then asked: 'Why did you ask Dar Luga about this new girl?'

'It is always wise to find out as much as one can before one questions a witness,' replied Fidelma shortly. 'I had not heard of the girl before so I wondered how long she had worked here. I remember a *dálaigh* who would only question a witness, wherever possible, in their own home. They argued that people reveal more of themselves in their own environment, where they are comfortable, than in other surroundings.'

A moment later the girl entered, after knocking on the door and being asked to come in. She was not what Fidelma was expecting. True, she was young and attractive, but under average height although well proportioned. She was crowned with a mass of curly, almost rust-coloured, hair, and blue eyes. Her features were inclined to be fleshy, the lips thick and the mouth a little too wide. However, she had an engaging, slightly nervous smile and stood looking from Fidelma to Enda and back again.

'You wanted to speak to me?'

'Just a few questions, Cainder.' Fidelma waved her forward. 'I am told that you might have been one of the last people to see Brother Conchobhar alive early this morning. Perhaps even the last person other than his killer. Tell me about it.'

The girl twisted her lips into a grimace, which implied she thought the subject was distasteful to her, but she spoke clearly.

'Dar Luga was in the kitchen. She usually is at first light, making sure everything is prepared for the first meal. Something irritated her. It seemed she did not have a good supply of hazelnuts for a dish she wanted to prepare personally for the King, your brother. So she told me to go to the apothecary and ask Brother Conchobhar if he could give her some.'

'I know you have not been long working here. Were you surprised that Dar Luga would ask the apothecary for hazelnuts?'

Cainder shook her head, grinning. 'I have learnt that the old "wolf-lover" was famous for his herb garden.'

Fidelma's eyes narrowed slightly at the familiar use of the meaning of the old apothecary's name.

'You knew Brother Conchobhar well?' she asked pointedly.

'Not well. I have had reason to take requests from Dar Luga to him several times since I have been here. He was a nice old man and reminded me of my father.'

'You seem familiar with the meaning of his name.'

The girl frowned. 'I think a lot of the attendants in the fortress call him by the nickname. It means no disrespect.'

Fidelma interrupted her by making a gesture with her hand. 'I know the meaning of his name. It is a familiar form but not usually used as one of respect for an elder,' she rebuked.

Cainder shrugged as if it was of no importance.

'So,' Fidelma said after a moment, 'continue. You say that you had been to the apothecary several times before? Then you were not surprised to be asked to go early this morning?'

'I went immediately.'

'Did you get Dar Luga's hazelnuts?'

'Of course. He had some jars and handed me one to take back to Dar Luga.'

'Give me some details. You went to the door of the apothecary? Then what?'

'The door was open so I went in. Brother Conchobhar was at the counter mixing something in a pestle. I asked him for the hazelnuts for Dar Luga and he went to a shelf, took down the jar and handed it to me.'

'He said nothing else?'

'We exchanged some banter, if that is what you mean. It

was in his nature to tease me and my nature to respond. That is all.'

'There was no one else in the apothecary? He was alone?'

'As far as I could tell. I had not cause to go behind his shop. I certainly would not venture into the room beyond as I heard that it is where he cut up bodies.'

'Where he performed autopsies,' Fidelma corrected pedantically. 'Did you see anything untoward when you were at Brother Conchobhar's place?'

'Untoward? I do not understand.'

'I mean anything suspicious, unusual, something that did not seem to fit the normal patterns.'

'Nothing.'

Fidelma sighed. 'The trouble is in placing this in the context of events. It was, of course, after first light?'

'I would say not long after first light. Dar Luga knew that he went to work early.'

'You came out of the apothecary and made your way directly back to the kitchens across the courtyard?'

'I did and . . .' Cainder suddenly paused with a frown forming on her brow.

'You have thought of something?' Fidelma prompted.

'I remember looking across the courtyard to the main gate and seeing you on that strange Gaulish pony that you usually ride.'

Fidelma gazed thoughtfully at the girl. 'While you stood there, did you become aware of Brother Conchobhar coming out of the apothecary behind you?'

Cainder looked at her blankly and shook her head. 'I just continued on to the kitchen.'

Fidelma put her lips together in a tight circle as if to whistle. 'Well, that's all for the time being. Thank you for your help.'

The girl hesitated, glanced at Enda with an inviting smile and left the room. Fidelma noticed and saw an expression of discomposure on the young warrior's features.

'You seem to have found an admirer, Enda,' she could not help commenting.

'Lady, the girl is . . . is . . .' Enda actually blushed.

'As Dar Luga described her? A little forward?' Fidelma chuckled.

'I did not encourage it, lady.' He protested. 'Why, that look was of . . .'

'Invitation,' Fidelma said, still amused. Then she became serious. 'Well, let us concentrate to the task in hand. Cainder's statement now gives us some idea of a timescale.'

'How?'

'Two people have said that Brother Conchobhar was alive when I left the fortress to go for my morning ride. So that is three of us who saw him. He was killed between that time and when you went to his apothecary to get the leeks for your barrack cook and found him.'

'Another person saw him,' Enda pointed out. 'Brother Laig says he saw you departing when Brother Conchobhar stood outside his apothecary and waved to you. Then he saw Conchobhar enter the apothecary with a tall, fair-haired woman who had been waiting outside.'

'Ah, yes: the attendant to Princess Blinne. The attendant Laig described so well but now denies it.' She paused thoughtfully.

'But you did not see the woman at the door of the apothecary nor did you see Brother Laig,' Enda pointed out.

'This is not inconsistent because the chapel runs at the side of the apothecary and there is a door into the chapel. If Brother Laig came out of that door, he would have been hidden from me by the angle of the chapel walls. As for the woman, I was leaving at that time, so concentrating on other matters.'

'But that means you would have been hidden from Brother Laig's view by the same angle of the chapel.'

Fidelma gave a quick smile. 'I know you have the makings of a good investigator, Enda, but this also is a possibility. Brother Laig came through the door, saw Conchobhar waving. Conchobhar turned into the apothecary. Brother Laig then walked out of the shadow of the chapel in time to see me disappearing through the gates. I did not see Laig as I was not looking back, but he was able to see me and realised that it was to me that Conchobhar waved.'

Enda gave a soft sigh. 'You always make things sound easy and logical.'

'That is supposed to be my task as a *dálaigh*,' Fidelma pointed out solemnly. 'However, let us not forget what Brother Laig said he then saw.'

Enda hesitated only a moment. 'He said he saw Brother Conchobhar with a lady.'

'Exactly so. With a lady, and he offered a description of her.'

'It was not Cainder,' reflected the warrior. 'But why didn't Cainder see this woman?'

'It depends on the perspective. Cainder left the apothecary and started across the courtyard to the kitchens. She glanced to her left and saw me on my horse going towards the gate. If the girl had left the apothecary and crossed directly to Dar Luga's kitchens, then Conchobhar would have been behind her. He exited after her so she would not have seen him do so. Neither could she have seen Brother Laig emerging from the chapel. She glanced to the gate and saw me leaving and simply continued on her way into the kitchens without glancing behind. I was not conscious of seeing her but I did see Brother Conchobhar wave to me – just a wave of acknowledgement. The tall blonde woman emerged from somewhere and went to the apothecary with Conchobhar.'

'If Brother Laig saw them together entering the apothecary at the same time, that means . . .'

'Means only that he could easily identify this lady and if his identification was accurate, it means that he has just lied to me.'

'Lied to you?' Enda was puzzled.

'His description was of someone tall, blonde and a lady. I thought it could only be one of my brother's guests. So when they were all gathered just now I asked him to identify her. He did not. He said he did not recognise the only tall, blonde woman in the room. Why mention her in the first place if he was not prepared to identify her?'

'Maybe it was someone else?'

'Do you know anyone else in the fortress at this time that fits that description?'

Enda thought about it and then shrugged. 'Not exactly.'

'Not *exactly*?' She found a humour in his response.

'Well, there is no one that I know of,' he corrected hastily, knowing how pedantic Fidelma could be.

'Very well,' Fidelma insisted. 'The only person I know of is the personal attendant to Princess Blinne, wife to the Prince of Ráithlinn.'

'I agree,' he admitted. 'I know her name to be Esnad.'

'Indeed, it is.' Fidelma rose to her feet as if she was suddenly very weary. 'Let us go and find her.'

They found Esnad in the company of Princess Blinne, strolling along the western walkway of the fortress, behind the buildings housing the royal chambers. The two women walked familiarly, arm in arm. Fidelma realised that Esnad could not be just an ordinary attendant. She clearly bore some relationship to the Princess Blinne.

She forced a smile of greeting at the two women.

It was Princess Blinne who spoke first.

'A sad day for you, Fidelma. I heard how fond you and your brother were of the old apothecary.'

'As you say, a sad day,' she acknowledged.

'How is your investigation proceeding? Do you know the culprit? Are we safe? If, as you told us, the tragedy is the outcome of some robbery, then it should not affect us?'

'It's too early to say anything definite, only what it seems to be,' Fidelma replied, glancing to the silent Esnad. 'You will forgive this intrusion but I just wanted to clarify something with you, Esnad.'

Did the woman pale slightly as she glanced at her companion before turning her face to Fidelma?

'What can I clarify?' She sounded puzzled.

Fidelma continued smiling. 'I was wondering if you had occasion to see Brother Conchobhar this morning?'

There was a pause before Esnad shook her head firmly. 'The first time I left the guest quarters was to come to the meeting in the great hall.'

'So if a woman was seen approaching Brother Conchobhar's apothecary this morning, it would not be you?'

'Most certainly not.' Esnad sounded indignant.

'I can vouch for her attendance on me this morning, Fidelma,' Princess Blinne intervened in a querulous fashion.

'It was just a report,' replied Fidelma easily. 'But perhaps the description was not accurate. Dar Luga sent one of her kitchen maids to get hazelnuts from Brother Conchobhar, so perhaps that is the answer.'

'That must be it,' Esnad said quickly, perhaps too quickly.

Princes Blinne was smiling. 'I understand a *dálaigh* has to check things and follow every lead.'

'Of course,' acknowledged Fidelma. 'My brother tells me that you and your husband, Prince Selbach, might be staying even after the Beltaine celebrations?'

'You are incorrect, lady. While it is beautiful here at the plains of Femen, I do long to get back to our island stronghold and the salt sea air before the summer starts in earnest.'

'It is some time since I visited your territory of Ráithlinn. I recall your fortress is on an island on the extreme border of the territory. It is a strange and impressive place, full of ancient tombs and standing stones.'

'So it is. An atmospheric island whose origins are in the time beyond time.'

'Wasn't Eógan Mór, our great ancestor, supposed to have named the island after his wife?'

'I know you are well acquainted with these things,' acknowledged Princess Blinne. 'Indeed, Eógan Mór – or the Servant of Nuada, as he liked to be called, having received the great sword from the god – did name the island as a special place.'

'We must move on,' Fidelma said abruptly, before smiling her farewell at the two women.

Out of earshot Enda looked at her in perplexity.

'What was all that about?' he demanded quietly.

'Two things. Esnad denied she was the women Brother Laig saw. Brother Laig, having clearly identified her, now also denies it. Yet his initial description was so precise. What has made him change his mind? When I entered the hall, I initially saw him standing with her as if he had been in conversation. By the time that I had finished speaking, he had carefully removed himself from her. I find there is some mystery here. Why tell me of the woman and then deny it?'

'True, that is a mystery but . . .' Enda began, then paused.

'Is he involved in this murder? If he is, then why was he of help to you in the first place?'

'I want to know more about Brother Laig,' she said. 'As he was sent by Abbot Cuán I shall have a word with Brother Fidach. He might know something of the background and Dar Luga may be right that he would logically know about reliquaries. Make sure you carry it safely.'

'Of course.' Enda sounded slightly affronted. 'But one more thing. Why can't you just tell this woman, Esnad, that you felt she was lying?'

'Because, without Brother Laig's identification, all I could say was she was a liar. What good would that do?'

'It could force her to admit it.'

'With only suspicion to back me, there would be nothing to force the woman to do anything. An accusation without fact is pointless. Anyway, we must move on to pursue more profitable avenues.'

'Am I missing something?' Enda frowned.

'If poor Brother Conchobhar was the victim of theft we must find out exactly what was stolen and what was not. I need to know more about the book shrine.'

'At least the sword was not stolen,' Enda reminded her. 'The household guards are now taking it in turns to guard it in the great hall. Just think of the furore had the sword been in the chamber when Brother Conchobhar was attacked and it had been stolen.'

The thought had crossed Fidelma's mind.

'We are long past those days when legends told us that he who possesses the sword of Nuada could claim to be the rightful ruler of all Muman,' she laughed. 'Now let us find Brother Fidach.'

They entered the dark oak doors of the chapel and paused to adjust their eyes to the dim lighting. Candles were burning at the far end of the chapel by the altar, but it was not enough to illuminate the interior. Suddenly a shadow moved quickly and Fidelma had collided with it before she could avoid it.

The figure was the first to recover and a curious voice said: 'Greetings, daughter of Failbe Flann, descendant of Nuada's servant.'

FIVE

The greeting was delivered in a strange almost hoarse tone. Fidelma took a moment to regain her composure and tried to focus on the tall shadow. It was as if the figure were clad in a dark shroud from head to foot, for there was little definition other than a long mantle encompassing it.

'Who are you?' she demanded, and felt rather than saw Enda edge closer behind her in support.

'I startled you, for which my regrets,' came the husky tone.

Fidelma was now aware that Enda was bending over something slightly behind her left shoulder. A moment later a faint light spread over the entrance to the chapel. It emanated from a small lamp. It must have been lit before but with the wick turned down. Enda had spotted it and simply turned it up to cause the illumination. The chapel had been constructed without sufficient windows, and those that there were had been put at angles so that the building was always in a state of darkness, lit by candles and lamps only for certain services.

The tall figure had immediately turned its head slightly away from the light. It was a woman, as tall as Fidelma, perhaps taller, and dressed in black robes that fell from the neck to the feet and a black head covering that obscured the features. It was a garb that was affected by the more devout female religieuse. What Fidelma could see of the features seemed strangely distorted by the covering. She had the impression of a mature woman somewhere between fifty or sixty years of age. But the lasting impression was of bright, pale eyes reflected in the light.

'Who are you?' she asked again.

'I am known as Sister Ernmas.' The voice still had that curiously throaty tenor while at the same time it was almost sepulchral in its quality. 'How may I serve you?'

'Sister Ernmas? I have not seen you here before,' replied Fidelma.

'We have not encountered one another before.'

'Did you come with Brother Fidach to serve in the chapel?'

'I am but lately arrived,' replied the woman.

'Have you have come from Abbot Cuán from Imleach?'

'The abbot is also Chief Bishop of the kingdom,' responded the woman in her throaty monotone.

For a moment Fidelma wondered whether to pursue the conversation. It was not often that newcomers were so reticent about themselves when arriving to serve the community of the principal citadel of the kingdom.

'You came seeking Brother Fidach.' The woman suddenly interrupted Fidelma's thoughts as if she had read them. 'You will find him in the far end of the chapel. But he will not be able to answer the question you wish to put to him.'

For a second Fidelma was stunned. By the time she recovered, the tall religieuse had turned and seemed to have vanished into the darkness.

'Where did she go?' Fidelma demanded of Enda.

The warrior moved forward, shaking his head. 'I did not see. I turned to trim the wick of the lamp to see a little better. She must have gone up the steps in the bell tower there.' He gestured towards the dark corner where there was an entrance into a stairway to the chapel's bell tower. 'Shall I follow her and call her back?'

Fidelma hesitated and then shook her head. 'There's not much point. We came seeking Brother Fidach. I presume that you have met Sister Ernmas before?'

'I can't say I have, lady,' replied Enda. 'But the religious who serve in this chapel are often changing. Indeed, Brother Fidach arrived here only a few weeks ago. I have spoken no more than a few words with him. For one of the New Faith he seems reticent about meeting people outside of his duties in this chapel.'

They moved into the chapel and made their way towards the far end where they could hear movement and see the light of a few candles in the gloom.

Fidelma recognised the figure of Brother Fidach. He was standing by the altar directing two of the religieuse, who were busy arranging icons on it, presumably for the service for Brother Conchobhar that evening. After the service the body would be taken to the burial ground below the fortress for its interment. Brother Fidach came forward to meet them with a brief inclination of his head to Fidelma. It was hard to be certain in the gloom of the chapel but his features seemed to express displeasure.

'Can I help you, Sister Fidelma?' he asked, laying a stress on the religious title rather than her secular name.

'I need to ask some questions in my role as *dálaigh*, Brother Fidach,' she replied, deciding not to point out that she had left the religious. She had made her reputation in law as *Sister Fidelma* and often found it more advantageous to let the misconception continue.

It was now clear that Brother Fidach was scowling as he moved forward into the light held by Enda.

'I prefer to be addressed as *an t-Athair*,' he replied curtly.

'*Father* Fidach is an unusual form of addressed among those of the New Faith,' Fidelma observed gently. 'Did not the Blessed Matthew write "call no man on earth your father for you have but one Father in heaven"?'

'The times move on,' Brother Fidach replied tightly. 'One hundred and thirty years ago, Benedict of Nursia told the religious communities to call the head of their communities "Abbot". What is that but the word *abba,* the Aramaic for "father", that being the language spoken by Christ?'

'I know we of the New Faith now use the term abbot only for the head of our communities. Like most of the followers of the New Faith in many lands, we call ourselves brothers and sisters unless we claim to be leader of some community.'

'As I say, times are changing and I am Father to all who come to confess to me.'

Fidelma's eyes widened a little. 'Ah, you would have people come to public confession rather than our most ancient system of soul friends? I therefore perceive you must be in favour of many of these recent reforms that come from Rome?'

'The reforms are necessary to bring people away from the path of darkness. The system of soul friends is an outlandish pagan ritual.'

'Many theologians would disagree with you.' Fidelma spoke softly, almost in a pitying tone. 'For two centuries, Rome, having embraced the New Faith, was teaching that confessing one's faults and misdeeds to one another was a good thing. Rome did not say all sins have to be specific or be confessed to a Brother of the New Faith. Doesn't the Blessed James say that we should confess our transgressions and faults to one another? That is why here, among the religious of this kingdom, we continue to use *anam chara* – soul friends – close friends with whom we can discuss our faults and wrong actions, and not necessarily formally confess them a priest.'

Brother Fidach had paled with suppressed anger.

'It seems, lady, you are replete in the knowledge of the old ways. I fear you follow the heretical teachings of our misguided countryman Pelagius?'

Fidelma let out a soft breath before gathering herself.

'That is a debate for another day,' she dismissed. 'I am here to ask questions as a *dálaigh*.'

Brother Fidach scowled again. 'I am obliged to answer only to my bishop or to the Chief Brehon.'

'Then I am obliged to instruct you on law. The *Bretha Nemed*, the Law of Privileges, will correct any false notions that you may have that you can refuse to answer my questions with impunity. I hold a degree where even a provincial King may not withhold information from me.'

There was a silence and Fidelma met the pale eyes of the priest resolutely, not flinching. Eventually the man blinked and dropped his gaze. She noticed a slight submissive reaction in the slump of his shoulders.

Without waiting for him to speak, she said coldly: 'There are two areas about which I would ask knowledge from you.'

Brother Fidach said nothing but did not refuse her.

'I wonder what you could tell me about a *cumdach* – book shrine.' She gestured to Enda, who had been carrying the box for her.

Brother Fidach examined it briefly.

'It is not one that belongs to this church nor have I seen it before. To whom does it belong? We have very few book shrines here. What book does it contain?'

'This one belonged to Brother Conchobhar, but there is no key.'

'So you wish to open it? There was a metalworker in the Abbey of Imleach who has made such things for the scribes who wanted to retain certain books in the library. I wonder if the smith here would possess such skills.'

Fidelma paused for a second and then realised that he spoke logically. Only a special metalworker would be able to open the box without destroying it.

'Is there anything else?' Brother Fidach's voice cut into her thoughts.

'When you came here as my brother's chaplain, were all the previous servers in the chapel replaced? I mean the two Sisters who assist you, did they come with you?'

'They came with me from the Abbey of Imleach. Abbot Cuán chose two of the younger brethren to assist me here,' he agreed.

'And Sister Ernmas – did she also come at the request of the abbot?'

'I have barely exchanged a word with that one. I thought she was here long before I came. I do not even know what role she fulfils here. She certainly does not participate in the main services.'

Fidelma concealed her surprise. 'And Brother Laig?' she asked. 'I presume he came with you from Imleach?'

'Not with me, though I knew him in Imleach. What about him? He is not here at the moment.'

'I just wonder what you know of his background.'

Brother Fidach regarded her cautiously for a moment.

'I know only that he was sent from Imleach to be physician here. I knew him briefly there,' admitted Brother Fidach. 'But I am no friend of his.'

'And your estimation of him?'

'I believe he is a competent surgeon, if that is what you mean?'

'Do you know anything else of his background?'

'I think he holds the degree of *druimclí*, the seventh order of wisdom, which, as you know, means he is considered to have a perfect knowledge of his art. He studied at the community set up by the Blessed Finnan Lobhar, on one of the islands in Loch Léin. I remember Brother Laig boasted of this once. He is possessed of that conceit of vanity.'

'The school has a reputation,' Fidelma conceded. 'It is in the territory of Prince Congal.'

'Why don't you ask him yourself about his background?' Brother Fidach asked in irritation.

Fidelma simply smiled. 'You have been a help to me, Brother Fidach.'

'I doubt it.' Brother Fidach was cynical. 'I shall look forward to debating further on the changing practices of the Faith.'

He turned away to attend to the two worried-looking religieuse, still holding their candles and waiting for instructions.

'Well, I can't see there was much to learn that we did not already know,' Enda said, as they left the chapel and started across the courtyard.

'There is always something to be learnt, even if it is not what you want to know at that moment,' Fidelma replied dryly. 'We now know that we have to consult a metalworker to get the book shrine opened. What is it?' she added as she noticed his expression.

'Didn't Sister Ernmas say that Brother Fidach would not be able to answer your question?' he pointed out. The thought clearly troubled him. 'How did she know what your question would be? Should we go and find her? You said that you wanted to ask her further questions.'

Fidelma hesitated a moment and then shrugged. 'She will have to wait. I want to finish finding out about the book shrine. But you are right. She seems a mysterious woman. Get the horses ready. We are going for a short ride.'

'Shouldn't we go to see the local smith?'

'I don't think he would be best suited to know about reliquaries or book shrines. His trade is shoeing horses, forging swords and spears and shields, and occasionally repairing carts. Metalworking at this degree, as Brother Fidach suggested, needs a different skill. Bring our horses to the gates, and don't lose the book shrine.'

'Where are we going, lady?' Enda asked, as they rode through the gates a short time later. Fidelma was leading the way down towards the township below.

'We are going to see my old friend Della,' replied Fidelma. 'Della is now one of the few people that if she does not know something then she knows someone who does.'

Della was a close friend to Fidelma but she had once been an outcast, a *bé-taide* or prostitute, whom Fidelma had successfully represented when she had been raped. Her successful prosecution of the culprit demonstrated that the law allowed protection for prostitutes if they did not consent to the sexual act. Since then Della had given up her former way of life and was now looking after an assortment of animals – ponies, a few cows and pigs – but also growing her own vegetables, and she had an apple orchard. Fidelma had been called to defend her once again when she had been unjustly charged with murder. It was during this time that Della had admitted that she was the mother of the warrior Gormán, whose abilities had already led him to become a champion of the élite Nasc Niadh, the Golden Collar, and then its commander. When he married Aibell, Gormán had retired and Enda assumed command. He, like others of the Golden Collar, had also shared many adventures with Fidelma.

Della had her small homestead on the western side of the township.

As Fidelma and Enda halted at her gate and dismounted, a dark brown dog came bounding to greet them, uttering short warning almost growling barks. It was a mixture of a wolfhound and a terrier, known as a 'half-dog', a *leth-choin*. Della had always been fond of the mongrel breed. Fidelma remembered how upset she had been when her favourite dog had been poisoned by a killer Fidelma had been chasing.

A commanding voice from the doorway of the cottage called the dog to be quiet and Della appeared. She was short of stature, about forty years of age, and yet the years had not diminished her beauty or the golden sheen of her hair. Her eyes lit up as she identified the arrivals. She gave another sharp order to the dog to sit, and then she came forward to greet her old friend with a hug, giving a smile and a nod to Enda.

'Come in and take cider with me. Gormán and Aibell will be sad to miss you.'

'Are they staying with you?' Fidelma asked in surprise. She

had not seen them for nearly a year for, after Gormán retired, they had gone to farm land bordering the territory of the Uí Fidgente.

'They decided to come for the Beltaine fair and celebration,' Della replied, leading the way into her cottage. 'They came a day or so ago and yesterday they went to visit an old colleague in the valley of Eatharlaí. They should be back later today. Can you wait to see them? Mind you,' she added thoughtfully, 'I suppose you did not come to see them?'

Fidelma shook her head with a laugh. 'I came to see my good friend.'

'I suppose you want some information from your good friend?' Della grinned mischievously. 'I should imagine that it has something to do with that object in the sack young Enda is clutching?'

Fidelma knew little escaped Della's attention. Nothing further was said until she brought them the mugs of cider. It was obvious she had chilled the jug in a stream so that the liquid was cold and refreshing.

'I must first tell you some bad news,' Fidelma said. 'Brother Conchobhar was murdered this morning. I have been asked to investigate by whom and why this evil deed was done.'

Della grimaced sadly. 'Bad news travels fast. I heard the death bell ringing from the fortress and, soon after, the news was spread about for whom it sounded. I intend to come tonight for the obsequies.' She had known Conchobhar most of her life and, indeed, he was one of the few people who had not condemned her when, being an orphan, poverty had forced her into her early profession.

'So how may I help?' she asked briskly, after a few moments, having gathered her thoughts. 'I need not add that I will do everything that I can to help find who is responsible.'

Fidelma motioned towards Enda to take the book shrine out of the bag and hand it to Della.

'It occurred to me that I should consult you as you know a lot about the area and such relics, Della.'

The woman grimaced. 'It depends. My knowledge is not specific. So what is it that you want to know?'

'Do you know anything about book shrines?' Fidelma pointed to the object.

'Not a thing,' Della replied immediately. Seeing Fidelma's disappointed expression, she shook her head and smiled. 'You know full well, lady, that I am no scholar and was not blessed by Ogma, the god of learning and literacy. All I know is that I have heard that some great scholars often keep their most valuable books in such bejewelled and metal cases. I have seen a few in my time.'

'You have more learning in you than most scholars I know,' Fidelma assured her.

'You flatter me.'

Della took the metal box gingerly in her hands and gazed at it, turning it over several times.

'I have seen reliquaries, but this is unusual. Only certain metalworkers, smiths, usually make this type of casket. It must be valuable because of those semi-precious stones with which it is embossed. But I wouldn't know what it is for, other than to keep a special book safe. What is inside?'

Fidelma pursed her lips for a moment. 'That's just it. There is no key to open it. It needs a special skill to do so. You know the area and who might have such skill. I hoped you might be able to tell me if the box was made locally; if there was something you could tell me about its workmanship.'

Della disappointed her with a shake of her head. 'I would not know that much, but the person you should see is old Gobán. He was once a smith at the fortress, but he left when Cathal Cú-cen-máthair became King of Cashel. Gobán said he was fed up shoeing warriors' horses and sharpening their weapons. He liked to make other objects of metal. He would probably know all about this type of box.'

Fidelma became enthusiastic. 'I do not know him but he sounds just the person I should consult,' she agreed. 'Would you know where he could be found?'

'Not far from here. Up the southern hill on the old bullock road. He still has his own forge there but does not welcome the simple tasks of shoeing horses or mending carts and the like. He is an artist in metals. This looks a valuable box and the sort he would know about.'

'A valuable box in more ways than one,' Fidelma replied solemnly, taking the book shrine from Della's hands and handing it back to Enda.

'Am I guessing that it has something to do with old Brother Conchobhar's death?' Della asked.

'I think it has, but I am not sure.'

'Knowing you, I am sure you would not be bothering with anything unrelated to your pursuit of the matter. Can it be connected with the sacred relics that Brother Conchobhar used to keep?'

'You knew about that?' For some reason Fidelma was not surprised at her knowledge.

'Everyone knew he was the Keeper of the Sword. That was his role at the Beltaine festival.' She suddenly looked anxious. 'Are the sword and other relics connected with the ceremony safe?'

Fidelma smiled thinly. 'The sword still hangs in the council chamber. You are anxious about that?'

Della's expression was serious. 'Did you know the fortress was once supposed to be a gateway to the Otherworld?' she asked.

Fidelma stared at her in surprise. 'I didn't realise you were interested in such things. There is hardly a hill or a cave in the land that is not said to be an entrance to the Otherworld. If the legend about the god Nuada emerging to give Eógan Mór his sacred sword were true, then I suppose it would be convenient that he would pop out of a hole up on the rock. But there are no caves unless . . .' She nearly mentioned the underground chambers and paused with a frown.

Fidelma knew that Della had long since abandoned any religion, due to her experiences in life.

'The problem about associating that legend about Eógan, the progenitor of the Eóganacht, to Cashel, is that he was a king many generations before Conall Corc made the rock the main centre and fortress of this kingdom,' Della pointed out. 'Still, it is true that people, in the retelling of legends, often distort the original. But, again, if you want to know about the legend of Nuada and the sword of the Eóganacht, you could do no better than talk to Gobán about it. I am mentioning this because Gobán is probably a believer in the Old Faith and the old knowledge.'

'I know there are still believers in the Old Faith,' conceded Fidelma.

'Gobán is not only a great craftsman in his metalwork but believes his power in art comes from the god smith Gobán. That is why he has adopted his name,' Della told her. 'Once you get him talking about the three great gods of all the crafts it will be hard to get away. He knows all the stories of the smith gods. And, moreover, he knows the symbolism and how and where things were created.'

'Then he might be able to explain more about this ceremony and what other relics Brother Conchobhar could have been keeping, which, if robbery were the motivation, might have led to his murder.'

It did not take long for Fidelma and Enda and their horses to ascend the old bullock road. It was a straight uphill track until it began to wind itself among a thick forest of yew and elder. Fidelma had passed this way less than a year ago on the way to Ráth Cuáin Abbey so she was fairly familiar with the terrain. They followed a narrow track through closely growing trees for a short while before the sound of metal being hit with a hammer had them pausing to locate its source off the main track. They followed the sound and moments later entered a small clearing with several buildings and a central forge.

They immediately saw the smith at work in his forge. There was no one else about and so Fidelma correctly presumed that this was Gobán. He was a slight-looking individual but his thin body was deceptive, for the muscles were strong and sinewy, hiding a strength few of the more stocky warriors could match. His flaming red hair hid the encroaching years, for he was past middle age. His bearded features were pleasant enough. His unusual green eyes, when levelled at her, danced with a hidden humour. She later learnt that he came from a long line of smiths who had served at the royal palace, each handing on the name originating from the word *goban*, a smith.

He paused in his task of shaping a piece of metal into a twisting and curious shape and, tongs in hand, thrust it into a water trough to hiss with steam, the vapour rising before he put aside the hammer and tongs and turned to Fidelma and Enda as they approached. His twinkling gaze moved from Fidelma to the golden collar of the Nasc Niadh, the torque, at Enda's neck, and then back to Fidelma.

'Welcome to my forge, Fidelma of Cashel,' he said gravely. 'I am honoured.'

'We have not met before, yet you know me,' Fidelma replied, puzzled, as she dismounted.

'I would be a poor soul if I could not add two and two. I last worked as a smith in the great fortress but left it when Cathal became King. I left to pursue my art in more seclusion and to make objects I wanted to rather than shoe horses and sharpen swords. I heard the toll of the death bell from the fortress. It is hard to believe old Conchobhar is dead. He seemed like the rock itself . . . indestructible.'

'How did you know it was Brother Conchobhar the bell was tolling for?' Fidelma asked.

The smith chuckled. 'I am not exactly a hermit here and the news quickly spread.'

'You were told how he died?'

'That he was killed when someone robbed his apothecary. I am truly sorry. He often passed this way gathering herbs. There will be a curse upon the evil soul that did this terrible thing. Conchobhar was the Keeper of the Sword and, as such, regarded as Gatekeeper to the Otherworld. That is what the New Faith now calls the House of Death. It is the nature of this New Faith to misconstrue it and teach people to fear it.'

Fidelma frowned uncertainly at the man's knowledge.

'I have not heard the term Gatekeeper to the Otherworld used in relationship to Cashel before,' she said. 'Why do you use it?'

The smith smiled knowingly. 'Why did Conchobhar dwell in the place over underground chambers on the great rock, which was once called the Ridge of the Otherworld People? It was one of the entrances to the place where, in time, we are all transported. Why did the great god Nuada hand over his sword for the chosen gatekeepers to defend the place where only the righteous should pass? That is why the Keeper of the

Sword is also designated as the Gatekeeper to the House of Death.'

Fidelma stared at the smith in astonishment.

'You knew of the underground chambers? Not even my brother or I knew of them.'

'Why should you? It was Conchobhar who was the Keeper of the Sword.'

'I was taught that the sword was merely the symbol of the authority of the Eóganacht kings.'

Gobán chuckled dryly. 'As one believes, so shall it be.'

'I am charged to discover the person that killed Conchobhar,' Fidelma explained, suddenly impatient. 'I need to ask a few questions.'

'I'll answer gladly, lady. I never go to the fortress these days, and while Conchobhar sometimes used to call here to exchange gossip when he passed along the old bullock road, gathering herbs for his apothecary, I have not seen him recently.'

'That's all right. It is about something else I wanted to ask you, but maybe it is connected.'

'Ask away, lady.'

'I am told you would know something about a *cumdach*, a book shrine.'

'I have made a few in my time, lady,' Gobán agreed without pride.

'Therefore you would know something of their construction and their age?'

'I do not claim to know everything, but what have you in mind?'

She turned to Enda, who had been carrying the sack in which they had placed the metal box. Enda immediately drew it from the sack and placed it on a side table. The smith took a step forward and began to examine it without touching or picking it up. His experienced eyes scanned the box.

'It is a *cumdach* right enough,' he said.

Fidelma restrained herself from replying that even her knowledge would stretch to recognising a book shrine, compared to an ossuary, if she could tell nothing else about it. However, the smith was continuing.

'You may know that there is a distinction in the way these

are made: each maker has his own peculiarities in constructing them. The shape, size, catch that closes it, the choice of precious metals and the stones and their polish . . . they all tell a story. Did you know that there was one of the New Faith – I think his name was Eusebius – who mocked at people of his own faith who insisted on having their books preserved either in these shrines or re-bound replete in gold and precious jewels, because the books had belonged to some sanctified person of their faith?'

He paused in his examination and exhaled in a long sighing breath.

'Can you tell us anything else about this particular *cumdach*?' Fidelma prompted.

'It is basically made of bronze, which is unusual for a modern book shrine. It is well constructed. I would say the metal was shaped by a master craftsman.' Gobán paused. 'Well, apart from that, the construction is unusual.'

'How so?'

'I suppose it is more the way that the metal is decorated rather than the box enclosure itself. Usually, in recent times, a book has a cross on the main face. It is usually covered in large gems, or rock crystal, and there are spaces between the arms of the cross that are filled with decorations that often depict something to do with the New Faith. That sort of motif is often repeated on the metal of the book shrine.'

'I can see that this has no such decoration,' Fidelma agreed.

'Just so, lady. Yet the bronze is covered with semi-precious stones and strange patterns on the metal.'

'Strange patterns?'

'Strange, if one considers symbols of the Old Faith to have no place here. Look at this central spiral and surrounding circles. It is curious that the central motif is the image of a sword, with the tip touching the beginning of an outer spiral, giving the impression that the sword point created the spiral decreasing as it moves to the centre. I do not think I have seen anything like it except on some of the old carvings on the ancient rocks.'

He stood back, shaking his head.

'Can you tell how old it is?' Fidelma asked.

'With a metal object?' Gobán smiled as if she had made a joke. Then he explained more kindly, 'Not with certainty, but I would guess that this is old. Perhaps it is older than the coming of the New Faith into this land. Bronze is not the fashion of book shrines today and the lack of Christian symbolism would make it more appropriate to the Old Faith. True, there are still quarters in the Five Kingdoms where the Old Faith clings tenaciously in the minds of the people, but they do not usually show it so outwardly as making an object like this. I see that the lid is secured by a lock . . . the *poll-eochrach*, the keyhole, has been recently scratched as if someone was trying to open it in a hurry. Do you have the key?'

Fidelma shook her head. 'That is why we came in search of you. We don't have the key. Obviously I would like to see inside but I do not want the shrine destroyed.'

'We might know more if we are able to open the box and see what kind of book is inside,' observed the smith.

Fidelma hesitated and then made a quick decision. 'Could you open it?'

The smith grinned. 'Are you asking me if I could open it without damage?'

'I am.'

'Then I shall do so.' The smith took a few items from his workbench and leant over the box, prodding and poking with several different instruments. It seemed only a few moments before he stepped back with the lid open.

Fidelma took a step forward and peered down into the open book shrine.

'It's empty,' she gasped in disappointment.

The smith shared her disappointment. 'I could only guarantee to open it but not what was inside it. However, from the wooden lining of the interior it proves there was something inside until recently.'

It was Enda who suddenly voiced an idea.

'You remember the piece of vellum or was it parchment that I found in the altar table? Maybe that's where the box used to be stored. Maybe the box was removed when Brother Conchobhar decided to hang the sword in the great hall. Perhaps he dropped that vellum then.'

Fidelma was prompted to search her comb-bag, where she had placed it. She drew out the scrap. It was the first time she had examined it in the light and she saw it was of vellum and fairly new. She felt disappointment, for its newness proclaimed it was not connected with the old book shrine. Nevertheless, she carefully held it between thumb and finger and stared at it. There were marks on it.

'This is what the ancient Greeks called *palimpsestos*, or scraped, a parchment made of untanned skin of goat, something akin to vellum, and dried under tension. It has been scored and scrubbed so that it can be rewritten on.'

'I know nothing of that,' Gobán sighed. 'Can you read what it says?'

'It is either a note or part of a word or sentence in the old alphabet but not entirely readable. It is as if it is a hasty notation. It could be the word *brionnach*, with some letters before and some after, but otherwise it is not decipherable and thereby meaningless. Then it says "emerald always to the east". It doesn't make sense.'

Fidelma shrugged and replaced the scrap in her comb-bag.

'Doesn't that word *brionnach* mean "false"?' asked Enda.

'It could be. It depends what were the words before and after it, which we do not know.' She turned to Gobán. 'Thank for opening the book shrine anyway. I must reimburse you for your time.'

'I need no reimbursement if I am helping to find the person who killed Conchobhar,' the man replied with dignity. 'I wish I could do more. I assume the book shrine was a part of the artefacts Conchobhar maintained?'

'It was,' Fidelma confirmed.

'I have not heard of a book shrine being used in rituals. Doubtless, it was what it contained that was important.' Gobán hesitated. 'I suppose I should add that the metal box was probably made in this area.'

'Why do you say that?' Fidelma asked in surprise.

'I judge that by the way the lock was made.'

Fidelma glanced with renewed interest at the lock. 'How so? Surely a lock is a lock?'

'Each locksmith has their own methods,' Gobán replied.

'The key to this is not made straight. See how the actual key hole is shaped like the letter "L" of the Latin alphabet, which we have adopted in place of Ogham?'

Fidelma had seen such keys before so had not really given it much thought. 'So the key, when inserted, has to conform to an L-shape so that it may fit into the lock and be turned?'

'Exactly so. It is a trick in key making that has a local tradition.'

'I did not realise that. So, even if it is an old key, we may presume that this *cumdach* was made within this area?'

'It is wrong to give an assurance when one is not sure.'

'But we can presume that it was made by some local smith?' she demanded sharply. 'Very well. Have you ever examined the sword? The sword of Nuada?'

Gobán looked shocked. 'Only the Keeper of the Sword and the hand of the rightful king should be privileged to touch it.'

'At the moment, the sword hangs in the great hall where the council of seven princes will be meeting. As you have long known Conchobhar, I thought he might have let you examine it.'

'Never! That would have been sacrilege,' declared the smith.

'A pity. I was just wondering how the metalwork of this box matched, or did not match, with the workmanship of the sword.'

Gobán's face assumed almost a mask of horror but she noticed something else in his eyes. It was as if it were an act and that some amused cynicism lay behind it.

'Lady, are you telling me that you have no faith that the ancient sword was made in the Otherworld city of Findias? No one should question that the sword of light was made by Gobán the Smith-God on the instruction of the great god Lugh. That the sword was given as a gift to Nuada, who handed it on to Eógan Mór as a symbol of rightful kingship? If you question that, you do not believe the great saga of your own family's origin.'

'What I am asking is, could the smith who made the *cumdach* be the same as made the sword?'

'Do you know the sight of that sword could cause great armies to march into conflict with one another? Just by the lifting of that sword would battalions march across the land causing princes to tremble . . . or so the legend goes. It is all to do with symbolism.'

'Brother Conchobhar had access to the sword and many other symbolic relics. I have now learnt that they are valuable enough that some people would resort to murder to lay hands on them. I find it amazing that so many believe in the power of symbols and not reality.'

Gobán smiled softly and spread his hands. 'As you believe, so shall it be.'

'What does that mean?' she asked irritably.

'It means that you must decide your own answers.'

SIX

After they left the smith and were returning to the fortress, Enda asked in a puzzled voice: 'Does any of that really help progress the inquiry as to who killed Brother Conchobhar, lady? I mean, things like gateways to hell and all that? I can understand it if they had stolen the sacred sword, for everyone knows what that symbolises to most people. But it was not stolen.'

Fidelma gave a shrug. 'We can assume the book shrine was something old and made by a local craftsman and to do with the relics. But what was in it? That is the important thing. I would say the Ogham writing on the more recent parchment was significant.'

'These days not even scholars use Ogham much,' the warrior observed.

'Unless it was something Brother Conchobhar had been copying. Perhaps it was a note from whatever had been in the book shrine. He used that type of writing material.'

'I know parchment; I know vellum and have even seen books constructed on pages of papyrus. However, I did not quite understand what you meant with that word you used . . . ancient Greek, you said?'

'*Palimpsestos*? It is where the writing on the goat or calf hide has been washed and scraped off so that it can be written on again. This way, scholars could make notes, drafts of their texts or other matters. It is not as efficient as the method we generally use, the *ceraculum* or wax tablet, on which the wax to be written on is held in a wooden frame, and then it can be warmed, smoothed and used again.'

'But all this does not seem to get us far.'

'It is only a possibility, but the scrap might be Brother Conchobhar's notes on the content. Although why would Brother Conchobhar need to make notes about the contents when he had the book? He knew Ogham; he taught me the ancient hieroglyphs.'

Enda sighed. 'Too many questions and not enough answers.'

'If we accept the fact that the text he was making a note of was of ancient origin we have the word "false", and I am thinking that the few letters on the torn side might be the item that was "false".'

'You said there were other letters, which meant nothing,' the warrior pointed out.

'In themselves they mean nothing, but put together would be a different story. I do not like making guesses.'

'But you have made a guess?' Enda prompted with a grin. 'What were the few letters after it?'

Fidelma could not disappoint the eager young man. 'The letters were *c, l, a* and *i*.'

Enda repeated them slowly and then struggled. 'Plenty of words beginning with *clai* . . . For example, a harpist, a female leper, a wave of hair . . .'

Fidelma shook her head disapprovingly. 'And you call yourself a warrior, Enda.'

He was puzzled.

She continued with a smile: 'The biggest group of words beginning with such letters are to do with *claidbed* – a sword and its uses.'

Enda closed his eyes and groaned softly. 'One always overlooks the thing that should be the first to spring to mind. Then it is a reference to the sacred sword?'

'It might be. But, as I said before, "might" is an important word.'

Enda's features showed his perplexion. 'If the reference to "false" applies to the sword, I cannot see how. Your brother has identified the authenticity of it and it hangs in the great hall where Brother Conchobhar placed it. It is guarded now by two of my warriors.'

'We must return to the immediate problem,' Fidelma replied firmly. 'We must find out why Brother Laig refused to identify Esnad when his initial description of her was so accurate. This seems to me important. Why was Brother Laig persuaded to change his mind about his identification, let alone why did she deny speaking to Conchobhar when she was seen by Brother Laig?'

As they entered the gates of the fortress, a couple of stable lads came quickly forward to take their mounts. They had begun to cross the courtyard towards the apothecary when a strong male voice called Fidelma by name. She swung round to find Conrí, the warlord of the Uí Fidgente, moving rapidly forward to intercept them. He was a tall, well-muscled man with a shock of black hair. His eyes were grey and sparkling, enhancing the white scar that ran across his left cheek, which would otherwise have given him a sinister impression had it not been offset by his lopsided smile and general air of good humour.

'We have not been able to speak with one another this morning, lady. I just wanted a quick word with you.'

'How may I help you?' Fidelma returned his smile. She had known Conrí and shared adventures over several years. It was thanks to Conrí's co-operation that a peace had finally been declared between the Uí Fidgente and her brother. Now everything depended on the coming council's approval.

Enda was about to move off but the warlord of the Uí Fidgente motioned him to remain.

'It is nothing that you should not hear, Enda. It seems that you both had other distractions earlier today. I thought I would take this opportunity to speak now. I did not know Brother Conchobhar but knew of his reputation. My commiserations. Does your investigation go well?'

'It is early times yet,' Fidelma replied.

'I am apprehensive, lady,' the warlord went on. 'It is sad that the forthcoming Feast of Beltaine will be marred by his death.'

Fidelma was uncertain what he wanted to say but waited for the man to continue.

'As you know,' he finally said, 'this is the first time that we of the Uí Fidgente have attended the Beltaine council. We well understand that this council is for the Eóganacht princes to approve the treaty of peace between ourselves and your brother Colgú. We are merely onlookers.'

'I know this has been explained to you,' Fidelma agreed.

'If the other princes do not agree with it, we also understand that it could mean a challenge to your brother's kingship as well as a return to our old antagonistic relationship.'

'Do you fear their decision?'

'We hear that Brother Conchobhar played a special role in these proceedings: that he held the title of Keeper of the Sword that must be raised to bestow legitimate kingship on your brother at the end of the council.'

'This concerns you?'

'As Brother Conchobhar has been killed, the question is whether his death has anything to do with the formal approval of Colgú and the kingship, and thereby the treaty with us? Do you think the council will be cancelled?'

Fidelma was startled. Her friend had raised an aspect not even she had thought about. She noticed Enda was starting to look uncomfortable.

'Your pardon, Conrí,' she said, handing Enda the sack in which she had been carrying the book shrine. 'Keep this safe for me, Enda, and I will join you shortly in the apothecary.'

She waited a moment, watching him trot towards the apothecary, before turning back to Conrí. 'The office of the Keeper of the Sword does not die with the holder,' she said in a serious tone. 'Did someone lead you to believe that the council would be cancelled? Or that the princes would try to remove my brother from the kingship?'

Conrí looked worried. 'We have known each other a long time, lady, albeit in the shadow of the enmity that formerly existed through the feud of our different kings.' He paused. 'I have to say, rumours are spreading about the circumstances of the old man's death.'

Fidelma grimaced in annoyance. '*Fama, malum qua non aliud velocius ullum.*'

Conrí's expression was blank.

'Virgil says nothing travels faster than rumour, especially if there is some scandal attached,' she explained.

'Then there is nothing to the rumours that are being spread?'

'I have not heard them. What rumours link Conchobhar's death and my brother's kingship? Surely nothing should be of more concern than resolving the murder of a wise old friend. He was more a father to my brother and me than our own father, who died when we were young. It is finding his murderer and motive that is my first concern.'

'I'll be honest, as I have always been with you,' Conrí replied firmly. 'Because of our past conflicts with Cashel, I would hate that any suspicion might unjustly fall on Prince Donennach, who has done much towards obtaining this new alliance between us.'

'Suspicion . . . of killing Brother Conchobhar?'

'I think you know what I am saying. At the ceremony some people who dislike the idea of the treaty between us will say it was we who sought a reason to destroy the treaty; that we might create an excuse to depose your brother from the kingship.'

'Who spreads such a rumour?' Fidelma asked, astonished.

'Rumours spread but one never knows the origin. I just thought I should mention it.'

'As you have,' Fidelma commented dryly. 'I would hope that you would accept that I do not act on rumours, unless there is some other substance?'

Conrí looked uncomfortable. Fidelma caught the expression.

'You think there is some substance?' she asked quickly.

'Not substance. But it is also known that my lord Donennach has had a cough for the last day or two.'

Fidelma was bewildered. 'What has that to do with this matter?'

'The same rumours might point out that Donennach has sent his bodyguard, Céit, several times to seek Brother Conchobhar's help to provide something to alleviate the condition.'

'And did he?'

'Céit bought back *orafunt*, horehound, to be made into a drink with hot water to use as a tonic.'

'Are you saying that Céit went to the apothecary this morning?'

Conrí immediately shook his head. 'Not this morning. But he went yesterday, I think.'

'And why would a previous visit by Céit to get some medication for Donennach implicate the Uí Fidgente in Brother Conchobhar's murder?'

'I just wanted to make things clear in case you hear about

visitations to the apothecary by Céit that might be presented with some other interpretation.'

'Am I likely to hear it from another source?'

'Perhaps; especially if someone wanted to circulate stories to cause alarm and raise suspicion by suggesting his death was due to the Uí Fidgente,' Conrí declared. 'Anyway, I tell you now that Céit, Prince Donennach's bodyguard, will have been seen visiting the apothecary regularly during these last days. I have heard a certain prince and his wife discussing it.'

Fidelma shook her head. 'Of itself, that means nothing, though I will have a word with Céit to confirm what you say. I presume you will name this prince and his wife if there is a serious accusation as to the purpose of Céit's visits to the apothecary? You will appreciate that telling me this does not exonerate Céit. It merely exonerates speculation. We will see what emerges at the council. Do you and Prince Donennach still intend to remain beyond the Beltaine ceremonies?'

'That was our firm intention, lady,' Conrí declared. 'We had expected to seal our treaty during this council. That is why we came here.'

Again she frowned. 'You speak with a past tense.'

Conrí's features formed into a broad grin. 'You are sensitive to the use of language, lady. Very well; I still hope that we can have the treaty fulfilled and honoured.'

He raised a hand towards his brow in a half salute and left her, making his way towards the guest quarters.

Fidelma gazed thoughtfully after him. She felt slightly remorseful as suspicion entered her mind and a Latin phrase came unbidden: *Si fecisti, nega!* If you did it, deny it! Even as it did so, she dismissed the very idea that Conrí could be playing a false game with her. She compressed her lips for a moment and then relaxed with a shake of her head. She had known Conrí too long to think him guilty of duplicity. The trouble was, she was just realising that any number of people could have reasonable excuse for visiting an apothecary. Brother Conchobhar not only supplied herbs but any plants from his garden that people in the fortress used in cooking. All of them would call on him when and as often as they needed them.

She glanced across to the apothecary in search of Enda to
see him already coming towards her. He gestured beyond her
towards the gates. She turned, becoming aware that an argument had suddenly arisen there. Two of the household guards
appeared to be blocking the passage of a man who was obviously trying to leave, and the man was shouting. She recognised
who it was with a sinking feeling.

Prince Selbach, Prince of Ráithlinn, was a short man but to
say he was stocky would be to pay him a compliment because
he was just fat and indolent in appearance. He was a full head
shorter than Fidelma, with a mass of dirty grey hair and a
straggling beard. His cheeks were red, lines of tiny veins
forming unhealthy patterns on them. His nose was pudgy and
his lips were thick, the eyes sunken into the surrounding flesh
but shiny like tiny dark pebbles. When he walked his bandy
legs gave him a rolling motion, like someone whose life had
been spent at sea. Fidelma often thought he could not be truly
an Eóganacht but she knew by his lineage that he was, claiming
direct descent from Corc. Her second thought, for which she
felt guilt, was: how could someone like Selbach have such a
young and attractive wife as Blinne?

While Selbach wore a hat of conical shape, a custom among
princes and nobles, his straggling hair spilt unkempt down to
his shoulders, not even cut short in front above the eyes, as
was the fashion. The result was left to the mercy of any breeze
and he had the habit of frequently raising a hand to brush it
away from his features. The mannerism irritated Fidelma and
she wondered why his wife, the Princess Blinne, never advised
him to have his hair attended to. She was, after all, very
particular about her own headdress and clothing.

All in all, Fidelma had to admit that this western cousin
was an uncouth and rather unwelcome visitor, his untidy, dirty
appearance demonstrating his character. However, he was one
of the seven senior princes of the Muman, and Fidelma realised
that she had to overcome her dislike and apply herself to
resolving the dispute at the gate.

She approached him with a firm expression. 'Is there a
matter that I can help with?' she called loudly. Enda came to
stand behind her right shoulder.

Selbach drew his arms away from the restraining hands of
the guards, turned and scowled at her.

'I am being denied exit by these . . . these . . .' he began
spluttering in indignation.

'These guards were only doing their duty and obeying the
orders of the King,' Fidelma responded mildly. 'I think it was
clearly announced in the council chamber that, because a
murder is being investigated, no one should leave the fortress
without special permission.'

He glared her. 'I fail to see why I should be locked in this
fortress,' he replied. 'The day is good and I had arranged to
go hunting with my cousin Furudrán. These men actually dared
to restrain me. I am Prince of Ráithlinn. What have I to do
with the murder of some old apothecary?'

Fidelma's lips compressed for a moment in an effort to
control her temper. Then she relaxed.

'Did you seek permission to leave the fortress from my
brother, as announced? If so, show the guards the token to
that effect and then they will let you through.'

'Of course I did not beg permission. Do they not know who
I am?'

'You are well known to me, Selbach. Yet once my brother
gives an order, he expects it to be obeyed. The order was that
no one should leave the fortress without permission until the
killing of Brother Conchobhar is resolved. The only exception
is when the burial takes place tonight. But as a *dálaigh,* I can
pass you through the gates.'

Selbach scowled. 'Then do so. At once!'

'Let us take a turn along the walkway and talk awhile.' She
indicated the fortress walkway above before saying to Enda:
'Wait for me here. I shall not be long.'

After a brief hesitation and realising that he could do nothing
else, Selbach ascended the stone steps after her. She paused
on the stone-flagged walkway that surrounded the fortress,
which, in times of danger, was usually manned by the King's
lucht-tighe or household guard.

'I think you were told the reason in my brother's hall not
long ago, cousin, why it was thought prudent to keep a watch
on those coming and going from the fortress. Brother

Conchobhar was not merely "some old apothecary". He was a mentor to my brother and me. I want to complete my investigations while we are all in one place.'

Selbach turned and spat over the stone parapet. Fidelma narrowed her eyes in disgust.

'The matter is irrelevant to me. I have nothing to do with it. I was late abed and had to be roused for the first meal of the day. I know nothing about this death.'

'I am pleased to hear that you slept well,' Fidelma replied with black humour, for she knew well that the likely cause was Selbach's addiction to strong spirits. 'Was it some malady that caused you to go to bed late?'

Selbach did not reply.

Fidelma continued, 'So you rose late? When did you hear of Conchobhar's death?'

'Already my wife was gossiping with her attendant, saying that the apothecary had been found dead.'

'Was your wife, the lady Blinne, also late rising as well?'

'I would not know. She was outside the bedchamber door with her attendant.'

'The attendant being . . .?'

'Esnad, a cousin of my wife.'

'A cousin? So has Esnad been her companion a long time?'

Selbach reached up a hand and rubbed his forehead. 'Yes; a long time. Why do you ask?'

'I was just wondering when Esnad brought the news about Brother Conchobhar's death to your wife?'

Selbach stared at her for a moment as if trying to work something out.

'Why do you ask that?'

'Just to make sure I have things in the order they occurred.'

He shrugged. 'It was late morning and one of the kitchen maids had carried up a tray of fresh baked bannock and honey. That, and a jug of cider. That is my breakfast. It never varies. As I say, it was well past my usual hour.'

'I don't suppose you know the name of the kitchen maid?'

Selbach grinned for a moment as he reflected. It seemed a lewd expression on his coarse features.

'A winsome young wench. She bore the name of one of the

three daughters of the famous Medb of Connacht. What was it now . . .? I forget.'

Fidelma smiled grimly. 'Cainder?'

Selbach nodded. 'That was it. She brought in the tray and woke me. That was when I heard my wife's voice. She was talking about the finding of the corpse of Conchobhar. Her voice first thing in the morning is not something I can stand after a night of serious drinking. I told her to go away and give me some peace.'

Fidelma paused for a moment, putting the information into a sequential context.

'Whom were you drinking with last night?'

'I drank with Furudrán, who was to join me in the hunt today. The sooner you have done with your questions the better, and then you can pass me through the gates. The day is getting late.'

'I have done for the time being,' declared Fidelma, turning to leave. Then she paused at the top of the steps leading back to the gatehouse. 'You say Esnad is your wife's cousin? It seems odd to take her cousin into service as an attendant. Who is your wife's family?'

Selbach frowned. 'My wife is a daughter of Foirchellach of Uí Echach.'

Fidelma's eyes widened slightly at the mention of a small but influential clan.

'So she is an Eóganacht by blood also?'

'Distant, but that her ancestry claims descent from Corc is clear, and she is proud of that heritage.'

'And Esnad?'

'She is the daughter of Blinne's uncle. Why such questions?'

'It was remiss of our *seannachaí* not to fill me in on the lineage of all our guests who are attending the council and festival.' Then she realised that the task of *seannachaí* now fell on the new librarian; it would be he who had to memorise and recite the ancestry of the guests when they arrived.

Selbach smiled complacently. 'I am sure the man justly thought it was only necessary to recite my lineage, which goes back to Eógan Mór, who—'

Fidelma sighed impatiently. 'I am aware of your ancestry, Selbach. I had not appreciated that you had married a distant cousin. Thank you for your assistance.'

'You were going to pass me through the gates,' the man reminded her petulantly.

Fidelma smiled. 'Did I say so? You and Prince Furudrán must be patient a little while longer, I'm afraid. I will inform my brother when you can leave the fortress.'

Selbach stared at her angrily. 'I don't see why the delay,' he challenged. 'Unless there is something . . .' He hesitated. 'I have heard the rumour.'

'The rumour?' she parried.

'The rumour is that when Brother Conchobhar was killed, many of the sacred relics were stolen. Is it correct? That does not augur well for a king facing possible censure.'

She stood there with a faint smile on her lips, staring him straight in the eyes but saying nothing. Selbach stared back, trying to keep a belligerent mask on his features. But he was the first to drop his gaze and turned away muttering. Fidelma watched him moving down the steps from the walkway and across the courtyard with his stumpy, swaying posture.

For a moment, she leant against the parapet of the fortress, gazing moodily out across the township below and towards the Plain of Femen, which stretched south to the distant mountain range. She realised just how little she had by way of solid information to resolve the death of Brother Conchobhar. The only curious thing was why Esnad denied being with Brother Conchobhar, having been seen by Brother Laig, and then why they both had denied it had been so.

Hearing her name called, she pulled away from the parapet, realising Enda was still waiting below for her. She started to descend the steps back into the courtyard. The next task would be to take the book shrine to the library to see if she could find out more about its likely contents.

She had just reached the bottom step when a trumpet sounded from one of the watchtowers. She knew from the tone that it was an alert to let everyone know that a strange rider, or riders, was approaching. She moved to stand at the gates with Enda, joining the guards, watching a single rider moving up the incline from the township to the gates.

Luan, Enda's second in command of the household guard, moved out to meet the horseman. As Luan approached him the rider suddenly halted and surprised everyone with a shout.

'Stay back!' The order was almost one of panic and carried to the watchers beyond Luan. 'Stay back! Do not dare to come closer.'

Luan halted, hand going protectively to his sword at his waist.

'What is this? Is it some joke?' the warrior called. 'You challenge me not to come near you? Why?'

'It is no joke. I tell you to stay back. I am here just to warn you; to spread the dreadful news. I tell you as I have been telling those I have encountered along the way. I carry word of warning to the King!'

Fidelma took a few steps forward to join Luan. She scowled and called to the horseman: 'Of what are you warning us? I am Fidelma of Cashel. Who are you?'

'I am come from the Abbey of Árd Mór. I am in the service of the Prince of the Déisi.'

Fidelma knew Árd Mór, the abbey standing on the cliff above the harbour. She had often set sail from its tranquil waters and broad bay under the shadow of that abbey that the Blessed Ciarán had built.

'So what is the meaning of this warning?' she demanded. 'Do you bring us news of some kind?'

'Two days ago a trading ship from Gaul came into the bay at Árd Mór. We tried to stop people disembarking, for two thirds of the crew were found dead aboard her.'

Luan and Enda both gasped simultaneously and took an instinctive step backwards. Words seemed to freeze in Fidelma's mouth. It was as if a coldness had gripped her entire body.

'Found dead from what?' she finally asked with a dried mouth.

'The *Buidhe Conaill*, lady, the affliction some call the Plague of Justinian . . . the great pestilence has returned!'

SEVEN

'A plague ship at Árd Mór?'

Colgú was aghast as he gazed from Fidelma to Enda. They had come directly from the gates to deliver the news in private but already it was being spread throughout the fortress. The messenger from the coastal port of Árd Mór had not even dismounted but had ridden on to spread the news elsewhere. Fidelma sat with her brother while Enda stood fidgeting impatiently, awaiting orders. It was clear that the news was going to induce panic among the inhabitants of the fortress as well as through the farms and villages across the countryside.

'The messenger said the ship had been destroyed by fire,' confirmed Fidelma. 'But three men escaped from it. That is the danger.'

'The plague,' Colgú intoned softly, shaking his head. 'I thought it had disappeared after the ravages it left on its last visit.'

The plague was a frequent visitor, and with little warning of its coming or going. The start of the last spread of the pestilence had been in the year of the Council at Hilda's Abbey of Streonshalh, in Northumbria, which Fidelma had attended and where she first met Eadulf. Over the next five years, it had devastated the population. But there had been no outbreaks during the last five years.

'It not only devastated the five kingdoms but all the kingdoms between here and Constantinopolis, where they called it Justinian's Plague,' Fidelma agreed sombrely. 'As you say, it has not been seen here for several years. It has raged through the known world for periods from the last century. The pestilence is not easily forgotten.'

Colgú seemed to sink deep into his thoughts.

'We should make an announcement,' Fidelma prompted him. 'Perhaps assure people that the ship bearing the plague has been destroyed by fire.'

Colgú appeared not to hear. His face was a mask of gloom.

'The pestilence spreads rapidly and does not discriminate between the status of men or women. Even our High Kings Diarmait and Blathmaic fell to its strange fever. Our cousin King Cathal Cú-cen-máthair died from it here in this very fortress.'

Fidelma suppressed a slight shiver as she remembered being summoned to the dying king's bedside so that he could give instructions to her to investigate a murder at the Abbey of Ros Ailithir. He was dead by the time she had resolved the matter and her brother Colgú, as heir apparent, had assumed the kingship.

'I remember it well,' she confirmed. Fidelma glanced at Enda and asked him to bring in Luan so that he could confirm exactly what the messenger from Árd Mór had told them.

When the grim-faced warrior stood before them he cleared his throat nervously.

'I only repeat what the messenger said. The ship was a *ler-longa*, a Gaulish merchantman. It appeared in the bay of Árd Mór and, apparently, there were enough unaffected members among the crew for them to anchor it offshore. However, the sails were left hanging. That was thought unusual. Three men rowed ashore but avoided the people and did not respond to questions. They ran off, disappearing into the forest that spreads nearby. So the Brehon of the abbey and a couple of the local seamen decided to row out to the ship to find out what was wrong.'

Colgú interrupted. 'You say the ship was a Gaulish merchantman?'

'That was the report. The Brehon and his comrades climbed on board and found people sick. There was nausea and vomiting, others were suffering with fever and chills, and some bleeding from their eyes and mouths as if their blood was not thick enough to congeal. Others lay prone and weak, covered in their own faeces. Their skin was discolouring – the condition known as *galar buidhe* – like a jaundice.'

Colgú frowned. 'It was said that there were some alive?'

'Alive but dying, without the power of movement.'

'Go on,' prompted the King grimly.

'When the Brehon and his men saw that, they realised the Yellow Plague had returned.' Luan paused awkwardly.

'Yet three men landed from this ship and fled into the nearby forests?'

'The messenger told me that Cummasach, Prince of the Déisi, happened to be staying at the Abbey of Árd Mór. He was the one who ordered that the local Brehon set fire to the plague ship.'

The Déisi territory was one of the largest in Muman and covered the coastal area including Árd Mór. Neither the Déisi nor their prince, Cummasach, considered themselves Eóganacht and had no seat on the council.

'It was Prince Cummasach who took charge personally?' queried Colgú.

'The prince ordered his men to chase the three who escaped from the ship. The messenger from Árd Mór said to assure you that Cummasach is determined to stop any spread.'

'It was he who gave the order to set fire to the ship,' Fidelma asked quietly, 'yet with the sick and dying on board?'

Apart from a tightening of the jaw line, Luan kept his features immobile.

'They would all be dead before long. The messenger said that Cummasach had archers lined up with fire arrows and they shot into the ship. It was burnt and sunk.'

Colgú swallowed nervously. 'But there were some alive still on board?' he pressed.

'No one dared to find out. Prince Cummasach was absolved from any sin in his actions by the Abbot of Árd Mór,' Luan added in a flat tone, glancing at Fidelma for reassurance. 'What else could be done with a plague ship?'

'But what news of the three men who escaped?' Colgú asked.

'At the time the messenger left Árd Mór, Prince Cummasach had sent trackers and warriors after them. I was assured that they would not get far.'

'Which way were they heading?'

'It was thought that they fled through the forests to the east.'

Colgú rubbed his chin thoughtfully. 'Not far along that coast they would reach Garbhain's fortress and there is a harbour there. From there they could get a boat and be anywhere, even get to another port in this kingdom without being detected. And what of the welfare of the Brehon and boatmen from Árd Mór?'

'I think they volunteered to go into isolation outside of the port when they returned to shore.'

Colgú exhaled deeply.

Fidelma could see the thought agitated her brother and she reached forward to lay a hand on his arm.

'Luan confirms what I said,' she told him. 'You can do nothing at this point, brother, except let people know this news and seek advice as to how we can deal with this matter. For as much as it seems harsh and callous, perhaps Cummasach's solution was the right one to stop the contagion coming ashore in our land.'

'We live in evil times when we have to be so callous,' muttered her brother. 'I will ask this new physician his thoughts. Perhaps he can advise how best we might be able to deal with the return of this pestilence.'

'If it begins to spread once again,' Fidelma pointed out. 'At the moment, the only physician in the fortress is Brother Laig. Doubtless the advice he would offer is what I heard in Rome during that year of the last major outbreak.'

'Which was?'

'*Cito, longe fugeas et tarde redeas* . . . Leave quickly, go far away and return slowly. It was from some medical tract written by a physician called Celsus.'

'That is of no help at all,' Colgú snapped angrily before realising that his sister had spoken with her usual ironic humour. 'I will have to summon the council members who have already arrived here and give them this news. We must see what advice they can offer.'

'The more advice the better, for I confess I was not impressed with Brother Laig.'

Colgú glanced at her and she interpreted the unasked question.

'I just don't like his attitude of superiority. He does not win my confidence. I wish Eadulf was here. At least he has studied the healing arts and has knowledge of this pestilence.'

'Well, we have no one else to turn to now. Brother

Conchobhar lived through the devastations of the plague here but . . . if only we had his knowledge. Eadulf knows much but even if he were here, he never completed his medical studies at Tuam Brecain. Still, he knows more than most of us.'

'I think we can spare a rider to go to Imleach with this news, and ask Eadulf to return,' Fidelma suggested.

'If it is the intention to summon a council to inform people,' Enda suggested, 'then perhaps it should be immediately. The longer the people are without knowledge, the more unrest will follow.'

Fidelma nodded. 'I suppose now is as good a time as any,' she said. 'The sooner the problem that faces us is known, the better.'

Colgú was clearly apprehensive but agreed. 'Have the bell sounded for the meeting of the council, Enda, and spread the word that all the senior advisers in the fortress are to attend as well.'

For the second time that day, the great hall of Colgú was crowded. Indeed, the news was already being spread and it was clear apprehension and fear were gripping the people as they crowded into the hall. As before, the princes and their wives and attendants took their places while the senior advisers to the King seated themselves. The great stag rampant banner of the Eóganacht, over which hung the great sword of Nuada, in its scabbard, was still in place behind Colgú's ornate chair on the dais. Fidelma not only took her place as legal adviser to her brother but was again deputising for Fíthel, the Chief Brehon. Brother Fidach, as senior priest, was there with the two religious who helped in the chapel. Fidelma looked in vain for the tall, dark figure of Sister Ernmas. Brother Laig, as the only physician, was there. Dar Luga was also in attendance, as was the new librarian, Brother Dáire, ready to make a record.

Fidelma was surprised and delighted to see, among those who entered, her old friend and companion in many adventures, Gormán, the former commander of the bodyguards to the Kings of Muman. He came quickly up to greet her.

'I was glad to hear from Della that you and Aibell were visiting her,' Fidelma said before he could speak.

'My mother told me that you had called at her place earlier

and told her the news about poor Brother Conchobhar. I was on my way here to see you and discuss matters when I heard the bell summoning the council and was told the reason.'

'Your help is going to be needed,' Fidelma assured him.

Colgú had seen him and left his chair to greet him.

'It is good to see you, Gormán. We need clear heads such as yours.'

From her seat Fidelma saw the rest of the chamber was crowded with household guards, together with the master of the stables, the fortress's own smith and other officials.

It was Enda's role as commander of Colgú's bodyguard to call the council to order. Usually, at a proper council, the call would be made by the King's *techtaire* or herald. As there was already a growing hush in the room it did not take long for quiet to reign in the chamber.

'We all know why this council has been called,' Colgú told them at once. 'The news from Árd Mór is terrible. Our council finds several members and advisers missing. Not everyone has gathered yet for the full council that precedes the Beltaine festival. Many are still on their journey here: the Chief Brehon, also the Chief Bishop of Cashel; even my own *rodamna*, my heir apparent, Finguine, the Prince of Glendamnach, is absent, as is the Prince of Árann. Yet even though we constitute five of the seven senior princes, it is the law that a king cannot arbitrarily move forward without the approval of his *ceithirfine,* the fourth circle of kingship. Does not the law ask: who is greater – the king or his people? The answer is the people, for they ordain the king; the king does not ordain the people. So be it. I am here to hear the advice of the council in this matter before I act.'

He paused before continuing. 'At this time, my *seannachaí* is absent by the simple fact that since he retired no new appointment has been made. I have made Brother Dáire my new librarian to undertake that role.'

He indicated the nervous young man who now sat at a scribe's table, to one side of the chamber, bent over papyrus with a goose quill and inks at the ready.

Colgú gave him a swift encouraging smile. 'Brother Dáire, the task falls to you to record our decisions.' He paused and looked around the hall. 'We have all heard the report that the messenger from Árd Mór brought here. Do we have further news?'

Enda cleared his throat and took a step forward.

'I have posted scouts to the south with orders to report if anything further is known among the farmsteads or villages nearby. There is nothing to add. The countryside seems calm for the moment.'

Colgú now turned to Fidelma.

'As my personal legal adviser, my sister stands in place of the Chief Brehon of this kingdom. I will ask her to speak first.'

To his surprise Fidelma shook her head. 'I will reserve my thoughts until we have heard what the princes who form the council have to say. I would just remind them that this gathering's immediate purpose is to discuss how best we may protect the people should the pestilence advance here.'

'In that case,' Colgú replied, 'we should first seek professional advice. As you all know, Brother Conchobhar, our learned apothecary, can no longer provide us with his sage advice. In his absence we have only one physician, Brother Laig, to counsel us.'

The polished young physician pushed his way forward and stood before the King before addressing the council.

'As we lack news for any other learned physician to make observations,' he began in his superior tone, 'I suggest that I ride for the Abbey of Árd Fhionáin and see if they have any news that would help. The abbey stands on the banks of the River Siúr to the east of Cluain Meala, where a new wooden bridge spans the waters into the territory of the Déisi. It is the best place to gather news. As a physician I could decipher the progress of the disease from the stories that I would understand better than most. I could learn whether we need be in fear of this plague. I could be there well before dark if I left now.'

Fidelma exchanged a glance with Enda and it seemed she was having trouble keeping a straight face at the physician's earnest plea. It was obvious to her that this was not his intention at all. Colgú glanced at her and he interpreted her meaning.

'We cannot spare Brother Laig for such a task,' he replied solemnly. 'And as the only physician, it is now essential that he stay here among us.'

Brother Laig was clearly not happy and seemed about to raise an objection when Fidelma intervened.

'Perhaps Brother Laig misunderstood the question. Our purpose was to seek advice on how best to treat or prevent the pestilence if it comes upon us. I am sure news will reach us if it is spreading. Apart from that, Brother Laig is helping us resolve Brother Conchobhar's murder, which still remains an immediate task, no matter the spread of the plague.'

'This is true,' Colgú approved. 'For those who have lived through the worst years of the *Buidhe Conaill*, the great plague, we know just how virulent it was once it seized an area. Our countrymen dropped in their thousands. It spared no one, either by virtue of rank or their closeness to God. So those with medical knowledge are essential. Brother Laig, we need your advice as a physician about what we can do as a defence against the return of this pestilence.'

It was Brother Fidach who unexpectedly intervened in a loud, booming bass voice. He had been barely concealing his agitation. Now he pushed to his feet, his whole body quivering in emotion.

'Do? What can you do? You dare ask that? Have you forgotten how to pray for forgiveness for our sins? Pray! Admit that you have strayed from the path of righteousness. God sends his plagues to cleanse us of the unholy. Pray and fast for the cleansing of your souls. Cast out your demons! Turn aside from the honeyed voice of heretics. Did God not make the Nile red as blood? Did He not cause the frogs to devastate the land? Gnats, flies, locusts – these entire pestilences did God send to remind us that we must be obedient to His will. He caused sores and boils to afflict the evil ones. Now he has sent this pestilence again as a reminder of the punishment that awaits the unbeliever. Hear me! Darkness will soon encompass this land; darkness will fall and you will mourn the death of your first-born.'

There was a shocked silence at his outburst. Only Fidelma responded, raising her eyes towards the ceiling in an exaggerated expression. 'I thought the New Faith taught that this is a God of love and forgiveness,' she commented loudly. 'It doesn't sound as if Brother Fidach concurs with the saintly teachers who brought this Faith to us.'

Brother Fidach began to splutter in anger. In the inarticulate state that the priest was reduced to, Colgú took the opportunity to address the physician again.

'What medical methods do we have to counter this plague when it arrives?'

The man was sulky at being thwarted in his attempt to leave the fortress and move somewhere to safety, for that had indeed been his intention, as Fidelma had guessed. There was no doubt in her mind that, had he left, he would not have been seen again.

He did not respond for a while until he realised that he must say something.

'People should gather sweet-smelling flowers to perfume the air. They should drink cider when it has reached the state of becoming vinegar, then mix it with rosewater.'

'You say that this will keep the plague at bay?' Colgú asked, cynicism in his voice.

'So it has been taught,' the physician shrugged. 'Better to simply avoid the contagion, turn your back on those who have it and burn the bodies as they did at Árd Mór.'

'What of those who still live?' It was Brother Dáire, the librarian, who raised his head from making notes. 'You would burn them also?'

'If you get near them you will surely die, for they are accursed of mankind,' shouted Brother Fidach. 'It is God's will and we must obey Him and accept the Fate He has ordained for us. If God has deemed that we die from this pestilence, then we must accept our fate.'

'There must be something else to do instead of becoming murderers of our brethren?' Colgú pressed angrily. 'As I recall, the Yellow Plague caused swellings to appear on the bodies. Not everyone died; some were cured. I seem to recall that it was recommended an application of onions and leeks, chopped, was then applied to the swellings, which were a mark of the plague. Some argued tree resin and roots of the white lily were to be put on the open wounds, and this had some effect.'

Enda sniffed in disgust. 'It does not sound as though it was a particularly efficacious medicine,' he remarked.

'It's probably as good as anything we have at this moment,' observed his comrade Dego.

Colgú gazed round the great hall as if seeking inspiration.

'In the years since the plague last devastated us we must surely have learnt something by now? It is the nature of man to learn from the disasters that afflict him. Has everything that we learnt during those terrible years been forgotten or cast aside? I am asking for any ideas that we may practically use to fight off the return of the plague. What are we to do?'

Prince Furudrán of the Airthir Chliach now rose to his feet, quivering with emotion, but whether it was in fear or antagonism it was hard to discern. His territory lay to the north of Cashel and his was an influential voice.

'I'll tell you what we must do.' He sounded angry but controlled. 'We must all retreat behind the walls of our own fortresses and ensure that no one is allowed in after we have closed the gates. Let the pestilence rage outside and when it is over then we must demand restitution from those who did not foresee the return of the *Buidhe Conaill*.'

Colgú was puzzled. 'I do not understand what you mean, Furudrán. No one could have foreseen the return of this plague. Whom do you seek restitution from?'

'Is it not said that a wise ruler should be prepared for all contingencies?' Furudrán asked in almost a sneering tone. 'As we are not prepared, perhaps we should look for a new and wiser ruler.'

Colgú leant forward in his chair with an angry movement. Fidelma reached out and laid a hand on his arm. She spoke quietly.

'Prince Furudrán, when we are fearful we say things that are not wise. Our task here is to examine if there are ways of remaining safe in the face of the fact that pestilence has apparently visited our shores. At the moment our information is too scant for us to do anything else. A plague ship tried to land at Árd Mór. It was destroyed. Three men, seemingly fit, managed to make it ashore and are now being pursued towards Garbhain's fortress east of Árd Mór. They may or may not carry the plague. This has caused concern but no more than concern. The plague may not have come ashore at all. Wisely, my brother has called this council to see if there are any ways we can be prepared and to deal with this matter if – and I stress the "if" – the pestilence *has* come ashore with these three men. All we know for certain is what the messenger from Árd Mór told us.'

She spoke slowly and deliberately. She paused for a moment, a trick of emphasis she often used to effect when presenting a case in a court room. Then she continued: 'Prince Furudrán has offered us his solution. He says we should all withdraw into our fortresses, shut the gates, and ignore the world outside until the pestilence has passed. Did I understand you correctly?'

Furudrán glowered angrily at her. 'There is nothing else we can do except stay inside and close the gates so no contamination can harm us.'

Prince Selbach rose slowly from his chair. Fidelma had a poor estimation of the Prince of Ráithlinn's manners but he seemed able to keep calm compared to his fellow prince. 'We are here in council to reflect on ideas, but let us do so seriously.'

He gazed thoughtfully at Furudrán for a moment before continuing, 'The Prince of the Airthir Chliach suggests, and correct me if I am wrong, that each prince returns to his own fortress and barricades himself inside. Can I ask, what does a pestilence know of barricades? This moment finds us here in Cashel for an important task, for the council to approve the decisions and treaties that our King has made during the last year, before the Feast of Beltaine. I would say that it is essential that the princes remain in this fortress and fulfil their obligation to meet in council.'

Furudrán shrugged. 'I have no objection to the idea of us fortifying ourselves in this stronghold. So long as the country folk do not think they can repair here for safety for, be certain, they will bring in the disease with them.'

'Is it not our task to protect our people?' Prince Congal of Loch Léin commented. He was a mild man who rarely raised an opinion but seemed to genuinely care for those he governed.

'Are you suggesting that we get as many people inside the fortress as want to come in?' asked Gormán. He had been frowning, trying to follow the argument. 'What of the entire township below us? The outlying farms and so forth? How many can we hold in here? For how long? And when the pestilence reaches us, when do we know if it has passed? What does it look like, what does it smell like? And while we are waiting for the answer, how much food should we store? And how much water? How can we be sure that our food and water is not contaminated by the breath of this unseen virulent disease?'

Fidelma frowned, surprised at Gormán and the harshness of what the former champion was saying. Gormán had paused and looked at those gathered as if he expected them to respond although he had posed too many unanswerable questions.

It was Colgú who finally replied. 'We cannot lock ourselves in and ignore the people outside who might be crying for help. You talk about seeking restitution, Furudrán. I know you did not specifically name me, but it is implied. As a member of this council, are you prepared to suggest solutions? I presume *you* did not foresee the coming of this pestilence or prepare for it? As a prince of your people you would be answerable to those people for the same reasons that you suggest I am.'

Fidelma decided to intervene as the atmosphere grew tense.

'Furudrán has articulated several questions. Sadly, they cannot be answered. I must suggest that Prince Furudrán has not really helped our deliberations.'

Selbach was immediately on his feet. 'I would urge Fidelma to be moderate in her views. She should know, as a *dálaigh*, that each of the seven princes is entitled to express his views. In the end, judgement is reached. There is a difference between brother and sister, and the sacred sword of Nuada in the hands of a righteous prince will point the way as the final arbitrator.'

While Fidelma was trying to understand what Selbach meant, Furudrán was standing again, quivering, making sounds as if having difficulty breathing. He finally raised a hand, pointing a finger at Colgú. He almost choked as he spoke.

'We all know that Fidelma has a gift for oratory, but words often obscure the truth. I warn you, Colgú, that come Beltaine, when you seek the applause of your people, they may not be so lenient with you if it is found that you have led them into this disaster that now waits on the shores of Muman. Already the plague might be traversing the country. Already there are rumours spreading through the fortress that the sacred sword of the Eóganacht will no longer be yours to hold up to claim your authority. Once the pestilence begins to devastate this kingdom, the kingdom will no longer be yours to govern.'

EIGHT

There arose angry cries from some of those gathered in the great hall. Enda and several warriors of the household guard had moved forward, Luan actually loosening the sword in his scabbard.

Colgú stood up with hands raised as a gesture to halt them.

'Furudrán of Airthir Chliach, I speak to you as a cousin, as well as a member of the *ceithirfine*.' His voice had that same quality of tone that Fidelma used when performing her judicial duties. 'I say this to you. It is well you say these things in council where all may speak their minds freely and without fear of retribution. That is the nature of our council and you are at liberty to approve or disapprove of my actions as your king. Yet this is not the time or place for such a debate. We are here to discuss ways of dealing with the plague, should it come upon us. All else is irrelevant and so I shall ignore things that are said in hot temper. However, I will tell you this, Furudrán, you are trespassing on your privileges. Have I made myself clear?'

It appeared that Furudrán was about to speak again but his wife, Moncha, rose, bent to her husband and whispered something in his ear. His jaw clenched for a moment and then he raised and spread his hands in a gesture of submission.

'I have spoken as I felt, for which I ask no apology. It is my right to speak my mind at a council meeting. I am not only of the *ceithirfine* but of the *indfine* and have a right to challenge where I think it appropriate. I have done so and am content to leave it as I have.'

Clearly Colgú would have liked a retraction of some of the statement but he merely resumed his seat, as did Furudrán.

In the uneasy silence, Fidelma spoke. 'We have not heard what others advise. Congal, you were about to remind us of our duty to safeguard our people. What do you have to say?'

Congal of Loch Léin, the mild and nervous man, had been

sitting head forward, shoulders hunched, his mane of long silver-grey hair flowing into an equally long beard that came to his chest. He had also recently succeeded to the princedom and was the very antithesis of his predecessor, Slébéne.

As her glance fell on him, Congal reluctantly rose. He was clearly uneasy. Fidelma wondered how this thin, furtive-looking man could have been chosen to govern the Eóganacht of Loch Léin. Certainly, Congal could boast a line of descent from Conall Corc, and was a senior prince in the council of Colgú. However, Slébéne, with his loud voice, had used a great bellow of laughter as a means of punctuation. He had been tall, with a barrel chest and muscular arms. Fidelma remembered that a favourite trick of his had been to seize two of his largest warriors by their leather belts and lift them over his head with his arms extended. But Slébéne had proved to be a devious and evil man and, in the end, perished because of it.

Looking at Congal, his placid successor, Fidelma almost shook her head as she remembered a remark Slébéne had once made: 'Age is a heavy load but the groans of the aged are often heavier than the load.' Certainly Congal seemed to be bearing a heavy burden. There was little of buoyancy in his character or dynamism for one who was prince of a territory and an influential voice on the council.

'Well, Congal,' encouraged Colgú, for the prince always waited to be invited to speak.

Congal began his reply with a sigh. 'I wish I was back in the land of the Cow Goddess.'

'Is that your solution? You just want to be back in your fortress at Daingean Uí Cúis?' Colgú replied, trying to restrain his cynical tone.

Congal spread his arms, palms upwards in a gesture of helplessness. 'Not exactly there. It is too crowded and the Yellow Death, as I remember it, loves to work its evil in crowds. I would isolate myself in my summer fortress under the shadow of Sliabh nDaidche, the great mountain, with its protection behind me and the sea in front of me. The plague passed over it once before, years ago, and it will do so again.'

Furudrán gave an unexpected roar of approval. 'Well, that

is good sense. The more I think about it, the more convinced I am that we should leave Cashel at once and go back to our own territories, isolate ourselves and avoid the oncoming pestilence.'

'Are you not concerned at the fate of ordinary country folk if we barricade ourselves in our fortresses?' Fidelma asked.

'We must do what we can for them,' agreed the prince, 'but we can't do anything if we perish. We must provide charity, for did not the Blessed Paul tell the Corinthians that the greatest thing of all was charity?'

Fidelma was about to respond when the morose-looking Prince Elódach of the Áine rose. 'I have recently come to the leadership of my people, following the unexpected death of my brother in a hunting accident. I presume that I have permission to speak in this council?'

Colgú stirred in surprise. 'You do not have to seek my permission to speak. You are of the *ceithirfine*.'

'I am not one of the learned and experienced Eóganacht princes, who are familiar with its protocols,' replied Elódach, as if it explained his reticence.

'Are you not the descendant of Crimthann, son of Eochaidh, son of the great Oengus Mac Nad Froíc, whose father, Conall Corc, found this rock and built his principal fortress here?' Colgú asked in a kindly tone. 'Were not my father and your father of the same blood? Did they not shed it in the same battles? You do not have to seek my permission to speak at this council. It is your right as it is also the right of the other princes.'

'I wished to be sure that no one challenges my right to be heard, for some may well do so in the light of past events.'

'What happened in the past is buried with the past,' Colgú replied immediately. 'We do not refer to it. What is it that you have to say?'

'What I have to say is that I am not a coward and I will stay and fight whatever terrors descend on my people. I will not scuttle to safe havens, island fortresses or to the extreme ends of the western peninsulas. I am an Eóganacht, proud of my descent from Eógan, who was gifted this land by the gods themselves. Did not Nuada give Eógan the sacred sword to raise in defence against all enemies, whether they be external or internal? Here I stay and here I will fight until victory or until death.'

There was a moment's silence before a howl of anger erupted from Furudrán, and even Congal's mild features re-formed into a disapproving mask.

This time Colgú was on his feet, using his height to try to dominate his relatives and bring them to order.

'My cousin Elódach has as much right to announce his intentions when faced by this pestilence as anyone else here. Perhaps he might have chosen his words a little less forcefully but it is good to know that he wants to defend this territory. But defence implies more than defiance and courage. I am still asking for ways of fighting a pestilence, not an army.'

Donennach, Prince of the Uí Fidgente, suddenly rose to his feet but hesitated until Colgú motioned for him to speak.

'I find myself in new and uncharted waters. For as long as can be remembered the Uí Fidgente have been in conflict with the Eóganacht of Cashel. We have claimed, over this period, that we were descendants of Cormac Cas, elder brother to Eógan Mór, and have the right to be recognised as princes of this kingdom. Many have died in the conflict that was our burden down the ages. So it rested on me to agree a peace and alliance with Cashel. This I have done and, for the first time, I come here to witness this alliance and to lend my voice to the approval of Colgú when the sacred sword of Nuada confirms this alliance at the Feast of Beltaine.'

He paused and even Fidelma found herself leaning slightly forward, wondering what Donennach was going to say. Indeed, even Conrí, Fidelma's friend, was looking apprehensive. Céit, the commander of Donennach's bodyguard, had moved slightly nearer to his prince as if ready to defend him.

Donennach glanced round for a moment as if to assure himself of their attention.

'I would say this, that Furudrán gives good advice. My response to this plague is to leave Cashel at once and to return to my own fortress of Dún Eochair Mhaig by the peaceful river waters.'

Elódach laughed harshly and for a moment, to Fidelma's surprise, the vision of the introverted and nervous young man vanished. 'What else would we expect of the Uí Fidgente?' His tone was sneering. 'It is not the first time they have run. The Áine saw them turn their backs to our warriors at battle on the Hill of Áine.'

It was Céit who called back in anger: 'And some of the Áine could do nothing other than watch the conflict from a safe distance because they feared to take part in that battle!'

There seemed a collective inhalation of breath. Elódach had leapt to his feet, his hand going for his scabbard but finding no sword hilt there. It was a rule that no one other than the King's bodyguards could enter the great hall armed. Already Enda was at Elódach's side and a hand with steel fingers had closed over the prince's right wrist.

'Everyone . . . resume your seats!' Colgú commanded the princes. 'This is a council of senior princes, not a brawl in an ale house. Sit down!'

When quiet descended the King continued. 'The courtesy I gave you, Elódach, forbidding people to mention the past, must not be abused by you. Courtesy is a two-way thing.'

Colgú sank back angrily in his chair. Some reference to an old event had been understood by several in the council, although not Fidelma.

Donennach was still standing, demanding attention. 'I would apologise to this council if insulting words were uttered by one of the Uí Fidgente. As the King said – let the past be buried with the past. He has already shown magnanimity in doing so and, as Prince Selbach said, the sacred sword of Nuada points the way. It hangs over the person of Colgú. Let us be content. Indeed, we have other matters of more immediate concern and these must be resolved by us as grown men and not as squabbling children.'

Colgú leant backwards in his chair, looking at the Uí Fidgente prince. 'Do you wish to add something more?'

'I do,' Donennach responded quickly. 'What I would have said before I was interrupted was this: I made the point that we would all like to fly away to some safe haven if we are being approached by the pestilence. It is a human instinct to flee to some familiar bastion. But that cannot be. There is one thing you overlook that binds us all here for a while.'

Even Colgú looked uncertain. It was Donennach who had
to supply the answer.

'The fact is that we face an invisible enemy who can find
us wherever we try to hide. So whether we stay or go, it will
be the same.'

Fidelma, thinking that Colgú was beginning to look tired,
decided to speak again.

'I have heard nothing that answers the question we were hoping
that this council would answer. I will ask it one more time. What
practical means do we have if we are to face the return of the
Yellow Plague?'

'I have told you,' Brother Fidach shouted again. 'Repent
and pray!'

Fidelma saw Dar Luga surprisingly raise her hand and
coughed nervously. She drew her brother's attention to her.
Colgú's eyes widened, for this was unusual in a council. Dar
Luga was only the household's *airnbertach*, housekeeper of
the royal residence and, as such, should not offer opinions.
After Beccan, Colgú's steward, had become involved in a
conspiracy against him, Dar Luga had taken on all the tasks
of the stewardship as well as those of housekeeper. Colgú had
been so content with the arrangement that he had not sought
to appoint another steward and several times Fidelma had
chided her brother for not giving Dar Luga the role in name
as well as in fact. The important fact was that a steward of
the fortress could claim a voice in council but a housekeeper
could not. He finally gestured his assent with his hand.

'Speak, Dar Luga,' he encouraged. 'You have earned the
right to be heard.'

The plump woman rose to her feet nervously and kept her
focus on the King.

'There are two things I should say. The first is that we
should be diligent in our cleanliness. We are a land blessed
with rivers and streams; we are blessed with springs. We should
be cleansing our physical bodies regularly. The second thing
is, this is a spacious land and we should not go crowding upon
one another. We know from the past that when we crowded
together the disease passed from one to another more quickly.'

'Is she saying that we should do nothing more than we do

already?' was the sneering comment from Blinne, the wife of Selbach.

'I know that it is common among the nobles here to bathe regularly,' explained Dar Luga. 'I do not have to remind you all that I and my assistants ensure that the *dabach* is filled each evening with hot water so that the *fothrucud,* the evening bath, can be taken. Do not I and my assistants ensure that, each morning, water is ready for the *indult,* the washing of hands and feet, and that a fresh bar of sweet-scented *sléic* is placed for lather according to the laws in the *Críth Gabhlach*? Do we not ensure sanative herbs are collected ready to be used in the bathing?'

'This much is done already, Dar Luga,' Colgú pointed out gently. 'But what is the point you are making?'

'The point is that we must instruct everyone, from noble down to servant, to follow these rules on bathing, on keeping clean, for in cleanliness I think the plague will pass us by. When I was a girl we bathed regularly in the upper reaches of the rivers and streams, always making sure that where the river rose there was freshness in the water, for lower down, cattle, sheep and other animals can pollute the waters and contribute their own diseases. So in clean, fresh water, there is health. It is there and free for everyone to use.'

'This is useful advice,' Fidelma said, 'but the fact is that it also means people would have to be able to move in and out of this fortress freely to obtain water, for we have limited supplies here within these walls and certainly not enough for all who reside here to bathe so frequently.'

'Unless, we ask a battalion of our warriors to be prepared to act as carriers of fresh water so as to continually supply it to the gates here.' Heads turned to Gormán, who had made the suggestion.

'Are you advocating that warriors act as menial carriers of water?' gasped Luan in disgust.

Gormán grinned at his former comrade. 'When the warriors march as a *sluagh,* when we cover long distances heading into battle, who carries water for us, my friend? We are all water carriers as well as soldiers. What man denies carrying water for his comrades?'

'But we are not marching to battle,' protested Luan.

'Aren't we doing that very thing?' Gormán replied, unmoved. 'Warriors are in the forefront of battle. They stand and are prepared to die in the fight against the enemy. Is not the oncoming pestilence the enemy? Is it not a war that we are facing? What is the difference whether we fight the enemy with the sword or whether we fight the enemy by other means? The purpose is to defeat the enemy that kills with disease just as surely as an enemy fighting with swords. As warriors we are asked to throw ourselves into the *barna baoghaill* – the gap of danger – the weak part by which the enemy seeks to enter the territory. So should we not throw ourselves into that gap now?'

There was a growing mutter of approval.

Enda was sceptical. 'The *lucht-tighe*, the household company, has to remain in the fortress but we should use a *catha*, a reserve battalion of warriors. We have one in training nearby. We can be well supplied if hands are needed to keep us in water.'

'I'd rather have fifty good physicians at the moment than fifty warriors,' scoffed Brother Laig.

Fidelma was approving of the former warrior's suggestion and ignored the physician. 'As Enda says, the training camp outside the township has a battalion ready in training according to law.'

'I could command such men,' Gormán volunteered. 'They could be used as scouts to give us warning of any disturbances or spread of the plague. In this way it would allow Enda to continue the urgent duties he is carrying out here with the lady Fidelma.'

While all men of the *céile* class were expected to come forward for voluntary service if needed, their service was strictly defined in law. The King was bound to pay each man for the service and compensate his family if he was lost in battle. It was said that it had been Cormac Mac Art who had founded colleges for the instruction in the arts of warfare at Tara. The Eóganacht kings had also established such training camps. The King, in times of peace, usually had one battalion, or *catha*, in training every year.

'It shall be done.' Colgú was enthusiastic. 'Gormán will

take the rank of *cath-mhilidh,* or commander, as he formerly held, but Enda remains commander of my household guard.'

Enda and Gormán exchanged glances of agreement.

'Then it is agreed,' Colgú announced.

'I will send the scouts with instruction that if any news of the approach of the plague come to them, then they will light beacons, the *tendal,* as they did in the old times,' Gormán suggested. 'I will make my headquarters in the training camp, just outside the township below, and send patrols and scouts to our borders for the purpose of picking up any news relating to the spread of this unseen enemy, if it has come ashore from this plague ship.'

'Then we will follow this plan,' agreed Colgú. He seemed relieved something positive had been decided. 'Perhaps Gormán and Enda can consult with each other on how best this intelligence may be relayed and how we should go ahead if there is need for us to lock ourselves in the fortress.'

There was a nervous cough. Brother Dáire, the librarian, had risen to his feet, seeking permission to speak.

'I may be wrong, but if I act *in loco autem scriba,* in place of your official scribe, then I believe I have a right to voice a view.'

Colgú looked confused and turned to Fidelma, who simply expressed her approval. 'The librarian does have the right,' she conceded, 'and perhaps he has knowledge that might help.'

Her brother turned back to the nervous young man and gestured for him to continue.

'It is said that the only thing people learn from history, is that people do not learn from history. Knowledge is quickly tossed aside and forgotten.'

'Well?' Colgú was puzzled.

'There are two matters that are related to the discussions that we are having. I am surprised that no one has referred to them. We have in our library a copy of the book called *De Bellico Perico* by Procopius of Caesaria. Our version is a Latin translation from the original Greek.'

'What has that to do with what we are talking about?' Colgú was bewildered.

'As the pestilence has been here before, I would say that

whoever was librarian at the time decided it would help us to have a copy of this work. In it there is a whole section on the Justinian pestilence. Procopius knew the plague well, for he was in Byzantium when he contracted it. He survived. That was a century ago, when the pestilence first came out of Egypt, from Pelusium and Alexandria, by way of merchant ships into the ports of Byzantium to spread over the known world. It is said that the deaths were uncountable – millions died – and we know how it swept across the five kingdoms.'

'You say that this Procopius wrote about this at that time?'

Brother Dáire picked up a leather-bound book from the table and began to turn its pages.

'Procopius writes that the plague visited as a sudden fever, which came on them as they roused from sleep or, sometimes, when walking or working. The disease spread in a languid manner and sometimes neither the sick nor physicians had any suspicion of danger until a swelling called a bubo took place in a particular part of the body – below the abdomen, or under the armpit or behind the ears.'

Some of the women present began to look uncomfortable.

'Do we need these details?' Furudrán asked.

'The first step,' the young librarian replied, 'is to be able to recognise the pestilence when it appears. The full details are described by Procopius. He says that the symptoms were not understood. Some supposed the disease centred in the bubonic swellings. They decided to investigate the bodies of the dead and opening some of the swellings they found a strange carbuncle that had grown there. Death had come in some cases immediately, in others after many days, and in some the body broke out in black pustules about as large as a lentil . . . all succumbed to death. Many were vomiting blood without visible cause. Importantly, he said that in this disease there was no cause that came within the province of human reasoning for in all these causes the issues were different and unaccountable. Tens of thousands died daily. However, some died and some were saved in spite of different methods of treatment. What worked for some did not for others. Initially it was thought that those who survived were those whose swellings reached an unusual size and then discharged pus; they survived and returned to health. Women in the process of giving birth died at the very time of childbirth but the babies survived.'

The young librarian paused and looked at the pale, frightened faces of the council members before resting on the arrogant features of Brother Laig.

'If you have not read this, I would suggest you come to the library and examine it. You should be then better equipped to know the enemy.'

Brother Laig's face reddened and he made an inarticulate sound in his throat.

Colgú's intervened quickly as he saw the growing anger in the physician's face.

'Does the account tell you the best way to treat it?'

'I would take Procopius's text with another,' Brother Dáire replied. 'A thousand years ago the city of Athens had a quarter of its citizens wiped out in a similar plague.'

'Athens?' Prince Selbach cried in frustration. 'Some eastern city? Who has heard of Athens and who cares about it?'

'Athens was then ruled by a man called Pericles,' went on Brother Dáire, not reacting to the man's ignorance. 'He was considered a great ruler, making Athens influential in the eastern world. His authority and its authority were undiminished until the arrival of a plague that broke the Athenian morale and they turned on Pericles, blamed him and removed him from office. He eventually caught the plague and died.'

Colgú frowned and cast a quick anxious glance at Fidelma before turning back to the librarian.

'And your point?' he prompted.

'Forgive me,' the young man replied softly. 'I do not know how much this company may know but in the library here we have a volume by Thucydides, an Athenian who also writes about this plague, which wiped out a third of his city. Living at the same time was a great physician, Hippocrates. Even most of our own physicians have now heard of him and his work. He wrote a treatise, *Epidemics* – that is on the study of plagues.'

This time Brother Laig did intervene.

'Hippocrates is not relevant to this part of the world,' he announced in a tone filled with derision.

'I would differ,' the young librarian said stoically. 'He makes the point that no religious rituals or incantations or even the most exotic medical formulae would defeat a pestilence such as that which visited Athens in his lifetime, and I would say the same of the one we are faced with now.'

He paused and smiled towards the plump housekeeper.

'What Dar Luga advises is good and may well protect the majority of us. But we are a people who like to be close to one another and we are not always so punctilious about our hygiene. But Thucydides reports that Hippocrates found an important factor in examining the plague. Those people who fell into despair before the pestilence reached them quickly succumbed to it. Further, those who flocked together, like sheep, quickly passed on the infection, especially when they crowded seeking care and comfort from one another. They succumbed to it in droves and had the highest number of mortalities. So what are the lessons? True, we must be clean, as Dar Luga says, and we must avoid banding together in crowds with strangers. We must also keep a positive state of mind. We must not panic nor must we despair.'

Fidelma was beginning to regard the young man with growing admiration.

'Brother Dáire speaks good sense as, indeed, does Dar Luga,' she commented loudly.

'There is one another thing that Thucydides also warns against,' called the young librarian. 'In the times of such disaster and pestilence, crime began to rise. Evil doers used the fears and needs of the people to commit the worst of evil acts, even stealing food and water from the sick, feeble and dying. Thieves calculated that those in charge would be too busy facing the pestilence to bother with them and so they would escape detection and punishment.'

Colgú shared Fidelma's appreciation of the advice that had been given. 'You have spoken good sense, Brother Dáire,' he said. 'For this, from now on you are my official librarian and *scriptor*.' He turned to Dar Luga. 'And you are now confirmed as my *rechtaire*, the steward of the royal household.'

'This is wrong!' came the angry voice of Brother Fidach. 'You are turning your back on the New Faith, the only path by which you can be truly saved. We should all hasten to the altars of the church, stand naked before God and confess our sins. God visits plagues on you to punish you when you have done wrong. So it was in ancient times and so it is now!'

Fidelma ignored him while looking approvingly at Brother Dáire.

'One thing that Brother Dáire says that I see already emerging among this council: the rise of panic and despair. If it rises unchecked, then, as Hippocrates said, it will lead to ruin and we will destroy ourselves even before the pestilence arrives here. I agree – we must maintain a positive mind. We do not even know if the pestilence has gained a hold on our shores.

'Meanwhile, I must remind you that I have the matter of Brother Conchobhar's murder to investigate and I shall be continuing to do so. You must hold yourselves available for answering my questions if and when I need ask. That means that no one – whatever the temptation – must leave the fortress without permission. You have heard good advice here and I suggest you follow it.'

NINE

After the great hall had emptied, Fidelma joined her brother, together with Gormán and Enda, in the King's private chamber. Gormán was given the white wand of office and his instructions were confirmed to organise the *catha,* or battalion, of warriors to serve as scouts and a defensive force if needed. When he had left the fortress, Fidelma, having indicated to her brother that she wanted a private word with him, asked Enda to wait outside.

'There are two matters I want to raise,' she announced as they seated themselves.

'I thought that you might want to,' her brother smiled grimly.

'I see you have left two of the household guard warriors in the great hall to keep an eye on the ceremonial sword. Furudrán seemed to suggest the sword might be connected with a question of your authority when the princes have their formal council.'

'At least he has warned us,' Colgú replied. 'It might be used as a focus of a demonstration against me. I have to admit that this particular year some of the princes are not happy with decisions I have had to make, especially about the treaty with the Uí Fidgente.'

'Furudrán infers that the council may raise objections to your rule,' Fidelma pointed out. 'What if this sword had gone missing? Was the purpose of the killing of Brother Conchobhar to steal the sword? Are people so superstitious that a missing sword could topple you?'

'The simple answer is – yes. Its symbolism is a focus. It would have been easier, though, to steal it from the great hall before I placed guards on it rather than steal it from the secret caves, which even I did not know about.'

'The thieves obviously did not know it was hanging in the great hall where Brother Conchobhar had placed it the evening before he was killed. However, could there be a second sword?'

Her brother glanced at her in surprise. 'I know of no other. What makes you say that?'

'Just remnants of a note Brother Conchobhar probably wrote. Nothing specific. Now that Brother Conchobhar, being the Keeper of the Sword, is dead, how does that affect the ceremony? Who hands you the sword? Someone must do so.'

Colgú thought for a moment. 'I was once told by old Conchobhar that the Keeper bequeaths the role to another before death. I don't know all the symbolism involved.'

'If there is no Keeper of the Sword, it might inspire a lack of confidence,' pointed out Fidelma. 'But we can't govern by symbols and superstition.'

'We will have to wait until the Chief Brehon Fíthel returns. He will know who the new Keeper is.'

'The guards must be doubly vigilant if there is such meaning in this symbolism. Do you really think there is such discontent among the princes at your rule?'

Colgú sighed moodily. 'I do not think that I have behaved badly as King.'

'Furudrán of Airthir Chliach is one of the influential Eóganacht princes,' Fidelma pointed out. 'But the tradition of the council is that all the Eóganacht princes have to be in agreement. You are Prince of the Eóganacht Chaisil, and one of the seven princes, so your opinion does not count. Finguine of the Glendamnach is another but he is already your *rodamna*, the heir apparent. He has been supportive of your decisions. Indeed, he has been part of them. Of the other five, we could say that Selbach of Ráithlinn seems critical and that leaves the princes of Áine, Loch Léin, and Árann. They must agree. Are you saying that you have cause to be worried?'

'You must know that I have not received unanimous support for several of my decisions,' admitted Colgú somewhat bitterly. 'My decision not to take more punitive measures against the Uí Fidgente when they were defeated at the battle of Áine – that was one of my first acts as King and it was unpopular, especially among the princes whose people suffered in that campaign. I was criticised for that.'

'The battle at Cnoc Áine was six years ago.'

'But still remembered vividly. Unrest and conspiracies

among the Uí Fidgente continued until last year, when I agreed that treaty and alliance with Prince Donennach. That treaty has yet to receive the approval of the council at the forthcoming meeting but it is already condemned by several.'

'Surely the council would prefer peace than to continuing the conflict?'

'That is to be seen. There are other events. I have been condemned for not leading an army against the King of Laigin in retaliation of his conspiracies against Muman. You were involved in uncovering the conspiracy involving Osraige. For the sake of peace, I decided to turn a blind eye to the involvement of the Prince of Osraige although I did force him to increase his tribute to Cashel. Then, of course, there has been much criticism about my forthcoming marriage to Princess Gelgéis . . .'

'But she condemned her cousin, the Prince of Osraige,' Fidelma pointed out. 'Do you really think there is such hostility on these matters among the princes? Are you sure that you are not seeing enemies where there are none?'

'Perhaps I am, perhaps not. I know that I have felt resentment but maybe I am exaggerating it. I think the main hostility is among the territories that border the lands of the Uí Fidgente.'

'If Furudrán reflects such an antagonism, at least I am warned. If Brother Conchobhar was attacked so someone could get their hands on the symbols of kingship as part of a plan to overthrow you, it still brings me to the question why they – whoever they are – did not take the sacred sword of office from the great hall instead of going to the apothecary and killing Brother Conchobhar.'

'Maybe they did not want to come into the open yet,' Colgú answered in a resigned tone.

Fidelma pressed her lips together and made a pushing motion with her chin as if to indicate a negative.

'I still have some way to go in this investigation.' A thought struck her. 'You know most people who serve in this fortress, don't you?'

'I would truly be a bad king if I did not know most of them. Why?'

'What do you know of a Sister Ernmas? I did not see her

attending the meetings with Brother Fidach and the other religieuse.'

Colgú seemed puzzled.

'I was not aware of any religieuse by that name serving in the chapel. Are you sure that is her name?'

'Brother Fidach told me that she was serving here when he arrived,' Fidelma said. 'In the brief exchange I had with her, she said she was from Imleach.'

'Certainly Brother Fidach arrived with the authority of Abbot Cuán. He had two young religieuse with him but I do not recall her at all.'

Fidelma rose from her seat with a shake of her head. 'It's curious. Anyway, I must continue the investigation. Within the next day or so, the rest of the princes will be here to participate in the council. Also, Abbot Cuán and the Chief Brehon Fíthel. Then it will be Beltaine. It would help matters if I could get this mystery solved before then.'

'That is if there is going to be a festival at Beltaine now,' her brother added bitterly. 'All we really needed is the threat of the return of the pestilence.'

'As Abbot Cuán will be coming from Imleach, I suggest that you send a messenger to request that he bring at least another physician and an apothecary, or more if they are available. If the pestilence does strike, I don't think we can put much faith in Brother Laig.' Fidelma suddenly looked concerned. 'If Eadulf insists on returning, I think it should be put to him that little Alchú should remain in Imleach. It may be a safer place for him than here.'

She left her brother and went in search of Enda.

'Where do we begin, lady?' Enda asked as they emerged into the courtyard.

'We have heard the opinion of Gobán, the smith,' she replied after a moment. 'Let us go to the library and have a word with the new librarian. He impressed me when he spoke in the council.'

'Brother Dáire?' Enda queried. 'He is young to be in this role. I do not think he has been more than a few weeks at the fortress, lady.'

'From what he said in the great hall, I thought he knew more than most there. You still have that book shrine?'

In answer, Enda held up the bag in which he was carrying the metal box. 'You told me to keep it safe, lady.'

Fidelma led the way to the library. At other times she was always happy visiting the great library, which the Eóganacht kings had taken great pride in accumulating. It rivalled the libraries of many of the ecclesiastical and bardic colleges. It was placed to the north-west of the complex of buildings that made up the fortress. They went through the doors that led into a small antechamber, which was where the librarian worked. No one was there. A single door at the back of this small room gave entrance into the large library room where all the books, most hanging from hooks in their individual book satchels, were stored. Tables were placed for those who wished to sit and read. At first there seemed no one inside this room but then Fidelma spotted a movement in a dark corner.

'Brother Dáire?' she called.

The fair-headed young man came forward from the shadows. He wore an expression of concern. He seemed to be constantly looking round and searching his surroundings. He gazed at her with pale eyes, and then recognised her.

'Lady Fidelma,' he acknowledged. 'How may I serve you?'

'I am seeking some advice, that is all.' She nodded to Enda to hold forth the sack with the book shrine.

The young librarian took the bag and placed it on a nearby table on which an oil lamp gave plenty of light. Reaching into the bag, he drew out the book shrine and placed it on the table.

'It is a *cumdach*, lady,' he announced gravely.

'Indeed, it is,' she replied solemnly, holding back an impulse to make a comment that this much was obvious. 'I was wondering if you could tell me what manner of book would be encased in it. A smith tells me the workmanship is unique, old and might even be dated before the coming of the New Faith two centuries ago.'

Brother Dáire surprised her with a quick smile.

'It is certainly ancient. I can confirm that,' he observed. 'But then I have seen it before.'

Fidelma tried not to show her astonishment.

'Where have you seen it?'

'I saw it last week.'

'Where was that?'

The young librarian blinked at the sharpness of her retort. 'Why, here, in this library.' He sounded surprised.

'Are you saying that this *cumdach*, this book shrine, is the property of this library?' she demanded.

'It is not. It is . . . was,' he corrected, 'the property of Brother Conchobhar.'

Fidelma gave an exasperated sigh. 'Then you must tell me all you know of it. How did you come to see it?'

Brother Dáire was clearly puzzled by the question and the agitation in her tone. However, he gathered his thoughts.

'When I came to serve in this library, my first task was to check an inventory of the books that are being held here.' He glanced round at the rows of book satchels hanging on the racks as if to indicate them and smiled. 'I am still working on it. The library here is quite substantial. As you know there has been an expanding of works being produced in the last two centuries, especially after the general adoption of the Latin alphabet. But we also have many books in Greek and in Hebrew as well. And there are the books of our own *Filí* or poets. We hold the earliest work of our own Seanchán Torpéist of the Eóganacht of Airthir Chliach and—'

'I am well acquainted with some of the works held here, Brother Dáire,' Fidelma interrupted dryly. 'I was born in this fortress. So let us concentrate on this book shrine.'

The librarian flushed a little at the rebuke.

'It was an edict of your brother that the inventory of books be made up to date. He ordered that a list of all the works here, secular and of the religious, be listed without exception. Because of that, Brother Conchobhar felt it was incumbent on him to bring me some works that he personally held as part of his official office as custodian of the sacred sword. Among other items he held were some ancient books on the healing arts and attendant subjects. He brought this *cumdach* in order that I might list the contents before it was returned to a place where, so he told me, unauthorised hands would not touch it. In fact, while he was here, he took the opportunity to make notes from its contents and went to one or two other volumes that we have, as if to check on references.'

'So the shrine was opened and you saw the contents of the book that it held?' pressed Fidelma excitedly. 'You knew that he held some ritual items connected with the kingship of Muman?'

'I did.'

'And what was the book?' she demanded, trying to control her impatience.

'Why, have you not seen the book itself?' Brother Dáire unhooked the lid and saw it was empty. He seemed puzzled.

'As you see, Brother Dáire, the book shrine is empty and that is the state in which I found it, apart from the fact it was locked and had no key when we came on it,' she said in considered tones. 'The contents have been removed. That is why I am asking you to tell me what was in it.'

Brother Dáire seemed startled as he considered this.

'You mean that the book itself has been stolen? So Brother Conchobhar found the key? He lost it when he was in the library.'

Fidelma closed her eyes for a second. 'I am confused. He lost the key?'

'When he had finished, he shut the shrine and took it away. Later that evening he came back and said he found it locked when he left here and had mislaid the key here in the library. He was going to come back next morning to have a thorough search of it. But how was the shrine locked and the book missing? Was it stolen when Brother Conchobhar was killed?'

'I want you to hold this as privileged information under law. You are not to mention it to anyone else. I just need to know what was in it.'

'I understand the need to keep this secret, lady. The *cumdach* contained a text of a *forsundud* with instructions to be given at the ceremonies when the assembly approves the installation of the king, giving validation for the legitimacy of his dynasty.'

'Was it an Eóganacht *forsundud*?'

'Your brother's ancestry?' queried the librarian. 'Yes. Some of it was, but it was mainly a smaller text in the ancient alphabet.'

'A text in Ogham? What was it about?'

'I can't recall the details offhand, I just copied the title.'

'You have no recollection of the title?'

'I had to list a lot of books to make the inventory. I can't recall offhand.'

Fidelma was about to reach for the *cumdach* when she stopped.

'You said that you listed the book in your inventory? Can you show me the list?'

Brother Dáire eyes widened at her logic. 'How stupid of me. Of course, I did. I tried to be specific about the content. I will find it, but I am now prompted that the *forsundud*, the praise poem, started with Eógan Mór and how he was renamed the Servant of Nuada when he was given the sacred sword and blessed by the god.'

'Was that the section in Ogham?'

'I think so. I do remember one thing. While I was making my inventory, Brother Conchobhar gave an exclamation and asked me where I kept the library copy of the poems of Seanchán Torpéist. When I told him where it was, he took it to a table as if he were looking something up. I know he took a quill and made a note on a piece of parchment. He looked at it and was nodding as if satisfied. He said one thing that puzzled me . . . he said: "The fists are the wrong way. To protect, hands do not attack."'

'What did he mean by that?'

'I've no idea.'

'He made a note as if he were copying something Seanchán Torpéist had written?' Fidelma echoed, trying not to sound excited.

'Just so.'

'Where is the volume?'

Brother Dáire went to one of the book satchels and drew out a small volume. It was a parchment book of scarcely a score of pages. Fidelma took it and carefully turned over the pages. But nothing seemed to be of any connection to what she was expecting. Then something caught her eye.

'You said Brother Conchobhar took a quill to make notes?' she asked Brother Dáire.

'As I told you. He made just a short note.'

Fidelma turned back to the page where she had noticed

a line under which were several pin pricks as if made with
the point of a quill. The words leapt out at her. *Bráthair
agus derbsiur* – brother and sister. What were these lines of
Seanchán Torpéist? 'Brother and sister are not the same,
one is false.' False! The word was clear – *brionnach*! Just
as it said in the strip of *palimpsestos* they had found. But
the context meant nothing. The poem appeared to bear no
relationship to sacred swords. Was it about some mytho-
logical story of two children who claimed the same father
– one was genuine but the other was false? What had that
to do with this matter? The quotation seemed to have no
connection at all.

Brother Dáire had returned with his inventory and laid it
on the table.

'I tried to be as concise and informative as I could,' he
explained as he unrolled the vellum on the table, before starting
to trace the lines with an ink-stained forefinger.

'Ah, it should be here, lady,' he smiled as he turned the roll.
'It should . . .' his voice trailed off.

'What is it?' Fidelma demanded.

She moved forward and bent over the librarian's shoulder.

There was a rectangular shape cut out of the vellum. It had
obviously been executed with the sharp point of a knife, the
lines clearly cut and not torn. The piece that had been cut out
was not discernible unless someone unrolled the scroll to this
point.

Brother Dáire looked very upset. 'How could anyone desecrate this work?' he muttered.

'The important question is, when did this happen?' Fidelma
asked slowly. 'How long after you saw the work that Brother
Conchobhar brought here to show you?'

'I cannot tell. I remember Brother Conchobhar waited while
I noted the titles. But he was busy doing some research. I
haven't looked at this inventory since I made it,' he replied.
'But look at the edges of the cut. They are bright and fresh.'

Fidelma's mouth tightened. 'After he wrote his note, did he
put the material back in the *cumdach* and leave?'

Brother Dáire frowned. 'No, I remember him holding the
notes in his hand and picking up the *cumdach* and leaving.'

'But he must have put the book back and locked it before he left?'

'He must have.'

'But it was locked when he saw Dar Luga, for he was concerned about having lost the key.' Fidelma frowned. 'And when we opened it, it was empty. At some stage it had to have been opened, emptied and relocked. Was there anyone else in the library at the time he was here?'

'I think so,' the librarian was frowning. 'You don't think the contents were stolen here and the box closed and locked so that he merely picked it up and only checked later, finding the key missing as well?

'Who has been to the library? Do you know, for example, if a religieuse has been asking about this document? She's very tall and clad in black robes.'

'Do you mean Sister Ernmas?' The librarian stared at Fidelma in surprise. 'I don't know her well but I made a note of her name for my records. But she is certainly a tall woman in black.'

Fidelma hid her excitement. 'So she uses the library? When was the first time you saw her?'

'Last week, not long after I first arrived here.'

'What can you tell me about that?'

'I was finishing my work. I saw a figure in the further end of the library examining some scrolls. I had not even seen her enter. But the library is open most of the time and one can even enter it from the gardens by a side door. I went forward to see if she needed help. As you described her, she was a woman dressed in dark robes and with a skin that was so pale I would have felt she had no blood in her. Her eyes were like pieces of ice in the dead of winter. Most of the time she kept her face in the shadows.'

'That sounds like a very poetic description,' Fidelma observed, unmoved. 'Did she say her name at that time or give any indication of her role in the fortress?'

'I do not think so.'

'I presume that you know when she uses the library?'

'Not regularly. You know the library is never locked, lady.'

'As the librarian, I would have thought that you would know all who serve the New Faith here.'

'Obviously I do not,' replied the young librarian dryly. 'There was a period last week when Sister Ernmas was in here for many long hours searching for some obscure text.'

'And she asked you no questions? What was she looking for?'

'To be honest, I do not know. She said she had been to the library before and knew what to look for. As I had only just arrived at the fortress then, I was pleased to leave her to her own devices. I did notice the manuscript she was examining was about the House of Death. I think it was something about Donn, the *aistréoir* – the Gatekeeper to the House of Death.'

Enda gave a slight shiver. 'Gatekeeper to the House of Death?' he muttered.

'It was an old text; I have since checked up on it,' agreed the librarian. 'Donn was supposed to be a collector of souls. He took them to an island and, from there, he conducted them to the Otherworld. The world of the dead.'

'Did you know, according to an old friend of Brother Conchobhar, that he considered the Keeper of the Sword was synonymous with Gatekeeper to the House of Death?' Fidelma said.

'But that is the role of Donn in the ancient stories,' replied the young man. He paused: 'Who is this religieuse, Sister Ernmas? What does she do here?'

'That is what I am trying to discover,' Fidelma replied patiently. 'Anyway, the people who entered here this morning – do you know what they wanted?'

'The priest wanted to look at a copy we have of *Ignis creator igneus*, which is sung at the blessing of lighting the candles on the Fires of Bel, and extols the lighting of the fires. Brother Laig and Esnad were also here.'

'So what did they want?'

'That I cannot recall.'

Fidelma sighed. There was little point in continuing. She glanced at Enda and motioned him to pick up the book shrine to return it to the sack. Then she thanked Brother Dáire and left the library.

Outside she halted and sighed in frustration.

'It seems we have more questioning to do,' she said reluctantly.

'I do not know what it is we have learnt, lady,' the young warrior confessed. 'You heard nothing of significance?'

'Probably there was if I could recognise the significance,' she admitted with a frown.

Enda assumed a glum look. 'Well, here comes our arrogant friend,' he said.

Brother Laig was crossing the courtyard, heading towards the royal residence. He glanced at them and seemed to increase his pace as if to avoid them.

'You seem in a hurry?' Fidelma called, moving towards him.

Brother Laig did not appear to be willing to slow his pace.

'I have to see the King at once,' he said shortly. 'I need to leave for the Abbey of Imleach and have been told that I cannot leave the fortress without his permission.'

'You may halt,' replied Fidelma in a tone of command that actually made the physician hesitate and stop uncertainly. 'You will not get permission for two reasons. Understand that I speak as a *dálaigh* as well as my brother's adviser. You cannot leave until I say so, for you are now a witness in the investigation of the murder of Brother Conchobhar. Secondly, you are the only physician now in this fortress and your knowledge may well be needed in these coming days. I thought that was explained to you at the council?'

'The King will not need my advice on how the plague will affect the kingdom,' he said petulantly. 'He already rejected it.'

'I need to ask you some more questions.'

Brother Laig sniffed. 'I have already given you my opinion on the death of the old apothecary.'

'You have,' she confirmed, 'but you have told me a lie.'

The physician was in the process of turning away, attempting to dismiss further conversation. Now he swung back, a redness coming to his cheeks.

'What? How dare you? You will apologise . . .'

'I dare because I am a *dálaigh* investigating a murder, and when a witness tells me something that is not true, the punishment is severe.'

So sharply did she speak that the physician took a step backwards and his mouth opened and closed without making a sound as he tried to respond.

'Brother Laig, you told me that you saw a woman go into Brother Conchobhar's apothecary after the maid, Cainder, left it. Further, you gave a description of the woman, which left me in no doubt who it was. This is not such a large place that people can be mistaken for one another.'

Brother Laig remained silent.

'I will take your silence as an admission that you remember describing the woman? You remember you said she was a "lady" among the guests here. Therefore, she was easy to pick out from the guests gathered in the great hall? I asked you to confirm who the woman was. It seemed that you had spoken to her first so I was surprised when you told me she was not the person you had described. Do you follow me so far?'

Brother Laig still said nothing. There was an almost furtive expression on his face as his eyes moved as if seeking a means of escape. Fidelma waited a moment before continuing.

'That was a lie. I have talked with Esnad, the companion of Princess Blinne.'

Brother Laig did not know that one of Fidelma's tricks, in questioning people, was not so much as to tell an untruth but to imply an untruth, which would make the person being questioned open up, thinking they had already been implicated in a greater lie. Brother Laig was no exception. He returned her gaze with one that mirrored guilt and anger.

'So Esnad admitted it was her?' he asked slowly. 'But she swore me to secrecy.'

Fidelma almost smiled with satisfaction.

'I saw you next to her in the great hall. I suppose you agreed to deny the story. You claimed not to have met her before. Why did you bother to describe her in the first place?'

Brother Laig's lips thinned. 'I described only what I saw.'

'Then why did you agree to lie after you talked with her?'

'I had seen her among your brother's guests. But, no, I had not met her before.'

'So the question remains: how did she persuade you to deny it was her that you had seen?' Fidelma pressed. 'This sounds curious. Are you sure that you had not met her or had dealings with her before?'

'I had not,' he replied almost indignantly.

'So did she explain to you her reasons for the visit to Brother Conchobhar's apothecary so early in the morning?'

'She has probably told you,' he shrugged.

'I am asking *you* what she said.'

Brother Laig hesitated. 'She said she had merely gone to purchase a herb. It was *mormónt*.'

'*Mormónt*? Wormwood?' Fidelma considered the statement for a moment. As far as she knew, it was not a rare plant but grew plentifully. 'Isn't that for digestive disorders?'

Enda, standing by, sniggered and Brother Laig looked uncomfortable. Fidelma frowned at them both in surprise. While she had a vague general knowledge of herbs she often relied on Eadulf as to their specific usages.

She turned to Enda. 'Does wormwood mean something to you?' she asked sharply.

Enda drew himself up with a faint flush of embarrassment. 'Sorry, lady. Being among rough warriors, you hear things being discussed. Wormwood is said to increase sexual desire and stimulate the sensual imagination.'

Fidelma's eyes widened a fraction. She turned back to Brother Laig. 'Is this true?'

Brother Laig grimaced dismissively. 'I have heard it is so but I have never had the need to try it myself. It is claimed for other usages, such as bad breath, but it is said, historically, that Roman legionaries found it a sexual stimulant.'

'I did not notice that the Lady Esnad had bad breath,' Fidelma remarked with irony.

Brother Laig was silent.

'So,' Fidelma continued, 'Esnad told you she had gone to the apothecary to get this wormwood? Did she acquire it?'

'I did not ask.'

'But she asked you to remain silent about her visit to Brother Conchobhar? And you agreed to do so?'

'That is so.' The response was unwilling.

'I'll tell you what troubles me, Brother Laig. What made you agree? This is a murder investigation and all witnesses are bound to tell the truth or suffer punishment of fines. You said that you did not know her and you had clearly recognised her leaving the apothecary. Why did you lie?'

She could see from the way Brother Laig's mouth seemed to clamp shut that she was unlikely to force a further response at that time.

'Very well,' she said. 'I will leave you to think about the consequences of withholding information when asked by a *dálaigh* in a case of murder. Think carefully on this.'

Brother Laig turned, and Fidelma and Enda watched him disappearing off towards the chapel building.

Enda was the first to move with a disapproving shake of his head. 'I can't say that I like Brother Laig.'

Fidelma grimaced with humour. 'I think you made that clear even from your first meeting with him.'

'Well, he does not make liking him easy. Also, I feel one cannot trust anything he says. He has some reason to lie and we should find out why. A little persuasion might be needed.'

Fidelma regarded him with some reproof. 'Information gained by force is worthless. Remember the ancient saying – when violence enters through the door of your house, law and justice leaves through the chimney.'

'So how can we proceed?'

'From the interesting point that Brother Laig has left us with.'

'Which was?' the young warrior asked uncertainly.

'The matter of wormwood,' Fidelma said with a thin smile.

TEN

At Fidelma's suggestion, they found Dar Luga in the kitchens busy checking on meal preparations for the King's guests. The formal appointment by Colgú, making her *rechtaire,* or steward, of the royal residence, had not changed her demeanour in any way. She preferred to oversee her kitchen personally and, indeed, do things herself rather than delegate them to others. It was a habit that Fidelma had never been able to coax her out of although she believed that Dar Luga often overtaxed herself. However, Dar Luga was a perfectionist in all things. But now she paused in making her lists and came forward to greet Fidelma with her usual motherly smile.

'How do you find your new position?' Fidelma asked with humour.

'No different,' she admitted, 'except it is good to have a word of praise now and then. I just hope I did not overstep my authority at the council, but no one seemed to be considering hygiene so I felt moved to speak.'

'It was a good thing that you should do so. In fact, you and that young new librarian spoke more sense than any of those so-called advisers who are supposed to offer counsel to my brother.'

'What can I do for you?'

'I have a question, if you don't mind,' replied Fidelma.

'If I can help you, all you have to do is ask.'

'Have you or any of the attendants, specifically those who look after the guest rooms, noticed anyone among the guests using wormwood?'

Dar Luga stared at her with a puzzled expression. It was clear that the mention of the herb registered with her.

'Wormwood, lady? Now, what makes you ask that?'

'It is just something that I am trying to work out.'

'Well, it is a coincidence.'

'Coincidence?' Fidelma prompted tersely.

Dar Luga gave a humorous grimace. 'It is just that young Cainder had the task of tidying the rooms this morning. She came to the kitchens and asked for hot water. She told me that the lady Blinne had requested her to fetch some hot water so that she could prepare a tonic.'

'And?'

'Cainder noticed that she had been preparing some worm-wood on her side table and so she assumed that was the base of an infusion that she wanted to create.'

'Are you sure this preparation was for the use of Princess Blinne?'

'Cainder simply said that the lady Blinne was the one preparing the mixture and asked Cainder to fetch hot water for it. One would presume that she was preparing the mixture for herself.'

Fidelma paused for a moment before thanking Dar Luga and leaving, followed by a perplexed Enda.

Once outside, he asked: 'Is that significant, lady?'

'You'll remember that Brother Laig's story was that Esnad claimed she had visited Brother Conchobhar to acquire worm-wood. You told me its use is as an aphrodisiac.'

Enda flushed. 'As I said, lady, it is common knowledge among the warriors.'

'So now we must ask if the wormwood was for Esnad or for Blinne, and why would either of them need such a medi-cation? They both seem virile young women.'

'You forget, it has uses in other forms.'

'I have borne those in mind but discounted them,' Fidelma assured him. 'And speaking of Brother Laig, I saw him going into the apothecary just now. He should have had these few moments to reflect on matters so we will go and have further words with him.'

She hurried across the courtyard with Enda at her heels.

Brother Laig was in Conchobhar's apothecary, taking down some jars from one of the shelves. He turned, slightly startled, as they entered. A moment later his expression re-formed in a distrustful mask.

'I am the only physician here and entitled to take what herbs

I deem fit to prepare for the pestilence,' he exclaimed defensively as he saw the inquisitive look on their faces.

Fidelma considered him without changing expression for a moment. 'I don't question your entitlement, Brother Laig. However, you have had an opportunity to reflect whether you want to reconsider your answers to my questions or are prepared to face the consequences of not answering. Perhaps we can continue our discussion?'

Brother Laig's jaw was set firmly.

'I have told you all. I think it vindictive of you to advise the King to stop me leaving the fortress to check on the progress of the plague when I might be of greatest help elsewhere.'

Fidelma regarded him sombrely. 'At the moment the King needs a physician's advice. Also, you are a witness in a murder inquiry. I suppose that you were sincere in your intention of heading south to learn about the plague? You were not thinking of turning north to the safer peaks of Sliabh Eibhline?'

For a moment Brother Laig was quiet and then the anger of pretended outrage spread across his features.

'How dare you claim . . . claim that I . . .?'

'Keep calm,' Fidelma interrupted sharply. 'I serve the law and not maliciousness or spite. I require you to answer my questions.'

Various expressions of hate and defeat crossed the physician's face as he gazed at her. He stood without making any response. She paused, waiting for a few moments before continuing.

'You described Esnad as the woman you saw entering this apothecary with Brother Conchobhar early this morning. Then you changed your story and said it was not her. Then you changed your mind again and said she admitted to you that she had gone there for wormwood, which, she said, was for her use. You then admitted that she made you agree to say that it was not her that you saw.'

Brother Laig shifted his weight uncomfortably but did not reply.

'It would be better to tell me the complete truth now rather than later,' snapped Fidelma. 'Surely there must have been a *quid pro quo* . . . something for something. I did not think you would have agreed to remain silent without expecting something in return?'

'I have told you what I know,' muttered the physician. 'What more can I say?'

'The answer to this one question, which intrigues me. I want an answer, a truthful answer. If you try to answer without resorting to the truth then the consequences will be on your own head.'

It seemed for a moment that he would not respond and then he shrugged.

'Well, if you must know . . .' the words were finally spoken with ill-concealed anger, 'we agreed that I would subsequently benefit from her lady's favours.'

Fidelma's eyes widened slightly. It was not the answer she had been expecting.

'I doubt that you believe in these new esoteric ideas of celibacy from Rome. However, I'm surprised that the lady Esnad would have immediately made such a suggestion to a stranger.'

'That is what she offered me to keep secret that she had gone to see Brother Conchobhar to acquire the herb.'

Fidelma stared at Brother Laig for several moments. She had the feeling, in spite of his arrogance and dislikeable personality, he was actually telling the truth; no other reason seemed logical. She realised that she could only pursue the matter with Esnad herself.

Outside, after they had left the apothecary, Edna finally exploded in annoyance. Fidelma realised that he had been trying to hold his temper in check for the last few moments.

'By Áine's sacred breath! Did you really believe that?'

Fidelma regarded him absently with a frown. 'I fail to see why you need to invoke the name of the old goddess of love to bolster your point.'

'It is just unbelievable,' the young warrior retorted.

Fidelma looked at him in amusement. 'You do not believe that the lady Esnad would agree to such a compromising liaison with the likes of Brother Laig? He is, after all, a handsome man, for all his arrogance.'

'I do not believe she would make so bold an offer as the price for his silence. Besides, if, as Brother Laig indicates,

Esnad went to the apothecary to get a sexual stimulant for herself before even meeting Brother Laig . . . why would she need it? Why should she need such a stimulant if she could make such an offer so easily to Brother Laig? To make such an offer, she would have to be one who has little need for arousal. That proves he is lying or . . .'

'That she might have gone to pick up the stimulant for someone else?' Fidelma finished.

Enda's face registered sudden comprehension.

'So that was why you were asking such questions from Dar Luga?'

'That was one reason. However, I believe it is now time that we have another word with Esnad and this time confront her with the truth.'

It was some time before they found Esnad. One of the guards had seen her going into the gardens, which ran inside the outer walls at the back of the library and alongside the interior behind the apothecary, the chapel and to the back of the guest quarters. In fact, Fidelma knew the area, for it was one where there was a wooden table and chairs, which the afternoon sun used to strike. She remembered it as a place where, years ago, she used to sit on bright summer days when she could read scripts outside of the claustrophobic environment of the library.

She made her way, with Enda following, around the library walls into a sweet-smelling flower garden. She saw Esnad exactly where she thought she would be, seated with head bent over a garden table with a small manuscript book beside her. Esnad heard their approach and glanced up with a frown. She was obviously displeased at being disturbed.

Fidelma greeted her with a disarming smile and went to sit next to her without asking permission. She glanced at the manuscript book on the table.

'I see that you are reading the poems of Líadan,' she opened. 'She was a fascinating poetess and the beloved of the poet Cuirithir.'

Esnad drew back slightly as if distancing herself.

'Their love story is well known, but frowned upon by some of the New Faith,' she remarked slowly. 'It is a beautiful love story. I like Líadan's philosophy. Men's hands always confront like fists, while women's hands will always protect and are raised in peace.'

'Is it her comment on Abbot Ciarán when he forbade their love?'

'Yes; she had a beautiful way of expressing it.'

'I doubt whether Brother Fidach would find beauty in it,' Fidelma observed dryly. 'He seems to believe in the new esoteric teaching that celibacy brings you closer to the godly life, just as Ciarán supposedly did. It is an idea that has some support in Rome.'

'When true love is prevented by the prejudices of others, it is a sad matter,' the girl commented.

'So you do not agree that the Blessed Ciarán was justified in preventing the love of Líadan and Cuirithir?'

'Only those intolerant of human love and affection would applaud these man-made rules that are created for others' unhappiness. Celibacy is a perversion of the human condition.'

'You believe in love, then?'

'It is, perhaps, the best of all emotions.'

'And you have experienced it?'

Esnad suddenly frowned, suspicious as to what lay behind the question. 'What do you mean?'

'A simple question. I was just interested. It is not the question, however, that I wanted to ask you. I came because I suspect that you lied to me. You know deceiving a *dálaigh* is punishable under law?' Fidelma had not changed her even tone.

The girl flushed and her jaw thrust forward as if she would deny it but Fidelma continued, 'You told me that you had not seen Brother Conchobhar early this morning. You told me that you had not gone to the apothecary this morning. I am told you did. Furthermore, you asked Princess Blinne to support you in your declaration and stand as witness. Why was that?'

The girl was flushed. 'Are you accusing me? Are you saying it is otherwise?' She tried to sound indignant.

'I am simply saying that there is another witness who has decided to tell the truth.'

Esnad's mouth compressed for a moment into a thin line. She was silent.

'Do you now admit the truth? You went to see Brother Conchobhar early this morning? Brother Laig has confessed it, and also that he spoke with you.'

'He said he would not,' the girl replied in anger.

'Let us have the truth. This morning you went to the apothecary. Was that on your own account?'

There was a long silence before Esnad finally answered.

'I was asked to go to the apothecary and obtain an herb.'

'By your cousin, Princess Blinne? And she asked you to get wormwood?'

'It was,' the girl confirmed after hesitation.

'Tell me what happened.'

'Nothing. I saw the old apothecary outside his *potecaire* and I approached him. I asked him if he had this herb that Blinne wanted. He had. We went inside and he found it. I paid for it and I left. It was as simple as that.'

'Did you see Brother Laig outside at that time?'

'It was only later, just before the council was summoned to hear of the death of the apothecary, that he came up to me and told me he had seen me there.'

'Had you known him before you came to this fortress?'

'I had not. Only after our party arrived some days ago was he pointed out to me as the new physician here.'

'So you were already in, or outside, the great hall and he approached you?'

'It was just after everyone was entering the hall. He asked why I had gone so early to see Brother Conchobhar. I told him I wanted herbs. He asked what type of herbs. Stupidly, I told him. He recognised the herbs and their use and said something lewd about them. Something to the effect that we had no need to stimulate the carnal desires between us. I was rude to him and began to walk away.'

'That was the end of the encounter?'

The girl shook her head. 'He took a pace forward and caught me by the arm. He said he felt bound to tell people what he had seen. He pointed out that I had been with Brother Conchobhar just before the time of his murder and that I would be a suspect. I protested but he said that he could stop the suspicion. Then he said I was . . . was attractive and asked why I needed such stimulants as the herbs he saw me carrying. I denied that was their use but he was insistent.'

'You admitted to him that they were for Princess Blinne, whom you attend?'

The girl was startled. 'I did not tell him!'

'But they were for Blinne? Is that the truth?'

'I was not willing to tell *him* that.'

'Why not?'

'Because I knew the reason why Blinne sought their use.'

'She is married to Selbach? What harm then?'

The girl pressed her lips together. 'It was because she wanted them for another.'

'Another?'

'She has a lover. She is no longer young and this lover was younger. That is why I did not want to tell anyone and reveal her weakness. Anyway, Brother Laig said that if I wanted his silence about my visit there must be some exchange.'

'And what was the exchange?'

The girl lowered her head. 'He said he would not tell that he had seen me with Brother Conchobhar if I . . . that is, if I . . . Truly I did not know what to do. Everyone was now entering the great hall. I saw you entering and he said he was duty-bound to report the matter unless . . .' She hesitated awkwardly.

'He made you an indecent proposal? Let me get this clear. It was not you who made this suggestion to him?'

The look of shock on the girl's face was enough to confirm Fidelma's initial opinion that Brother Laig had lied.

'Did you agree?'

'What else could I do?' Esnad said with a trembling lip. 'I had to say something immediately. I could say nothing but inclined my head as if I agreed.'

'I presume that nothing further has transpired?'

'Of course not, and neither will it now that I have reconsidered the alternatives. I could not do that, even for the lady Blinne's sake.'

'For Blinne's sake? Very well. Let us forget Brother Laig for the moment. When you saw Brother Conchobhar to purchase the wormwood, was there anyone else in or near his apothecary? I want to be sure of that.'

The girl had no hesitation. 'I had a clear view of the working rooms that make up his apothecary and there was no one there. That I can swear to.'

'So why did you purchase this herb for Blinne? Who is it that she is enamoured of?'

'That I do not know. I think he may be one of the young warriors. However, I could not take an oath on it.'

Fidelma shook her head sadly. 'Well, as Hippocrates once wrote, *"primum non nocere"* – "above all do no harm". And if she is doing no harm . . .?'

Esnad pursed her lips. 'I do not think Selbach cares much about what she does.'

'There is always divorce, anyway. There are plenty of grounds for divorce stipulated in law, and several that are classed as obtainable without fault, where neither the wife nor husband is liable. If their union is amicable then there is no problem. I will not mention this conversation. But in trying to conceal the nature of the matter you nearly landed yourself under suspicion of Brother Conchobhar's murder.'

'I have been a friend to my cousin since we were born. When she realised that there were other things that she needed in life, apart from being Selbach's wife, I have been happy to assist her.'

'Would she not have been better to divorce him?'

'I do not think that she would like to give up the power of being wife to the Prince of Ráithlinn,' admitted the girl.

'And Selbach is one of the seven senior princes of the Eóganacht,' Fidelma added thoughtfully. 'I admit, I do not know much about him as a person.'

'Even though he is a senior prince, I think that he believes that his branch of the Eóganacht has been excluded in many things,' offered the girl.

'Excluded?'

'That they should have been princes of a greater territory than the one he now rules.'

'Kingship is not something to be given,' Fidelma corrected her. 'It has to be earned. And as I recall, the Eóganacht Ráithlinn extend along the southern coast from the territory of the Cenel nÁeda to the territory of the Béara. The island that is his principal fortress is one whose size and beauty is easily overlooked by conflicts that arise on the mainland. The sea separates it. I certainly would prefer living in such an area.'

Esnad shook her head. 'I am afraid Selbach is of a philosophy that beauty counts as little without power. But, at least, the stretch of water would provide a better protection if the pestilence descends on us. Selbach takes great pride in Árd na Rátha, his fortress, which he adorns as if he possesses great wealth and power.'

'But Blinne and you, yourself, are also related to the Eóganacht?'

'So distant that it is not worth the mention. We are of a small clan, minor farmers, even if we are called the Eóganacht Uí Echach.'

'But growing in influence, I hear,' Fidelma added.

Despite her modest reply, the girl was obviously as proud of her connections as any of the princes.

When Fidelma and Enda made their way back to the main courtyard, the commander of the household turned to Fidelma once again, showing his confusion.

'If we believe her, what do we do now? Are we going to see the arrogant Brother Laig and call him a liar again for blaming the girl, and then see if we can get further information?'

'I don't think he has much more information to give. I believe we have learnt the truth from Esnad as to her visit to the apothecary. I will put a watch on Brother Laig. I would not put it past the physician to try to leave the fortress if he can. I think he would do so for no other reason than he is scared of the pestilence.'

'He will not be alone,' Enda smiled thinly. Then a thought seemed to occur to him. 'If there was an attempt to rob Brother Conchobhar because it was known he was the keeper of some of the sacred artefacts of kingship, then it strikes me that Selbach might be worth questioning. If the girl is right, and he thinks that he should have more powers, then what more power could he attain other than the kingship itself?'

'Perhaps,' Fidelma admitted quietly. 'But don't forget that this desire might be shared by all the princes.'

'Very well,' Enda said with a sigh. 'So what path can we take? It seems we have considered all the avenues that are open.'

'Then we must try taking the avenues that are closed to us at the moment,' replied Fidelma.

Enda was puzzled and was about to speak when Fidelma held up her hand to still him.

'I've just remembered something that Conrí said that I wanted to follow up.'

Enda's face brightened. 'If there is any plot in this, and you discount Selbach, then the next suspect would be one of Uí Fidgente. Donennach would be the obvious suspect,' he offered.

Fidelma regarded him with disapproval. 'It occurs to me that you have named several obvious suspects, Enda,' she said dryly. 'Anyway, Donennach has made an alliance with us; remember that. And Conrí, his warlord, has been a friend of mine over the years.'

Enda shrugged, slightly bewildered. 'Then we have no suspects at all?' he complained.

'Suspects? No. But we do have an unexpected area that I should pursue and you have just reminded me of it. Do you know if Céit, Donennach's bodyguard, is quartered in the guest house?' she asked.

'He was given quarters to be nearer to Donennach.'

'I wonder if he is there now. Let's go and find out.'

'Do you think he is a suspect?' Enda asked in surprise.

'Cannot I question anyone without them being arraigned as a suspect?' Fidelma sniffed disparagingly as they made their way to the guest house.

The first person they saw on entering the complex was Conrí himself.

'Any more news of your investigation?' he greeted cheerfully.

Fidelma knew him well enough to know he was without guile.

'I thought I should just have a word with Céit, following what you said earlier.'

The warlord of the Uí Fidgente frowned. 'Is it necessary? I only told you so that you might take it into account, following the rumours and veiled accusations that I have heard. In fact, I thought at the council Donennach made some good points in the face of the anger from Selbach.'

'No need to worry,' Fidelma assured him. 'As a *dálaigh* my task is laborious. I have to check every little detail. I just want to confirm with Céit the details of the times he went to see Brother Conchobhar. I think you said it was *orafunt*, horehound, he was asking for, to make an infusion to ease Prince Donennach's cough.'

'Perhaps you could check that with Donennach himself,' Conrí said seriously.

Fidelma smiled. 'I could but he was not the one who went to the apothecary. I suspect you think I am double checking out of suspicion. In fact, there is another reason for me to do so. If Céit went to see Brother Conchobhar several times to get this herb then it might well be that he saw someone else hanging around the apothecary. One has to check all details, for what one can miss, someone else can observe.'

Conrí was at once contrite. 'My apologies, lady. I did not mean to imply that I suspected your motivation. I think that the Uí Fidgente have had enough bad leaders over the years for you to suspect many things of us. Finally, we have a good man in Donennach and it is good we have now agreed an alliance with Cashel.'

'Is Céit in the guest quarters?' Fidelma asked.

'I think he is across at the stables opposite. You will find he is good at his job but not given to much imagination.'

Fidelma frowned. 'What makes you say that?'

'Oh, because he has a blunt tongue. You must remember him from the time you came to Donennach's fortress?'

'I suppose so. But I won't hold that against him.'

'Let me tell you this. He commanded a company of our warriors at Cnoc Áine,' Conrí pointed out. 'We would not want a bitter tongue to be a reason to unjustly accuse him.'

'The battle at Cnoc Áine was a bad time for everyone but it was some six or more years ago,' Fidelma reflected, not for the first time.

'To some it seems like yesterday. You will find the memories of the Prince of the Áine have not faded yet.'

'Prince Elódach? I thought he made good sense this morning.'

'But I think the memory of Cnoc Áine has not faded in his mind,' repeated the warlord. 'As you know, he was accused of cowardice there. Only his mother, Princess Aincride, supported him. His father and brother led the charge that devastated the Uí Fidgente in the battle.'

'But not before the Uí Fidgente laid many of their champions and nobles into an early grave,' Fidelma pointed out. 'Elódach lost his father and others of his family.'

'I was a young warrior there, lady,' Conrí continued reflectively. 'I saw Elódach commanding his company of élite archers. Later I was told that his father had ordered him to remain there unless the charge against us failed. So he stayed there and witnessed the charge in which his father was killed. It was his brother who turned the offensive into victory: his brother, who became prince and, not knowing his father's orders, thought his brother stayed on the hill because he was a coward. His brother put him under a *geis*, to henceforth call himself Elódach.'

Enda gasped. 'So that is why he bears the name, which is surely an insult. The name means a fugitive . . . one who escapes from their duty.'

'Exactly so,' Conrí confirmed grimly. 'He bears that name because his brother believed he had deliberately shirked his part in the battle. It might have been placed unjustly upon him but a *geis* is a difficult thing to discard.'

The *geis* was an ancient belief that was still practised and believed. Fidelma herself had once been put under such a *geis*, or injunction, by no less a person than the High King. It was a powerful taboo or prohibition to undertake a specific task or not to do something, and was a point of honour and more serious than any crime.

'But Elódach is the prince of the Áine now,' Enda pointed out.

'He succeeded his brother earlier this year,' Fidelma agreed.

'Then surely the *geis* is broken?' pointed out Enda. 'He does not have to obey it. He could discard the name Elódach and adopt his original name?'

'Not in his eyes,' Conrí said. 'We heard much about Elódach. He was the favourite son of his mother, Princess Aincride. She was a very powerful woman and swore she would make him Prince of Áine, making his elder brother repent the slight he did him. She apparently encouraged him to keep the nickname his brother had given him because she was of the Old Faith. I heard it said that she was a *taiscélaid,* a believer in omens. So Elódach, like his mother, believes that the sacred injunction stands until he has mitigated it by some course of alternative action. He is filled with bile at suffering this disgrace. He feels that only by some other deed would it be wiped out.'

'But what deed?' Enda asked thoughtfully. 'Does he want to provoke another war with the Uí Fidgente to atone for it?'

'I don't think he has the courage,' Conrí replied after some thought. 'No, I suspect the real war he wants is with his dead brother, who forced the *geis* upon him. He can't have that now his brother is dead and he has succeeded as prince of his people.'

'A war with the dead would be a difficult war to instigate.' Fidelma smiled without humour.

'It sounds, however, as if it was his mother who wished to provoke discord,' Conrí said. 'After all, now her favourite son is prince, what more would she want? Surely it is time to move on from all these feuds and squabbles. One should follow the lead of Donennach and your brother, Colgú, and bury the past with such matters.'

'I wish life were that easy,' Fidelma sighed. 'Céit is in the stables, you say?'

At Conrí's affirmative, she raised her hand in thanks and set off with Enda at her side.

The stables lay directly opposite the guest accommodation and were separated from it by a wide space where the horses were often taken and led around for exercise if they couldn't be taken out of the fortress and down into the surrounding fields and forests.

They were crossing towards the stables over a flagstoned area. Fidelma was walking slightly in front and to one side of Enda. It was quite a warm day. The sky was still clear and blue, but the afternoon sun was now dropping in its westward position, lowering over the buildings of the fortress. Fidelma was trying to think of anything she might have neglected during her investigation. She wondered if she had wasted time in taking a wrong path from the start. Maybe this was not the intricate plot that her brother and she had begun to imagine. Maybe it was just a simple robbery in which Brother Conchobhar had emerged at the wrong time and wrong place. Perhaps the trap door into the chambers below the apothecary had been opened and the thief had just seized an opportunity. Maybe she was being misled . . .

She was contemplating this when suddenly Enda leapt on her, sending her sprawling into the flagstones, knocking the breath from her body. She heard a cry of agony, a strange brief moment of reflection as she realised that she had not uttered it. Then she felt the painful tearing on her arm, grazing it before she made contact with the stone flags. Then there was a moment of bewilderment as the weight of Enda's body fell on top of her. A pain in her forehead. Then all was suddenly dark.

ELEVEN

She awoke in blackness. The immediate sensation that Fidelma experienced was a stabbing pain in the right side of her temples. Then the blackness was beginning to dissolve and take on shapes; grey twisting shapes, swirling and floating like smoke caught in a breath of air. She was struggling to breathe, trying to reach out to clear the meandering smoke away; to clear her vision. Dimly she felt something had happened to her. But what? She thought she was beginning to scream, fighting for air. The smoke suddenly lightened and for a few seconds everything came into a blinding focus. The light made her want to close her eyes.

The face of Eadulf seemed to be coming towards her, his expression mirroring concern.

She tried to speak but then his face rapidly receded, as if being drawn back through a long tunnel, and the swirling greyness returned and everything was then absorbed into blackness. Total blackness again.

She awoke again. Her temples were throbbing. Everything seemed out of focus, distorted. She eventually realised that she was lying flat on her back in her own bed. She found it difficult to keep her eyes open. She blinked rapidly and forced them open. Then she felt she was warm; too warm. The blanket that covered her was hot and seemed to be damp. The bed felt alien but she knew it was her own bed. A hand with a cloth was dabbing something cold and wet on her forehead. She tried to focus properly and then with some difficulty recognised the concerned and kindly face of Dar Luga.

The first clear thought that came into her mind was for her son. Alchú! Where was her son? She frowned and tried to articulate questions but only a groan broke from her lips. Then water was being trickled against them. Drops entered her mouth, cold on her tongue. She swallowed a few and then started to cough. Hands supported her head and shoulders, helping her into a semi-sitting position. Then a cup was being held to her lips. This time she took a swallow, crying out in protest when it was taken away before she drank her fill.

'Easy, lady, easy,' she heard Dar Luga softly instructing. 'You should not drink too much yet.'

She blinked again, turning her eyes to the benevolent features of the plump woman.

'Where . . .?' Fidelma began. 'Where . . .?'

'You are in bed in your own apartment. You are safe, lady.'

Fidelma grimaced. 'Alchú,' she managed to mumble. 'Where is Alchú?'

'There, there! Do not concern yourself, lady. Your son is safe at the Abbey of Imleach. He is not far away. Conserve your strength.'

She shut her eyes. Alchú was in Imleach. He was with his father. Eadulf! She remembered Eadulf's face fading before her but when was that? She wished the throbbing in her head would stop.

She was pushing back against the pillow in order to raise herself into a sitting position when the voice of Dar Luga told her to lay still.

It seemed that she had fallen asleep for a moment because she awoke and was aware of someone coming into the chamber and taking charge. She realised it was Eadulf.

'What's happened?' she tried to say, but the croaking sound that came from her throat was almost unrecognisable. She pushed herself up into a sitting position and groaned aloud as the throbbing renewed like drumsticks bearing a tattoo on her temples.

Eadulf moved forward. He bore a cup of some concoction in his hand.

'What should happen is that you should take this and lay still for a while.'

'What . . .?'

Eadulf seemed to guess the questions that vibrated in her mind as she tried to articulate them. 'Alchú is safe still at Imleach. When I received the news of what was happening at Árd Mór I thought it better to come here by myself. I arrived at the fortress yesterday evening. You had an accident.'

'Yesterday? An accident?' She was confused.

Eadulf seated himself by her bedside, trying to make her sip the medicine from the cup. It was clear that she was determined to press her questions.

'I don't suppose you will take this until you have learnt what happened.'

She groaned again. 'Tell me!'

'You have received a nasty knock on the head,' he said. 'A knock on the right temple. I have cleaned it and bandaged it and you should be taking this infusion and resting . . .'

Her mind began to clear in spite of the throbbing in her head.

'Tell me.'

'I had just arrived and was coming through the gates into the fortress when I heard a disturbance from the stables. There were several people there. I went forward and saw you stretched out on the ground with blood on your forehead. I saw a couple of warriors lifting Enda off you. He had an arrow through his right arm.'

'Enda? An arrow . . .?' she repeated in a dazed tone.

Eadulf continued: 'You drifted in and out of consciousness while I quickly assessed your injuries. I would say, as you fell, you gave your head a crack on the stone paving. Luan and another warrior helped to bring you here to our apartments. Dar Luga came to help nurse you.'

'What of Enda?' she mumbled, trying to get her thoughts clear. 'You said Enda had an arrow in him?'

'He did. Thankfully, though it was bleeding profusely, it had just gone through the flesh. I pulled it out and dressed the wound. He is recovering now and in great anxiety at your own injury.'

'I still don't understand. What happened?'

'Isn't that enough to content you and get you to rest awhile?'

'What happened?' she insisted.

Eadulf knew when to give up.

'Apparently you and he were walking across the yard from the guest quarters to the stables. Enda told me that it was a sunny afternoon. He saw something glint and out of instinct he pushed you to the ground just as the arrow embedded itself in his arm. From the sounds of it, had he not done so, it would have struck you in the back of the neck. Someone made an attempt on your life.' The last sentence was spoken in a flat tone as he tried to control his emotions.

Fidelma took this in for a moment and then asked: 'Is Enda all right?'

'The wound will mend shortly.'

'Was the arrow kept?'

Eadulf smiled at the fact that, in spite of her condition, her mind was still working like that of a *dálaigh*.

'I learnt enough about arrows in our last adventure to know the importance of such evidence,' he assured her. 'I kept it safe, but now is not the time to think of that.'

'So Enda saved my life,' she muttered slowly.

'He did. And you can see him soon enough and thank him, but as for now, you must rest.'

'It happened yesterday? Have I lost a day?'

'You have been unconscious and asleep since yesterday evening.'

'Do you know what has happened here?' she asked anxiously. 'I mean to Brother Conchobhar?'

'I have had a long talk with your brother and with Enda. They have told me everything.'

'I have been here since yesterday?' Fidelma seemed annoyed. 'Did they bury poor Conchobhar last night? That was arranged.'

'They did so. I attended. It was done in ritual form and with all respect.'

She compressed her mouth in an expression of anguish as she lay back. 'There is much evil here, Eadulf.'

'Your first task is to have a proper sleep and rest and we will talk about it afterwards.'

'You have also been told about the plague ship at Árd Mór?'

'I have been told the full story,' Eadulf assured her. 'Enda also told me that you have no great faith in Brother Laig. I know the King's council is due to meet here within days and Abbot Cuán will be bringing a couple of physicians and an apothecary from the abbey. Meantime, I can help if an apothecary is called upon.'

'I am glad you have come back, Eadulf. I need your knowledge and support.' She reached out a hand and squeezed his.

Eadulf shrugged in embarrassment. 'And I need you to be well,' he replied. 'So drink this infusion and get some natural sleep. After you have rested, we can turn our minds to these matters.'

'Are you sure that Enda has filled you in on the details of our investigation and . . . and . . .?'

'Drink!' Eadulf commanded firmly.

She hesitated but then obeyed him. A short time later she was in a deep and natural sleep.

When she awoke early the next morning she had a vague memory of her brother coming to see her the previous evening. There were also memories of Dar Luga coming to bathe her forehead and hold a cup of some medication to her lips. It seemed that Eadulf was constantly at her bedside. But now she awoke feeling strangely refreshed, and although her head was still sore it was no longer pounding. At least the soreness was manageable. She raised a hand, touched the bandage and then smiled.

Eadulf entered and it took a while before she could persuade him that she was fit enough to be up, so she demonstrated it by having a good meal of fruits and a mug of fresh goat's milk mixed with honey. Then she dressed and went out into the fresh air where, with Eadulf's assistance, she walked in the gardens at the back of the guest quarters and chapel. It took her a little while to recover her proper balance, but the movement made her stronger, although it was exhausting. She noticed members of the household guard were constantly in the shadows. It was then she realised the deeper significance of Eadulf's words: 'Someone made an attempt on your life.' So, leaning on Eadulf's arm, she asked that they return to their chambers where a fire had been lit for her comfort.

The first visitor was Enda, with his arm in a sling. He immediately started apologising for pushing her to the ground but she waved him into silence.

'Don't be silly. Had you not done what you did I would now be dead. How is your wound?'

'It is nothing, lady. Friend Eadulf is a good physician. I

fear if I had had to give myself to the care of Brother Laig I would not be as well as I am.'

'I am no physician, Enda,' Eadulf corrected him. 'Anyway,' he moved to a corner and picked something up, 'this is the arrow.'

Fidelma glanced at the object he held in his hand.

'Do you recognise the arrow, Enda?'

The warrior held it up to examine it.

'I am afraid we will learn little from this. There are no distinguishing marks and it could have been fashioned by any one of a thousand fletchers.'

Enda handed Fidelma the arrow and she glanced at it.

'You are right. I see nothing remarkable except this is an arrow that is cheaply made. It is the sort that only a poor hunter might use and not even a professional one.'

'Surely that is at least something?' Eadulf commented.

'Not enough to lead us to what type of person owned this arrow, let alone who fletched or shot it,' she sighed, pausing. 'Now, remind me, for I have lost time with my injury, what were we in the midst of doing when the arrow was loosed at me?'

'You told me that you wanted to see Céit, the bodyguard of Prince Donennach. We were told by Conrí that he was in the stables.'

'Why did you want to see Céit?' Eadulf asked.

'Céit had visited Brother Conchobhar's apothecary several times. Conrí had mentioned this and said he had gone to get a medication for Prince Donennach,' Enda explained quickly.

'Donennach had a cough and Céit had been sent to get *orafunt* or horehound,' Fidelma began to remember. 'Conrí mentioned this as he felt it might make Céit a suspect. I just wanted to confirm the matter of his visits with Céit himself. We saw Conrí at the door of the guest quarters. He told us Céit was in the stables. It was when we started to walk across the yard from the guest rooms that the arrow was fired.'

Fidelma held up the arrow, seeming to examine it.

'We crossed towards the stables . . .' she repeated thoughtfully. 'Then the arrow was fired from behind us, and behind us were the guest quarters . . .' She paused. 'Who was behind us?'

Enda looked at her and became suddenly excited. 'We had just left Conrí. So Conrí of the Uí Fidgente was standing directly behind us!'

There was a silence for a moment or two and then Fidelma shook her head. 'My instinct is against even contemplating the idea that he would be the unsuccessful assassin.'

'But he is a warlord of the Uí Fidgente,' Enda pointed out. He clearly had his suspicions of the Uí Fidgente.

'I have known him for a long time,' Fidelma replied, thoughtfully. 'He was instrumental in brokering the peace. By the way, has anyone seen him since the incident?'

'I was told he was one of the first on the scene to help you,' Eadulf admitted. 'He has made several enquiries after your recovery.'

'Let me see if we can gather more information before dwelling on suspicion. Can one of you find Conrí and bring him here immediately?'

After Enda had left on this task, Eadulf picked up the arrow and placed it to one side.

'Enda is right,' he reflected uneasily. 'Conrí is an Uí Fidgente noble.'

'You think I am prejudiced on his behalf?' Fidelma asked. 'He did work towards peace several times over the years. When the Uí Fidgente was prone to war against Cashel, he remained a friend to us.'

'Wasn't it Aristotle who wrote: "*Amicus Plato, sed magis amica veritas*"?' Eadulf smiled thinly.

'Indeed, truth is more valuable than friendship,' Fidelma interpreted the meaning. 'But we have never known Conrí to tell an untruth.'

Eadulf shrugged. 'I have seen too many conspiracies since I have been here; I have become prejudiced in the opposite way. Everyone is suspect until they prove otherwise.'

'I try to think the opposite, Eadulf. Let us gather information before leaping to conclusions.'

'Presumably the arrow tells nothing at all?'

'As we have already discovered.'

'If this attack on you was to impede your investigation, you must have discovered something that has worried the killer.

Yet so far as Colgú tells me, everything has led to a dead end at the moment.'

Fidelma stared at Eadulf for a moment. Then she smiled. 'Now I know why we have a good partnership. You have an uncanny way of pointing out the obvious. All I have to do now is find out what could worry the person I am pursuing that would give them cause to make an attempt on my life. I am beginning to think my brother is correct about a motive for killing Brother Conchobhar.'

'Do you really think he was killed because of some plot to get the council to censure your brother and eliminate his kingship?'

'Without the annual confirmation of my brother's steward-ship of the kingdom, the future is uncertain.'

'And you believe it is the murderer's intention to appear at the council and persuade the other princes to refuse to approve your brother's actions during this last year?'

'Probably the murderer himself will not be the person to stand against him in council. If that were so, it would have to be one of the seven senior princes. He will be the leading conspirator. The murderer would be someone working for him . . .'

'If we follow your suspicions, then the killer is still here in the fortress and, that being so, you are still in great danger,' Eadulf pointed out.

'I have been in danger before, Eadulf,' Fidelma replied. 'But I will be honest with you. There is a flaw to this reasoning. While I feel that this deduction is the logical one, I am also thinking that if someone wanted to disrupt the ceremonial and council, why eliminate Brother Conchobhar as Keeper of the Sword, which the King has to raise at Beltaine as a symbol of approval? Why not just steal the sword from the great hall? And then, of course, the flaw is that the princes would not be swayed by symbols but by logical criticism.'

Eadulf certainly had no contrary arguments and said so. Then he suddenly chuckled. 'I suppose the sword in the great hall is the genuine sword? After all, what does an Otherworld sword look like?'

Fidelma was about to reply when she paused and examined him closely.

'I suppose,' she said thoughtfully, 'symbols are not things one can test the reality of. Anyway, we have already examined the genuineness of the sword. My brother says it is the real one and he is not superstitious.'

'It is what the people think, being generally superstitious, that is the serious problem, not whether it is a fake or not. That is the nature of symbols. However, a stupid question, perhaps, but has the sword been examined?'

Fidelma shook her head with a faint smile. 'It was the first thought that occurred to us and it sent my brother racing into the great hall. He examined the sword and declared it was the real one. But yours is a good thought.' She paused and then asked: 'Have there been any reports about the spread of the disease since I have been out of things?'

'Nothing so far. By the way, while I was at Imleach, I heard that Abbot Cuán had received criticisms about Brother Fidach, who does not appear to be making himself liked here.'

'He prefers the new Roman idea of calling himself *Athair* or "Father". Frankly, he is an autocrat and seems almost hysterical in defence of the dictates of Rome. He is a religious bigot who thinks that all we have to do is pray the pestilence out of existence. If the plague comes then we don't need hysteria.'

'It seems that he is best removed,' Eadulf sighed.

'I will have to ask Abbot Cuán to explain to Fidach that he must stay until the investigation into Brother Conchobhar's death is resolved. I don't think he will be of much help if the plague strikes.'

Eadulf's eyes widened. 'You mean he is a suspect in the murder of Brother Conchobhar?'

'At the moment, many are suspects. I have not been able to narrow the list of them. Fidach has to remain until the investigation is complete. Anyway, once we have let one person go, you can imagine the rush of people leaving here to avoid the plague.'

'I think you will find that Abbot Cuán is anxious to stay until the council is over. You can imagine the panic throughout this kingdom if faced with the return of the pestilence at the same time as the council split and there is an attempt to over-throw Colgú.'

'Be honest with me, Eadulf, if the plague does take hold again, is there little we can do? The physician is just as hope-less as Brother Fidach is.'

'I have talked to Dar Luga about him,' Eadulf admitted. 'Although some of his ideas are indeed hopeless, there is little more I know that I can be of help with. There was one recipe that was used when the plague struck my country eight or nine years ago. Some claimed it to be of help. It was that the shells of new-laid eggs of chickens should be taken and roasted and then crushed into a powder. People used a pestle to crush them with the petals of marigold flowers and put them in a pot of finely brewed ale, adding treacle made from honey and warmed over a fire. They then took one cup of this mixture in the morning and one cup at night.'

Fidelma stared at him incredulously. 'And this was to save you from the plague?'

'That is what they used to say. Among my people, the East Angles, they used to make a drink from the purple flowers of betony, what you call *bíattas*. Some physicians claimed it stopped the inflammation, the diarrhoea, and headaches. I will not endorse either of these methods nor will I denounce them. I'll be blunt with you, Fidelma: my experience is that there is no known cure. Even the best apothecaries have to guess and, indeed, it is in the lap of the Fates as to who survives and who does not.'

Fidelma shivered slightly. 'I have tried to put it out of my mind in recent years. But I remember the fear that it spread when I was younger. Will we know if it spreads near us?'

'There are signs,' affirmed Eadulf. 'It depends. Some people will start by sleepiness and delirium; others will be shivering, some with a fever and giddiness and they start to vomit. They become intolerant to light or have pains in many places, in the stomach, in the back or other limbs. The worst aspect is the later stages of the pestilence. That is when you find around the neck, armpits and groin, swellings, which are inflammations. They can range in size from being as small as nuts to being as round as apples. They are often filled with

the disease and some physicians came to the conclusion that
if you lance them and then apply the pulp of an onion or a
leek, or even vinegar to the open wounds, it will draw the
disease from the sick.'

'What would you do?'

'Frankly, I don't know. Personally, the hope is that one
survives the fever because I do not think there is much chance
once one passes to the other stages of the disease. Having said
that, I have heard of some miraculous cures.'

They sat in silence for a while, their minds filled with the
hopelessness that they felt over the plague.

They were disturbed by a tap at the door. Enda entered in
answer to Eadulf's call and then stood to one side to allow
Conrí, the warlord of the Uí Fidgente, to follow him.

Conrí went straight to Fidelma, examining her anxiously.

'Lady, I hope you are well recovered. I came as soon as
Enda said that you had asked for me.'

'I am well recovered, Conrí,' she answered seriously,
motioning him to take a seat before her. 'And I need you to
help me piece together the few moments since Enda and I left
you and went to the stables to try to find Céit.'

'I can add but little. You and Enda left me to make your
way to the stables and I turned into the guest house. It was
over in a moment. I had barely started to ascend the stairs to
my chamber, when I heard a great shouting. I turned back
to the door and saw Enda and you – at least I presumed at
the time that it was you – lying on the ground and people
running towards you. I started running, too, and by the time
I had reached you both, you were encircled by warriors and
stable boys. I pushed my way forward and, to my surprise,
saw Eadulf already bending over you. I later heard that he had
just returned to the fortress almost the same moment that this
happened.'

'When did you learn what had happened?' Eadulf asked.

Conrí shrugged. 'I suppose it was all in the same moments,
standing among the crowd. Enda still had the arrow through
his upper arm and was bleeding badly. You were attending
him while, at the same time, getting a couple of warriors to
take the lady Fidelma to her bedchamber. I was told that

someone had loosed an arrow at Fidelma, and Enda, in pushing Fidelma out of its path, took the arrow himself in his upper arm.'

Fidelma gazed at him steadily. 'You realise that the arrow was fired from behind us.'

Conrí's eyes widened a fraction and then a humorous smile crossed his face.

'Well, you can rest assured that I was not the person who fired it.' He glanced at the arrow on the table. 'Is that it? May I look?'

At Fidelma's nod of assent, he picked it up and examined it critically.

'I am afraid it tells you nothing. It is a cheap arrow, made more for a poor person's hunt than a warrior's bow. There are many such about.' He laid it back on the table. 'Seriously,' he suddenly said, his expression abruptly sombre and unsmiling, 'you did not think that I . . .?'

'I can see no reason why,' Fidelma answered, 'but the fact remains that the arrow was fired from behind us and . . .'

'And must have come from the guest quarters,' concluded Conrí. He sat rubbing his chin thoughtfully. 'It is a logical conclusion. But, if you accept I did not shoot it, that the arrow was not fired from the doorway where I had been standing, then it must have been loosed from nearby. But where?'

'I accept that there are other places in the building from which an arrow could be fired,' Fidelma pointed out.

'There are no other openings on that side of the building on the lower floor. There is just the entrance door,' Eadulf reminded her.

Conrí was thoughtful. 'The chapel stands to the right of the building.'

'Sheer walls until the upper part of the building, where there is a bell tower. Could that have been the positon from which the assassin shot?' Eadulf asked.

It was Enda who made a sudden clicking sound with his tongue. 'If the arrow was aimed at your back and struck me in the upper arm when I tried to push you out of the way, then it could not have been fired from the door of the guest house. The angle would be wrong. It had to be fired from a higher elevation. I saw the reflection of it in the polished metal stacked by the stable door. That is why I pushed you to the ground from behind at the moment the arrow struck me. It struck me at a downwards angle. Eadulf will witness that by the angle of the wound. That's when I fell on top of you, lady.'

'Allowing for a slight deviation,' Conrí agreed, under-standing the warrior's reasoning. 'So it must have come from . . .' Once more his eyes widened. 'Then if not at the ground floor where I was, but from the next floor, where there are three windows in that wall.'

Enda closed his eyes for a moment as if trying to visualise the formation.

'There is a window directly above that door. Who is that room allocated to?'

Conrí was looking worried. 'That is my chamber, lady. But I was not in it. I was still at the bottom of the stairway when the arrow was fired.'

Enda seemed to be trying to catch Fidelma's eyes. She sighed. 'I know what you are going to say, Enda.'

Conrí grimaced. 'If I were in your place, I would do the same. You want to search my chamber to discover if there is a trace of a bow and these arrows there. I have no objections. I insist on it.'

'I don't think it will prove anything,' Fidelma said after a moment's thought. 'If the assailant was trying to implicate you, he would have ensured more evidence was planted there. Otherwise, he would not leave his weapons behind, especially when he saw he had failed in his attempt.'

'Why would this assassin seek to implicate me?' Conrí demanded.

Fidelma regarded him with impatience. 'To stir up animosity against the Uí Fidgente.' She paused and frowned in thought. 'I was going to ask Céit about his early morning trips to Brother Conchobhar's apothecary just to confirm what you said . . .'

'And now he becomes a suspect?' Conrí asked bitterly. 'Does that make the Uí Fidgente suspects?'

'You were the first to alert me to the fact people might have seen him visiting the apothecary,' Fidelma reminded him. 'You felt that you should tell me before I started being suspicious about him. You felt I would get to hear of these visits. Was Céit among those who emerged from the stables and crowded round after the attack? Did you speak to him afterwards?'

She had noticed that a frown had started to furrow Conrí's forehead.

'I did not. I never saw him after that incidence but . . .' Conrí's voice trailed off.

'You have thought of something?'

'Céit's chamber is next to mine at the guest house. Yet I am sure he had left for the stables before you were shot at.'

There was a silence and then Fidelma let out a long exhalation of breath.

'Then we must speak with Céit.'

There was a sudden disturbance outside the door and Enda went forward to open it. An attendant was outside and seemed excited but lowered his voice to a whisper, addressing the warrior. Enda hesitated a moment and then stepped outside, also lowering his voice and shutting the door behind him.

'Now what?' Fidelma demanded impatiently. 'I hope this isn't the news of the plague spreading that we have been dreading?'

The door re-opened and Enda returned. It was clear he had bad news, although he was trying to keep his features immobile.

'There has been another killing,' he announced.

They were silent for a moment and then Fidelma asked in a measured tone, 'Tell us who is dead.'

Enda glanced suspiciously at Conrí before answering.

'It is Céit,' he said with heavy emphasis. 'Céit has just been killed by Prince Selbach.'

TWELVE

Conrí let out an oath and Fidelma started to rise from her chair.

'Where do you think you are going?' Eadulf called in alarm as Fidelma began to make for the door.

'To find out what has happened and why,' she replied without pausing.

'You are in no fit condition. You need to rest,' protested Eadulf.

'No one will rest unless I find out what has happened,' she replied grimly, over her shoulder.

Eadulf was about to protest again but the warlord of the Uí Fidgente intervened with a set and determined look.

'At worst we might have a blood feud on our hands. The Uí Fidgente might demand vengeance on the Prince of the Eóganacht Ráithlinn. There is much at stake, including the treaty. I must go to find Prince Donennach. With Céit dead at the hands of an Eóganacht prince, the idea of peace hangs in the balance.'

He was gone without waiting for permission.

Eadulf caught up with Fidelma outside. She glanced at him with a grim expression. 'I shall need your help more than ever, Eadulf, and you, too, Enda.'

'I don't have to I tell you that you have recently risen from bed after a bad blow to the head,' replied Eadulf. 'I would have preferred it if you had spent more time resting.'

As they came into the main courtyard, they did not have to look far before they saw where the incident had taken place. A crowd was gathered outside the main doors of the royal residence. There were several warriors there, most of them members of the household guard, with Dego trying to organise things. There were also a few hostile-looking men who were personal bodyguards in the households of the princes. Others, mainly attendants in the various households, stood by, unsure of what they should do.

In the middle of them, almost on the steps of the royal residence, the physician, Brother Laig, was on his knees, bending over the body of a man who lay flat on his back. There was blood staining his clothes and, nearby, a short distance from his open hand was an abandoned sword. It was easy to recognise Céit.

As Fidelma, Eadulf and Enda halted before the body, Conrí was just arriving with Prince Donennach. Both were grim faced.

'How was he killed?' Donennach demanded.

The question was addressed to Brother Laig. He did not respond, except to rise to his feet from where he had been examining the corpse. He brushed down his clothing.

'We await a response,' Fidelma snapped when it seemed he was ignoring the Uí Fidgente prince.

The physician glared at her. He still had not acquired the technique of modifying his superior attitude, even when addressing Fidelma.

'As you can see,' he gestured to the blood-splattered body.

'I am asking you,' snapped Fidelma, 'or are you saying your medical competence is not enough to give us the response that we are seeking? If so, I think Brother Eadulf here will be better qualified to tell us.'

The conceited physician flushed. 'The man was run through by a sword. It was a swift, clean piercing under the ribcage and into the heart. He was dead before he dropped to the ground.'

'Where are the witnesses to this?'

'Lady, everyone who was witness has repaired to your brother's council chamber.' It was Dego who answered.

'Everyone?' She was astonished.

'Luan, who was first upon the scene and saw the killing – he took them there with your brother,' he replied.

Fidelma glanced around. 'I was told that Prince Selbach was responsible for this man's death. Is he inside as well?'

To her surprise Dego shook his head. 'He went straight to his own chambers in the guest house. We were not sure of our authority to stop him.' The latter was said more by way of an explanation to Enda than anything else.

Fidelma turned to Prince Donennach. 'We will see my brother first,' she said as she stepped round the group by the body and, accompanied by Eadulf and Enda, led the way into the royal residence, closely followed by Donennach and Conrí.

The guards outside Colgú's private chamber immediately opened the doors for them. They made their way inside where a moody Colgú was sitting, head bent. Luan, Enda's second in command, was standing to one side. Next to him were two other men: one an attendant at the royal residence and the other the saturnine Brother Fidach.

'Fidelma, are you well enough to be here?' It was Colgú's first question as she entered.

'I would not be here if I were not,' she replied testily. 'Now what has happened? Why was the Prince of Ráithlinn allowed to leave?'

Colgú gestured to Luan. 'Tell my sister as you told me.'

'There was not much to tell,' the warrior said nervously. 'I was on duty on the other side of the courtyard, by the gates. I heard the noise of an altercation. Two men were shouting at each other. I glanced across the courtyard and, just in front of the doors of the residence, I saw Selbach of Ráithlinn shouting and waving his fist at a warrior. I have learnt that the warrior's name was Céit and he was one of the Uí Fidgente party. The sounds of their argument were very agitated. I did not hear what it was about but, on Selbach's part, it seemed very serious and very heated. I was about to cross the courtyard to intervene. Even as I looked, I saw the warrior called Céit draw his sword and threaten Selbach—'

'Wait,' Prince Donennach interrupted sharply. 'Are you sure about that? You saw Céit draw his sword first and threaten Prince Selbach?'

'I can only tell you what I saw. That *is* what I saw.'

'Go on. What then?' Fidelma prompted.

'Céit was waving his sword and Selbach suddenly had his sword in his hand and made a quick thrust under the guard of the warrior. The warrior fell back, dropping his weapon.'

Fidelma glanced at the attendant who stood by Luan. He was an elderly man who she had noticed was a cleaner in the King's apartments.

'It is exactly as Luan reported,' he said nervously. 'I do not know what the argument was about.'

As Fidelma turned to Brother Fidach, he met her gaze with a scowl.

'I can add but little. I was on my way here to press my demand to be allowed to return to the Abbey of Imleach. As I approached, I heard the shouting and then saw a man fall backwards. He had a sword in his hand, which he dropped before he fell to the ground. Prince Selbach stood over him, his sword still in his hand. That is what I saw. I do not know the reason for this conflict.'

Prince Donennach held Colgú's attention. 'I wish to point out a matter of contradiction. We hear that Céit drew his sword first and then, by magic, a sword is in the hands of Selbach. Also Céit was too seasoned a warrior to just have his sword in his hand, waving it about and apparently unable to parry or defend himself from the single thrust from this sword in the hands of his adversary. It makes no sense.'

Fidelma pursed her lips thoughtfully. 'I have noted that. But first let me get the overall scene clear.' She turned back to Luan. 'After the warrior fell back, what happened?'

'I started running towards the fallen warrior. Several other people had arrived, including Dego and others, who sent for the physician. Prince Selbach sheathed his sword. He said that if he was wanted, he would be in his rooms. I think Dego called him to stay but he did not glance back. In the circumstances, I decided to report directly to your brother and told the others as witnesses to come with me.'

'The others, with the exception of the man who had killed the victim,' Fidelma snapped.

'As I said, Prince Selbach said he would wait in his own chamber if there were any questions.'

'*If?*' The inflection on the syllable was obvious. 'Were there no other witnesses to the cause of this conflict?' she demanded.

Luan and two others shook their heads. Fidelma turned back to Luan. 'So you heard no words that would have told you about the nature of this argument?'

'I did not hear the words specifically but only their voices raised in anger.'

'But – and this is important – you say you saw Céit draw his sword first and it was in his hand . . .?'

'He held it in his sword hand,' Luan said thoughtfully. 'When I first saw him he seemed to be holding the sword in a defensive position.'

'When did you see a weapon in Selbach's hand?'

'Maybe I was too busy looking at the sword in Céit's hand to notice when Selbach drew his weapon,' Luan replied. 'Selbach had his left side towards me while Céit had his sword arm towards me.'

Fidelma's eyes narrowed. 'This is important. Do you think Selbach already had his sword in his hand?'

'I cannot swear to it.' Luan shrugged after some thought. 'All I know is that Céit had his sword drawn and was shouting at Selbach. The outcome was that Selbach had his sword in his hand and made the fatal thrust.'

There was an uneasy silence. Prince Donennach turned gravely to Colgú.

'If Céit drew his sword first then Selbach can claim he acted in self-defence. But this is not good, Colgú of Cashel. This matter must be explained, and explained very clearly. If this is the result of some personal argument and Selbach acted in self-defence then we must expect a full explanation as to what provoked it. It is worrying that Selbach was allowed to leave the scene without explanation.'

Colgú was listening, sitting slightly forward with hunched soldiers. He raised a troubled face to his sister.

'If it was wrong to allow Selbach to leave, the wrong is mine,' Luan intervened hurriedly before the King spoke. 'I did not know if I had authority to order the prince to remain.'

'No blame on you,' Fidelma assured him. 'It would have been difficult to restrain Prince Selbach.'

'But I agree with Prince Donennach,' Colgú admitted. 'Selbach may be a senior prince of the Eóganacht and that very fact now casts a shadow on him. Indeed, it casts a shadow on the honour of all the Eóganacht princes. If the matter is not resolved quickly then there will be obvious consequences.'

'I am well aware of that, brother,' she said firmly. 'I have worked long and hard to bring this treaty between the Uí Fidgente and Cashel for approval by the council. It is too important to see it dissolve in the smoke of a quarrel, personal or otherwise. I intend to question Selbach immediately. We have heard the witness statement from Luan, supported by Brother Fidach and this attendant. Now we must hear the story from Selbach. However, it might be difficult to summons him, a prince, to appear here.'

Her brother inhaled deeply and then let out a long, low breath. 'Knowing something of Selbach's character, I fear it will not be easy to question him,' Colgú agreed. 'I will accompany you to the guest quarters and stand as witness to your questioning.'

'I agree that we should go to Selbach's quarters immediately,' Fidelma said.

Prince Donennach moved forward. 'Céit was my personal bodyguard. He served me well. If he attacked Selbach, he was provoked, I have no doubt. As there is no *dálaigh* to represent Uí Fidgente interests, I insist on my right to come and hear this testimony.'

'If it comes to that,' Fidelma said thoughtfully, 'since Selbach has chosen the location of where he will give his defence, I suggest all of us make our way to his quarters to stand ready as witnesses in case statements are challenged and witnesses have to defend their statements.'

Colgú agreed with his sister. Selbach had chosen where to make his witness statement and she had proposed the logical means of hearing it.

It was as they were making their way to the guest quarters that Fidelma took the opportunity to raise a question with Brother Fidach.

'I suppose you have not encountered Sister Ernmas again? I ask because she seems a very elusive person. Not even my brother knows what authority she has to be serving in the chapel here.'

Brother Fidach gazed at her defensively. 'She does not have my authority. So you can't tell me anything more about her? Who she is?'

Fidelma's mouth compressed morosely. 'That's just it. No one seems to know.'

Brother Fidach frowned. 'What did you say her name was? Sister Ernmas?'

'That was the name I was given.'

'Extraordinary,' Brother Fidach commented.

'What is extraordinary?' Fidelma demanded.

'I heard that you were an expert at deciphering names. It should be an appropriate talent at this moment in time.'

'Appropriate?' She was momentarily confused.

'The name means "death by iron", which colloquially means "death by the sword".'

Fidelma looked startled. For once her memory of names and their meanings had failed her.

'Hardly a name to give a member of the New Faith,' she said thoughtfully. 'I remember now. Ernmas was the name of the mother of Macha, one of the three personifications of the old goddess of death and battles.'

Luan had been listening to their conversation. 'I thought that was a name that was never given,' he interrupted. 'Even in the time before time, even when the folk worshipped the ancient gods and goddesses. It was said to be an accursed name.'

Fidelma was surprised by the warrior's knowledge.

'You are right,' Brother Fidach confirmed. 'I would never have associated it with those serving the New Faith.' He turned to Fidelma. 'Are you sure that you heard the name correctly?'

'The new librarian heard the name, as did Enda,' Fidelma pointed out. She glanced at Enda, who assented. 'I think, when we are through with Selbach, we must institute a careful search of the fortress for this strange religieuse whom few people are privileged to see.'

Most of the group remained in the small antechamber of the guest quarters while Colgú, Fidelma, Eadulf and Prince Donennach ascended the stairs to the rooms occupied by Selbach of Ráithlinn.

He immediately dismissed his attendant, who had opened the door for them.

'I was expecting you,' he said gruffly to Colgú, but barely acknowledged the others.

'My sister is here in her legal capacity,' Colgú announced, 'so she will take your statement.'

'I thought she was ill?' replied the Prince of Ráithlinn, his voice carrying no trace of concern.

'Well enough to be addressed directly,' Fidelma replied irritably. 'I need your statement as to why Céit of the Uí Fidgente lies dead in a pool of blood on the steps of the royal residence. You will know why Colgú and Donennach accompany me, and Eadulf accompanies me as my assistant.'

Selbach gave a shrug as if it were of no importance to him. He turned and sat down. Although it was against protocol, he did not offer a seat to the King before sitting himself.

'Witnesses are waiting below in case of challenge and there is cause to re-examine them,' she explained.

'That will be a matter for you,' the Prince of Ráithlinn dismissed. 'I will tell you the truth as I see it.'

'I presume that you do not deny that it was your sword that killed the Uí Fidgente warrior?'

'Why should I deny it?'

'And the reason why you did so?' pressed Fidelma.

'It was an affair of honour,' Selbach returned, almost in a dismissive tone.

'Are you claiming it was a duel?' Fidelma asked in surprise. Of all the reasons she had been expecting it was not the one that Selbach now offered. Her companions were also surprised.

'Even the law recognises a duel,' the Prince of Ráithlinn said, like a teacher addressing a child. 'Doesn't the law say that a wound, even a mortal wound, is not actionable when received or given in a duel?'

'It does,' she agreed, 'but the text of the *Din Techtugad* does specify that a duel has to be arranged in a proper manner, and without prior arrangement it is not recognised. Even if the combat is witnessed as a duel then witnesses have to come forward to testify the legality of the combat.'

'So what makes you claim it was not prearranged? I tell you it was a duel, and the fact that I killed my opponent is of little consequence in law.'

'You should recall that your so-called duel was witnessed, and there appeared little preparation and no official witnesses aside from those who saw the argument erupt. It was seen almost as a brawl,' intervened Prince Donennach.

'Then the witnesses are blind,' Selbach replied.

'You should do better than claim that as a defence.' Fidelma's

voice was stern. 'If it was a duel then you should have repaired
to a level ground. Between the combatants there should have
been placed the *caam* – the wood of contention.'

The *caam* was a length of wood that was placed between
the adversaries and should not be crossed by either of them
during the conflict.

'You should have taken up your swords, standing feet wide
apart, and raised your hands with the swords before commencing
to strike at one another.'

'I am told that the New Faith condemns duelling and we
no longer refer to the ordeal as *fír nDé* – the truth test of God,'
Colgú commented.

Prince Selbach actually chuckled. 'Well, God's truth was
not weighed in the balance here.'

'The *Din Techtugad* also allows a judge to put fines on those
who break the conditions laid down,' Fidelma continued when
Selbach made no further comment. 'I have said the conditions
are strict. More important, adding to the prohibitions that my
brother speaks of, it is a fact that a duel cannot be fought in
the grounds of a king's house or that of a noble, or on church
land. Where you killed Céit is not in accordance with the law.
On those matters alone, you would be judged guilty of breeches
of the law; guilty also of disobeying the strictures in the
Audacht Morainn. It is said no one should undertake a duel
in falsehood.'

She paused and regarded Selbach in silence with a grim
expression.

'Do you want to reconsider your story?' pressed Colgú.

It was difficult to estimate whether Selbach was angry, for
red cheeks were his normal colouring. Eventually the Prince
of Ráithlinn exhaled with an angry breath.

'I did not lie when I said it was a matter of honour. Perhaps
I chose the wrong defence as I would argue that this man's
death was one of those seven examples listed in law that does
not require a *colainnéraic* or fine to be paid for those guilty
of homicide in self-defence.'

'So which of the seven do you cite in defence?' Fidelma
asked, slightly surprised by the man's knowledge as well as
his change of tack.

'A number of texts stress that it is permitted to kill in self-defence.'

'Are you claiming that Céit attacked you with the intention of killing you?'

'I say that the law states that it is lawful to kill someone if they have wronged you or your family. That you can defend your honour or family honour. Is this not so?'

Fidelma searched in her mind while Selbach pressed on: 'This man wounded my honour and does it not say . . . every counterwounding is free from liability?'

The words of the text came back to her and she was forced to agree.

'So you now claim that Céit wounded your honour to the extent that you could fight and kill him without the formality of a legal duel?'

'That is what it says and that is what I claim as a defence. My action is regarded as self-defence. It was a matter of honour.'

'His wounding of your honour has to be serious,' pointed out Colgú.

Selbach stared defiantly at them. 'You doubt the law?' he said scornfully.

'We do not doubt the law,' Fidelma replied sharply. 'I am not sure that I accept your interpretation. I will refresh myself on the matter as it is stated in the *Críth Gabhlach*. As I recall, it says that you will have to explain in detail what this wound against your honour was. It requires you to produce a witness to it.'

'It would save time if you took my word, the word of an Eóganacht prince, one whose antecedents are equally as good as your own,' he snapped back.

'Selbach, it matters not what your rank is,' pointed out Colgú. 'If your claim is untrue, the law does not give you immunity. Even a king can lose his honour price – indeed, his honour – if he cannot prove his claim. There is a more serious matter than proving that claim to a judge in legal terms. Unless you stand innocent within the law then we might enter into the realm of *dígal*. You know that will bring you and your family into a blood feud with Prince Donennach of the Uí Fidgente.'

Selbach gave a derisory laugh.

'We have been at war with the Uí Fidgente for generations and it has done us no harm.'

'This time it is different,' Colgú pointed out, before Prince Donennach could intervene. 'If you cannot prove that you acted under the law, nor offer the requisite compensation for this death, then none of the Eóganacht princes can legally support you if you go to war . . . even if you are Eóganacht. The Uí Fidgente can send out a party of avengers to exact their vengeance on you with immunity. You will have no recourse, nor can you call for protection. I believe that is what the *Críth Gabhlach* says. Am I not right, Fidelma?'

'You are right,' Fidelma agreed. 'So now I urge you, Selbach, to co-operate fully under the law or else the law has to denounce you.'

There were some moments of silence. Then Selbach raised his shoulders and let them fall as if he were helplessly pressed.

'Then you advise me that I must reveal the dishonour this man did to me and to my family? I would say this dishonours all the Eóganacht princes. That being so, the self-same *dígal* – that blood feud – may come about anyway.'

Fidelma exchanged a bewildered look with her brother. 'Are you now saying that your silence is a means to prevent a blood feud?'

'It depends on what you consider the best advice will be. If I speak, there will be blood. If I don't speak, you say there will be blood. Either way, blood may ensue.' He stared at Colgú with a smirk. 'Did Furudrán not say in council the other day that your kingship is one where many of the choices you have made have not been good for the welfare of this kingdom?'

'No more prevarication.' Colgú was close to losing his temper.

Fidelma was surprised when Selbach clapped his hands and a pale-faced, worried-looking Esnad appeared from the adjoining room. She kept her eyes lowered.

'Tell my wife that her testimony is now needed and that I will call for her to join us in a moment.' As the girl left, Selbach turned to Fidelma. 'Before I ask Blinne to join us, I must emphasise that this is done at the insistence of Colgú and yourself. I therefore ask Prince Donennach to agree that he has no wish to pursue a blood feud.'

Prince Donennach frowned. 'I will not be bound before I have heard what is to be said,' he declared. 'I wish only to hear the truth.'

'We will hear what is said,' Fidelma acknowledged. 'That is logical.'

'Then I shall ask my wife to join us,' Selbach agreed. The Prince of Ráithlinn clapped his hands again and Esnad entered, followed by Blinne. The wife of Selbach entered stiffly and stood before her husband. She was white faced but had a bruise and red blotch on her left cheek. Her lips were thin and blood-less. There was not the sparkle in her features that Fidelma knew to be usual with the attractive young woman.

'Tell your story,' Selbach ordered curtly. 'Tell them why I and my house have been dishonoured.'

Blinne was still standing erect but as she turned to face them she kept her eyes firmly on the ground.

'I should warn you,' Fidelma decided to point out before Blinne began to speak, 'that what you say has the force of an oath. Once you speak, you speak of your own free will. You are attesting to a truth that is punishable under the law if it is found later to be knowingly false. It is my duty as a *dálaigh* to caution you on this fact.'

'She knows this,' Selbach snapped.

'Then it is up to her to acknowledge it,' Fidelma returned. 'Lady Blinne, do you accept that you are now obliged to speak the truth?'

Blinne lowered her head with a quick bow.

'So what do you have to tell us?'

Blinne swallowed nervously and then, still looking at the floor, said slowly: 'The Uí Fidgente warrior raped me.'

Selbach immediately spoke almost triumphantly. 'You see? That Uí Fidgente swine dishonoured my wife and thereby dishonours my kindred. He dishonours all the Eóganacht.'

Prince Donennach gave a sharp inward take of breath and moved as if to step forward.

'Let us hear the details of the evidence without resource to expletives or the calling names,' Fidelma declared quickly. 'The details shall be heard fairly in accordance with the law.' She turned back to Blinne. 'Now, this is important as there are two types of rape, according to the law. There is *forcor*, forcible rape, and *sleth*, all other manners of rape. Even if the woman is not violently forced, if the woman does not agree to the intercourse, then it is rape. So when you say you were raped by Céit of the Uí Fidgente, I want you to understand the difference.'

Something was stirring in the back of Fidelma's mind. She was remembering the purchase of wormwood as a concoction for an aphrodisiac. Esnad had implied that Blinne was having an affair with a young warrior.

'I don't understand your question, Fidelma of Cashel,' Selbach intervened in annoyance. 'Of course, she understands what she is charging the warrior with.'

'It is not you to whom I am putting that question,' Fidelma replied immediately. 'There are certain things I must put forward in law. Given the two types of rape, and bearing in mind a distinction between an affair and a steady relationship, she has to think carefully on the question. What type of rape are you saying this man carried out?'

Selbach actually uttered a profanity.

'Are you putting words into her mouth? Are you trying to say that my wife was having an illicit affair with this Uí Fidgente scum?'

'I am trying to discover the exact charge that is being made,' Fidelma shot back. 'What type of rape was committed?'

Blinne set her shoulders as if with a sudden resolve.

'I will tell you the details. I was in the bedchamber next door.'

'Alone? Who else was in these chambers?' Fidelma asked quickly.

'I was in the chapel, talking with Brother Fidach,' Selbach immediately answered. 'Esnad was giving instruction on a matter of food to the woman in the kitchens.'

Fidelma ignored him and looked to Blinne to answer.

'That is so,' she agreed. 'I was alone in the bedchamber,

undressing. I wanted to change my clothing for the *etar-shod*, the midday meal. There was a knock on the door and Céit was standing there.'

'Did you know him?'

'I had seen him as part of Prince Donennach's retinue.'

'But did you know him?' pressed Fidelma.

'I don't understand.'

'Had you ever spoken to him before?'

'He was just a warrior. Why should I speak with him?'

'So he stood at the door, a man totally unknown to you? You had never exchanged words with him? There was no reason why he should come to your private chambers?'

'None.'

'So what happened then?'

'He suddenly pushed in, forcing me backwards and closed the door.'

'And you screamed for assistance?'

Blinne frowned. 'I can't remember. I was shocked. I was half clad. He started to proclaim his passion for me.'

'You protested?'

'I think so. He pushed me across the room towards the bed. I could not fight him off. He was strong; a warrior. I struggled but he was too strong for me.'

'And during all this time, you cannot remember if you cried out or screamed?'

'I was in shock,' she repeated.

'You are saying that he took violent possession of you; that he forced you to have intercourse with him?'

'That is what happened,' she mumbled.

'Then he left?'

'I heard Selbach returning. So the warrior sprang up and rushed to the window and climbed out. He apparently dropped to the yard below. A moment later Selbach, my husband, entered, saw me with my clothes in disarray and demanded to know what had happened.'

'You told him?'

'Should I have kept quiet?'

'I presume Selbach went to the window?'

'I went to the window,' Selbach intervened hurriedly. 'I saw a man hurrying away and I recognised him as the Uí Fidgente warrior.'

Fidelma turned back to Blinne. 'And this you take oath on as to the truth of what happened?'

'I do. This is the truth, as I told it to my husband.'

'And you were aware that this was the warrior called Céit?'

'I had seen him before in the retinue of Prince Donennach,' Blinne declared firmly.

'So there was no doubt of who this man was?'

The woman answered with a nod.

Fidelma turned to Selbach. 'You maintain that your wife clearly identified Céit to you. You were in no doubt as to the identification of Céit as the person who forced your wife to have intercourse with him?' When he affirmed this, she asked: 'What did you do?'

'I am an Eóganacht, the Prince of Ráithlinn. What was I supposed to do?'

'I need to hear what you did from your lips.'

'I took my sword and went racing down into the courtyard. I caught up with Céit in front of the doors of the royal residence. I challenged him. He drew his sword.'

'What was said, when you challenged him?' she interrupted.

'He denied it, of course. His insult was increased by that denial. So once again I challenged him. He drew his sword and he was angry and I knew he was going to strike and so I struck first.'

'For the record, you never thought to bring the matter before the law for judgment or arbitration?'

'Why should I? The evidence was clear and my honour was at stake; indeed, the honour of all Eóganacht.'

'There are certain matters to be considered now under law,' Fidelma commented thoughtfully. 'In normal circumstances when a woman is raped, even if it is under *forcor*, violent rape, the matter is heard before the Brehons and the punishment is the honour price of the victim's legal superior, or that of the victim herself, if that fits. In this case the maximum compensation would be the value of fifteen milch cows plus whatever the *eraic* fine would be. It would not be death, which is what Selbach claimed as his honour price. The law is not clear here and, indeed, there are eight categories even under forcible rape that have to be considered. So I must take time to consider these.'

At that moment she saw Prince Donennach appear to make a move to catch her eye.

'I will consider the matters raised and give my rulings later,' she interrupted before he spoke. 'I have other matters to contend with. I do believe there might be some connection between them all and—'

'That's absurd!' Selbach stormed. 'What other matters? There is only the matter of why and how I slew the Uí Fidgente rapist. That is unambiguous. Anyway, I am plainly without fault in my action.'

'As I was saying,' went on Fidelma calmly, 'there are many factors involved here, not the least, Brother Conchobhar's murder. Then there is the attempt on my life and now there is this matter. So when I have finished considering all these things I shall give judgment on each. In the meantime, I am reserving my right to reexamine all witnesses. Have I made myself clear?'

'I see no connection with those matters and the death of the Uí Fidgente,' Selbach insisted.

Colgú seemed to be agreeing. 'I have to say, Fidelma, there is nothing I have seen or heard that connects the two matters.'

'There is a possible connection, which I do not want to make public now,' insisted Fidelma. 'I hope you will allow me to keep that to myself until I have examined the matters further.'

'Then I must make a demand,' Selbach said. 'In a day or two, the council will be meeting. This matter must be resolved before the council or I will bring it up during the council when we discuss the confidence of the princes in the ability and authority of the King.'

'On that you have my assurance, Selbach of Ráithlinn, because you have pointed to the very concern that I have to consider and why I must not rush to judgment.'

For the first time since they had asked for an explanation, Selbach did not look so confident.

Standing in the courtyard again, after they had left the guest quarters, Eadulf turned to Fidelma with a perplexed expression.

'It is a peculiar story,' he commented. 'In fact, from what Enda has been telling me of what has been happening in the period I was away at Imleach, some very abnormal events have occurred.'

'This one, if not handled correctly, could lead to grave consequences,' she pointed out. 'This is such an event that could even lead to a bloody new war in this kingdom. That will result in the deaths of thousands.'

Colgú sniffed to disguise a bitter humour. 'That is, of course, if the deaths of thousands are not caused by the return of the pestilence beforehand.'

THIRTEEN

As Fidelma and Eadulf were crossing the courtyard to return to their own apartment, Conrí came hurrying up behind them, calling them to stop. Fidelma turned with a frown of disapproval.

'Did I not say, Conrí, that I have other matters to attend to before making judgment on Céit's death? I will be calling witnesses as and when I need them. I wish to hear no more evidence at this time. Selbach, unless he and Blinne are lying, has a good defence, which must be heard. I hope Prince Donennach understands that the matter needs more information and thought. I will not act in haste because a wrong decision at this stage would be fatal in more ways than one.'

'I understand. But there is the matter of Céit's burial, which, under law, should be at midnight tonight or tomorrow night.'

'What of that?'

'Can I take it that there is no legal objection to that and that Eadulf will be examining the body of Céit before it is prepared for burial?'

'Why Eadulf?' Fidelma was puzzled. 'Any one of the attendants here could wash the body and wrap the *recholl*, the winding sheet, around him, for the burial. There is no impediment to that.'

Conrí had an awkward expression on his face. 'But will he examine the body?' he said with emphasis.

'There is no need for an examination. There is no question that Céit was run through by Selbach's sword. He does not deny it.'

'Does there not have to be proof that Céit was guilty of raping the Eóganacht princess and was therefore slain in retaliation?'

Eadulf looked surprised. 'What has that to do with an examination of the body?'

'Are you worried that he will be refused burial because he

is deemed a rapist?' asked Fidelma. 'The corpse must be buried.'

'I would prefer Eadulf to examine the body,' Conrí insisted. 'I know Eadulf to be thorough, professional and truthful.'

Eadulf smiled thinly. 'I welcome the compliment, Conrí. But in this matter, anyone could prepare the body for burial.'

'I doubt it,' replied the warlord. 'However, you don't understand. It is essential that an examination takes place.'

'Are you trying to tell us something, Conrí?' Fidelma frowned.

'Did you know that Céit was divorced two years ago?'

Fidelma was puzzled and gave him a searching look. 'What has that to do with this matter? I don't understand.'

'Céit's wife divorced him,' Conrí elaborated. 'His wife divorced him under one of the second category of the separation laws, which state that a couple can separate without fault and the wife can take her *coibche*, her dowry, with her. This was what happened.'

'I have enough conundrums to unravel,' Fidelma replied angrily. 'Can't you say exactly what you mean?'

Conrí sighed. 'Without being crude, I refer to the law that says that a woman who is deprived of sexual intercourse by her husband can seek a divorce.'

'Are you implying that Céit preferred the cohabitation of men or even the company of boys, even though the wife desired him, but he refused to meet the marital obligations?'

'Céit was incapable of intercourse of any kind.'

Eadulf glanced at Fidelma before turning back to Conrí as the meaning began to dawn in his mind.

'Are you saying that he was sexually impotent and this was the reason for his divorce?' he asked.

'*Díbreith* is the legal term,' Fidelma acknowledged. 'How do you know this thing, Conrí? Usually in a divorce case the facts are heard before the Brehon and the decision is made public with the details of how the decision was reached.'

'That is why I ask,' Conrí said after a moment. 'I ask that Eadulf should examine the body. He may obtain proof of this impotency.'

Eadulf replied with a shake of his head. 'An examination

of impotency is not often a physical matter but a matter of attitude.'

'In this case,' Conrí replied in a flat tone, 'I believe that you will find it was a physical wound that took his manhood from him. That should be physical proof enough.'

Eadulf pursed his lips in surprise. 'Then I shall examine the body and attest the facts if they are there. Have the body immediately brought to the apothecary, where I shall examine it before it is prepared for burial.'

'And if Eadulf finds that Céit was impotent . . .?' Conrí pressed, looking closely at Fidelma. 'You know what that means?'

Fidelma's expression was grim. 'It means that the lady Blinne was lying about being raped. It also means that Selbach had no claim of self-defence for his killing of Céit. Indeed, it means an innocent man has been unjustly accused and slain. For that there could be a bloody price to pay.'

'He could put forward the defence of having been lied to by his wife,' pointed out Eadulf, who sometimes surprised Fidelma with his grasp of the law.

'Even that would be no complete defence for the action Selbach took,' Fidelma pointed out. 'Either way, Selbach would have to make atonement under the law.'

'I will await Eadulf's findings before I allow Prince Donennach to act,' Conrí announced. 'We will not be precipitous for we know the gravity of the situation. We wish to avoid any cause for bloodshed. We also want to see the treaty between Colgú and ourselves confirmed.'

Fidelma and Eadulf stood in silence for a few moments, watching Conrí walk back to the guest quarters.

'You had better get on with that as quickly as you can,' Fidelma instructed, and, as she saw Brother Fidach walking back to the chapel, she added: 'Perhaps you had better find a witness to your examination. He should be the very man.'

Eadulf examined her with some concern. 'You should go and lie down awhile. You should have had today just resting.'

Fidelma forced a smile. 'There are many things to do first. Do not be concerned. I feel perfectly all right at the moment.'

Eadulf knew that he was not going to persuade her to rest

and so made no further effort. He left her and hailed the priest to engage him in his mission.

Fidelma had to admit to herself that Eadulf was offering good advice and she ought to rest a little, but a thought had begun to irritate like an itch. She had not been able to dismiss the mysterious Sister Ernmas from her mind. She turned back to the library and found Brother Dáire was making notes from an old parchment scroll. He looked up and seemed pleased to see her.

'I heard that Prince Selbach has been fighting a duel with a warrior of the Uí Fidgente. Is it true the warrior has been killed? That does not augur well when a council meeting is due.'

'There is a specific matter I need to ask about,' Fidelma replied, getting directly to the point. 'You will remember our talk about Sister Ernmas?'

The young librarian smiled. 'I do. In fact, I was going to raise the matter with you. Our talk played on my mind and it was only a short while ago that a memory came to me. I had seen her one day at dusk. She was standing at the back of Brother Conchobhar's apothecary.'

'What made you remember it now?'

'It just came to me because we talked about her interest in the matter of the Otherworld. A short while ago I took a stroll to where I had seen her . . . out of curiosity, you understand?'

'And what did you find there?'

'She was standing by that old stone carved in Ogham.'

The stone had intrigued Fidelma since she was a girl and had inspired her to learn the ancient alphabet named after Ogma, the god of learning and literature. She knew the stone was also inscribed with the name of Corc, who had established Cashel as the seat of the kingdom of Muman. There were, however, some words that she had never been able to make much sense of. Not even old Brother Conchobhar who, in her eyes, knew just about everything, could make a clear translation from the ancient and worn letters. One word began with the letters SÍD and Conchobhar told her this could mean *sídhe* or hill, but the other letters he had no way of guessing. He had once thought that it might be *síd n-uailli* – seat of pride – because the Eóganacht had made Cashel the capital of the kings.

'I know that stone,' Fidelma affirmed.

'Well, I recognised Ernmas by the light from lamps the guards were lighting along the walkway on top of the walls. I have no doubt who it was.'

'I understand. So she was by the old stone when you saw her?'

'It was before those times that I told you I saw her in the library. She was standing by that stone and later in the library she asked me about the House of Death.'

'Does any other memory come back to you about this?' Fidelma pressed.

'Not a memory, but something that took place early this morning. After the ending of the *Matutinum*, the service before first light, which Brother Fidach insists on holding, she was already here. But so were a few others. They were Brother Laig, Father Fidach and the lady . . . I forget her name . . . she who is the companion of Princess Blinne.'

'What did this Sister Ernmas do?'

'She actually asked me a question.'

'Which was?' Fidelma asked impatiently.

'She wanted to know if the library had a work by the scholar Báetán of Loch Goir.'

'I've never heard of him,' Fidelma frowned, 'although I do know the lake. There is a small abbey on one of the islands. It is part of the territory of the Eóganacht Áine.'

'Well, I share your lack of knowledge on this writer,' Brother Dáire admitted. 'However, the woman showed me a reference in the manuscript she was reading. It said that he wrote something called *Doireóracht den Tigh na nDaoir*.'

'*Gatekeeper to the House of Slaves*?' Fidelma hazarded, struggling with the ancient term.

'Not exactly,' the scholar corrected. '*Gatekeeper to the House of Death* would be a closer translation.'

Fidelma gave a sharp exhalation of breath as she remembered that the old smith, Gobán, has used the same term.

'Was it a story of Donn, the god of death and collector of souls?' she ventured. 'You do not have such a work?'

Brother Dáire shook his head immediately. 'Alas, though it sounded intriguing, we do not have it. The reference was clear but it was not about Donn. The reference said that the House of Death was also known as Druimm Sidhe.'

'Druimm Sidhe? The Ridge of the Otherworld People? Isn't that the name . . .?' Her voice trailed off as she considered it. It was exactly what Gobán had said.

Brother Dáire smiled knowingly. 'It was the name that was given to this very hill, Cashel, before Conall Corc made it the capital of the kingdom. That was three or four centuries ago.'

'I have heard some local folk still retain knowledge of the ancient name. I had no idea of this connection.'

'Have you read the old Ogham stone out there?' He indicated to the back of Brother Conchobhar's apothecary.

Fidelma's eyes widened when it struck her what he was referring to.

'The stone says something about this place being a hill under which the old gods and goddesses dwelt,' Brother Dáire went on. 'As you know, the New Faith metaphorically drove the old deities into the hills. The people were not entirely willing to give up their gods and goddesses. So they call them the *aes sídh* – people of the *sídh* or hills. Now we use the word for "hill" as the word for dwellers in the hills, therefore beings with supernatural powers, magical powers. They are merely the old gods and goddesses who still exist in our minds.'

'Certainly they exist in the names we have given our landscape,' Fidelma agreed.

'Most hills are said to house such beings,' the librarian explained. 'Our myths and folklore are replete with them. Just look at the mountains to the south. Isn't that where Bodb Dearg dwells in the Mountain of Women, and he was the mighty son of The Dagda, the good god, father of the gods.'

'But why would this writer, Báetán, refer to Cashel as the Gate of the House of Death? As children we were always taught that it was Donn, another son of The Dagda, who was the keeper of the dead and took their souls to the west, to Tech Duinn, the House of Donn, which was considered the House of Death.'

'When I saw this brief reference, I asked the same question,'

Brother Dáire agreed. 'When you look at the Old Faith, you are told that the way to the Otherworld is not always a single and straight path. I have thought much about this. I even started making a search among the more obscure texts to try to find this book that the woman wanted. I admit my failure.'

'Did you encounter her after this?'

'I did. I saw her briefly in the library with Princess Moncha, the wife of Furudrán of the Airthir Chliach. They seemed to be exchanging information.'

'Whoever she is, if such a reference does exist, then it would be an intriguing story. I always thought the House of Donn was supposed to be on a single western island in the Great Sea . . . west off the coast of Béara . . .' She paused and shook her head. 'It was the god Nuada, who was Donn's brother, who gave the sacred sword of Findias to Eógan Mór. Eógan then called himself the Servant of Nuada. If this hill is considered an entrance to the Otherworld, then Nuada should be regarded as the Gatekeeper to the House of Death, not Donn.'

'If you follow that logic,' Brother Dáire replied with humour, 'then you have a problem with upsetting many scholars. Let us accept it was the god Nuada who gave the sacred sword, *Frecraid*, to Eógan Mór. Yet we are told the Eógan Mór was king in Muman eight generations before Conall Corc became king. It is accepted that it was Conall Corc who made Cashel the capital of his kingdom, not Eógan. How is it that the sword is also supposed to protect Cashel as the Gate to the House of Death?'

Fidelma's mind was racing as the words of Gobán the smith came back to her. Brother Conchobhar had believed that the Keeper of the Sword was also the Gatekeeper to the House of Death. It was a powerful symbolism.

'There are a lot of peculiarities here,' she finally agreed. 'I am certain that there is a need to find this strange woman.'

'You don't think that she could have killed Brother Conchobhar?' asked the young librarian nervously.

'She certainly did not steal the sword,' Fidelma replied. 'It is now carefully guarded in the great hall. Perhaps there is something behind the symbolism. They may all be pieces of the same puzzle but how do we make them fit together?'

The librarian suddenly said: 'You don't think that we are dealing with someone from the Otherworld?'

Fidelma was about to take the words seriously until she saw the humour on the young man's face.

'When people start to talk about the supernatural,' she replied, 'it is usually because they don't have a logical explanation for something that can be explained in very natural terms.'

'If only they could understand those terms,' added Brother Dáire. 'Even the New Faith resorts to supernatural beings when they have nothing else to offer.'

'Keep all this to yourself, Brother Dáire,' Fidelma said. 'This woman is real and we must find her.'

Eadulf abruptly entered the library, crossed to a chair and dropped into it as if exhausted. Brother Dáire saw he had something to say to Fidelma and, with a quick excuse, left them together.

'Well?' Fidelma asked after a moment or two. 'Did you examine Céit's body? What did you find?'

'What can I say except that Conrí was absolutely right,' Eadulf replied with a grimace of distaste.

'He was not capable of sexual activity?'

'No question that he was impotent. He must have suffered considerably when that wound was made. It was an old battle wound. I have seen nasty battle wounds but this was one of the worst. I have to say I admire the physician who worked on him. He saved much, but Céit would have been completely incapable of intercourse . . . even of attempting it.'

'So Blinne was lying?' Fidelma said thoughtfully.

'Believe me, there is no way that Céit could have raped her, nor attempted to do so.'

'So we must have further words with her.' Fidelma was thoughtful. 'On second thoughts, perhaps a few further words with Esnad before we confront Blinne.'

'You are not well enough yet. You have not rested properly,' protested Eadulf. 'And may I remind you, there is also the matter of the identity of the person who shot you. Are we saying that it was Céit and, if so, why?'

'Too many things compete for attention,' Fidelma replied

irritably. 'I will have to make choices as to which is the most urgent.'

'I would say the urgent matter is making sure you get well.'

'Or stay well,' she replied thoughtfully. 'To stay well, we need to resolve these mysteries and prevent any further killing.'

Eadulf made a noise at the back of his throat to express his disapproval. 'The least you can do is to let Dar Luga bring you a hot broth and then you should rest for a short while. You should never have risen from your bed in the first place.'

'So you keep telling me,' she snapped in annoyance. Then she added: 'I am sorry, Eadulf. I am now sure that there is a plot to bring down my brother or create dissension and war among the princes. There may be other matters involved that I can't understand. At the moment it is so frustrating but I cannot waste time. Get Enda to bring Esnad to our quarters at once. I want to talk to her but away from any prying eyes and ears.'

Eadulf rose hesitantly, paused as if he would argue and then left.

It was not long before Eadulf and Enda ushered the girl into their chambers. Fidelma did not rise from her chair. If the truth be known, she felt herself too lazy to do so. She was sitting, stretched before a fire, sipping the hot broth that Dar Luga had sent her. She found the liquid relaxing and rather soporific. Perhaps she had done too much this day. She frowned and tried to pull herself together. She motioned Esnad to take the seat opposite her while Eadulf and Enda seated themselves nearby.

Esnad looked defensive and her jaw set firmly. Fidelma felt the girl had prepared herself for this interview.

'Do you believe it when Blinne claims she was raped by Céit?'

'Why would she tell me a lie?' countered the girl.

'It was you who told me that Blinne was having an affair and that's why she needed wormwood,' Fidelma said without preamble. 'I presume she did not claim that Céit was her lover as well as the rapist?'

Esnad stared at her and found no reply coming quickly to her tongue. Even Eadulf looked startled at the suggestion and was about to point out that it was physically impossible. But

Fidelma had chosen the question as a means to block the girl's prepared responses.

'I didn't know who her lover was,' Esnad finally shrugged. 'She never said.'

'Well, rapist or lover, I am afraid she chose the wrong victim.'

Esnad was now puzzled, trying to determine where Fidelma was leading her.

'We know that Blinne was lying when she said Céit raped her,' Fidelma assured her confidently. 'So she is responsible for his death and that death was an unlawful act.'

Esnad was shaking her head. She seemed truly confused. 'How are you so sure that Céit did not rape her?' she began. 'Blinne claimed that—'

Fidelma cut her short. 'Perhaps Selbach chose Céit, and forced Blinne to make the claim so that he could kill him to stir up a conflict between Eóganacht and Uí Fidgente? He could use rape as a legal justification,' Fidelma suggested.

Esnad was silent for a few moments but not ready to concede.

'This warrior, Céit, could have done what she claimed,' she argued. 'Why do you say he could not?'

'Accept that I know,' Fidelma returned coldly. 'That it can be proved. So now we must come to why he was picked on by Selbach.'

There was a long pause before Esnad spoke.

'I have already told you that I was sure Blinne had a lover but who he was I had no knowledge. All I knew was that he was a warrior of rank. If you have proof she was lying then surely you must ask her?'

'Indeed I must, but as she could lie to the point where an innocent man was murdered why would she be willing to start telling the truth now?'

The girl was silent. Fidelma waited a while and then continued: 'This means that Blinne faces a serious punishment as a false witness, while Selbach loses more than his honour. According to the *Din Techtugad*, in which the law on this matter is written, it is said that there are three punishments of the gods on those who bear false witness. The first is that death will strike them. We have an innocent death whose responsibility lays heavily on Blinne and Selbach. Next there is a visitation of a pestilence. We have already heard of a plague ship landing at Árd Mór. The final curse is a lack of food and water. Should the plague spread, then we shall certainly encounter that. It seems the punishment of the old gods is already beginning.'

Eadulf shivered slightly, for he had not yet completely abandoned his pagan past.

Esnad's head was bent forward. 'What do you want me to say?' Her tone was no longer defiant.

'The truth. Show me that you are not like your cousin; that you are not giving *gúfíadnaise*, false testimony?'

'I swear I am telling the truth,' the girl said, her dry lips almost cracking with the force of saying the words.

'I ask you to reflect deeply. Do you know anything about this claim of rape? If, as it is said, you and Blinne are close cousins, she would have sought your comfort after such a traumatic incident.'

'She told me nothing. I knew nothing of this until Selbach summoned me to their chambers just before you came to question him. He told me that Blinne had been attacked by an Uí Fidgente warrior. I noticed she had bruising on her face. Selbach said that on Blinne's identification, he had sought the man out, challenged him and killed him. Selbach told me he was expecting you to come and question him. I was to stay with Blinne in the bedchamber and look after her and come when summoned.'

'You say Blinne had bruises on her face. Indeed, we saw them. Did she tell you how she got them?'

Esnad shook her head. 'She told me nothing at that time. I presume they were caused during the rape.'

'She did not tell you that it was Céit who inflicted them or, more likely, that Selbach had made the marks?'

'Selbach would not have struck her,' protested the girl immediately. 'He is not that type of person.'

'You know him that well?' Fidelma asked, amused. 'I doubt any woman knows to what point a man may be driven before he loses control of his emotions.'

'I know nothing more than I have said.'

'Nothing more?' For Fidelma it was always a signal that there was always more that could be extracted. 'You have implied that Blinne often had affairs. Would that not provoke him?'

'Of course not!' Esnad retorted without hesitation.

'You sound positive? I presume that such matters were not always one sided?'

'Selbach dwelt in his fortress called Árd na Rátha on the island of Raerainn while Blinne had a fortress called Dún Beg. They pursued their own affairs.'

Fidelma smiled thinly. 'So you confirm there was no reason for Selbach to make the excuse he did to kill Céit?'

Esnad's eyes widened as she realised what she had said.

'So they did not always share the matrimonial bed with each other?' continued Fidelma. 'If affairs were common to both, there seems little reason why Selbach became incensed enough to kill Céit. Why did he lose control to the point that he went after the person his wife apparently named, to strike him down? Does this seem logical?'

'I do not know,' replied the girl helplessly. 'Anyway, rape makes the difference.'

'If rape it was, it was certainly not by Céit. If we accept Blinne was having an affair, as you claim, can we presume this current one started after your party came to this fortress? You did not come to the fortress with any males in the retinue?'

'Selbach had two bodyguards but we left them to take quarters in a place outside the township. It was the place where the Beltaine feast and market will be held. I alone accompanied Selbach and Blinne as a companion into the fortress.'

'So when did she reveal she was having an affair? Was it after her arrival at Cashel?'

'In truth, she only made an oblique reference, and that was when she asked me to get the wormwood from the apothecary.'

'The point being that you believed that the affair was with a warrior in this fortress?'

'That was why I cannot deny it was with this man Céit.'

Fidelma stared at her for some time, as if searching out the truth with her examination. Then she finally told the girl to go back to her room. Esnad rose with alacrity and left the chamber quietly.

'Why didn't you tell her the reason why Céit was unable to rape Blinne?' Eadulf demanded after the door closed.

'Never give arms to your enemy while you are negotiating with them,' Enda intervened, thoughtfully. 'I learnt that during my training.'

Fidelma gave a soft chuckle of appreciation. 'Exactly so. Let Esnad wonder what information we have.'

Eadulf was not convinced. 'I think this is a mistake. Esnad will surely tell her cousin that you have some evidence that she has lied about Céit.'

'That is exactly what I am hoping she will do,' Fidelma confirmed. 'Meanwhile, Enda, can you make up a list of those who were on guard at the guest quarters or at the gates when the princes and their entourages began to arrive?'

'Of course, lady,' Enda replied. 'But only a couple of the princes brought their own bodyguards into the fortress. Selbach and Elódach did not do so.'

'The princes' escorts were told to make camp at Ráth na Drínne,' Fidelma said thoughtfully. 'So only a few personal attendants were allowed to stay in the fortress. It should not be difficult to get some idea who would be liaising with Blinne.'

Eadulf seemed surprised that the princes' warrior escorts were camped outside the fortress. 'Are the warriors encamped on the lands around the tavern owned by Ferloga and Lassar?'

'I do not have to remind you that Ráth na Drínne is deemed the centre of the festivities during the Feast of Beltaine,' Fidelma said. 'It is on those open spaces that the market and entertainments are held. Ferloga is master of the entertainments, as you'll recall from last year. It is an obvious place for the warrior escorts of the princes to set up their camps while only a few personal attendants came into the fortress.'

There was a sudden strident note from a distant trumpet. Enda rose reluctantly to his feet. 'That's someone approaching the gates. I'd better see what news is brought.'

It was not very long after he left that a warrior knocked on their door to inform them it was Gormán who had returned with news. He and Enda had gone straight away to speak with the King. Colgú had sent a request for Fidelma and Eadulf to attend him.

'Is it news of the pestilence?' Fidelma queried, her heart suddenly beating rapidly.

The warrior denied any knowledge.

In Colgú's private chamber, the King and Enda were deep in conversation with Gormán. Gormán and Enda started to rise as Fidelma and Eadulf entered. Colgú waved everyone to their seats.

'Is it news of the pestilence?' Fidelma demanded at once.

'Repeat your report,' Colgú instructed Gormán.

Gormán cleared his throat briefly. 'I am told that there seems to have been some instances of the plague in the territory of the Déisi. Prince Cummasach is treating the outbreaks with harsh measures.'

'What is the source of this information?' Fidelma queried.

'Some merchants who came across the River Siúr to Árd Fhionáin. They reported that they had seen a couple of villages burning beyond Sléibhte an Comeraigh.'

'Villages burning beyond the mountains?' Fidelma was puzzled. 'Deep in the territory of the Déisi?'

'The news is not first-hand, of course,' Gormán commented. 'One of my men talked to the merchants at the abbey when they arrived. He was also told that Prince Cummasach had warned people that he would burn down any villages where the plague broke out in large numbers. He was determined to use all in his power as a means of containing the spread of the disease.'

'These are very harsh measures, indeed.' Fidelma was quite astonished. 'Can Prince Cummasach be persuaded that there are better ways of containing the spread?'

'I only report the news that is brought to me, lady,' Gormán said, with a nod of resignation. 'But beyond the Comeraigh mountains, all along that coastline, it is Prince Cummasach who decides how to treat the pestilence.'

Colgú shifted uneasily. 'Indeed. He still might pay me tribute, acknowledge me King of Muman, as do all the princes of this kingdom, but Gormán is right: Cummasach rules his territory without interference.'

'Some others of my men are bringing in similar tales from the Déisi territory,' Gormán continued. 'Beyond the mountains, south of the Plain of Femen, either the Déisi or the Uí Liatháin rule their territories with a harsh grip, as you know. The fact is, the people may have started to panic. If the plague is spreading, the memories of what happened years ago are uppermost in their minds. Once panic really sets in, the people are like wild animals. Even if Prince Cummasach were more temperate in his policies to contain the pestilence, there would be no stopping the panic.'

'What do you mean?' Eadulf asked.

'Much misinformation is being spread. It is the uncertainty of what is reality and what are invented stories that causes people to behave in such disgraceful fashion. We hear that foreign seamen and traders found in the ports along the southern coast are now being attacked. Some have been injured, some have been killed. It has even been reported that members of the religious have been attacked and killed. It seems that many are blaming the religious for the return of the pestilence.'

'The religious? For heaven's sake, why?' Eadulf asked.

'The arguments of some of the religious, like those of Brother Fidach, have rebounded on them.'

'Rebounded? How, exactly?'

'Apparently, their exhortations that the plague is God's punishment for people not admitting their sins and seeking penance have been taken seriously. When the religious claim they are without sin and it is just the people who are the sinners, people are angry that the religious are not showing proper contrition for their own sins. They reason that is why the pestilence has begun to ravage the land once again.'

'That is insanity,' Eadulf observed. 'Not that I condone the religious for using such a stupid argument.'

'When people are in fear and dread they are capable of insane behaviour,' Colgú said. 'Logic is cast aside and they strike out like little children. They are thinking only of their own protection. There is another matter Gormán has raised that causes concern – theft.'

'Theft?' queried Fidelma.

'Faced with such an interruption of normal values, the greedy and immoral will prey on the sick and vulnerable. I have received reports of cattle raids, even sheep and pigs have been run off in some of the south-eastern areas of the kingdom,' Gormán explained.

'It might open a way for Laigin to take advantage and try to take over the Osraige.' Enda looked somewhat perturbed.

'I think Laigin will be concerned with conditions in its own territories,' Colgú replied. 'After all, they have ports that connect with more countries than we do, and it is from these ports that the pestilence comes. The rivers from these ports connect through the kingdoms.'

'We should be looking after our own security,' Gormán declared. 'A lot of people are now hearing stories from the Déisi territory and are becoming fearful that they will be left unprotected.'

'What do you suggest?' Fidelma asked.

'I said earlier in council that we are in a state of war with this plague.'

'And so?'

'All we can do at the moment is watch and control travellers along the southern routes. We must make sure that the fear does not spread.'

'This is an invisible enemy,' Colgú agreed. 'We could deploy whole armies along the southern borders and then find the pestilence has already passed us by, leaving the dead and dying in its wake.'

'This is true,' Gormán agreed. 'However, we might still be able to control the worst elements of the people taking advantage of the weak and sick.'

'There is something in that,' Colgú said thoughtfully. 'I am willing to give permission for you to raise more warriors to control any outrages.'

'I am already keeping enough sentinels in strategic places. They have fast horses equipped and ready. They can ensure the spread of the information as to where the disease is breaking out. I also have small patrols of warriors scouring the districts generally to detect any who are taking advantage of the situation.'

'Are our patrols allowed to go into Déisi territory?' Fidelma asked. 'Prince Cummasach is very protective about his territorial rights.'

'We keep a watch from the borders between us and the Déisi. As we have said, both the Prince of the Déisi as well as the Uí Liatháin are not of the Eóganacht, even though they pay tribute to Cashel.'

Colgú sighed irritably. 'Eóganacht or not, it is the same with all the princes and their territories. We have seen enough of Furudrán and Selbach's tantrums as an example during these last days. Has any message come directly from Prince Cummasach as to the extent of the spread of the disease in his territory? I presume that the three contaminated sailors from the plague ship managed to get away or have perished?'

'Prince Cummasach has made no attempt to send a report to us. One of the messengers we had from Lios Mór said that he had heard all three men were killed and their bodies burnt. But that could not have been before they contaminated others.'

Colgú ran a hand through his unruly red hair in distraction.

'To sum up, have you heard any reports that put the pestilence any nearer to us than the southern mountains? Is it still south of the River Siúr?'

'No reports have come to us placing it north of the river.'

'Then all we can do now is to keep watch. You are also alerting physicians and apothecaries whenever you find them?'

'I have issued that order to my men,' Gormán acknowledged. 'Eadulf has told us that Abbot Cuán should reach us from Imleach, perhaps by midday tomorrow, and is bringing two physicians and apothecaries with him.'

'Then there is little to be done except continue to try to solve the deaths of Brother Conchobhar and Céit.'

Gormán was startled. 'The death of Céit?' He had known Céit well and, of course, it was the first time he had heard of the death. 'What happened?'

'Céit was slain by Selbach, who claims it was in a duel,' Colgú explained briefly.

'A duel that might be a murder due to the fact it was provocation on an innocent man,' Fidelma added sharply. 'I hope to report a development soon.'

The meeting broke up as there was little else to do. Talking and companionship was merely a therapy to distract from the threat of the consuming darkness of the approaching plague. Finally, each went his or her own separate way with little more to be said. Eadulf had been right about Fidelma needing more sleep and that tiredness would soon consume her. Almost as soon as Fidelma laid down on her bed, she was in a deep, dreamless sleep.

It was some time before Fidelma realised that the thunderstorm she'd heard in her sleep was not a thunderstorm at all but a loud banging on the door. Eadulf was groaning in protest as he came awake at her side. She scrambled from the bed and hauled on her gown. Enda was at the door and it was clear that he, too, had been aroused from his sleep, for his clothes were askew and his weapons seemed hastily slung on their leather warrior's harness. Even as he stood there he was still brushing his tousled hair back from his forehead.

Fidelma's half-waking mind tried to make sense of his appearance.

'It's late,' she mumbled, still blinking. 'What is it?'

'Lady, I thought you should know at once . . .'

A cold fear hit her that it was more news of the pestilence. She tried to focus at him and drew her robe more tightly around her. She was aware that Eadulf had now joined her at her side.

'Go on,' he urged Edna. 'What has happened?'

'It's the Princess Blinne. She has been found on the rocks below the fortress wall. She must have fallen from the battlements. She is dead.'

FOURTEEN

'Are you sure that it is Lady Blinne?' Fidelma asked in a shocked tone as she regained her senses.

'I am sure,' Enda replied immediately. 'When the guard raised the alarm, I went immediately to examine the body.'

For a moment Fidelma closed her eyes as if she had been touched by a sharp pain.

'Then it's my fault,' she whispered. 'My fault.'

Eadulf stepped forward, wondering whether she had misunderstood what was being said.

'She fell? From where?' he asked Enda.

'The walkway on the south-east of the battlement.'

'Near the south-east tower?'

'One of the guards thought that he heard a scream,' Enda went on. 'He alerted the patrol below the fortress. They began a search round the walls. Even in the blackness it did not take them long to find the body. I was called and went to see it and I recognised who it was.'

'It was my fault,' Fidelma repeated. Hearing the tragic tone in her voice Eadulf and Enda turned to her in concern.

'You are not making sense,' Eadulf said sharply.

'When I told Esnad that we knew Blinne was lying about Céit, I thought she would immediately tell Blinne. I thought then Blinne would reconsider her story and come back to me with one bearing more resemblance to the truth, or that it would force her into a course of action from which we would find out the real reason for Selbach's attack on Céit.' She paused and gave another groan. 'I did not think her death would result.'

'You think she would throw herself from the walls because she lied?' Eadulf was aghast.

'No. I think she was murdered.'

It was Eadulf's turn to be shocked.

'I should have foreseen this possibility!' Fidelma was bitter in self-recrimination. 'Where exactly did she fall from?'

'Near the south-east tower that is accessible from the store-rooms below,' Enda replied. 'I have already given instructions for the storerooms to be searched as a matter of routine. There was no one there or any sign of anything untoward.'

'The storerooms are a good place for assignations, for there are a couple of connecting doors with the guest quarters,' Fidelma pointed out thoughtfully. 'You say the storerooms have already been searched?'

Enda nodded. 'I ordered Luan to take some men and search them thoroughly but to do it quietly. What should I do now?'

'Allow us a moment or so, Enda,' she replied. 'We will put on clothes and come and view the body.'

'There is nothing you can do there, lady,' the warrior pointed out. 'The woman's body is not a pretty sight. It is, forgive me, so mangled that you would learn nothing by viewing it.'

'Except that I must follow the procedures incumbent on a *dálaigh*. In the case of murder I must view the body myself. We must acquire all the knowledge we can, and it would be reprehensible of me not to examine the victim at this stage.'

In a very short time Fidelma and Eadulf followed Enda across the darkened courtyard to the main gate, lit by brand torches that danced in the slight breeze but provided little light.

'Any further developments?' asked Enda of the warrior who stood sentry.

'Dego and some men are still with the body,' the man answered. He turned into the guard room, asking them to wait a moment, and emerged with a lantern. 'It is dark, so you must go carefully.'

Enda took the lantern and led the way through the gates and down the slope to the base of the great limestone thrust on which the fortress was built. The dominating outcrop stood over sixty metres above the township that had arisen around the impressive seat of the kings of Muman. They turned off after a short distance and made their way towards the south-eastern side of the towering dark walls.

'I thought it better not to rouse the fortress by ordering horses,' Enda explained. 'It is but a short walk down to the spot.'

In fact they had not gone very far before they saw a group of shadowy figures standing around a lantern and heard Dego's voice come in challenge. Enda answered.

The lantern held at arm's length by Enda was enough for Fidelma to see that Princess Blinne's death had not been a pleasant one. The body was almost unrecognisable and covered in a dark substance that shone in the flickering lamplight. It was clear that it was blood. The clothes were torn where they had encountered the sharpness of the rocks below the walls. Fidelma stood aside so that Eadulf could bend and quickly view the twisted remains of the corpse.

'There is nothing I can tell you,' he said, rising after a moment. 'The body is so badly damaged I could not say whether she was knocked unconscious or killed before she fell. Nor could I say whether she was pushed over the wall, jumped or fell. It is also impossible to say whether she was killed by the impact of the fall or a blow before the fall. The impact on the jagged rocks below inflicted terrible damage.'

'I said there was nothing to be learnt, lady,' Enda muttered. 'Shall I order the remains to be removed?'

'Take them to Brother Conchobhar's apothecary,' Fidelma agreed, trying to hide her emotions. She felt guilt that she had not foreseen the possibility of this outcome to what she had told Esnad. 'Let us go back and see what can be discovered at the spot from where she fell.'

Luan was waiting outside the main storeroom door. The fortress was still in dark silence. Luan led them directly to the walkway by the south-east tower. He held up his lantern so that Fidelma could examine the area, leaning over the rampart to judge the exact spot from which Blinne had fallen. Even with the lantern it was too dark to see any detail in its flickering light. Luan told them that he had already searched through the large storage areas and corridors constituting warehouses. He had especially examined the doors that led from the guest quarters into the storerooms but had found nothing suspicious. Finally, Fidelma dismissed Luan and his men to go back to their usual duties.

'What now, lady?' Enda asked as they followed the warriors out of the storeroom and paused in the courtyard.

Fidelma glanced up at the sky. The dark clouds seemed to be lighter in the east.

'It will soon be light,' she pointed out. 'I suppose we should go and inform Selbach of his wife's death, if he does not know already.'

Eadulf seemed surprised at this cynical addition. 'What makes you say that?'

'I thought you knew Cicero's famous dictum.'

Eadulf thought for a moment but made the excuse it was too early in the morning to think. Enda simply stood in puzzled silence.

'"*Cui bono?*"' she said dryly when she saw they did not know. '"For whom is the benefit?" At the moment, the only known person who gains from Blinne's sudden silence is Selbach.'

'There is one point in his favour,' Eadulf countered. 'I can't see him panicking after drawing such attention to his defence of killing Céit. Slaughtering his wife in this manner makes no sense, for it leaves him without a defence to fall back on.'

Fidelma realised that Eadulf had made a good point but she said nothing. They walked into the guest quarters without a further word. The household guard came forward out of the gloom and stiffened in respectful attention when he recognised them.

'Have you been on duty long?' Enda asked quietly, trying to remember the duty roster for that night.

'Since midnight,' the man answered.

'Has nothing disturbed you during your watch?'

The guard frowned with a shake of his head. 'Should something have disturbed me?' he countered.

'You have heard no movement from any of the guest chambers? Have you seen any of the guests leave their rooms?'

'No movement that I am aware of. Things have been as quiet as the grave.'

'And you have been here all that time? You heard no movement, for example, from the chambers of Prince Selbach?'

'Those quarters are on the upper floor at the back of the guest house. I have been here at this front entrance most of the time.'

'Stay here then,' Fidelma instructed, before turning and leading the way to mount the stairs to the upper floor.

Selbach's chambers were entered by a single door from the corridor, which held a line of several such doors that gave entrance to various guest chambers. At a signal from Fidelma, it was Enda who rapped sharply on the door. There was no answer. Impatiently, Fidelma motioned him to knock again. There was still no answer. In dealing with a senior Eóganacht prince, it was not politic to enter without this ritual. Now Enda reached forward and tried the handle of the door. To their surprise the door was unlocked and opened with quiet ease. Enda entered first. He was still carrying the lantern and he took a few steps forward, holding it high.

The light of the lantern fell on a tidy but empty room. This, as Fidelma remembered, was the small reception chamber where Selbach had sat making his defence of slaying Céit. She pointed silently to the adjoining door. This was the bedchamber shared by Selbach and his wife. Enda went forward and knocked again, according to protocol. Silence greeted them. This time Fidelma moved forward and turned the handle of the door herself, but Enda held her back from entering first. He gently pushed her to one side and passed into the dark chamber, holding the lantern before him.

The bed was rumpled and untidy but it was devoid of occupants. Enda swung round to allow the lantern to illuminate the entire room. It was clear the room was deserted. It seemed as though the inhabitants had left in a hurry as some of the travelling boxes had their contents crumpled as if they had been hastily rummaged through. A few things were discarded on the floor. The light from the lantern flickered wildly as Enda went on his knees and peered under the bed before climbing to his feet again.

He shook his head mystified. 'No one here at all, lady.'

'He must still be in the fortress,' Fidelma said. 'Those boxes contain clothes that would not be left behind.'

'Unless he was fleeing from the consequences of his action,' pointed out Eadulf.

'His action? You think he threw his wife to her death and has fled?' Enda asked.

Fidelma shook her head. 'I don't think so.'

'But it is a possibility?' pressed Eadulf.

'A possibility,' Fidelma conceded, turning to Enda. 'I suggest we institute a search of the fortress for him. Firstly, I want to have a quick word with Esnad. We'll see just what she did after she left us; whom she spoke to. I suspect that she would have gone immediately to speak with Blinne.'

They left Selbach's quarters and turned along the corridor to where the other guest chambers were. Esnad, as a companion, had her room positioned along the corridor at the rear of the guest quarters. Enda led the way, holding the lantern, with Fidelma and Eadulf following. They came to a halt outside the room and Fidelma was about to knock when what sounded like a female groan of pain came to their ears. Automatically Fidelma grabbed the lantern from Enda and, at the same time, motioned him to kick in the door. Each of the guest rooms was fitted with a lock or a bolt and it did not occur to anyone that this would not be drawn across. Enda stepped back, raising his right foot so that the flat of it crashed against the door just above the lock. He put such force behind it that the wood splintered and the door burst inwards.

Fidelma entered with the lantern. The room had been in darkness. She was aware of two figures lying on the bed. A woman screamed in shock. A man was cursing as he leapt naked from the bed and stood facing them.

An expression of surprise crossed Fidelma's features as she confronted the naked form of the Prince of Ráithlinn. The figure in the bed was trying to pull a cover around herself. It was Esnad. Fidelma glanced back to the man, allowing a grim smile to spread across her lips.

'Cover yourself, Selbach,' she admonished in a dry tone. 'You look ridiculous.'

Selbach was already pulling a robe around him.

'How dare you?' he spluttered, lacing his angry words with expletives. 'You will pay dearly for this intrusion. You will . . . you will . . .'

'I will counsel you to remain silent for the moment, Prince Selbach,' Fidelma advised coldly before turning to the flushed face of Esnad, who had now succeeded in covering herself. It was clear that what they had heard was not a groan of pain but one with the opposite cause. 'Light another lamp, Enda,' she instructed.

'I am going to call the guard. I am reporting you to your brother, to the Chief Brehon. I shall see you punished for this affront . . .' Selbach continued to splutter profanities as Enda bent to light a nearby lamp.

'I repeat my advice, Selbach. Remain silent,' Fidelma repeated in an icy tone. 'In fact, I order you to be quiet. Eadulf, you and Enda will escort Selbach back to his own chamber. Use force, if necessary. He has already demonstrated what he is capable of with a sword so make sure you watch him well and keep any weapons from his grasp. He is not capable of trust.'

Enda had already unsheathed his sword, placing the point at Selbach's throat. Selbach made to speak in protest but Enda placed the tip of his weapon so that it pricked the man's flesh, causing him to wince in pain.

'Are you coming quietly of your own free will?' Enda demanded in a quiet but threatening tone. It seemed that he enjoyed giving orders to the Prince of Ráithlinn. 'If you prefer, you can be bound and dragged to your chamber.'

'I will go,' Selbach grunted reluctantly. 'But you will all hear much more from me on this affront to my honour.'

Fidelma allowed her smile to remain fixed. 'That is exactly my intention, Selbach. We have heard much about your honour but I hope the next time we hear about it we will hear some truths.'

As her companions left with Selbach, Fidelma turned to the figure of Esnad, who was now sitting upright on the bed, the coverings drawn tightly around her. Fidelma gestured to the broken door, hanging crookedly from its hinges with the splintered wood.

'I regret that for the moment we cannot ensure privacy during our talk,' she observed in an amused tone, drawing up a chair and placing it so that she could sit facing Esnad on the bed. The girl did not reply but the flickering light of the lamp could not distort the hatred that twisted her features as she stared back. She made no effort to break the silence between them. Fidelma took her time.

'So, Esnad, the obvious question that I must ask is – how long has your affair with Selbach been going on?'

'What if I am having an affair? Point me to the law by which it is forbidden,' Esnad returned in a defensive sneer.

'It is not the fact in itself but the circumstances of the act that are sometimes called into question before the law,' Fidelma replied evenly. 'In this case there are a lot of circumstances that seem questionable. So, should I assume that you have been Selbach's mistress for some time or is this the first time you shared your bed with him?'

'Assume what you like. Selbach is an Eóganacht prince and you cannot do anything against him.'

'Do you think so?'

'Oh, yes; the most you can do is to make him pay fines you will levy on Blinne for telling him an untruth about Céit raping her. He will swear that it was what he was told.'

'How long have you and Selbach been here?' Fidelma changed the subject but did not enlighten Esnad. 'I mean in this bed?'

'That is my affair.'

Fidelma felt it best not to be sharp with the girl immediately but wait until the appropriate time.

'I think not,' she replied, still keeping to a soft tone of amusement. 'Unless you co-operate, things will go very ill with you. So let me start by suggesting that when you left me earlier you went to tell Blinne that I had proof that Céit could not have raped her?'

'You told me not to tell her,' countered the girl.

'I told you in the belief that you would do so. And I will lay a wager you did.'

'As Blinne's cousin, I had to warn her,' Esnad replied, keeping her defensive tone.

'But she or you also told Selbach? Is that not so?'

Esnad's hesitation confirmed Fidelma was correct.

'How did Selbach take that information?'

The girl thought for a moment. 'He simply laughed.'

'He laughed?'

'He said that he would be happy to pay the fines for her lies. Whatever the outcome, Céit was dead and therefore the dice had been cast.'

The phrase reminded Fidelma of something. Suetonius had written '*alea iacta est*' to indicate there was no going back when he commented on the decision of Caesar to cross the Rubicon, and how Roman soldiers would use casting dice to decide on a course of action.

'So Selbach had taken a step from which there was no going back? Do you know what he meant by that?' she asked.

It was as if the thought had never occurred to Esnad before.

'I think it was the decision he took that his honour must be avenged and because he believed what Blinne had told him.'

Fidelma knew all about the extremes to which *coim-enech*, the noble's honour, was taken. The word *enech* also meant 'face' and putting on a good face was a passion to many nobles.

'So he felt that he should act the outraged husband. In the circumstances it sounds illogical. Both he and Blinne were having affairs.'

'Affairs can be accepted, but a rape was an affront to his honour,' the girl replied.

'How would you describe your liaison?'

Esnad seemed indifferent. 'I can only say that our situation is one of openness and ease. Blinne knew of it. We broke no law for you to pry into.'

'Is that what you think?' Fidelma shook her head. 'I ask you again, how long have you and he been here in this room?'

The girl saw that Fidelma was insistent.

'If you must know, it was after midnight that he came. It was not long after, as he waited until everyone had retired for the night.'

'Not long? And since then has he been constantly here with you? Did Selbach say he had left his wife in their bed when he came to your room, or did he come later when Blinne had already left their bed in search of her lover?'

'He said she had left already to see that secretive lover.' The girl sounded defiant, almost happy. 'So he decided to visit me.'

'He accepted this as natural? He displayed no concern about Blinne? When you told him that I knew she had been lying about the rape, are you sure he was not concerned?'

'As I said, he simply laughed. I suspect he even knew who

this lover was. Apart from fines, you can't do much to him or
to Blinne if you claim she was lying to him. You can't do
anything to Blinne.'

'There I can agree that you are right. In fact, no one can
do anything more to her.'

An uncertain look spread crossed Esnad's features.

'What do you mean?' she demanded.

Fidelma's expression did not change; her eyes were sharply
upon the woman.

'You will take an oath that Selbach came to your bed shortly
after everyone retired and has stayed here ever since?'

'Why should it be a matter for me to take an oath?'

'Blinne was pushed over the wall of this fortress a short
time ago. There is not much left of her.'

The reaction – her expression and gasp of surprise and
horror – seemed genuine enough to Fidelma. She leant forward.
'Now here's the thing . . . once the lie was known, who was
it that decided that Blinne was of little use to them any more?
When you told Selbach, did he see it as an opportunity to get
rid of her and make a legal arrangement with you? Or when
you told Blinne, did she rush to her lover, this unknown warrior
that you have told me about, and he, seeing suspicion mounting,
decided it would be very convenient to get rid of her? Either
way, it is an event you were indirectly responsible for.'

'I have nothing to say,' the girl said quietly.

Fidelma glanced at the shattered door and turned to Esnad
with an almost malicious smile.

'We should do something about that door soon, for the sake
of security. After all, Blinne met her death falling from the
tower that rises from the storerooms on the other side of that
wall.'

'I don't understand,' the girl protested.

'It depends, of course, whether it was Selbach or the
unnamed warrior who is responsible for this deed.'

Fidelma stood up abruptly, turned and left the chamber.
As she made her way along the corridor she realised the light
had strengthened. A new day had dawned now. Strangely
enough, she did not feel at all tired, even with the exertions
of the previous day and the shortness of the night. She felt

curiously invigorated. She paused as she found Eadulf outside the door of Selbach's chamber. He looked a little morose.

'It's going to take a strong will to deal with the arrogance of that one,' he told her, jerking his thumb towards the door.

'Is Enda with him?'

'Enda has the ability to just shut his mind to the insults that the man has been levelling at him. I had to step outside for some fresh air.'

'Come with me,' Fidelma instructed. 'I will have a word with Selbach.'

When they entered, Enda was standing stoically by the door, his eyes fixed to the ceiling as if trying to ignore Selbach. The Prince of Ráithlinn had meanwhile seated himself in a chair.

'Enda, I want you to organise a couple of guards on permanent duty outside here. They are to keep watch on Selbach, and on the girl Esnad. Ensure they are confined to their rooms.'

Selbach used a choice of invective that Eadulf had difficulty following and demanded that Fidelma fetch her brother, Colgú, to him.

Fidelma stood unmoved, turning to add to Enda, 'When your men come, make sure a constant watch is to be kept on Selbach until I am ready to interrogate him.'

'Interrogate me?' Selbach shouted. 'May you be spat on by every assembly you ever attend! I am not one to forgive and forget, Fidelma of Cashel. I am as much an Eóganacht, even more so, and I have just as many and more rights as you do.'

Only now did Fidelma turn to look him directly in the eyes.

'Selbach of the Eóganacht Ráithlinn,' she intoned heavily, 'it is my duty to tell you that your wife, the lady Blinne, is dead. She was pushed from the storeroom tower to the rocks below the fortress walls. She was murdered. Your rights are diminishing.'

There was a silence and Selbach took a step backwards and sat down heavily in the chair that he had momentarily risen from. He said nothing, but the bewilderment on his face was clear.

'You will remain in this room until I am ready to question

you,' continued Fidelma. 'Guards will be placed outside to ensure that you do so.'

She motioned Eadulf and Enda to follow her, then she shut the door and turned the key firmly in the latch.

Enda was already calling an additional guard up from the entrance to the guest house. Fidelma and Eadulf waited until the orders had been issued and then she led the way outside.

The fortress was beginning to stir and there were sounds of activity from various quarters. Fidelma glanced up at the sky. It was nearly full daylight. Outwardly, as people hurried about their morning tasks, it seemed nothing unusual had taken place. They paused in the courtyard.

'What now, lady?' Enda asked when he had rejoined them.

'You have been up most of the night,' she pointed out. 'I suggest you have a nap and something to eat.'

'Are you sure you don't need me further?' Enda was reluctant to leave them.

'Not immediately. You are no good to me in a tired state if things become busy. I have a feeling that things will become very busy before this day is older.'

Enda accepted her advice and left them for the direction of the *laoch-tigh*, the barracks housing the *lucht-tighe*.

'To be honest, that advice was the same that I gave to you,' Eadulf remarked as they watched Enda walk away.

Fidelma was tempted to follow Eadulf's advice but other things occupied her mind.

'We will join my brother for an early breakfast and discuss the events of the night. Frankly, Eadulf, I am now worried. There appear to be too many unconnected events. Yet I am sure that they are all connected in some way. Usually, there is a hint of purpose behind things once we begin to investigate. Yet in all this I can see nothing that makes a logical connection.'

Colgú sat looking down at the remains of his *primchutig*, the first meal of the day, which had been served by Dar Luga. His expression mirrored the heavy responsibility that he felt. He had hardly eaten anything compared to his sister and Eadulf. Over the meal she had informed him of the events of the night. His facial expression had grown longer and longer.

'This is not turning into a good time,' he declared as Fidelma finished explaining as much as she could about the events of the night.

'What time is ever good when there is murder involved?' Fidelma asked rhetorically.

'You now have three deaths to explain to the council,' Colgú pointed out.

'I believe they are all connected, even Selbach's unlawful killing of Céit. I also think that you are right to be worried about the council.'

'You are usually talented at spotting connections when others do not see them,' Colgú observed morosely. 'Is there no glimmer of light at all that you can see that will lead you to connecting and resolving these mysteries?'

'What are the reasons that you feel the council will stand against you this year?' she asked. 'You raised this. So who do you suspect is plotting against you?'

Colgú flung out his arms in a helpless gesture. 'Only by agreement of the seven senior princes does this kingdom hold together in the traditional forms of government. You saw some of their attitudes at the meeting the other day. You heard what Furudrán said.'

'They are not all like Furudrán.'

'He is an articulate and eloquent orator once he is allowed to speak. Do not underestimate him. His territory is essential to our entire northern border.'

'You appear to believe that he can persuade others to follow him and there will be support enough to oust you from the kingship.'

'I know it can be so. I know it in my bones. If your report about Selbach is accurate, that is a second prince who will not look kindly on me.'

'Feelings in bones are not good auguries,' pointed out Eadulf. 'Who is behind this plot? It has to be a majority of the seven senior Eóganacht princes. Moreover, they would have to be in Cashel for the majority to cast their vote against you. Who are they? I know you are one of the seven . . . so that leaves six others?'

'Anyone could serve as an agent for the conspirator,' Fidelma corrected. 'Whether a senior prince is involved or not, he does not have to be physically present. Do you have news when the other princes are likely to arrive here?'

'They will arrive in a few days,' her brother replied. 'Maybe even later today.'

'Perhaps the news of the plague ship might prevent the council from meeting?' Eadulf suggested. 'If the princes are reluctant to travel here, the council could be put off until a later date?'

'We are bound by tradition,' Colgú replied firmly. 'Bound not only by the tradition of Beltaine but by the fact that this will be the seventh year in which the seven princes meet in council to approve my stewardship of the kingdom.'

Eadulf had to admit he was not entirely sure of the symbolism of the councils.

'If there is a plot to declare me a weak king it could not happen at a better time,' Colgú declared.

'I don't see how,' Eadulf said. 'If the plague has returned and spreads in the south, it will mean that the southern ports to Gaul and beyond are closed. That means the princes of the Déisi and Uí Liatháin will not be able to attend.'

Fidelma was shaking her head. 'They don't have any say in the initial choice of kingship for they are not of the seven princes of the Eóganacht that meet in council. The lesser princes pay tribute to Cashel, as does the prince of Osraige; as will the Uí Fidgente once the treaty with them is approved. But they are not of the council.'

Even as she explained, Fidelma could see that this was getting them nowhere. 'Let's change the subject. How are we going to deal with Selbach? If there is to be a hearing before a Brehon, I would have to hand over the matter to Fíthel, as Chief Brehon, to judge.'

'Do you think Selbach really killed his wife?' her brother asked.

'I would say that the odds are against it,' Fidelma replied, surprising him. 'He was as shocked as anyone when I told him. It makes no sense if what Esnad says is true.'

'There's a lot of "ifs" in your thoughts. Do you think what she says is the truth?'

'That is a question to be decided,' Fidelma conceded. 'However, we have to question him again, especially now that he realises his position is serious.' She began to rise from her seat and then paused. 'I don't suppose you have heard any more about this mysterious Sister Ernmas?'

Colgú grimaced sarcastically. 'I hear weird stories about my palace being a gateway to hell; a place where the souls of the dead are taken on their journey to the Otherworld. I suppose I should accept strange beings like this Ernmas to haunt it.'

'I am not responsible as to what stories are told,' Fidelma sniffed. 'I had no idea the palace was considered a gateway to the House of Death.'

'I suppose that did not fit in with the New Faith.' Her brother made an oblique reference to the fact that Conall Corc was hailed by the ancient scribes as the first King of Muman to convert to the New Faith.

'Even with the Old Faith I was always taught that only Donn was considered the Gatekeeper to the House of Death,' Fidelma said.

'That is so. But now there are stories that Ernmas was mother of the triple goddesses of death and destruction, of Badh, Macha and the Morrígan. In some stories she was mother of Fiachna, who appears in some ancient stories as King of the Dead.'

Fidelma stared at her brother in surprise. Colgú caught her look and started to chuckle in spite of himself.

'Don't worry. I have not turned into a scholar of the ancient stories. After you mentioned the name Ernmas to me, I took the opportunity to summons young Brother Dáire for a talk. He had been working on the references that you went to speak to him about. He told me this story about the ancient goddess.'

Fidelma grimaced with an almost helpless expression. 'I wish we could find this strange woman bearing a name that means death by iron; clearly death by the sword. These stories and the curious encounters are all we need to create unease at this time.'

At once her brother resumed his serious expression. 'We do not have much time to sort the matter of Brother Conchobhar's murder even if Selbach is complicit in his wife's murder,' he reminded her again.

With sombre faces Fidelma and Eadulf left Colgú's chambers. They made their way across to the guest quarters beyond the chapel. A couple of the household guards were on duty in the antechamber. Another of the guards was lounging against the door of Selbach's chamber. He straightened immediately as he saw them approaching along the corridor.

'Any problems?' Fidelma asked as they paused before him.

The guard shook his head. 'He has been in there as quiet as a lamb, lady. Not a word or sound out of him.'

'It seems that the death of Princess Blinne has struck the verbosity out of him,' Eadulf murmured.

Fidelma turned to the door. The key was still in the lock and she turned it and went in without knocking. Then she halted so abruptly that Eadulf nearly collided with her. She frowned, examining the room in a swift glance. Then she hurried to the adjoining bedchamber, the door of which was slightly ajar. She pushed it fully open and stepped inside. Eadulf rushed past her and began a frenetic search. There was no sign of Selbach. This time Fidelma knew, with cold certainty, that they were not going to find him in Esnad's bed.

FIFTEEN

The guard outside Esnad's chamber had barely time to stiffen in deference as Fidelma, with Eadulf, brushed by and flung open the door. Esnad was still in her bed, though apparently wide awake. She started up with a nervous cry as they entered. The bedchamber was small enough for them to see immediately that Selbach was not hiding anywhere.

'Where is he?' Fidelma demanded without preamble.

The girl stared at them in bewilderment.

'Who?'

'Don't play with me,' Fidelma replied coldly. 'Selbach has escaped from his room. So where is he hiding?'

For a moment the girl looked surprised and then a cynical smile spread over her features.

'I do not know, but if I did I would not help you.'

'Are you saying that he has not contacted you?'

The guard who had been outside was standing in the doorway. He moved forward nervously, having overheard what Fidelma was saying.

'Lady, I have been outside this door since a guard was ordered. I can assure you that no one has entered or left this room since I have been here. No one has been near this door. I swear it.'

Fidelma raised her chin. 'So no one has even been along this corridor?' She could not help her sarcasm born out of frustration.

'I did not mean that,' protested the guard. 'This corridor leads to and from many of the guest chambers. The Prince Furudrán and his wife as well as the Prince Elódach have passed along. Some other attendants have also been along here but none even glanced at this door.'

'They all passed together?'

'They passed separately. Firstly, Prince Elódach, then Prince Furudrán and his lady came by within moments, and then some attendants. They did not stop and they went down to the stairway.'

'What of the other guests? Prince Donennach, for example,' Eadulf asked.

'I have not seen him,' the guard said. 'I have not seen any others. The Uí Fidgente rooms are at the front of the building so would have no business in this corridor.'

It fell to Eadulf to ask another question. 'When people passed along here, did they seem surprised to see you, a guard, stationed here? No one asked why you were here?'

'They barely glanced at me . . . except lady Moncha did look at me as if to ask a question, but then she changed her mind and went on down to the main doors with her husband, Prince Furudrán. I heard voices so perhaps the question was asked of the commander of the guard below.'

'Other than that, you saw nothing unusual during your time here?'

'Nothing, lady,' the man assured her.

Fidelma turned back to where Esnad was still sitting in the bed. Perhaps she had been mistaken in accepting Esnad's word that Selbach had been with her all night. The Prince's flight seemed to confirm that he was guilty of murdering his wife.

'So it seems Selbach has deserted you and thought to escape himself,' she observed grimly. 'Now perhaps you will tell me the truth.'

'He did not kill Blinne,' the girl spoke angrily. 'I told you the truth. He was with me through the night until you interrupted us.'

It was clear the news of Selbach's disappearance had shocked her but only increased her defiance.

'Well, the fortress is secured,' Eadulf commented. 'He will soon be found somewhere, unless he has the ability to fly over the walls.'

There were sounds of someone hurrying along the corridor and the guard turned, hand on his sword, ready to intercept them. It was only Enda.

'I was making a final check of security, and the guard at Selbach's chamber tells me that he had vanished.'

'I told you to get some rest,' returned Fidelma irritably.

'Time for rest later,' Enda replied. 'I see he is not here. Have you found out how he escaped from his chamber? The guard told me he was stationed outside the whole time.'

'There were only two ways in or out of that chamber – the door or the window,' she said. 'We seem to be able to discount the door as an exit, so it must be the window.'

'But it is a long drop from that window to the ground below,' Enda pointed out.

'Not if you have a rope,' Eadulf suggested. 'Let's go and see.'

'What about me?' The protest came from Esnad. 'Am I being starved? No one has brought me food yet.'

'For the time being you are being detained,' Fidelma told her firmly. 'I shall have food sent to you.'

She turned to the guard and gave the order. 'Keep a sharp watch on her,' she added to the guard as he shut and locked the door after them.

Returning to Selbach's chambers, Fidelma immediately saw that she had missed the fact that the window in his bedchamber was open. There was no sign of a rope, although just below the opening was an iron ring whose fixings were driven into the wall. This was not unusual for there were many like it in the buildings of the old fortress. Such fixtures had been placed there so that the constructors could scale the walls for renovation and repair. Brother Conchobhar had once told her this when, as a little girl, she had asked the purpose. But there was nothing attached to the iron ring.

Enda had been right when they peered from the window. It was a long way to the ground. The space directly below was a rough garden between buildings of the guest house and outer northern wall of the fortress.

'Maybe a rope attached to the ring would allow an agile person to descend safely,' Eadulf suggested.

'Agile or not,' replied Enda, 'that would need a strong rope. There is no rope still attached.' He bent forward to examine the ring and then sucked in his breath loudly. 'But there was. Look, there has been some rubbing on the ring. A rope fixed on that could have made its mark.'

Eadulf was perplexed. 'How would a person tie the rope,

climb down and then be able to undo the knot? Are you saying that Selbach had an accomplice? If he fixed a rope on it to lower himself to the ground, an accomplice would have had to come in to untie it and take it away afterwards. The only person who could possibly have done so is the guard outside. That means the guard could have lied to us. But I think not. If the guard was involved, why not let Selbach out of the door without the necessity of climbing down a rope?'

Enda was not put out. 'Selbach could have tied the rope to the ring himself,' he suggested. 'He could have used what we call a *snaidm retha fair.*'

'What's that?' Eadulf asked.

'A slip knot is one that might be loosened by pulling one end to withdraw a loop. He could well have the knowledge to do so, provided he had a rope long enough and not too thick. As a warrior, it is one of the first knots we are taught.'

Fidelma had been examining the wood frame of the window while they spoke.

'He seems to have made a clumsy exit,' she ventured. 'Look at the splintered wood to the top of the frame. It's as if he had dug the point of a knife in it and twisted it.'

'Curious,' Enda observed with a puzzled expression. 'There are some strands of string in it.'

'However curious, I think we are forgetting the important point,' Eadulf said. 'Somehow, he got to the ground below but that means he must be hiding somewhere in the fortress. The guards have kept a special watch at the gate from the time Brother Conchobhar's body was found. So they would stop anyone exiting without authority. He could not have passed through the gates.'

Enda was in agreement. 'Escaping from this window with a rope is one thing, but using the rope to escape over the walls of the fortress in daylight is another. He would need an extra-long rope for that. Also, we should not forget that Selbach is not a young warrior. From what I saw of him, he is an indolent prince – begging your pardon, lady – even if he could swing down the rope with determination.'

Fidelma glanced round the room in case she had missed something.

'We best examine the ground below this chamber window and perhaps we might trace which way he has gone,' she directed.

From the lower floor there was a door by which they could enter the gardens at the back. While it was easy to ascend these ramparts here by way of the steps in the watchtowers, which were placed at strategic points, it would have been impossible to descend from the outer wall, even with the aid of a very long rope. The guard patrols along the walkways between the towers were more frequent after the event of the previous night.

The intervening ground was used for growing vegetables. Footprints were easily spotted by Enda and these headed to the western side of the grounds, towards the back of the apothecary. With Enda's keen eyes for tracking, the first thing they discovered was the coils of strong rope pushed under some nearby bushes. Knotted through one end of the rope was a length of lighter string.

'That's curious,' Eadulf remarked. 'If any weight was put on that string, then it would have just snapped.'

Enda stood looking at it and a smile spread over his face. 'I think I know how it was used. It's a trick I've seen on campaign.'

'Bring the rope,' Fidelma said. 'But first let us follow Selbach's prints.'

Enda was already moving on, swinging the rope over one shoulder. He followed the prints to where the garden ended and narrowed into the area of land behind the apothecary, which Brother Conchobhar had devoted to his herb gardens. At the end was the small Ogham-inscribed stone. Beyond that was the open space before the library. This was a paved area and so the prints ended. South of the library were the main kitchens with their separate entrance, and beyond that the royal residence with its permanent guard standing outside. Across from this were the chapel and the apothecary.

Enda went and had a quick exchange with the guards but they had seen no sign of Selbach.

'I'll check with Brother Dáire, who, I see, is already in the library,' Fidelma decided. 'Enda, you and Eadulf have a look in those chambers below the apothecary. It could well be that

Selbach might try to hide there, thinking that we would not bother. Oh, and leave the rope there so that we can pick it up afterwards and you can show us your trick with the knot.'

It was only a short time before they reassembled in the courtyard. There was no trace of the Prince of Ráithlinn.

As Fidelma was considering the next move, the door of the main kitchen opened and the maid Cainder came through, carrying a small wooden keg. She halted and looked round as if disappointed and began to move back to the kitchen. Fidelma hailed her. She replied negatively to Fidelma's question as to whether she had seen Selbach.

'He has not come through the kitchens, lady. I have been working there since early this morning.' She looked around again with a disappointed expression. 'It is later than I thought.'

'Later than what?' Fidelma asked, picking up on her disappointment.

'I wanted to ask Rumann if he had some more *corma,* but he has already gone. We need another barrel in the kitchens and Dar Luga asked me to order it while Rumann was here.'

Rumann was the tavern-keeper in the centre square of the township below.

'Did Rumann come up to the fortress this morning?' queried Fidelma.

The young girl nodded quickly. 'He was delivering some ale that Dar Luga had already ordered and was taking away the empty casks.'

Fidelma knew that next to his tavern Rumann had his own brewery and stables. She had once had to investigate the finding of a body in one of the big casks where he brewed his ale. She was about to leave the girl when an idea suddenly occurred to her.

'Did Rumann deliver ale here this morning?' She wanted to be sure.

'Why, yes, lady. He does that regularly.'

'So he came in a wagon? He delivered ale in the wooden casks and then took away the empty casks. Is that right?'

'That's right.' The girl seemed perplexed that Fidelma was repeating herself for confirmation on what she thought was a normal practice.

'Where did he park this wagon when he was delivering the casks?'

Cainder made an encompassing motion with her free hand. 'He can't be long gone. He left the wagon here where it is easy to unload and replace the empty casks.' She pointed up to where a beam thrust from the side of the building. There was a chain and pulley on it and it hung above a doorway. 'When he had finished, he came in to have a drink before returning to the township. He is my uncle, lady,' she added.

Fidelma compressed her lips but a moment. 'He does not do this work alone, does he?'

'Oh, no. It takes two men to shift the bigger casks, even when empty. One of our men helps with lifting the barrels when they are swung into the storeroom.'

'Are you saying that the wagon stood unattended with some empty casks in it once the task of unloading and loading was complete?'

'It was a normal thing, lady.' The girl grew more concerned. 'Have I done anything wrong?'

Fidelma patted her shoulder. 'You did nothing wrong.' She turned to her companions. 'I think we should go to the township immediately. I am afraid we have found the way that Selbach might have left the fortress.'

'You think that he smuggled himself out of the fortress on Rumann's wagon inside an empty cask?' Eadulf asked.

There was no need for Fidelma to reply. The first stop was at the gates where Luan was once more in charge.

'Rumann left some time ago,' he confirmed, glancing at Enda, preparing to justify himself if something was wrong. 'The orders were only to stop the guests staying in the fortress and ensure—'

'So you didn't search his wagon?' Fidelma tried not to sound critical.

'I had no orders,' Luan protested, looking to Enda to support him. 'I did not think I had to stop regular traders like Rumann with his ale casks.'

'You did right,' Enda agreed firmly. 'There is no fault of yours.'

Enda was always prepared to stand up for his men if they

did the right thing. Fidelma immediately realised that Enda
was right and added her own assurance.

'But I have a feeling that our guest has long gone. As we
are not absolutely sure Selbach escaped in this way, although
it seems fairly certain, Eadulf and I will go down to Rumann's
tavern immediately. Get the stable master to bring our horses.
Quickly!'

Luan was already running to the stables before she had
finished speaking.

'Enda, you stay here and continue the search to make sure
he is not hiding somewhere we have overlooked.'

Enda was not too happy. 'If Selbach went out in Rumann's
wagon, it means he has no horse. So at least the likelihood of
him being able to find his way to join his bodyguards at Ráth
na Drínne is remote.'

'Rumann probably has a stable and horses,' Eadulf reminded
him.

Further conversation was cut short when Fidelma's grey-
white Gaulish pony and Eadulf's roan cob were brought. They
left the main gates at a fast pace down the incline that led to
the township.

It was quieter in the township than the day before, when
Fidelma had noticed several people leaving almost in panic,
having heard the news of the plague ship. Somehow Gormán
had calmed people down and she saw several of Gormán's
warriors here and there about the town. But as she and Eadulf
crossed the main square towards Rumann's tavern they saw
his wagon had not yet been put away and Rumann himself
was standing agitatedly by it. For a wild moment, she felt
excited that the tavern-keeper had apprehended Selbach. But,
as Rumann turned towards them, she saw he was not in the
best of moods. He hurried forward to meet them.

'I've just had one of my best horses stolen,' were his first
words before she could greet him. 'It was one of your brother's
guests!'

'He was hiding in your wagon?' Fidelma asked.

'In one of the big ale casks,' replied the tavern-keeper
angrily. 'The man claimed he was a noble and, if I delayed
him, I would taste his steel.'

'You did not call for Gormán's warriors to help you?' Fidelma asked.

'He threatened my son,' Rumann replied simply. 'He stole a horse and left. I have alerted Gormán just now. There was nothing I could do. He was crouched in one of the empty casks that I was bringing back to the brewery. When I stopped and was climbing down from the wagon, he hauled himself from the barrel with a knife in his hand, which he held to my throat. He bade me choose my best horse. I could lose the horse or lose my son. What could I do?'

'It's all right,' Fidelma reassured him. 'But you saddled him a good horse?'

'This man knew his horseflesh. If I had tried to saddle a horse that was just used for hauling a wagon, he would have known.'

'Then what happened?'

'He mounted and that was it. I immediately sent my son to find Gormán as I knew he would be at his mother's farm. I am waiting for him now.'

'Did you see where the man went?'

'He went straight into the forest, due south, rather than going the easy way across the cow road.'

There was a sudden shout and, as if on cue, Gormán came trotting up to the tavern with Rumann's young son mounted behind him. If Gormán was surprised to see Fidelma he did not show it.

'What's this about a stolen horse?' he began.

'No more, no less,' replied Fidelma. She quickly filled him in on the story. 'Do you have a good tracker?'

'I know of none better than myself,' chuckled the former commander of her brother's bodyguard.

'I know better than to argue,' she replied. 'Can you find half a dozen of your warriors? We are in pursuit of the Prince of Ráithlinn. I will explain along the way. I think Selbach intends to meet up with some of his own warriors at Ráth na Drínne.'

Gormán called instructions to a nearby warrior.

'He'll have a good start on us, lady,' he added.

'Maybe.' She did not sound alarmed. 'Don't forget that he

might not be so familiar with this part of the kingdom. The unfamiliar territory might slow him down. It depends where he is making for after Ferloga's tavern at Ráth na Drínne.'

Fidelma turned to the bewildered Rumann and asked him to send his son back to the fortress to inform Enda of the situation and instruct him to remain there.

Rumann had listened to the exchange in surprise.

'Are you saying the man who robbed me was the Prince of Ráithlinn, lady?'

'I am afraid so. Don't worry, you shall have the return of your horse and the compensation due.'

'But why would a prince descend to theft?' Rumann was bewildered.

Fidelma could not help an ironic smile. 'How else would he become a prince?'

Gormán gave her a disapproving glance. 'I am not sure your brother would agree.'

'Sometimes humour is the best way to examine history,' she replied impatiently. 'How soon before your men join us?'

'Maybe getting his party together at Ráth na Drínne will slow Selbach down, if he went to collect them.'

Before she could express further impatience, half a dozen of Gormán's warriors joined them. With Gormán leading the way, they set off immediately southward. It would take only a short time to go through the forests towards the crossroads where Ferloga and his plump wife, Lassar, ran their tavern and farmstead. Ferloga had chosen a good location as it was one where merchants, farmers and religious frequently travelled, passing on their way to many markets. More importantly, next to the complex of buildings around the tavern itself was the great ancient circular construction called Ráth na Drínne – the Fortress of Contentions. This was where contests and games had been held from the time beyond time. Particularly popular was the great fair of Beltaine of which, in recent years, Ferloga was appointed the Fair Master.

Fidelma knew during these last few weeks Ferloga had been busy preparing the entertainment for the market and fair at the request of her brother. Performers of many types, the acrobats, tumblers, jugglers, jesters, athletes and others, came to show their talents. Among the popular contests were horse racing, team games played with a ball and sticks such as *cumán* or *immán* or *lúbóc* and other sports. Of course, there was always music and dancing. The festivities of Beltaine could last many days and even well over a week. Ráth na Drínne was an ideal location for the encampments of merchants as well as the various bodyguards of the attending princes.

'From Ráth na Drínne, Selbach will have to strike southwest if he intends heading back to his own territory. We should easily catch up with him,' called Gormán, reassuringly.

Although they rode along one of the lesser trails from town, through the forest, it was a more direct route, heading straight south over the hills that eventually emerged on the great Plain of Femen. It was named after one of the brave warriors of myth and was the fertile land at the root of the power and wealth of the Eóganacht Kings of Cashel. It abounded in both legend and history, running southward from the tall limestone rock to the high mountains; the mountains associated with the homes of the various old gods and goddesses, from the Bodh Dearg, the warrior son of The Dagda, to the beautiful Caer, the lover of the Aonghus Óg, the god of Love.

It was a short ride, and as they entered the grounds of Ferloga's inn, the first thing Fidelma noticed was the number of young men lounging among the numerous tents and shelters that had been erected. She recognised several bodyguards of the princes by their leather harnesses and weapons as well as the emblems and standards. But there were other people – merchants, musicians, acrobats and other performers – who were obviously early arrivals for the coming days of performances and festivities.

Groups of people paused to stare with curiosity as Gormán halted his small troop outside the tavern. Fidelma was about to dismount when the door opened and Ferloga himself came out. He recognised Fidelma immediately and came forward with a warm greeting. He was followed by the smiling, plump figure of his wife, Lassar.

'We have not seen you for many months, lady,' he began.

'We cannot pause long, Ferloga,' she interrupted. 'We are in pursuit of an absconder from Cashel, wanted for questioning.'

'A richly dressed man?' he queried. 'He had warriors encamped here. I recognised their banner as Eóganacht Ráithlinn.'

'That is the man,' she confirmed at once.

'He and his men left in a hurry. There were eight warriors who had been camping here. When this noble arrived, he barely had time to wait for them to saddle up and join him. Oh, true that he reluctantly threw me some coins for my payment. It barely covered the amount of drink they had consumed. I knew he was not one to be trusted, in spite of his finery. He only paid because he knew I would delay him and these other men would help me if he created trouble.'

With a lifetime of being a tavern-keeper, Ferloga's proud claim was that no guest had ever succeeded in cheating him of his fees. Fidelma knew his boast that, whether noble or peasant, he could tell at a glance what a guest's calling was and whether he was trustworthy.

'You say he was joined by only eight men?' Gormán asked.

'Warriors,' confirmed Ferloga with emphasis. 'Don't underestimate them. They were professionals, like the rest of the lads here who are bodyguards to the princes here for the festivities. These did not seem to mix with the same free-hearted spirit of the other warriors.'

'Which way did they go?' Fidelma asked.

'I was too busy collecting the coins that he threw at me to notice,' the tavern-keeper replied angrily, glancing at his wife.

Lassar, who had been standing slightly in the background, now came forward.

'I can tell you, lady. They took the road due south to Cluain Meala, to the Field of Honey.'

It was a little township by a ford crossing the River Siúr.

'They rode directly south towards the River Siúr? That's straight into Déisi country.' Fidelma tried to contain her surprise.

'Are you sure of this?' Gormán demanded of Lassar.

'I believe I can tell which is south and which is north, son of Della,' Lassar admonished. As she had known Gormán since he had been a baby she did not feel uncomfortable using a familiar bantering form with the tall warrior.

'Due south?' muttered Fidelma. 'Strange they did not take

the road west into the territory of the Múscraige Breogain.' The offended look on Lassar's face made her apologise quickly. 'It is just that it is an unexpected direction.'

'We overheard from some of the travellers that there is supposed to be a plague in Déisi territory,' Lassar said. 'But none of the travellers here knows details. Anyway, if the people you pursue be men of Ráithlinn, then they came from the south-west and would have gone back that way. They would have not gone directly south across the mountains towards the coast. But the truth is that they did so.'

'Lady,' Gormán interrupted anxiously to Fidelma, 'we should not delay if you want to overtake them.'

Fidelma uttered a brief word of thanks to Ferloga and Lassar, and turned her horse back to the road, followed by Gormán and his men.

'It's a good, well-kept road between here and Cluain Meala,' Gormán said as he rode alongside her. 'We could maintain an easy canter as it is better not to risk tiring the horses by a gallop.'

At her acquiescence, he gave the command as they increased their pace to a canter across the Plain of Femen towards the distant southern mountains. The riding was easy. Fidelma found herself almost enjoying the soft warm breeze and the rocking motion of the canter. It was a pleasant day. The blue skies were flecked with small white round clouds with fraying edges, as if a host of dandelion puff-balls had blown into the sky. The sun was already westering to their right as they crossed the green plain with its crisscross pattern of little waterways, each feeding the great 'sister river', as the Siúr was named. The name came because the river rose in the mountains north of Cashel and wound its way south and east before joining its sisters, the Bhearú and the Fheoir, at Port Lairge to empty into the great sea. Fidelma did not have to be reminded that the River Siúr was also the border between the Eóganacht Chaisil and the territory of the Déisi.

Not for the first time since Lassar had told her the direction in which Selbach was heading, she wondered why he was taking that route. She had expected him to turn south-west towards his own territory. Was Selbach trying to mislead her, throw off her pursuit?

It was still warm and the sky was light when Fidelma led the small band of warriors into the tiny square of the settlement known as the Field of Honey. The first thing she noticed was an air of tension among the small groups of people that were about. The tiny township stood as a market for people on both sides of the ford and yet it seemed curiously deserted. On the southern side it marked the main route leading south through the mountains to the great abbey of Lios Mór and thence on to Árd Mór, one of the major southern coastal ports. In fact, the port was the nearest and most important for bringing goods to Cashel.

As they rode across the main square, Fidelma could see a group of armed men at the ford, a point at which she knew the river could be crossed on horseback. Not far away was the place where those more timid could be pulled across on a ferry, no more than a large raft, from one bank to another.

She did not pause but led her companions directly to the shallow crossing.

An armed man demanded that she halt and turn back.

'We wish to cross the river,' she replied in surprise.

The man shook his head firmly.

'I am ordered by my prince not to let any further riders cross here.'

'Further riders? When was the last time anyone crossed south from here?' she demanded.

The man was indifferent. 'That should be no affair of yours. The fact is that you cannot cross and that should be sufficient information.'

'It is my affair. I am a *dálaigh*,' Fidelma snapped.

Only then did the man notice the golden torque of the Nasc Niadh around Gormán's neck, and he modified his tone.

'*Dálaigh* or not, there is a pestilence thriving on the other side of this river and I am ordered that no one else should be allowed the cross until this has been dealt with. So do not attempt to cross.'

'Who ordered you to prevent me crossing?' Fidelma demanded, slightly puzzled. 'I am Fidelma of Cashel.'

The man looked slightly impressed but did not change his position.

'The far bank is the territory of the Prince of the Déisi. I can only accept orders from the prince. I am just obeying orders.'

'You say people have crossed recently? Who were they?'

'Men crossed here not so long ago. My prince met them on the other side of the river. I am now forbidden to allow anyone else to cross here.'

'When did these men cross?' Gormán insisted. 'How long ago?'

'At best, no more than a fraction of a *cadar*.'

A full *cadar* was a quarter of a day. Selbach had obviously pushed his men and horses at a fast pace from Ráth na Drínne.

'Are you saying Prince Cummasach was here at that time and allowed them to do so?'

'He did so.'

'Then if he allowed them, why do you refuse me?' she exclaimed. 'My brother is Colgú of Cashel, to whom the Prince of Déisi pays tribute.' Impatiently Fidelma was about to ride into the river ford, ignoring the man, but Gormán reached forward to hold her rein.

'I think we might have lost them, lady,' he said softly. 'If they have crossed and made their way into the hills and forests beyond it will be difficult to follow. It might take me a long time to sort out their tracks and perhaps, up in some of the peaks, the stony ground would become their accomplices, disguising the way they went.' He paused as she sat irresolute and, it seemed, about to disagree. 'There are other arguments,' he added.

'Other arguments?' queried Fidelma.

Gormán simply pointed to the crossing and the far bank. They were outnumbered and most of the opposing warriors had their bows ready. At a signal from their commander Fidelma's party would not even reach the centre of the river.

'It will be dark by the time we get back to Cashel, even if we start back immediately,' Gormán advised. It was clear that he was reminding her of the possible consequences of going into the territory where the pestilence had been reported.

She thought for a moment. She realised that Selbach could be dealt with later. In the circumstances he had forfeited his right to sit at the prince's council. Her priority now was to resolve the mystery at Cashel.

As if he read her thoughts, Gormán said: 'More important that you have some facts to deliver to the council and to Fíthel, the Chief Brehon. Even if Selbach reaches Ráithlinn and locks himself in his fortress there, he still remains answerable to the Chief Brehon and to the King.'

'You don't have to convince me, Gormán,' she sighed. She glanced at Eadulf and shrugged. 'Perhaps the positive point is the fact that we still hold Esnad. Being abandoned, she might start revealing something of the truth that I am seeking. I would suggest that we have our men rest for a short while, get fodder and water for our horses, and then start back to Cashel before it becomes too dark.'

Fidelma allowed Gormán to order the men to return to the main square of the settlement. She was aware of an uneasy silence in the township in spite of the fact that several people had now gathered in the square. Glancing back to the river crossings, she saw even more warriors had clustered on the far side as if gathering to defend the river from any attempted crossing. She realised that there had been no way she could have made any successful attempt to follow Selbach.

She was confused. Why had the Prince of the Déisi been there? It was surely a coincidence that he had been there when Selbach and his escort had crossed into the territory. Why had he taken extreme measures to contain the pestilence but then allowed Selbach to continue on south? In fact, why prevent people going south when the idea surely was to prevent the pestilence spreading north out of his territory?

As they rested ready to journey back to Cashel, she realised a curious group of the inhabitants was closing around her. Gormán returned protectively to her side. A middle-aged man approached them. His body language proclaimed that he was used to being in command although he possessed a face whose expression seemed to imply that he was understanding and kindly. He recognised the golden torc at Gormán's neck and obviously knew the significance.

'Forgive me, we had no notification of your coming, lord,' he bowed. 'I am afraid the Déisi have only just closed the ford. There is a pestilence said to be raging on the other side of the river.'

Gormán regarded the man grimly. 'This is Fidelma of Cashel,' he indicated, and the announcement caused surprise.

The man flushed and turned apologetically to Fidelma. 'Forgive me, lady, for not recognising you. It is that I have only just succeeded my uncle as *bo-aire* and it has been a while since you have graced the Field of Honey with your presence.'

'And you are?' Fidelma asked.

'My name is Arard. How may I serve you?'

'Were you consulted about this closure of the crossing?'

'I was not,' Arard replied, sounding indignant. 'I find that strange enough. There has also been a lot of movement witnessed on the southern side of the river. I have not known the like of this even in the days when the Yellow Death last visited.'

'What do you mean by "movement"?'

'Warriors have been seen making camps on the southern side of the river. Several fires have appeared on the far side of the mountains. We have been told the fires were villages that had to be torched because of the spread of a pestilence. So, I suppose, it was obvious that the crossing of the river should be closed. But as *bo-aire* I should have been consulted.'

'Yet those men, those whom we were pursuing, were allowed to cross south without any problems,' Gormán pointed out. 'Were you consulted about them?'

'I gathered from the gossip that the man who led them was a prince. By the time I arrived, they were across the river. His demeanour was not one to challenge lightly. They paused awhile in the tavern here, their horses were exhausted but they were awaiting someone to arrive south of the river.'

'Awaiting someone?'

'When they arrived, one of their number went to speak to those on the south side of the river. We saw a rider was dispatched and the rest of them waited here. They did not engage with the villagers. I only just arrived and was about to speak to this prince when I saw the Prince of the Déisi arrive on the far bank. I recognised his banner. It was then that they crossed.'

Fidelma was thoughtful. 'So it seemed that Prince Selbach was waiting to get permission from the Prince of the Déisi, to cross south of the river? How long did he wait here?'

'Not very long,' Arard replied. 'My farm is some way out of the village; that is why I did not arrive sooner. One of my people said he overheard this prince . . . he overheard him say that he wanted to get to his ship before the evening tide.'

Fidelma was startled. '*To his ship*? Are you sure he said that?'

'That is what my man said. Surely, nothing unusual in that? There is a lot of coastal shipping beyond those mountains, several fine ports too; anchorages with good protection against the tides.'

Fidelma knew every port along the southern coast of Muman.

'So they were looking to reach the coast before the evening high tide?' she asked Arard.

'They all had fine horses and so should easily manage it,' agreed the magistrate. 'That is, provided they do not insist on pushing them continuously at a gallop. But each determines his own course, lady. If it were me, I would have preferred to stay safe. But there are others who follow other paths that I have no understanding of. I was surprised they insisted on passing into Déisi territory, especially with the news of the pestilence.'

'Well, if we could finish getting water and feed our horses,' she said, resigned to the fact that Selbach had succeeded in his escape, 'we should then start back to Cashel at once.'

Arard glanced critically at their mounts. 'You have cantered your animals for some distance.'

'We will rest them a short while,' Fidelma reassured him. 'We must be back before nightfall.'

However, they had to take their time, moving almost at an ambling pace along the road back to the fortress. Fidelma let her mind slip into deep thought. Eventually Eadulf asked her what was bothering her so much.

'A plague ship is destroyed. The Prince of the Déisi is supposed to be ensuring the pestilence has not come ashore and spread. Selbach and his men escape and are then greeted by the Prince of the Déisi, who allows them into his territory.

We are not allowed to follow because, we are told, no one is allowed into a possible plague area. We are informed that the pestilence is spreading, villages are being burnt, and the Prince of the Déisi has sent his warriors to guard the borders in order to contain the plague. There is something very strange in all this.'

'Closing borders could be a logical containment policy,' Eadulf replied.

'It is not an unusual policy to restrict movement from a plague territory,' Fidelma agreed. 'But what is unusual is allowing movement *into* a plague territory.'

Gormán, riding alongside, caught the point.

'What I find odd is that it seemed Prince Selbach sent word to the Prince of the Déisi asking to be allowed to cross and waiting while the prince himself came to meet him. And that remark overheard by the *bo-aire*'s man.'

'About the ship?' Eadulf queried. 'Why didn't he come with his entourage by land?'

'It would be easy to bring his party from his fortress at Raerainn along the southern coast to land at one of the ports,' Fidelma pointed out thoughtfully. 'The question is which port? The nearest choices would be Eochaill, Árd Mór or the fortress of Garbháin.'

'Even if Selbach had landed his ship at Árd Mór before the arrival of the plague ship, why would he be heading back there, having heard the story of its arrival?' Eadulf pointed out. 'We may soon discover the answer to that question.'

'How so?' Fidelma asked. Then she realised that there could be a simple answer. 'You mean that Esnad might start telling the truth when she realises that Selbach has really deserted her?'

SIXTEEN

It was dark when Fidelma and Eadulf left Gormán and his small troop of warriors outside Rumann's tavern before making their way up the slope to the gates of the fortress. Luan was in charge of the guard and he called on the stable boys to take their horses. He told them that Colgú and Enda had been waiting for them, indicating their concern at the long absence. In fact, Colgú had personally intervened to delay the burial of the bodies of Blinne and Céit in case legal requirements needed the presentation of the bodies as both had been unlawfully killed. This needed Fidelma's approval.

She found her brother and Enda in the King's private chamber and immediately related the details of their chase to the Field of Honey and what had happened to prevent them from following Selbach's crossing of the River Siúr into the Déisi territory.

'It would have taken several days' ride overland to Selbach's fortress,' Colgú commented. 'It would be logical that Selbach and his party had made the journey here by a coastal sailing vessel.'

'I think you have missed the point,' Eadulf ventured softly. 'Surely it would not have been the best way to *return* to his territory.'

'How do you mean, friend Eadulf?' Colgú frowned.

'If he had landed at Árd Mór, which, granted, is the easiest and most logical port from which he would travel here, I see no problem. But to return that way, with the news of the plague ship at Árd Mór, is foolish. Would the captain and crew of his vessel still be waiting around in Árd Mór after the plague ship came into that port?'

'Exactly,' Fidelma agreed. 'He should have crossed westward into Uí Liatháin territory from there, and headed to the port of Eochaill. Or why go through Déisi territory at all with the plague threat?'

'We spoke of this curiosity on our way back here. We are hoping Esnad will enlighten us on the matter,' Eadulf added.

'Did you hear anything about the spread of the plague while you were in Cluain Meala?' Enda asked. 'Did Gormán's scouts have anything to report?'

'There was something I found curious, related to Selbach's actions,' Fidelma said when they did not pick up on the thought that crossed her mind.

There was a bewildered silence.

'You, Enda, have already sent watchers along the southern border with the Déisi. We have seen patrols of Déisi warriors along those borders, which is excellent if you consider the need for containment. Observers have seen fires at night, which are thought to be villages being burnt to contain the plague. Yet at Cluain Meala only Selbach and his men crossed and then the border was closed in both directions. More importantly, we were told that the Prince of the Déisi had arrived to meet Selbach.'

'It is confusing,' Colgú agreed, anxiety edging his voice. 'We must have answers to all these mysteries soon as the rest of the princes will start to arrive tomorrow or the day after.'

'Doesn't Selbach's action negate him from using his influence and casting a vote at the council?' Eadulf asked.

Colgú glanced in query at Fidelma on the legal point.

'It is not a personal vote at the council,' Fidelma explained. 'Selbach could simply nominate his heir apparent to represent the Eóganacht Ráithlinn on the excuse that he is physically incapacitated in person.'

'But that is not true!' Eadulf protested.

'We are talking technicalities in law,' she sighed. Again, it seemed no one was picking up on the possibility that she was implying. She decided not to pursue it for the moment. 'Well, it is no use going over these events without more information. I need some sleep, for it has been a long day. Tomorrow we will go and question Esnad again.'

The next morning, having washed and eaten, Fidelma led Eadulf and Enda to the apothecary where Enda had left the coiled rope that Selbach had used to escape from his chamber.

Then she led them to Selbach's former chambers. Once inside Fidelma made her way to the window and seemed intent on examining the splintered wood in the frame at the top. She removed the small strand of string, examining it with a frown. Then she turned and examined the rope and gave a subdued chuckle.

'Enda, you said that you have seen warriors perform the trick by which Selbach could have escaped from this chamber. I think I know how. But there should be an item in here that would have been essential to the trick.'

'I saw nothing immediately.'

'Probably because we were not looking for it until we found the rope and the string,' she agreed. 'Would you mind checking again? I would imagine all you have to do is look under the bed.'

Eadulf glanced at Enda and shrugged. However, Enda bent down to peer under the bed. He made an exclamation and reached under it, returning to his feet holding an arrow.

Fidelma took the arrow and examined it. 'I suspect it will be found similar to the one extracted from your arm, Enda.'

The young warrior raised his eyebrows a fraction in surprise as he looked at the shaft and its feather flight.

'It would appear so, lady. Are you saying that it was Selbach that . . .?'

She frowned. 'The archer that loosed this arrow took their position down in the garden and shot it up from that spot so that it embedded itself in the wooden frame above the window.' She pointed. 'Just where the wood is splintered.'

'So what is the meaning of this?' Eadulf asked.

'You saw this rope that Selbach discarded down in the garden? How did Selbach have such a rope in these chambers and how could he use it?'

'By the trick that I suggested,' Enda replied. 'A light piece of string tied to the rope. The arrow was fired, bearing the string behind it. Selbach took the string by which he was able to haul up the rope and secure it.'

'A simple explanation,' Fidelma agreed. 'The rope was attached to the long string that was fixed to the arrow. The arrow was fired up at the window from the garden. It embedded itself in the upper frame. Selbach then removed the arrow rather roughly and in a manner that caused splintering of the wood. He hauled up the string to which was attached the thicker rope. He tied the rope to the iron ring outside, the ring being one of those builders' attachments that you often find in the walls for repairs or scaffolding. He tied it with a slip knot. He tossed the discarded arrow under the bed to confuse us. Then he climbed out, descended to the garden below and loosed the slip knot. The rope fell to the ground. He then hid the rope under the bushes where we found it. This left no immediate sign of how he had left his chamber. I presume he hoped to delay us by this ruse, to give him time to leave the fortress.'

Eadulf was nodding as he followed her points. 'There is one point you do not mention,' he said thoughtfully.

Fidelma's smile broadened with almost self-satisfaction. 'Indeed. You are about to mention that Selbach was not alone in this escape. Who was it who fired the arrow from the garden with the string attached so that he could haul the thicker rope up and attach it?'

Enda was rubbing his arm, still healing from the arrow wound. He was frowning in concentration.

'Are you saying that the person who fired the shot at you when we went to the stable, the arrow that hit me when I pushed you out of the way; are you saying that was done by an unknown accomplice of Selbach?'

'Certainly the arrows were fired by the same person. That person wanted Selbach to escape. But was Selbach the conspirator or the accomplice? I am not sure. Indeed, Selbach is central to this entire mystery . . .'

'Are we talking about one mystery or several?' Eadulf queried. 'Do the actions of Selbach link to the murder of Brother Conchobhar?'

'I am sure of it,' Fidelma confirmed. 'Some things do not make sense but others do fit together easily.'

There was a call from the main entrance below. It was one of the guards. 'Gormán's wife, Aibell, is waiting at the gate for you.'

'Is anything the matter?' Fidelma asked in concern as she

approached Gormán's attractive young wife, who was waiting by her pony at the main gate.

'Only that Gormán thought that you should know of a new report from one of his men from Árd Fhonáin. It arrived this morning.'

'Is it further word about the spread of the plague?'

'Only that of new fires. They have now been seen beyond the river in Déisi territory.'

'There have been fires there ever since we had word of the plague ship.'

'Gormán told me to tell you that the fiery hue that has been seen in the skies is stronger, according to the scout's report. The fires are unlike the previous fires, which it was thought were villages being burnt to contain the spread of the plague. These observed last night were more controlled, like the accumulation of regular campfires. He says that you will know the significance of this.'

'Campfires?'

'It was reported that they were like the fires of a *sluagh*, a battalion of warriors, on the march,' added Aibell.

'Is it possible that Gormán could get someone to approach nearer in order to make certain what they were?' Fidelma asked.

'This is why he sent me. He has taken some men and ridden to the abbey to reconnoitre, and beyond it, if possible.'

'So he thinks this is significant?'

She nodded. 'After you returned from Cluain Meala last night, Gormán was discussing with some of his men how Déisi sentinels were placed along the borders at the crossing points of the river. He is suspicious that something is afoot. Gormán also received a report this morning that Finguine, the Prince of the Eóganacht Glendamnach, and his party, are proceeding through the glen of Eatharlach. Apparently Fíthel, the Chief Brehon, is accompanying him. They should reach here later today.'

'That will be good news for my brother, at least,' Fidelma replied, knowing Finguine was usually a firm supporter of her brother. The Prince of Glendamnach was the *rodamna*, or heir apparent, to Colgú. It had taken Eadulf a long time to understand that the law of primogeniture did not apply in the five kingdoms. Sons did not always succeed their fathers by right, even in kingship. While it was true that they had to be of the same bloodline, a gathering of the family, descendants from a common ancestor, met and elected the most worthy to become head of the family and assume the title, where appropriate.

While Colgú's father had been King Failbe Flann, after Failbe died, three of his cousins, after the deliberations of the seven senior princes, had succeeded to the kingship, starting with a prince of the Eóganacht Áine, then a prince of the Eóganacht Chaisil, and the last of these had been Cathal Cú-cen-Mathair of Glendamnach. Colgú had been elected as his heir apparent. When Cathal had died of the Yellow Plague, seven years before, Colgú had succeeded. By the same system Finguine of Glendamnach, the son of Cathal, had been elected as Colgú's heir apparent. Finguine had always been a good, steady support and friend to him.

Fidelma thanked Aibell for bringing the information and then turned back to her companions. Eadulf sensed the rapid working of Fidelma's mind behind her furrowed brow as she considered the news.

'What now?' he finally prompted. 'Do these new fires mean something?'

'At the moment, we can only go on what we know. We must continue to proceed as we initially intended,' she decided firmly. 'We will go to question Esnad. I hope she has reconsidered her decision on giving us information now she realises that Selbach has fled without her.'

As they turned towards the guest chambers, they saw the youthful librarian, Brother Dáire, hurrying across the courtyard. He was heading to the doors of the royal residence. When he saw them, he hesitated, and then changed direction towards them.

Fidelma and her companions halted and awaited his approach.

'Are you looking for me?' Fidelma asked.

'It was about your question to me of the other day, lady.'

'My question?'

'About the religieuse with the strange name – Sister Ernmas.'

'Ah.' Fidelma's face brightened. 'You have more news of her? Do you know where we can find her? I certainly want to speak with her.'

To her disappointment Brother Dáire shook his head.

'I can't say I know where you can find her but it happened just after you left the fortress yesterday. I was coming out of the library when I glanced to the herb garden at the back of old Brother Conchobhar's apothecary. I thought I heard some movement there so I went to the corner of the apothecary to get a better sight across the herb garden, but further along where a lot of things are grown for the use of the fortress.'

Fidelma was impatient. 'And what did you see?'

'I saw the tall, dark-clad woman in the vegetable garden.'

'What was she doing? Not looking at the old Ogham stone again?'

'She seemed to be bending down looking at the plants.'

'Looking at the plants?' An idea came to Fidelma. 'Do you mean looking at the bushes?'

'That was where—' Eadulf began, but Fidelma cut him short.

'What did you do?'

'I knew that you wanted to have words with her, so I called to her. I was going to ask her to contact you.'

'How did she respond?'

'She did not. She stood up suddenly with her back to me and moved away quickly. The angle of the wall there obscures your vision when a person moves close to the building.'

'So she went to the shelter of the walls where there is an entrance to the guest quarters? Could you see if she entered them?'

'I am afraid I did not. I imagine that she did, for there are no other ways to exit along there than through the buildings. When I saw you standing here, I thought you should be aware of this.'

'It is much appreciated, Brother Dáire. My thanks.'

'Well, that doesn't help us much,' Enda said as soon as the librarian had moved out of earshot.

'On the contrary, it adds to our knowledge,' Fidelma said. 'As Eadulf was about to remark, I think the lady was looking for the rope we found there, perhaps in an attempt to take and hide it to add to our confusion or disguise the fact that Selbach had an accomplice.'

'Well, no sooner do we see this woman than she vanishes. It still doesn't help.'

Eadulf started. 'You mean that this Ernmas was the archer that helped Selbach escape?'

'Perhaps she was only sent by the archer to pick up the rope. It confirms the suspicion that Selbach was not acting alone. As we intended, we shall go to have another word with Esnad.'

'On the way, I'll pick up the rope. I left it on the bed in Selbach's chamber,' Eadulf admitted.

The chamber was now devoid of any sign of the rope. He peered about desperately before looking at Fidelma's grim face. She called the guard from the passageway and asked him who had been into the chamber since they left.

'Only the religieuse that you sent to pick up something,' the man replied cheerfully.

'A tall woman in black?' Fidelma queried.

'That's the one.'

Fidelma gestured that the guard could leave and turned to the woebegone faces of her companions.

'It cannot be helped. It might have been evidence but we can construct the case without it. At least we know that we must find this woman.'

'Well, if Sister Ernmas has it,' Eadulf commented, 'it did not take her long to follow our trail and find where I had left the rope. She is clever, this dark lady.'

'I don't like this,' Enda said. 'How is it possible that this woman can come and go and no one can discover where she is? It's uncanny. Does she possess the *ceó druidecta* . . .?'

Fidelma stared at him in disapproval. 'The Druidic's Mist is just an old tale when people thought evil spirits could move around in a cloak of invisibility. We have better things to do than go down that path.'

The lover of Selbach scowled at them as they entered her room. This time Esnad had washed and dressed and was sitting in a chair with the fingers of one hand tapping in agitation on the oak wood arm.

'You have probably heard that Selbach escaped the fortress?' Fidelma began.

Esnad simply smiled. 'He will be back. He would not leave me,' she replied confidently.

'Believe it or not, he has,' Fidelma replied. 'He seems to be heading for the mountain pass on the way to Lios Mór. That's the territory of the Déisi and, by the way, the Prince of the Déisi was seen to welcome him into his territory when he crossed the River Siúr.'

The girl responded with a short brittle laugh. 'You are playing games with me. Why would he be heading into that plague area?'

'That's what we would like to know,' returned Eadulf.

'You are trying to trick me into revealing where he is?'

'Rest assured, he is gone. Nor is he heading south-west back to his own territory. He seems to have gone south towards the coast. He can't think much of you to leave you here.'

The girl raised her chin in pugnacious fashion. 'He would not leave me here. I know it is just a trick to get me to help you find him.'

'He has left you here,' Fidelma assured her firmly. 'The fact that he fled raises the question as to whether he killed his wife and that you were providing him with an alibi. After all, he killed a man claiming the man raped his wife. If you are involved it means that you could be next to be dealt with.'

Esnad hesitated and then tried to be humorous. 'If he has escaped, then whom am I in danger from?'

'We know now that Selbach had an accomplice, the person who helped him escape. That was not you. So the accomplice remains here in this fortress.'

For a second the girl looked nervous. Fidelma seized the opportunity to continue.

'You should be worried. The interesting fact is that someone helped Selbach in his escape, whether you accept that he has abandoned you or not. This places you in a very dangerous situation. Even if Selbach was innocent of killing his wife, then the person who helped him escape certainly was the culprit. Are you not concerned that this person remains here? Selbach has left you to face the consequences of his actions by yourself. Perhaps you might think of telling us what you know before you have to answer for the consequences.'

The girl's lips parted with just a slight movement of her facial muscles.

'I am not stupid,' she asserted. 'You tell me that he had escaped and he was heading directly south into Déisi territory. That's where this plague is supposed to be. Selbach would never go there. You heard what he said at the meeting the other day. He would have gone south-west through the territory of the Muscraige Breogán and if he went as far as the River Siúr, he would have crossed it to go directly west towards the territory of the Muscraige Mittine and the Cenel Loegairi.'

Fidelma regarded the defiant girl for a few moments. Then it seemed that she suddenly changed the subject.

'I presume that you intend to return to the island of Raerainn by the same means as you arrived?' she asked with an innocent air. 'It is a long way into the territory of Ráithlinn. It would have taken you and your party days to travel the distance from Raerainn through the mountains to here.'

'It would have if—' The girl caught herself.

'Yes, it's easier by boat,' Fidelma smiled. 'But I have been in small coastal vessels along our southern coasts. The seas can be pretty tempestuous at times. What made Selbach choose that particular route to come to Cashel?'

Esnad's jaw tightened and she was silent when she realised the trap Fidelma had set. Then she shrugged and said nothing.

'Selbach was trying to return to his ship when he fled from here,' went on Fidelma. 'Where did you land? You could have landed at Árd Mór and made your way across the mountains, perhaps over the River Siúr at the ford at the Field of Honey. But with the plague, it is not the best way to return. Of course, there is another good anchorage. However, there is also Eochaill, from which you could have come up An Abhainn Mór, the Big River, as far as the abbey at Lios Mór. Wasn't that the better way?'

'If you know so much, you tell me,' the girl replied petulantly.

Fidelma put her head to one side as if considering the question. She was also considering the fact that Selbach had been greeted at the ford by the Prince of the Déisi himself.

'I think Selbach would have chosen to land in the Big River,' suggested Fidelma. 'It is a more secluded approach.'

She watched the girl carefully and saw the slight start and the quick attempt to control her features.

'Apart from the eight warrior escorts that were left at Ráth na Drínne, did Selbach bring anyone else from the ship?'

Once again the girl remained silent. Fidelma considered. Would Selbach have chanced crossing into Déisi territory unless he had a good reason? In normal times, there was certainly no reason why Selbach should not prefer to use the sea route from his island along the coast. However, it seemed odd, especially in view of the news of the plague ship at Árd Mór, to have expected his vessel to remain at anchor there waiting for his return. But it was clear the girl was not going to tell her anything further at this time. She exhaled sharply in frustration and rose to her feet.

'Can I leave the fortress?' Esnad demanded as they prepared to leave.

'You must remain in the fortress until the end of my inquiries. So must all the guests,' Fidelma said, as she made towards the door. 'You will be wanted as a witness. Of course, if you know nothing other than what you have told me, then, as I say, I shall remove the guard from your door and you will be free to leave your chamber and go where you will within the boundaries of the fortress.'

'Of course,' Eadulf added, 'it might be wise to restrain yourself to your quarters and accept the guard outside. The person who helped Selbach escape might want to ensure that you remain silent.'

'You must do what you will.' Esnad tried to sound diffident.

'Very well,' Fidelma said, pausing at the door. 'As a precaution, you will remain here. You will be sent meals but think well what I said.'

Outside, in the passage, Eadulf turned to Fidelma and said: 'In spite of her bravado, I think you have left behind a very frightened girl.'

Fidelma returned his gaze with a complacent look. 'That was my purpose. She might soon have further thoughts about protecting Selbach. But she is very stubborn.'

They left the guest quarters and were returning to the royal residence when Fidelma saw a merchant's wagon coming through the main gates. She paused thoughtfully as she saw the guard commander checking it.

'Enda,' she suddenly said, 'do you remember that I asked you if you could find out who was on duty at the gates when Selbach and his party arrived?'

Enda uttered a profanity, then immediately apologised for it.

'I forgot, lady. I did gather the information but then things began to happen. I'll go and get the person who commanded the guard.'

'Bring him to our chambers.'

They had barely reached their apartments when Enda arrived with Dego, who immediately confirmed that he had commanded the guard when the Prince of Ráithlinn had arrived.

'Can you remember who was with him?' Fidelma asked.

The young warrior rubbed his forehead for a moment as if by some magic it would cause the memory to come.

'His wife, the lady Blinne, and her companion, the lady Esnad. He had no bodyguard. I gathered these were bivouacked at Ráth na Drínne.'

'No one else? Isn't that unusual? How did Selbach's party arrive?'

'There was just the driver of their wagon. I understand that he had been accompanied by warriors as far as Ráth na Drínne, where the festival would be held.'

'So, he had no other with him when he entered the fortress?'

'I am certain,' Dego confirmed.

'What of the driver of Selbach's wagon? Was he a warrior?'

'The driver of the wagon was no warrior. As soon as the baggage was unloaded and taken to the guest quarters, the driver had orders to turn the wagon back to Ráth na Drínne.'

'So we can be sure that the mysterious Sister Ernmas didn't enter the fortress in his party in some other disguise?'

Dego seemed to be amused by the idea. 'I had particular

reason to pay attention to Selbach's arrival. So I can reject that notion.'

'Explain why?'

'His arrival coincided with the arrival of the Prince of the Áine.'

'Prince Elódach? Why does that event cause you to remember it?'

'Prince Elódach arrived on horseback. His belongings followed in a small wagon driven by a male with one male attendant. Once the wagon was unloaded the prince and his attendant went to the guest quarters. The driver of the wagon was making to turn out of the gate when Prince Selbach's wagon had difficulty at the gate because of the two wagons passing. This meant there was a brief hold-up. Words were exchanged between the two drivers.'

'So what happened?' Eadulf asked.

'Nothing much. The wagons finally passed each other and that was that.'

Fidelma regarded Dego with indecision for a moment.

'What happened to Selbach's wagon driver?'

'I am told that he went to rejoin Selbach's company of warriors at Ráth na Drínne,' Dego replied confidently.

'But neither a wagon nor its driver joined Selbach when he and his warriors fled to Cluain Meala,' Eadulf pointed out.

'That's easy to explain.' It was Enda who answered. 'Why take the wagon, which would have slowed them down? Also, what need of a wagon? He was escaping with no baggage and neither his wife nor his mistress was with him.'

'So maybe the wagon driver is still at Ferloga's inn?' Eadulf suggested brightly. 'It would be worth sending someone to see if we have overlooked him.'

Fidelma turned towards Dego. 'As you could recognise this driver, will you ride to Ferloga's tavern and, if the driver is still there, bring him back here? But do so quickly. Put him on the back of your horse, if need be. You do this on my authority.'

After Dego had left, Fidelma compressed her lips in frustration. 'Even if the driver just confirms what Dego said, we still will not know how this woman, Ernmas, came into the fortress.'

'She must have been here for some time,' Enda suggested,

'even though we cannot place her. Abbot Cuán must have given her authority to be here.'

'And not told Brother Fidach? I begin to believe she entered here only *disguised* as a religieuse,' Fidelma said firmly. 'I don't think she is one. She must have some connection with Selbach to help him escape when we had confronted him. In spite of what Dego says, I think Selbach arrived with three women: his wife, now killed, and Esnad, his lover, who refuses to tell us anything further, and this tall woman who calls herself Ernmas. This mystery is frustrating.'

'I think Dego is reliable enough,' Eadulf said. 'If he says that she was not part of Selbach's party, then we must trust him.'

He waited for Fidelma to suggest something. Fidelma usually had some path to follow, even if it proved negative, but it was rare that she admitted that she had no idea how to proceed further.

'Anyway, with Fíthel, the Chief Brehon, wanting some account, we should start looking more diligently for answers to the questions that I cannot answer.'

Eadulf caught the faint bitterness in her tone. His mind flooded with memories of when he and she actually separated over a disagreement about her determination to become Chief Brehon. Eadulf knew well that her ambition of becoming Chief Brehon of the kingdom had not diminished.

On enquiry, they found Prince Elódach strolling round the northern battlements of the fortress. He greeted them in a friendly fashion and raised his right hand to gesture to the mountains that rose to the north-west of Cashel.

'How I long to be back among the peaks of Sliabh Eibhlinne,' he said wistfully. 'See how the sun strikes those distant ridges? A natural fortress against all enemies. I'd feel safer there than just being confined here and waiting for the pestilence to spread.'

'Those mountains are a natural fortress indeed,' Fidelma agreed. 'I have spent some time among them. But if the pestilence is to come, I do not think it cares about mountains. It can cross oceans, for did it not devastate many lands and cities before it arrived on our shores?'

'So I have heard,' admitted the prince in a serious tone. 'Yet up in the mountains one has a feeling of safety. I would prefer to be there than here.'

'Yet, in council you were the one who stood up for my brother and declared that you would stay here in Cashel and not be chased away like Selbach. At least you did not think about hiding until the dangers passed.'

Elódach shrugged. 'I am a pragmatist, lady. I was a younger man when the plague passed through this land last time. I remember with shock when even the joint High Kings, Diarmait and Blathmaic, could not escape it and were struck down in Tara. Then Cathal, our own King at Cashel, perished. Prelates and sinners alike expired and, as you will recall, where great populations once lived, their fortresses and townships became ruins and wastelands. This kingdom is in trouble, lady, whether from the pestilence or the envious eyes of Laigin or, indeed, those who would destroy it from within. So I decided that as I am now one of the seven senior princes of the Eóganacht, I should be here when the great council meets.'

'You mention those who might wish to destroy this kingdom from within,' Fidelma said. 'It has been attempted many times by those seeking power but no one has been successful.'

Elódach seemed to smile but there was no humour in his face.

'And will do so again. I am sure.'

'My brother does his best to ensure that no one has any grounds for discontent.'

'There are always grounds for discontent. You saw that at the meeting the other day.'

'That was why it was good that you declared that you stood ready to support my brother, come the great council before the Beltaine feast.'

'Indeed, I did so and, curiously, so did Donennach of the Uí Fidgente.'

'Curiously?' frowned Fidelma.

'The Uí Fidgente and the Áine Chliath have long been enemies and constantly in conflict, if not in all-out warfare; continually raiding across our borders for cattle and sheep. However, it does not prevent us agreeing strategy.' He suddenly looked at her with a searching expression. 'I know you are engaged in investigations. Have you come to ask me specific questions?'

'Not really,' Fidelma replied easily. 'I think you will soon learn there is more news about Selbach. You have probably heard that his wife was killed and he, rather than face questions, has fled the fortress?'

'News travels swiftly,' he conceded.

Fidelma went on: 'I actually came to ask you or your attendant whether you had encountered a tall religieuse by the name of Sister Ernmas.'

Elódach shook his head. 'I have even heard rumours of this woman. I confess I avoid religieuse of the New Faith. My mother adheres to the old ways, while I remain quiet on such matters. I would not like to see strangers haggling over my soul. That man, Fidach, is enough to destroy any religion in you. He is an arrogant man who tries to put himself on the same level as the nobility. He tried to order me to call him "Father". I am looking forward to Abbot Cuán's visit here soon. I shall demand the abbot return this arrogant man to the cloisters to learn humility before I make him answer his insults to honour. "Father", indeed!'

Fidelma had to admit that Elódach had a point.

'Fidach has his own way of interpreting the New Faith, which is apparently in line with some new fashion among those interpreting the Faith in Rome. Once we were all addressed as "brothers" and "sisters", but now Rome is allowing all the clerics to be addressed as "father" even though that it is prohibited in the sacred writings. Yes; I know what you mean.'

'Well, I will not attend his services as my brother princes do. I will not even sing Colmcille's hymn "*Noli Pater*" as a protection against the *blefed,* the pestilence.'

'So you have seen nothing of a tall religieuse in black robes?' she summed up.

'Not as far as I am aware? There are two female sisters serving the chapel but I have seen none clad in black robes.'

'Your attendant, would he have seen such a person?'

'My attendant, Máen? He is a lazy man and barely moves from the chambers allotted to us. But he has been with my house since I was a child. Anyway, I have but the one attendant because my needs are simple. He would tell me if he had seen such a bizarre creature. Why do you ask about this particular religieuse?'

'As you say, she seems a bizarre creature and only a few people here seem to know of her and what she does. I have only seen her briefly.'

'Is she so important to find?'

'It is curious to find someone in the fortress that no one knows about nor, apart from myself and the librarian, even admits to having seen.'

Elódach gave an amused chuckle. 'This is an appropriate place to witness apparitions. But, rest assured, I have not seen this woman, although there do appear to be enough deaths and mysteries without anyone being conjured from the Otherworld to slaughter them.'

'An appropriate place?' queried Eadulf. 'Why so?'

Elódach chuckled. 'Where else will you meet shades of the Otherworld than at the so-called gate of death?'

SEVENTEEN

'Elódach seems possessed of a humour,' Fidelma commented lightly, after the prince had taken his departure and left them to stroll along the wall of the fortress.

Eadulf, however, was serious. 'I hope he means it as humour. These old beliefs can have substance.'

Fidelma was often reminded that Eadulf had only converted to the New Faith when he was a teenager. Now and again he showed signs of a belief in his pagan upbringing and concerns for the supernatural.

'I scarcely think that the person we seek is a denizen of the Otherworld,' she smiled reassuringly. 'Anyway, Beltaine celebrates the end of the dark half of the year – it's a festival of light and new beginnings. It is the first month of summer. It is not really the time for the shades of the dead to haunt us.'

'I know that the dark half of the year starts after the summer quarter with the Samhain Fest,' he agreed. 'Let's hope the Otherworld keeps an accurate record of the year cycle.'

For a moment Fidelma was unable to decide whether he was being serious or ironic until she noticed the twinkle in his eye.

Outside the royal residence, they left Enda to organise yet another search of the buildings for the elusive figure of the strange Sister Ernmas and went to report matters to Fidelma's brother. He met them in his private chamber.

'I do not really understand the import of the message from Gormán,' Colgú confessed. 'What is Prince Cummasach up to?'

'That is the pertinent question. Whatever it is, I feel there is something wrong. It is curious that hardly any merchants or travellers have come out of Déisi territory since the early reports of the plague ship.'

'But surely that would be normal in the circumstances?' suggested Colgú. 'Cummasach is keeping the border tight so that the plague does not spread.'

Fidelma grimaced sceptically. 'But you will remember when the plague was spreading years ago it was impossible to keep the territorial borders so tight. True, now and then it is reported that fires are seen and it is presumed that a village is set fire to when the inhabitants were all consumed by the pestilence. But not to the extent we are hearing reports. I suspect that something is going on in Déisi territory.'

'Such as what?' Colgú asked helplessly. 'I am more concerned with the feeling that I have that something is being planned against me here at the council meeting before Beltaine.'

'I have a theory,' began Fidelma.

But she was interrupted by the sound of a trumpet at the main gates.

'I would guess that is the arrival of Finguine with Chief Brehon Fíthel,' Colgú sighed. 'I think Brehon Fíthel will want more than a theory.'

He did not notice the angry flush spread on his sister's cheeks. Eadulf glanced in warning at her.

'Aibell brought a report that they and their entourage were near. They had been seen coming through the glen of Eatharlach,' he said quickly to distract Colgú.

A few moments later there was a knock on the door. At Colgú's command, Enda entered the council chamber.

'Prince Finguine and Brehon Fíthel have arrived. Will you see them immediately?'

'At least you'll have the Chief Brehon of the kingdom to support your investigation,' Colgú spoke dryly as he motioned Enda to bring them in.

Fidelma knew her brother shared her irascible humour but her disinterest in Fíthel's support was genuine. She was conceited enough about her own abilities to resent the idea that she needed support from anyone of her profession. It was some time since she had put herself forward before the Council of Brehons to ask for recognition to be Chief Brehon of Muman. She had been so single minded in the task that she had formally left the religious life. Most people still used the prefix 'Sister' because it was by that title she had gained her reputation in the five kingdoms and even beyond. The matter had even caused a temporary split between Eadulf and herself.

Her legal peers, however, had decided in favour of the more experienced Brehon Fíthel. Even now there was still a little antipathy left in her when they met.

'Well, you will have support in the council through Finguine,' she pointed out waspishly to her brother.

As greetings were exchanged, Colgú asked: 'Is there any word about Abbot Cuán coming with the physicians and apothecaries, as I was told he promised?'

Finguine was a year or two younger than Colgú and bore a shock of red curly hair, a humorous smile and twinkling blue eyes. He could easily be placed as Colgú's brother.

'In fact, I already saw the abbot in the township,' Finguine reported. 'He will be along shortly. I am told his intention is to leave one of the physicians, who have accompanied him from Imleach, in the township in case of emergencies there. A second physician and an apothecary will come here. Is there further word of the pestilence?'

'None that makes sense,' replied Colgú.

'We have heard the terrible news about old Brother Conchobhar.' The sharp, dark-faced Brehon Fíthel glanced expectantly at Fidelma. 'We also heard vaguely of the killing of an Uí Fidgente warrior in a duel by Selbach of the Eóganacht Ráithlinn. I will, of course, expect a detailed report.'

Before she could reply, Colgú intervened.

'And you shall hear all about that, but first, I am a poor host not to offer hospitality on your arrival from your journey.' He clapped his hands and summoned an attendant to provide drinks and traditional *bairgen* or small pastries. When the ceremony of hospitality was over and everyone was seated, Fidelma saw the eyes of Brehon Fríthel turned to her. He and Finguine sat still and silently as they listened to Fidelma taking them through the events of the last few days. She did it simply, putting forward the facts without adding any speculations.

'Are you then searching for this Sister Ernmas as a suspect?' Brehon Fíthel asked after she had finished.

'I have yet to finish my investigations,' she replied. 'Sister Ernmas is a possible suspect in the killings of Brother Conchobhar and Princess Blinne. We cannot find out how and when she came into the fortress or, importantly, where she is hiding, But, critically, I feel her appearance in the fortress is the key to everything.'

'What of the killing of the Uí Fidgente warrior?' Brehon Fíthel asked.

'There is no doubt that Selbach provoked and killed him, but I think the purpose behind that is also connected to Brother Conchobhar's death.'

'But Selbach has escaped?'

It was Colgú who voiced his opinion. 'I have this suspicion that my rule is to be questioned. I had thought Selbach of Ráithlinn was a supporter of my policies but his actions and flight from the fortress are disturbing.'

'So, what stage do you think you have reached with your investigation into Brother Conchobhar's murder and matters you see as relevant?' asked Brehon Fíthel of Fidelma.

'They are not at a stage where I can even give you a hypothesis,' Fidelma responded.

'That is not good,' the Chief Brehon replied. 'Anyway, the bodies of Céit and the Princess Blinne must certainly be interred by midnight. I suppose you have no objections?'

'I have no objections,' Fidelma replied. 'As for the situation not being good, I cannot make it otherwise at this time.'

Another knock at the door interrupted them. It was Enda once more, his eyes seeking out Fidelma.

'Your pardon, but Prince Donennach requests permission to speak with you, lady,' the guard commander said.

Fidelma immediately arose with a general apology. She hesitated at the door and glanced to Brehon Fíthel.

'I presume that I am still in charge of the investigation?' she asked rather sharply.

The Chief Brehon did not smile. 'Until there are grounds for me to take over. I know you will investigate assiduously in an attempt to resolve the matter before the princes meet. Obviously, I am sure you are aware that Selbach is suspended from the council until such time as he surrenders himself and explains his behaviour. He might, of course, send his heir apparent and personal Brehon to come and speak in the council in his behalf, thus representing his people.'

'I am aware of the law,' Fidelma replied coldly. She glanced at Eadulf and, seeing her expression, he rose to his feet with an apologetic word to the King and went to join her as she left the King's chamber. Her mouth was tightly set and Eadulf realised that she had been angered by the Chief Brehon's remarks. Sure enough, as they followed Enda out of the royal residence, Eadulf heard her mutter tightly: 'Until there are grounds for him to take over!'

Enda led the way to the guest chambers and it was Conrí who opened the door of Prince Donennach's chamber when Fidelma knocked. His face was solemn as he stood aside to let them enter. Fidelma indicated to Enda that he should wait for them in the corridor. As they entered the room, Prince Donennach rose to greet them, his expression grave.

'You sent for us?' Fidelma asked brusquely, still thinking of the Chief Brehon.

'Far be it from me to send for you,' Donennach replied uneasily, a little in surprise at her querulous tone.

Fidelma realised she was being impolite. 'You will excuse me, Donennach. I had other things on my mind.'

'Ah, I have heard that Chief Brehon Fíthel has arrived,' Donennach said in a low voice. 'Surely he cannot criticise your investigation?'

'What can I do?' she said, avoiding the question.

'We have heard that Blinne, the wife of Selbach, was thrown from the walls of this fortress. There is no need for me to repeat she told her husband a lie when she said that my body-guard, Céit, raped her. That was the excuse Selbach used as a defence for killing him.'

There was a silence.

'Therefore?' Fidelma prompted.

'We asked to see you so that we may officially reaffirm that we had neither knowledge in this matter nor in the subsequent death of Blinne.'

'Let us sit so that you may explain this to us in more comfort,' Fidelma suggested.

The Prince of the Uí Fidgente motioned them to take seats.

'Conrí has known you a long time, lady,' he began awkwardly.

'Five years have passed since Conrí and I first encountered

one another at the time of the Badger's Moon,' she replied gravely. 'Thanks to Conrí I have come to know you a year or so ago and trust your word.'

'Just so,' Donennach said appreciatively. 'Without our working together, we would not have thwarted the plot of certain members of the Uí Fidgente to continue to make war on Cashel.'

'Conrí's advice in helping negotiate the treaty agreement with my brother, which you are honouring by your attendance here, has been invaluable to seeing the possibility of peace move to reality.'

'Indeed.' Donennach hesitated as if unsure how to proceed. 'We are also aware that the treaty has to be endorsed by the meeting of the seven major Eóganacht princes at this council before the Feast of Beltaine.'

Fidelma looked from Conrí to Donennach.

'It would seem that you suspect that I would conclude that you were responsible for the killing of Blinne?' she asked. 'Presumably this would be interpreted as a revenge for her false claim that Céit had raped her. Is that your concern?'

Conrí and Donennach quickly exchanged looks.

'That is exactly what we thought,' admitted Donennach. 'I have watched from time to time the processes of your mind, lady. Once we heard of the killing of Blinne, and no one was caught, I saw that it was the route along which your thoughts might travel.'

Conrí added hurriedly: 'Blinne acted falsely and caused the death of an innocent man. We want the truth to be known as soon as possible. Rumours spread quickly and matters could escalate into a *dígal*, a blood feud. That is the last thing that we should be involved in at this time.'

'There is often a great deal of difference between what should be and what is,' Fidelma sighed. 'I have already reminded Conrí of the exhortation of the ancient philosophers – *Si fecisti, nega!* If you did it, deny it! So just accepting it is so because you say it is so does not resolve matters. But I take your point – a blood feud would be pointless at this time. So, tell me, how did you come to hear about the rumours?'

'From the guard in the guest chambers.'

'Useful fellows in spreading information,' muttered Eadulf in annoyance.

'Did the guard also tell you that we knew positively that Blinne had lied? On Conrí's advice, Eadulf found out that much when he examined the corpse of Céit. We questioned Selbach on this matter after we found Selbach in bed with his own mistress soon after Princess Blinne's body was discovered. They both swore that they had been together throughout the night and thus each gave the other an alibi. However, Selbach has confused the issue by managing to escape from confinement before we could investigate further. The problem is, the alibi seems a sound one. That means someone else killed Blinne.'

Prince Donennach was shaking his head. 'Then all we can say is that it was not I, nor was it Conrí.'

'And, of course, you have your own alibi for the time of Blinne's murder?'

'As you know, I and my companions came as guests in this fortress unaccompanied and alone. We have left our main bodyguard encamped at Ráth na Drínne. I have no lover waiting in my bedchamber to give me false testimony,' Donennach replied fiercely.

'We are told that Blinne had a lover. She lied about Céit to disguise the identity of her real lover. To her cousin, Esnad, she described her lover as a warrior.'

Conrí's jaw tightened, his mouth forming a thin line. 'All I can say is I am not he. I am not involved in this matter.'

'Well, since we are together,' Fidelma shrugged, 'tell me how you came to Cashel.'

Donennach looked bewildered. It seemed a sudden change of subject.

'How did you arrive here?' pressed Fidelma.

'We came by horse. Three of us came to the fortress but the escort of nine warriors stayed at Ráth na Drínne.'

'A small party for the Uí Fidgente travelling in Eóganacht territory,' commented Fidelma.

'Leaving Uí Fidgente territory until the treaty between us is approved is difficult,' Donennach pointed out. 'But I had a company of warriors, ten warriors. They went straight to their bivouac. We knew each dignitary was allowed only one or two attendants or guards in the fortress. That is why Céit accompanied us here.'

Eadulf had a sudden thought. 'Would it not be logical to have been escorted by a Brehon?'

'Why so?' demanded Donennach. 'There was no reason to suspect the treaty would be challenged since the basis was drawn up by Brehon Fíthel and Fidelma, and agreed by my Brehons before we came here.'

'So you arrived at the fortress, just the three of you, with only the baggage you carried on your horses?'

'That is so. We are warriors and used to doing without attendants.'

'Tell me, in your time here, did you mix with any of the religious?'

This brought a further exchange of surprised looks.

'Brother Conchobhar was always welcoming,' Conrí admitted. 'But we did not regard the apothecary as one of the religious.'

'Who else did you see?'

'We did not like Brother Fidach and his affectations,' Donennach replied. 'In fact, I could not bring myself to go to any of his services after the first one. The young librarian, Brother Dáire, was worthy of conversation. I saw a couple of others, whose names escape me, but not that they intruded into one's space.'

'What of Sister Ernmas?'

'Sister who?' Donennach asked hesitantly. 'Oh, yes. The strange religieuse. We have not seen, nor do we know anything of her.'

'I believe I have seen her,' Conrí said suddenly, surprising them. 'I think she was in the courtyard outside the chapel small door. But I have never spoken to her.'

'You saw her in that small area at the side door of the chapel?' Eadulf pursed his lips. 'That is almost next to the apothecary?'

'When was this?' Fidelma asked.

'It would have been some days before Brother Conchobhar was found murdered,' Conri admitted.

'You don't know anything further about her?'

'What is there to know? A religieuse is a religieuse.'

'In this case I would say perhaps much more.' Fidelma abruptly rose. 'I have taken into account the concerns you have. I am determined to resolve these matters.'

She thanked Donennach and Conrí, promising to be in touch with them soon. She motioned Eadulf to follow her. Outside Enda was waiting for them.

'What now?' Eadulf asked as they followed her along the corridor. There were guards still in evidence, including the two who still stood outside Esnad's room.

'I keep thinking that I have overlooked something,' confessed Fidelma as they walked slowly from the guest quarters, around the chapel to Brother Conchobhar's apothecary. 'Wait for me in the library while I just check something.'

Fidelma entered Brother Conchobhar's workshop, with its familiar odours, with a sense of loss that went with the memories that the aromas brought to her mind. Soon the apothecary would be turned over to someone else to manage. Brother Conchobhar, with all his skills and wisdom, would just become a distant memory. Indeed, in time he would even be forgotten. She was suddenly reminded of something she had read by the Roman lawyer, Cicero: *'Nihil est aeternum'* – 'Nothing lasts forever'. The happiness of today would be a fading memory of tomorrow. She would not have been the person she was without the advice, the mentorship, of old Brother Conchobhar. He had taught her so much, not especially his wonderful knowledge of the properties of plants and herbs and human anatomy, but his philosophies, the way he could read the signs of the sky, know when a storm was brewing, or the ways of the winds and its directions, the positions of the stars in the sky. So much . . . so much had he taught her.

She allowed herself a gentle sigh to quell the strange pricking that came to her eyes. Then she moved on into the second room where, and she had almost forgotten, the battered body of Blinne lay carefully washed in a winding sheet, ready for the burial that evening. She presumed Dar Luga had arranged some of the female attendants to wash and prepare the body after Luan had brought it back into the fortress. Nearby the body of Céit was wrapped ready to be taken to the grave area where it would be placed with broom branches to cover it.

It was then that she saw that the trap door in the floor of this room was still open and she could see the top of the ladder in place. A frown crossed her features as she stood uncertainly trying to remember whether it had been closed after they had exited the underground chambers. She was sure the trap door had been shut as it had been dangerous to leave it open. Nothing had been touched in the apothecary but the open trap door worried her. She felt she ought to make a final check of the strange underground chambers below and now it saved her time and energy as the ladder was already in place. She saw a candle placed on a shelf and, by it, a flint and steel. She hesitated. She knew it took her some time to ignite a flame to light a candle and she was not noted for her patience in doing so.

After a moment's hesitation she took the candle and exited the apothecary. She made for the nearby door of the chapel. She was hoping that there were lights there from which she could light her candle. Her luck was in for there was a lamp already lit and its flame still fluttering. There was no one else about and so she took it and returned to the apothecary, shielding the lamp with one hand, and managed to pass into its interior without the lamp being extinguished by the gentle passage of the air.

She paused only a moment before starting down the ladder, carefully carrying the lamp into the darkness below. At the bottom, she turned and peered around. It seemed strange that she and her brothers had been born in this place but had never known of the existence of these underground rooms. *Were* they a gate to the Otherworld, hewn out of the solid limestone rock of the fortress? They were chambers known only to old Brother Conchobhar for all these years. She wished the walls could speak and reveal the secrets they had witnessed. Was it from here that the Otherworld hosts emerged in a vision to the swineherds, Cuirán and Duirdriu, and told them to inform Conall Corc that if he kindled a fire on this limestone rock and made it his capital, his dynasty would last for ever?

She smiled, remembering the anachronism of an even older

ancestor, Eógan Mór, having a similar promise from the god Nuada, who gave him the sacred sword *Frecraid*. She had been raised on such legends as a child; stories that, even in these days of enlightenment, some still believed. She abruptly stopped smiling and shivered slightly at the idea of the emergence of Otherworld forces appearing at this very spot. Even the New Faith did not dismiss such stories but merely gave a different explanation for them.

The noise was slight but loud enough for her to start, head to one side, trying to locate its origin in the echoing whispers of the chamber.

There was another light now emerging through the narrow twisted aperture between the two chambers. Someone was making their way into the chamber from the second one where the ritual artefacts had been stored, including the book shrine. Because of the way the narrow passage between the chambers twisted in their construction, the light could not be spotted until the person holding it had started to emerge through the link towards the main chamber.

Fidelma found herself standing completely still. However, in spite of her effort to control herself, her heart started to beat faster as she waited for the holder of the light to emerge.

The young face of the librarian, Brother Dáire, emerged blinking at the increased light caused by Fidelma's lamp. Then he squeezed into the chamber holding a small lantern in his hand.

'Lady,' he seemed surprised. 'What are you doing here?'

She adjusted her position quickly, relaxing and hoping Brother Dáire had not seen her apprehension.

'I am here because I am a *dálaigh*. You should know that,' she answered tightly. 'What brings you down here?'

'I had been thinking about the book shrine that you had showed me. The empty one and the scrap of parchment you found by it.'

'A scrap of *palimpsestos*. Stretched goat's skin akin to vellum,' she corrected pedantically. 'What were your thoughts?'

'I think the important item when Brother Conchobhar brought it into the library was not the *forsundud,* the praise poem, but the notes on the rituals and the sword. That is what made

Brother Conchobhar start looking and making references. He
left the book shrine open to one side with the manuscript. I
knew Sister Ernmas was in the library around that time. When
Brother Conchobhar returned to the table, the shrine had been
closed and relocked. He picked it up. Perhaps his thoughts
were diverted and he thought the book was still in it. Maybe
he forgot he had not closed or locked it.'

'So you think the shrine was left for Brother Conchobhar
to carry away while Sister Ernmas took charge of the contents?
Why was the book more valuable than the shrine?'

'It was not the praise poem. It was the notes about the
ritual.'

'So, what is your theory, Brother Dáire?'

'I believe that even Brother Conchobhar realised there was
some significance in the book other than the poetry. That's
what he was trying to copy out, but his notes were taken. He
paid for that secret with his life.'

'But what of the other artefacts? Why not take the sacred
sword?'

'The ritual items? I suppose they were worth taking although,
admittedly, the prize would have been the sacred sword.
Anyway, it is still hanging safely in the great hall. The thief
has realised that, now the King has put a guard on it, it is
impossible to take. But something may have been in that book
that Brother Conchobhar noticed was important. That's why
he had the sword hung where all could see it and thus prevent
it from being secretly removed.'

Fidelma sighed softly. 'Something important about the
sacred *Frecraid*? Well, no one has attempted to steal it yet.'

'That is what worried me and then I thought . . . was he
killed to stop the theft or was it to stop him revealing what
that book actually said?'

'Revealing it to whom? Who would be interested in what
an old book said?'

'Several people seem to be interested in ancient rituals. The
new priest, for example.'

'Brother Fidach?' Fidelma was incredulous. 'With his fanaticism for the New Faith, he would be the last person who cared
about ancient rituals.'

'But he went to the library to see the text of *Ignis creator igneus*,' pointed out Brother Dáire. 'The blessing of the candles to commence the rituals of the Feast of Beltaine. Once the sacred flame to ignite the Fires of Bel is lit, the King is supposed to step forward and be acclaimed.'

'I still do not understand your point.'

'Bear with me, lady,' replied Brother Dáire. 'As the feast day was coming up shortly, I had occasion to look at the manuscript that Brother Fidach had asked for because I wanted to make sure that I also knew of the rituals.'

'Go on. The next part of the blessing is well known. I have attended the Feast of Beltaine.'

'It is the moment the blessing is made and the King steps forward and the Bishop of Cashel begins to chant the blessing on the King. It is a ritual older than the New Faith, whose prelates once tried to absorb it.'

'I do recall the ceremony. The Keeper of the Sword steps forward holding *Frecraid*, The Answerer, the sword of Nuada, high, and hands it to the King. He holds it up and is thereby acclaimed the righteous ruler of the people.'

Brother Dáire smiled in acknowledgement of her memory.

'This is correct. But there was something in the words of instruction that worried me. Worried me because of the idea that the sacred sword might have been the object of the theft.'

Fidelma was growing a little impatient.

'You are confusing me, Brother Dáire.'

'I do not mean to do so. But something in the instructions irritated me until I went and looked them up a short time ago.'

'Which was?' Fidelma snapped impatiently.

'The text says that the Keeper of the Sword hands it to the King and it is held with hands palms outwards, signifying protection to the point of the blade, the sacred emerald to the east. Then comes the phrase, "It must be the true sword and not its reflection".'

Fidelma frowned. '"Not its reflection"? Are those the exact words? But what does that mean?'

'Exactly my reaction, lady.' The young librarian seemed pleased with her questions. 'The words say not the *scáth ar claideb*.'

'It is an odd choice of words. "Not the reflection of the sword".'

'The words could also mean "an image of the sword",' Brother Dáire pointed out.

For a moment she looked at him. 'Are you saying that the way it is written means that the sword used in the ceremony could be only an image of, and not a true sword?'

'I think that a better concept would be *aithris* – an imitation.'

'What you are saying is that the sword of office that hangs in the great hall is not genuine but a copy? A duplication of the original sword?'

'That would be one conclusion.'

'I am afraid that the thought had already occurred to me. My brother had the sword taken down and examined it. He declared it genuine and, after all this time, he ought to know. However you hold it, right or left hand, the emerald is to the east.'

'It crossed my mind that Nuada had his right arm severed in the war between the gods. The god of healing, Dian Cécht, had to make him an arm and hand of silver. After that he could only be able to wield the sword with his left hand.'

'But held in either hand the sword still has the emerald pointing to the east. So that is not a guide. And why did Brother Conchobhar place it in the great hall on the evening before he was murdered?' Fidelma asked.

'That was after he read that text. Maybe he had an indication that someone might attempt to steal it. Or, the thought occurred to me, he placed a replica in its place.'

Fidelma stared at him for a moment, realising the young librarian had made a very logical speculation.

'If it is a replica, it has fooled my brother.'

'It was only by accident that you found the note Brother Conchobhar made, even as incomplete as it is. The thief did not want even that knowledge to be known. Remember that my note on the content was stolen.'

'The contents just gave a clue to the rituals.'

'Which were valuable with regard to the smaller artefacts taken. The sword was the most valuable. Was it taken or was a replica taken?'

'My brother is sure that the sword in the great hall is genuine. Are we sure there was a second sword?'

'Its reflection,' Brother Dáire confirmed softly. 'The reference is clear.'

'I have to accept my brother's knowledge,' Fidelma said.

'Then I will show you that there is a reflection. Come and look again in that second chamber.'

Fidelma followed the librarian, squeezing through the aperture and emerging into the second chamber. At first glance it seemed that nothing had been altered.

'What did you see while you were here?' the librarian asked. 'As you can see, on the top of that altar are the silk markings that clearly show where the ancient sword was usually kept. You could see the indentations. You said you opened a small area at the side, where there was a lever, and that when pressed, it opened the front panel. That's where you saw the vellum. Is that so?'

'That is so,' Fidelma confirmed.

The young librarian went to the place she indicated, opened it and put his hand inside. It was clear he had already tried this before. There was a click and the front panel opened, revealing the long empty spaces, as before. Fidelma stared in silence. The top shelf showed a velvet covering. Brother Dáire held his lamp close and bade her look. From the impression on the velvet the marks showed a sword had rested there, very similar to the velvet area on top of the altar-like box.

Brother Dáire was watching her expression.

'You would agree?' he asked quietly. 'See what I mean? Why have two resting places for one sword? One on top and the other inside.'

After a few moments, she told him to relock the panel. Once back up the ladder into the apothecary she had gathered herself together.

'I think Eadulf and Enda are across in the library,' she said. 'We'd better join them.'

Eadulf and Enda were not alone in the library. They were in the company of Brother Laig.

'I say again that I know almost nothing of this Sister

Ernmas,' the physician was saying. 'If you want to know about
her ask Brother Fidach.'

'We have already asked him but he has seen this woman
only a few times,' Enda volunteered.

'Well, perhaps he knows more now.'

'How do you mean . . . he may know more now?' Fidelma
asked, entering the conversation.

'I saw him but a short time ago, inside the chapel in a rather
animated conversation with her,' replied the physician.

Fidelma's eyes widened slightly.

'Did you now?' she breathed softly. 'What do you mean by
"animated conversation"?'

'I meant there was a lively reaction between them.'

'Were they arguing or were they just talking as if they
knew one another well?'

'I would have said that they were arguing,' Brother Laig
said.

'How did you recognise her as Sister Ernmas?' Fidelma
pressed.

'I saw her previously in the library poring over some manuscript in the company of the lady Moncha.'

Fidelma was irritated by reminding herself of what Brother
Dáire had previously told her.

'So you saw this curious religieuse with Moncha; that is,
the wife of Prince Furudrán?'

Brother Laig looked at her almost pityingly. 'Is there another
lady Moncha in this fortress?'

Fidelma was too busy sorting out the implications to give
her usual waspish response to his sarcasm.

'You say this happened only a short time ago in the chapel?'
At his nod of confirmation, she asked: 'Did either of them see
you?'

'Why should I care? I have a right to be in the chapel.'
Then he paused. 'In fact, I do not think they did see me. They
were too busy with their argument. I was going to pass across
the chapel to the door that connects it with the living quarters
set aside for the clerics. My room is there. Before I entered
from the antechamber into the main chapel, I realised that I
had forgotten something in the library. I hesitated for a few

moments, and this was when I saw them in conversation. So I turned and went back to get the item I had forgotten. We were just talking when you came.'

'I'd like to be clear on this,' Fidelma said. 'Where were they having this animated conversation?'

'They were standing behind the altar table.'

'And you saw them clearly?'

'The candles were lit at the altar. They were standing together at one end of the altar. I was the one in darkness so that's why I don't think they saw me for the brief time I stood there after I became aware of them. Now, have you finished with me?'

'You didn't hear any word that passed between them? Only the tone of the conversation?'

'As I said, it was an animated conversation. I would just say that Brother Fidach's voice was raised in a disapproving tone. Come to think of it, he was gesticulating. He kept pointing downwards as if to his feet.'

'To his feet?' Fidelma frowned. 'What was wrong with them?'

'I have no idea. As I said, they were standing behind the altar table so if he was gesturing at something it was hidden behind it.'

'Very well, I have done.'

The physician turned with a snorting sound, blowing air through his nostrils as if in an expression of disgust, and moved off towards the apothecary.

Brother Dáire was staring after him. 'I certainly do not like that fellow,' he observed. 'He is too arrogant for his own good.'

'I think we can concur on that,' Fidelma nodded. 'So now let us find Brother Fidach and hear what he has to say about this matter. The mystery of this woman Sister Ernmas is irritating me to the extreme.'

The chapel was in darkness when they entered. There were certainly no lit candles on the altar table.

Eadulf tripped in the darkness and would have fallen had it not been for the steadying arm of Enda. Eadulf let out a soft oath.

'It's no problem,' said Enda, feeling his way to the ledge where candles were usually kept.

Like all warriors of his class, Enda carried at his belt a small bag containing flint, steel and tinder, which was known as *teine creasa*, fire of the girdle, or often *tenlam*, hand-fire. The tinder, *sponc*, was the dried leaves of coltsfoot, and all warriors were trained to produce a fire in the quickest possible time. Indeed, Enda had lit the nearest *innlis*, or tall candle, before they were aware of any time passing in his attempt to do so. It fell to Eadulf to light a second candle from the dancing flame of the first one.

It was fairly clear the chapel was deserted.

Eadulf went to stand by the entrance of the bell tower to peer upwards, as if half expecting the tall woman to make an appearance.

'Brother Fidach must be in the quarters of the religious,' Fidelma sighed as she pointed to the door at the far end of the chapel. She had gone a few steps when Eadulf uttered a sharp gasp.

'What's wrong?' she demanded, turning back.

'I felt something on my neck,' he complained. 'There! Again!' He raised a hand and wiped it across the nape of his neck. It was wet and sticky. Maybe it was an insect. 'Devil take it!' he exclaimed. 'Something wet fell on my hand.'

As he withdrew his hand from his neck, Enda, who was standing nearby, moved closer with his candle raised and looked forward.

'Careful, Eadulf. It is droplets of blood,' the warrior proclaimed. He raised his candle. 'Move aside from the steps.'

Eadulf had been standing close to the bottom step of the bell tower. He moved away. Enda then crouched down and examined the steps leading into the tower.

'What is it?' asked Fidelma, returning to the entrance.

'The splatter of spots here and on the wood of the stairway . . .' Enda indicated them with his hand. 'They are spots of blood, lady.'

Even in the darkness, the young warrior read her thoughts. 'I'll go up and take a look.'

He did not ascend the wooden steps into the bell tower far

before they heard him halt. There was some movement and then his steps descended. He reappeared and stood facing them in the candlelight. Although the flickering flames of the two candles distorted his features they could see that he was concerned.

'What is it?' Fidelma demanded again.

'It is the priest, Brother Fidach. He is dead. His throat has been cut.'

EIGHTEEN

As a warrior, a member of the élite bodyguard, the Golden Collar, Enda was no stranger to death. Violence was his profession. He had encountered death in many forms during adventures escorting Fidelma and Eadulf in their investigations. It was five or six years ago that he had first been sent to accompany Fidelma, along with his comrades Dego and Aidan into the hostile territory of Laigin to rescue Eadulf, who was about to be hanged by the vindictive Abbess Fainder of Fearna. Since then he had seen more than enough deaths in conflict as well as murders. Yet he still retained an apprehension of death outside of battle, and especially of a religious for, even in the time of the Old Faith, it was a terrible deed to kill a priest. It was considered just as horrendous as *fingal*, or kin-slaying, which struck at the heart of the kin-based structure of society.

Enda stood aside and motioned to Eadulf to ascend the wooden stairway. He moved up to where Brother Fidach's body was balanced over the edge of the circular flight of stairs with one foot trapped under one of the wooden steps, which prevented him falling completely back down the stairs. He lay on his back. His head was flung backwards so that the blood from his severed throat dripped down.

Noting the blood was not congealed, Eadulf realised that the event had not long taken place. He moved carefully in order not to dislodge the body. He examined it in the light of the candle Enda handed up to him. Even in that light he noticed a strange, almost surprised look on Brother Fidach's features. The cut was obviously done by a very sharp knife, a swift upwards cut into the throat before the knife was pulled across, causing a gushing slit in it. He checked that again, for it was not a tear, which confirmed in his mind that the cut had been made with an exceedingly sharp instrument.

The one thing that puzzled him was the position of the body. If Brother Fidach had been ascending the stairs then the assailant must have been standing a step or two above him. If the attacker was the mysterious Sister Ernmas and she was as tall as she had been reported, then she would have obviously had to bend forward to achieve the cut. But then it would have been difficult, almost impossible, to have succeeded in making the upwards thrust under the chin from that angle. If she had been below him on the stair, she would surely have had to stretch upwards and so lose the force necessary to inflict the wound.

Fidelma called impatiently from below.

'A moment,' Eadulf replied, giving a quick glance around, holding his candle high, to ensure he had not missed anything. Then he moved down to join her. On the bottom step he gave her a quick summary.

'I'd better see for myself,' Fidelma finally said. 'I am the *dálaigh* and I am bound to do so.'

She took the candle and went carefully up the steps.

Eadulf turned to Enda with an ironic grimace. 'I am told that no one knew the ancient story that this was supposed to be a gate to the House of Death. If they didn't know before then they will do so now.'

A moment later Fidelma reappeared. 'We'd better bring the body down and then have it removed to the apothecary. I'll ask Dar Luga to have it attended to. Abbot Cuán should arrive soon so we will leave it to him and his physician to attend to the rest of the matters. At this rate, we should have had a mass grave dug. Apart from poor Brother Conchobhar, we now have three more bodies to bury.'

Eadulf exhaled as if exhausted. 'What now? Another potential path to finding this mysterious woman is blocked.'

'Are you forgetting one other thing that Brother Laig told us?'

Eadulf frowned and then silently rebuked himself for his forgetfulness. The mysterious woman had been seen in the library with Moncha, the wife of Prince Furudrán, looking at a manuscript.

'We should find the lady Moncha and question her?' he suggested.

'You have taken the words from my mouth,' Fidelma remarked tartly.

It took a short time to make the arrangements with Dar Luga, whose features were now pale and fearful. Having to wash and prepare four bodies in as many days was unprecedented in her experience.

Fidelma and her companions were now heading back once more to the guest quarters when a warrior hailed them in the courtyard. It was Dego, in the company of an elderly man. They waited while the two approached.

'I have found Selbach's driver at Ferloga's tavern.' He indicated the elderly man at his side. The man was bent in that curious way that wagon drivers seemed to adopt after long years of bending over the reins of a team of horses. The old man looked uncomfortable, bowing in respect as he raised a knuckled hand in salute to Fidelma.

'What is your name?' she asked him.

'Echdae, lady.'

Fidelma tried to hide her smile. The name meant 'horse god', and anyone looking less like his name she had yet to see.

'I am told you are the wagon driver for Selbach of Ráithlinn.'

The man moved his weight nervously. 'Not exactly, lady.'

'I was told . . .' she began uncertainly, looking at Dego.

'I drove him and his party here, that is all. I mean that I am not of his household. He hired me to bring him and his ladies, escorted by his bodyguard, to the fortress. The bodyguard and I were to wait in the place called Ráth na Drínne in case they needed my services after the Feast of Beltaine. He paid me good money in advance,' the man added in satisfaction.

'In advance?' echoed Eadulf in surprise.

The old driver grinned wryly. 'He did promise to send one of his warriors to slit my throat if I did not remain at Ferloga's tavern until he needed me. Even when I heard he had collected his bodyguard and ridden south, I felt I should remain there until I knew that he had truly gone. I cannot say I enjoyed my service with him.'

'So you were hired? You are not from the territory of Ráithlinn?'

'I am of the Uí Liatháin. I do a lot of work for the religious at the abbey of Dairinis.'

'Dairinis?' Fidelma repeated thoughtfully.

'That's where I was employed by Selbach. He was staying at the abbey on Dairinis. I was asked to take his party and luggage from the abbey to Cashel. As I say, we were escorted by warriors on horseback, who came as far as Ráth na Drínne. I left Selbach and his women here, while I returned there to wait for further instructions.'

'But you knew Selbach and his warriors then left?'

'But not his women. So I remained there in case I heard further.'

'Had Selbach and his party already arrived at this abbey of Dairinis when you were hired to drive them here?'

'They had. There was a ship anchored there and I was told that they had arrived on board it. My stable is not far away from Dairinis on the Uí Liatháin side of the river.'

Fidelma had a satisfied expression. 'I shall probably need to speak to you later, Echdae. There are some matters I have to attend to first.' She turned to Dego. 'See to it that this man is given his fill of food and drink, and ensure that he does not leave the fortress until I ask for him again.'

Fidelma and her companions continued on in silence to the guest quarters and went up the now familiar stairs. As they passed the chamber of Esnad, a guard was still standing on watch outside.

Fidelma murmured: 'After we have spoken with Moncha, we will see if that girl has come to her senses and decided to tell us what she knows. She's had time to dwell on the consequences. If she refuses, we now have the driver's evidence of where they landed, which might be a means of extracting further information from her.'

It was Furudrán himself who opened the door of his guest chamber.

'Moncha has just gone to the library,' he answered when Fidelma enquired for his wife. 'She is a great scholar, you know. She is a poetess of the fourth order, a *cano*,' he added proudly, as if an excuse were needed. 'She found some interesting volumes in the library here.'

'I would hope to hear her read her work.' Fidelma returned pleasantly. 'But we have recently come from the library. She was not there.'

'She probably went through the passage that leads into the chapel and you cross through it to get to the library. She often takes that route to avoid the winds and rain crossing the court-yards.' He paused and then said: 'One moment.' His voice was suddenly serious. 'I would like to say something. Come in for a moment.'

It was clear that he was addressing just Fidelma and so she asked her companions to wait before she stepped inside. Furudrán closed the door behind her.

'I hear that Selbach's wife has been killed and that he is a suspect.'

'That is so,' Fidelma confirmed, curious at his change of attitude from his usual hostility displayed in the council.

'Is it true that he has fled the confinement of this fortress and gone south with his warriors?'

'It is true, but where did you hear this?'

Furudrán shrugged. 'News spreads quickly among the guards, even if it is whispered. I was not surprised to hear this.'

'Why not?' Fidelma asked, restraining her quickened interest.

'You remember the arguments in the council when we were told about the re-emergence of the pestilence?'

'I do.'

'I voiced some distinctive views. You will know that I have some criticisms of your brother, Colgú. I still hold those views; well, not that I wish your brother harm but I think he has made some wrong decisions.'

'The council is the place to discuss that. Not with me.'

'I agree,' Furudrán replied hurriedly.

'What is the point that you want to make, Furudrán?'

'I make no point but wanted to warn you. I may disagree with your brother but I do so according to the law.'

'Warn me?' she frowned.

'A short time after that meeting, Selbach approached me. He had been striding up and down the walkway behind the guest chambers here. He was angry but seemingly controlled and I would say he had a curious vengeful humour.'

'I am not sure I follow what you mean.'

'He talked about your brother the King in angry terms, saying that he would not last long in the kingship. He said that Colgú's time was limited to the next council meeting. He swore that Colgú would be ousted by the princes. He supported entirely what I had said and advised me to join with him and others who have become tired of weak peacemakers like Colgú.'

Fidelma tried to keep her features expressionless.

'Are you saying that there is going to be an attempt at assassination?'

Furudrán shrugged. 'Assassination was not mentioned. I think any sane person would know it would result not just in a blood feud but in an all-out war. One prince against another. On the other hand, a council decision by the seven princes would be legal and peaceful. No army would be raised against another. We would remove him and no one could call it illegal or unjust. War between the princes would thus be avoided.'

'Was Selbach saying that Finguine, the heir apparent, would be appointed to the kingship? I know that the seven senior princes, or a majority of them, have to agree first.'

'It is known that Prince Finguine is so close to your brother as makes no odds. They move locked in step. Finguine's father sponsored Colgú as his heir to the throne, and now Colgú sponsors Finguine. The princes were happy to confirm the annual passing of power so far. Since then we have had the problems with how he has dealt with Laigin, Osraige and the Uí Fidgente.'

'You were saying that Selbach invited you to join him against my brother?'

'When someone wants power badly, then a conspiracy will start. I will not join a conspiracy but I will express my views. I have that right to dissent but only to act under the law.'

'If Selbach puts himself forward against my brother in council why would he think the princes of this kingdom would support him to succeed my brother? Selbach does not have the character to be a popular king.'

'My impression was that Selbach did not consider himself

in contention,' Furudrán declared. 'I believe Selbach is guided by another prince who might command authority enough to assert his claims. And, before you say, that prince is not me.'

'Then it is hard to see which prince. Colgú's vote is obvious, and Finguine's. So we know Selbach's position. That now leaves you, and you deny your interest, Elódach of Áine, Congal of Loch Léin, and Tigernach of Arann.'

Furudrán shrugged. 'I told you my position. Anyone who can prove they have a direct bloodline to Eógan Mór can command sufficient force.'

Fidelma frowned. 'Are you suggesting that . . .?'

'I suggest no one, lady. I do say that even Donennach of the Uí Fidgente already makes a claim to be descended from Eógan Mór, as does his cousin, a prince of the Uí Corpri. My wife is a good scholar and has seen some of the genealogies of the descendants of Eógan Mór.'

'The last prince of the Uí Corpri was killed at the Battle of Áine,' Fidelma pointed out.

'Reputedly killed in the battle by your brother,' Furudrán declared. 'It is thought that the last of the Uí Corpri had a young son called Dáire.'

Fidelma was quiet for a moment. Then she shook her head. 'The Uí Fidgente have agreed a peace and alliance with the Eóganacht,' she pointed out. 'Even if their claim of descent from Eogán Mór's elder brother, Cass, is inaccurate, it gives us a new and peaceful way forward. I do not think that the seven Eóganacht princes would accept a claim from outside the *ceithirfine*.'

'I am not giving a prophecy,' Furudrán smiled dryly, 'just pointing out possibilities.'

'I accept that. And we assume that Selbach was aware of the effort to topple my brother from the kingship. He needed a majority of the seven princes. So whom was he relying on?'

'What I am saying is that even minor princes pay tribute to one or other of the seven Eóganacht princes. If there is a war it will become a very bloody one. It might be the minor princes who dominate. It's just a thought.'

Fidelma was deep in contemplation as she and her companions made their way once more to the library. It was as they entered the ante-chamber that a scream rang out. It was a sharp and sudden sound followed by the crash of someone falling and a piece of furniture being overturned. Within a moment, Enda rushed into the long gallery with its rows of book satchels and shelves. They heard another crash from the far end, which Fidelma knew was where there was the doorway to the back garden in which she had often sat. Fidelma and Eadulf were not as fast as Enda, running through the rows of the book satchels. They saw Moncha was sprawled on the ground, a heavy *tamlorga*, or single supported writing table, overturned beside her. Enda was already disappearing through the open door into the garden. A large number of books had been knocked from the shelves nearby. There was no sign of the librarian, Brother Dáire.

Eadulf knelt down beside the prone form of Furudrán's wife. She was groaning and trying to focus, blinking her eyes rapidly. There was blood on the side of her head.

'Lie still,' he instructed sharply. 'Fidelma, get me some water.'

'I . . . I am all right,' muttered the woman, raising a hand to her head.

'I'll tell you if I think that you are,' Eadulf sharply assured her, peering closely at the wound. 'Did you get hit on the side of the head?'

Fidelma returned with a jug of water and Eadulf used it to begin to bathe the woman's bloodied head.

'How does your head feel?'

Moncha's lips turned down. 'I wish it would stop pounding. What happened?'

'Well, I don't think I need to tell you that you were attacked. The question is – who by?' Eadulf said. 'Where is Brother Dáire?'

No one answered.

Fidelma bent down to help raise the woman into a sitting position on the repositioned fallen chair.

'Did you see who did this?' she asked.

Moncha grunted in pain as she turned towards Fidelma. 'It was a woman from the chapel. She had been studying in here a few times and we had even spoken before. She suddenly turned and attacked me.'

'Sister Ernmas? A tall woman dressed in the black robes of a religieuse?'

Moncha frowned. 'You know her? I was struck by whatever it was she held. I must have been knocked backwards and fell, sending the chair flying. It was a shock. I think momentarily I was unconscious.'

Eadulf finished bathing the wound and stood regarding his handiwork critically. 'There's no cut as such, just an abrasion that has bled, but it will heal. However, there will be a bruise. You will doubtless have a headache. It is lucky we reached you when we did.'

Moncha was massaging her temple with one hand as Enda re-emerged through the open door. He looked doleful and was shaking his head.

'I lost her, lady,' he said in answer to Fidelma's glance and unasked question.

'She can't have gone far. How could you lose her?'

'She moves like a ghost,' muttered Enda in self-defence. 'One moment she was there and the next . . .' He lifted a shoulder and let it fall eloquently.

'Please,' it was Moncha, now growing ill tempered, 'is someone going to answer me about what is going on here?'

'If you can walk, Moncha, I think we should go to the kitchens and get Dar Luga to produce a strong drink for you. Then we can discuss what has taken place.'

When they were seated in Dar Luga's little administration office with a small flagon of *corma*, and Moncha was recovering from her shock, Fidelma explained.

'You were attacked by the woman who calls herself Sister Ernmas. As you admitted, you were seen together working in the library. How well do you know her?'

'Know her?' Moncha's eyes were wide in surprise. 'Only that she asked me some questions.'

'We hoped you might be able to tell us who she was. Sister Ernmas just tried to kill you. She is probably the same person who killed Brother Conchobhar and who has now killed Brother Fidach. Had we come to the library a moment later we could have found you dead. So what do you know of her?'

Moncha was regarding Fidelma as if she was mad. She shook her head in disbelief.

'Are you trying to tell me that a Sister of the Faith tried to kill me? I am not a credulous person. You will have to explain this to me.'

'We have been searching for this mysterious so-called Sister Ernmas for some time. I am told you were looking at some ancient books together. Is that not so?'

Moncha was still staring at her with incredulity, but there was no doubting the concern in Fidelma's voice.

'You think that she attempted to kill me? But for what reason?'

'That is precisely what we are trying to find out. So we would appreciate that you co-operate with us.'

'How can I do that when I do not know anything to co-operate about?'

'By answering the first question. What did you talk to her about those earlier times in the library?'

'Just about some ancient texts we were both looking for. Or rather, she was asking my opinions about.'

Fidelma did not disguise her sigh of exasperation. 'What ancient texts?'

'Of the poet Seanchán Torpéist and of Báetán of Loch Goir.'

'When was this?'

'I suppose it was no more than a week or so ago. My husband and I had just arrived at the fortress. Knowing there was such a library here, I wasted no time in visiting it. The young librarian was new, so he was only just coming to know where books were kept.'

'You had never seen this Sister Ernmas before you came here?'

'No, I had never seen nor met her until we came here. Is that clear and specific enough for you?'

Fidelma actually smiled at the woman's defensive aggression. 'It is specific enough. You just met her seeking references in the library?'

Moncha was now fully recovering her spirits. 'You probably don't know but I am a poetess and of the degree of *cano* . . .' she began with a patronising tone.

'I know that very well,' Fidelma assured her.

'Then it should follow that I know that your brother's library contains many treasures. You have a great collection, including the secular works of Seanchán Torpéist and other great poets of this kingdom. It should be logical, therefore, that I would be fascinated to view works, especially the works of the *forsundud*, the ancient praise poems. It was in search of these that I met this woman.'

'So you came to the library. I presume you found the manuscripts?'

'I did so. This library contains several works connected with the descendants of Eógan Mór.'

'And these are what interested this woman?'

'This is so.'

'I presume that you asked what her background was?'

'She told me she was of the Uí Liatháin and was studying at Mael Anfraid's abbey.'

Eadulf immediately confessed that he did not know it.

'It is a small abbey on the Island of Oaks, Dairinis. It is towards the mouth of An Abhainn Mór, the great river.'

'Dairinis?' Eadulf glanced at Fidelma, recognising the name of the abbey mentioned by the old wagon driver.

'We were in that territory last winter,' Fidelma reminded him quickly, as if to cover his look of surprise. 'If you remember, we boarded a boat at Eochaill, the town of the yew wood, to make our way home. As we started up the river, there was an island on our east bank. I don't know it but I have heard it has many learned scholars there. One scholar, called Ruben, is interested in collecting the laws being adopted by Rome concerning the New Faith.'

Moncha looked impressed as Fidelma explained. Fidelma caught her glance and was dismissive.

'It is part of my profession to be aware of scholastic activities connected with law in each territory.'

'I would have thought the Council of Brehons were against these laws; I think they are called Penitentials.'

'We have our own law system, which I consider a better one than any that relies on physical punishments. But because we are against such a system we have to acknowledge that many of our misguided clergy are trying to force these new ideas from Rome on us. Therefore we must understand their reasoning and the nature of these new ideas. However, go on. This Sister Ernmas says she comes from Mael Anfraid's monastery on Dairinis?'

'She said that she was studying there.'

'Well, she certainly wasn't known at Imleach, which is what I thought she told us,' Enda muttered.

Fidelma's look told him to be quiet.

'Anything else?' she asked turning to Moncha. 'You said she was interested in the genealogies?'

'Of the Eóganacht princes. She seemed interested in their symbols.'

'Did you not find it strange that she would be interested in such a thing when the Uí Liatháin are regarded as minor kindred of the Uí Fidgente?'

Moncha nodded quickly. 'You have the right of it, Fidelma. Their ancestor was the son of Dáire Cerbba and not an Eóganacht at all. But scholars do not have to confine themselves to studying their own kindred.'

'Did you ask what her particular interest was? What symbols she was interested in?'

'She was vague on that. But I had the impression that she was particularly interested in the symbolic structure of Cashel itself. One of the manuscript books I found her poring over was a text called "The Finding of Cashel". It is—'

'I know it,' Fidelma said shortly. 'It is the story of how Cashel was made the principal fortress of the kingdom.'

'But the woman seemed more interested in what was here before that time – when Conall Corc became a Christian and when it was called the Ridge of the Otherworld People . . . when people considered it the gateway to the land of the dead. That is why she was looking for the work of Báetán of Loch Goir. He was a poet from the Eóganacht Áine territory.'

Fidelma found Eadulf staring in astonishment at this information.

'It is an old tale,' Moncha went on indifferently. 'It wasn't of much interest to me, and Báetán's work does not find favour in the New Faith.'

'The important thing is that we want to find her and there-fore, how?' intervened Enda, feeling the conversation was beyond him. 'How does she keep eluding us, hiding in this fortress? Why did she kill the priest and did she kill the apothecary?'

'You are scaring me,' Moncha declared, realising that they had not given her the full story. 'Why would she attack me?'

'Do you have an attendant?' Fidelma asked abruptly.

'I have. I came with my attendant, and my husband has a personal bodyguard. We were accompanied by twelve warriors. But it is a sign of respect that the main bodyguard remain outside the King's fortress. They are at Ráth na Drínne, as are the bodyguards of the other senior princes.'

'I would advise you to remain in your quarters until we have sorted out this matter,' advised Fidelma. 'Stay close to your husband and your attendants. This mystery woman may be a danger to all of us and we have seen enough killing in this fortress. We do not want to encourage any further deaths.'

'But why me?'

'You know what she is interested in. Maybe that is enough for her to try to stop you from relaying this knowledge. Maybe it is the same reason why Brother Fidach was killed.'

Moncha shuddered. 'I would not have come through the passages that lead through the chapel had I known he had been killed.'

They accompanied the woman back to the guest chambers after Eadulf had pronounced her well enough to move. After they left her, Eadulf raised his arms helplessly.

'Does any of this make sense?'

To the surprise of her companions, Fidelma replied: 'I am beginning to see a pattern. Perhaps the pattern is becoming the revelation of a plan. It is a curious one.'

'Are we to be let in on it?' Eadulf said after waiting in vain for an explanation.

'I don't have enough information to be confident to argue it as a possibility, only as an idea. Anyway, I want to see Esnad and finish with her story. As I said before, I think she now has had time to dwell on things. And we have old Echdae to back us up if she has not.'

As they approached the door of the girl's bedchamber the guard stiffened and saluted formerly. Fidelma sensed that the guard was relieved to see her.

'Is all well?' she asked. 'There has been no activity from the prisoner?'

'All is fine now. The lady Esnad has been rather vociferous in her complaints and, I am afraid, I have incurred the wrath of the Prince of the Airthir Chliach.'

'Prince Furudrán? Why? What is the problem?'

'He passed down the corridor and asked me if he could see the lady Esnad. I told him – no. I hope I did the right thing, lady?'

'It was because you refused his request that you incurred the wrath of Furudrán?'

'Your orders were explicit, lady, that no one be allowed to speak to her without permission. When I remained firm on this point, the prince was not pleased but desisted when he saw I was not to be moved.'

Fidelma exchanged a meaningful glance with Eadulf and then smiled at the guard.

'You did exactly the right thing.'

'I wonder why Furudrán was so anxious to speak with Esnad?' murmured Eadulf as Fidelma instructed the guard to unfasten the door.

Esnad sprang up from her chair as they entered. She seemed more subdued than before. Fidelma motioned her to be re-seated and glanced at the remains of some food on the table.

'You have been brought food, I see. I hope you have rested and can now speak to us.'

The girl scowled. 'I told you the truth, that Selbach was in my bed all night when his wife was killed.'

'So why did he flee from this fortress? Why try to escape, which was not an easy task to accomplish?'

'He did not flee. You lie. He would not desert me. You are still trying to trick me.' Yet again the girl was stubborn.

'Nevertheless, that is precisely what he has done. So it would be best if you tell us the complete truth. He and his men went back to where you harboured your boat.'

A silence fell in the room. It seemed Esnad had reluctantly come to realise that Fidelma was being honest with her.

'Has Selbach really left the fortress? Has he deserted me?' Her voice was almost a plea.

Fidelma looked with sympathy at the girl. 'You may believe it or not. If you need an oath, you may choose one. So far as I am concerned, my word as a *dálaigh* is sacred.'

The girl suddenly sighed and sank back in her chair, her shoulders hunched as if in an attitude of surrender.

Fidelma perched herself on the end of the bed while Eadulf leant against the wall. 'So now tell us your story, Esnad. Let us start with the coastal ship that brought Selbach, his wife and you here.'

There was a pause and the girl shrugged. 'You were right, of course. We did make the journey in a *serrcinn*, a coastal sailing ship. As well as Selbach, there was Blinne and myself and twenty of his warriors.'

'Only twenty?' Fidelma had been expecting more.

'A few warriors were left to guard the boat and only a company came with us. These we left at a place not far from here called Ráth na Drínne.'

'So you sailed from Selbach's fortress on the island of Raerainn and along the coast . . . to where?' encouraged Fidelma.

'To the mouth of An Abhainn Mór, the Great River. This leads up to Lios Mór. We made anchorage at the small abbey not far up this inlet.'

'Were you told its name?' Fidelma knew full well but wanted to make sure of the girl's story.

'Dairinis, the Island of Oaks.'

'Why was that port chosen?'

'I think it was arranged by Selbach. He had horses waiting for us there as well as the wagoner. We disembarked there and spent the night while the warriors encamped outside the abbey. I remember a small party of horsemen came to meet Selbach.'

'Who were they?'

'All were *flaith*, nobles, by the look of them. There were only four of them and we remained among the community while Selbach rode off with them. He was gone for the best part of a day. That evening Selbach rejoined us. He looked very pleased with himself.'

'Did he explain why?'

'I could not ask him at the time. On the morning of the next day, we set out. Blinne and I were in the wagon with the escort of warriors. Selbach rode with them. I don't know the countryside but we followed the eastern bank of the river, which eventually crossed over the mountains and into the great plain before Cashel.'

'Has Selbach ever explained what his meeting was about? Did he tell Blinne? Did she tell you?'

'I tried to ask, several times, but all that he would say is that I would soon know.'

'Did you see anyone else at this little abbey? For example, a tall, religieuse clad in black: Sister Ernmas?'

'Our party was exactly as I have told you. No more; no less. I have seen no one from that abbey.'

'Now tell me about the night Blinne died.'

The girl thrust forward her chin determinedly. 'I told you that I have been Selbach's lover for some time. With Blinne dead I need make no secret of it. On the night that Blinne fell over the wall of the fortress, he was with me until the moment you burst in. And that is the truth of it. I have no cause to lie.'

Fidelma hid her disappointment. She had a feeling that she could now believe the girl for there seemed no logic in her not sticking to her story, having admitted so much.

'Tell me some more about your cousin, Blinne,' she suddenly said. 'You have told me that she had this warrior lover and so I suppose she did not mind that you had become lover to her husband.'

'That is true. Why should she mind? There is no law forbidding it.'

Fidelma admitted there was none, although with the coming of the New Faith there were new concepts entering society. They were a direct blow to the tolerant customs permitted under the Brehon laws.

'It is still unexplained why she claimed Céit raped her,'

Fidelma sighed. 'Was that her idea or was it an excuse dreamt up by Selbach and she was asked to lie by her husband as a defence for him? If Selbach so freely preferred the old laws on what the New Faith consider the laxity of relationships, it is obvious that his excuse about rape disguises some other reason?'

'That's easy,' the girl responded. 'Céit was an Uí Fidgente and there was much blood spilt between them and the Eóganacht. Don't forget that this new treaty with the Prince of the Uí Fidgente is not liked by all. I know enough to say that many Eóganacht princes, like Selbach, see Donennach as a usurper who should be eliminated. The fact that the treaty your brother agreed to goes far in accepting the claim of the Uí Fidgente to be descended from Cormac Cass, the elder brother of Eógan Mór, has caused many to hate your brother.'

Fidelma thought about this for a few moments, remembering what Furudrán had said. 'Selbach found the treaty with the Uí Fidgente abhorrent? Did he plan action himself or did that abhorrence rely on other princes?'

'I do not know what you mean.'

'In killing Céit was Selbach acting on his own? Was it just an excuse to kill an Uí Fidgente warrior? If I accept your alibi for Selbach, then someone else must have killed Blinne. But was the killing of Céit his idea to create a blood feud between the Uí Fidgente and the Eóganacht or was someone else dictating this? Are you sure that Blinne had a lover, a warrior, as she told you?'

'She never used to hide things from me,' replied Esnad. 'I am certain she had a lover and she did say he was a noble warrior. That is all. She did mention something that I felt was interesting.'

'Which was?'

'She hoped Selbach did not have second thoughts about the main purpose of this coming Beltaine.'

'The main purpose? What did you understand by that?' Fidelma asked sharply.

'I understood nothing. All I know is that I once overheard Selbach saying something about Beltaine being the time when choices had to be made between the brother and the sister.'

Fidelma's eyes widened. 'Between the brother and the sister?'

'I didn't hear the rest properly but that was the main point.'

'To whom was he speaking?'

'It was to one of the princes.'

'You know which one?' Fidelma asked quickly.

'I do not know. I did not see to whom he was speaking.'

'So there are some princes who are going to make their views known at the council meeting here in a few days' time?' she murmured rhetorically.

Eadulf spoke for the first time. 'Isn't that what councils of princes are supposed to do?' he asked.

'Maybe something more was meant by that phrase,' Fidelma said sharply.

The girl shrugged. 'The politics of princes are of no concern to me. All I know is what Selbach said: that he and other princes were angered by the treaty Colgú had proposed. He said . . . the princes . . .' The girl suddenly paused and frowned as if a thought had struck her.

Fidelma leant forward. 'Something has come into your mind?' she prompted.

'Just a vague comment,' Esnad admitted. 'When Blinne was talking to me about the warrior she said she was having an affair with, I remember she once used a curious phrase. She said that he was a noble warrior and one whom Selbach would have to respect.'

'All warriors consider their role as noble,' murmured Eadulf.

'Perhaps it might indicate that he was of rank, like a member of a bodyguard to one of the princes,' Esnad pointed out. 'But even so, it would not mean that Selbach would respect anyone of lesser rank.'

'A final question,' Fidelma asked the girl. 'Have you come across a Sister Ernmas while you have been here?'

'You mentioned her earlier. There are a couple of religieuse serving the chapel but I don't know their names.'

'You might remember this one. She was tall, taller than I am. She was dressed in black without any colour relief and she always kept a covering on her head, making it hard to distinguish her features. She was not young, perhaps fifty years of age or more.'

Esnad shrugged. 'I might have seen her. Tall and dressed in black robes, you say?'

'Are you sure you wouldn't know her?' pressed Fidelma.

'Yes. Although I remember Blinne making a joke about such a person.'

'A joke?'

'She went to meet her lover – an assignation in the chapel – and saw him in conversation with such a person. When she entered, they seemed to break apart and the tall one vanished. Blinne's lover seemed nervous and when she asked about her he told her that the religieuse was asking if he knew about the rituals of the Beltaine Feast.'

'Anything else?'

'No. She just thought it was bizarre that her lover would be bothered to even speak to one of the New Faith. Blinne was not exactly interested in religion of any sort. But she told me that her lover apparently still believed strongly in the Old Faith and the prophecies of the ancients. So when she returned she told me about it and we had a laugh, pretending her lover was having an amour with this strange woman who was old enough to be his mother.'

Fidelma glanced at Eadulf before turning back to the girl.

'Did Blinne say anything more about her lover?'

Esnad shrugged. 'Only that this lover set much store by prophecies and symbols.'

'Prophecies and symbols?' repeated Fidelma softly.

'Blinne was not interested in such matters.' The girl tried to sound assertive. 'I have answered all your questions to the best of my ability – can I now be released from this imprisonment?'

Fidelma shook her head. 'I am afraid that you must remain here until I have finished my investigation. However, it will not be long. I must add that it is for your own good . . . for your own safety. I fear your life may be in danger.'

Esnad's eyes widened. 'From whom?' she demanded.

'The person who killed Blinne.'

'So you accept Selbach was not guilty of that?' The girl could not help a tone of triumph in her question.

'Since I accept your word that he was in bed with you, that is the logic. However, Brother Fidach has been killed and the lady Moncha was attacked. It was by the same person that I am now certain killed Blinne. I am also sure it was the same person that killed Brother Conchobhar. I think that person will now think that you know too much.'

'But how? Who is it?'

'We are getting near to that identification,' Fidelma said.

Esnad regarded her with a helpless expression. 'But I know nothing.'

'You know more than you understand. So for the time being, you will stay here under guard.'

NINETEEN

'I want to have another word with Furudrán,' Fidelma announced after they had left Esnad locked in her room with the guard still outside.

Fidelma seemed preoccupied with her thoughts so Eadulf made no comment as she led the way back along the corridor to the rooms occupied by Furudrán and his wife. There was a guard outside his door, as she had instructed, in case of a further attack on Moncha. Inside they found the prince in a state of agitation. He held a finger to his lips, nodding towards the adjacent bedchamber.

'Your warrior escorted my wife back and told me what happened. It seems that I owe you much, Fidelma. Have you found this strange woman, Sister Ernmas?'

'Not yet,' Fidelma admitted. 'Is Moncha recovered from her ordeal?'

'She is lying down. As you saw, it was a nasty blow on the head.'

'If the headache does not go away soon, send for me,' Eadulf volunteered. 'I have some infusions that will alleviate the headache like *midaige*, balm mint, and the squashed root of valerian.'

Furudrán thanked him, then asked: 'Was it to see how she felt that you have come?'

'It was also to ask you a further question,' Fidelma conceded.

Furudrán glanced towards the closed door and then said quietly: 'Let us step out into the corridor, so as not to disturb Moncha.'

Outside Fidelma was direct.

'When we left you to find your wife, you went straight to the chamber of Esnad and demanded to see her. She was confined there on my orders and I had left a guard outside her room. I understand that you tried to overrule my instructions to the guard. Why?'

Furudrán did not seem to be put out by the sudden sharp inquisitiveness in her tone.

'After you left I was remembering something and needed to have my mind refreshed by the girl. I had heard rumours that, while Ráithlinn is one of the seven senior princes, times are changing. The Uí Echach are thinking of challenging Selbach in his own territory as they have grown stronger.'

'The Uí Echach?' Eadulf frowned. 'Isn't that the minor branch of the Eóganacht from which Esnad and Selbach's wife, Blinne, come?'

'So, the question remains . . .' prompted Fidelma.

'I am thinking that the Uí Echach not only claim descent from Eógan Mór,' Furudrán went on, 'but they have marital connections with the Uí Fidgente as well as the Uí Liatháin and the Déisi. When you put all that territory together, it extends from almost the south-west along the entire south coast of the kingdom to Port Lairge. Isn't that worrying in the light of what we have been discussing?'

'Yet, if you go far back in our ancestries, we are all related to one another at some stage,' Fidelma pointed out. 'What did you hope to learn from Esnad?'

Furudrán smiled thinly. 'Did you know that Esnad's brother, Cas, is prince of the Uí Echach?'

'What are you suggesting? That the Uí Echach are trying to seize the kingship even when their ruler is not one of the senior princes? That they were controlling Selbach in his attempt to persuade the other princes to censure my brother?'

'I was hoping that Esnad might divulge something if Selbach had revealed his plans to her. I now believe that Esnad was ignorant of the details. But Selbach must have some backing to make him so confident. The other thing of concern is that he claimed in the council that only a righteous prince, a *flaith fírian*, could claim the sacred sword of Nuada. He said he would prove that. When the time came the sword would point the way.'

'The sword hangs safe in the great hall,' Fidelma reminded him.

'He said the matter would soon be resolved. That the choice between brother and sister was obvious. The brother and sister were unlike.'

Enda, remembering the argument in the council, was puzzled. 'I never fully understood what that curious statement Selbach made was supposed to mean. Was he suggesting there was some choice between your advice and that of your brother, Colgú?'

Furudrán grimaced thoughtfully. 'I can think of no other brother and sister than you and your brother Colgú who have more power in this kingdom. However, the other alternative is that of Esnad, who you now know was Selbach's mistress, and her brother, Cas, prince of the Uí Echach.'

'It doesn't make sense, either way,' Fidelma replied. 'Selbach needed the support of all the seven senior princes, not the minor princes who pay tribute to them.'

'I have to be honest and declare that I do not approve of the treaty, as the Uí Fidgente borders my territory. Selbach was trying to involve me in his plotting.'

'Are you involved?' she demanded.

'Not in any conspiracy,' Furudrán affirmed. 'I express my views openly and not surreptitiously. I do so in council and defend myself there.'

'Then we will await the meeting of the council and see if the sword of Nuada does point the way.' There was a little irony in Fidelma's voice. But she was thinking of the references she had heard relating to a 'brother' and 'sister'. It did not seem quite right. Her thoughts were interrupted by the sound of a trumpet at the gates.

'I suppose that this means more problems,' Eadulf observed in a woeful tone.

It was only a short time before one of the guards came looking for them.

'The King is asking for you in his private chamber, lady,' the man announced. 'He has Gormán with him. He also asks for Eadulf and Enda to attend.'

Colgú and Gormán were together in the King's private chamber as Fidelma led Eadulf and Enda in. From the expression on their faces it was clear that they were discussing the problem. Her brother was sprawled in his chair by the central fire while Gormán had risen from a nearby seat.

'Is it news of the pestilence?' Fidelma asked immediately.

'The rest of the princes, our cousins, are beginning to arrive.

We must start making decisions,' Colgú interrupted in a frustrated tone. 'The council must be held tomorrow morning.'

'There are still lots of things that do not make sense,' Gormán responded to Fidelma.

'Let us deal with first things first,' Colgú admonished. He turned to Fidelma. 'Are you close to an answer about the death of Brother Conchobhar or any of these problems?'

'I have suspicions,' Fidelma replied reluctantly, 'but nothing that would allow Brehon Fíthel to make an immediate decision in law. However, I hope that will be rectified before morning.'

'Time is not on your side.' Her brother's tone was terse.

'Such matters as these are not dictated by time,' she replied defensively.

'In this case, I think they must be,' Colgú said. 'Tomorrow at noon the council of princes will meet in the great hall. Even if Selbach does not attend, I am told that Brehon Fíthel will allow Selbach's *rodamna*, his heir apparent, to speak for him and the Eóganacht Ráithlinn.'

Fidelma sank into a chair opposite her brother and sighed. 'There is some conspiracy here and if a majority are determined to overturn you there is little to be done.'

'What can you present?' demanded her brother.

'That Selbach was making an attempt to discredit you and persuade the other princes to do so.'

'It is his right to criticise my decisions unless you can show he is doing so as some sort of plot outside the council,' her brother said moodily.

'There is another point,' said Gormán, almost apologetically.

Colgú invited him to continue.

'As you know, when we heard news of the plague ship and then received the cautionary warnings from Prince Cummasach of the Déisi that he was trying to contain it but closing his borders, Colgú placed me in command of scouts to watch things from our side of the River Siúr, mainly to listen for news of the pestilence spreading.'

Fidelma made an impatient gesture. 'And so?'

'You already know the curiosities that occurred when we were chasing Selbach after he fled from Cashel?' Gormán asked.

'I now have an explanation as to why he did so. He came here by a coastal vessel and anchored it at Dairinis on the Déisi side of the Great River,' Fidelma explained. 'He was making his way back to where his vessel was.'

For a second Gormán looked disconcerted. 'So you knew why Selbach was not putting himself in harm's way by crossing into Déisi territory?'

'I realised why he was not afraid of the plague. Because Selbach knew there was no plague.'

There was a silence. Colgú and Gormán exchanged glances of astonishment.

'You knew there was no pestilence?' Colgú gasped.

'I suspected. The stories of the pestilence were only meant to distract us and allow Prince Cummasach to gather his Déisi warriors in camps to make them ready to march against Cashel. The idea was to do this once the council has declared against my brother. I think they will also be joined by some of the southern territorial rulers, the Uí Liatháin and Uí Echach, who will join with warriors of the Ráithlinn.'

'Then you have proof? You can present it to the council?' asked Gormán.

'But at the moment there is no evidence, and Chief Brehon Fíthel always demands evidence,' Colgú pointed out. 'And what can we say? Some merchants managed to evade the Déisi warriors patrolling the southern banks of the Siúr and made their way across the river at Árd Fhionáin. They reported that behind the hills, just across the river, they saw camps. They reported it as a *marcshluagh*, a cavalry battalion training. That I found significant. If the Déisi are joined by others—'

Fidelma was interested and turned to Gormán, interrupting her brother. 'You found cavalry significant?'

Gormán thought: 'Indeed, lady. Cavalry could move fast and be here and deployed in less than a *cadar*.'

A *cadar* was a quarter of a day. Colgú was clearly worried. 'Our scouts were seeing training campfires and not villages or places burning. Gormán was suggesting that I ought to raise warriors against the Déisi but this might be seen as an action to prevent the council meeting.'

'I don't think Prince Cummasach will order his men to

move on Cashel until the decision of the council is known,'
Fidelma suggested.

'That is a logical strategy,' Gormán agreed. 'But you say
only one prince behind this plot is identified?'

'Selbach,' Fidelma repeated.

'Gormán's scouts report that a number of travelling enter-
tainers coming from Eochaill to take part in Beltaine came up
the Great River to Lios Mór. Some have crossed through
Muscraige Breogain territory and so avoided the Déisi territory. They had disturbing news.'

'Which was?' Fidelma's tone showed her exasperation at
her brother's dramatic pauses, although she realised that it was
also a habit that she had acquired, especially when making a
case before a judge.

It was Gormán who continued. 'At Eochaill they noticed
seven *laech-lestar*, seven war vessels, sailing for Dairinis.
Others went on to Árd Mór. They were filled with warriors.'

Fidelma's face was grim. 'Selbach's warriors, I presume?'

Eadulf now spoke. 'I know that Prince Cummasach controls
a large territory but I did not think even Cummasach could
deploy his warriors with any hope of success unless he was
supported by some of the seven major princes of the Eóganacht.
Selbach has to have more conspirators in this plot.'

Fidelma looked at Gormán. 'Are there any reports of military
movements from other territories?'

'There are reports,' Gormán admitted. 'Consolidations rather
than advances.'

'Then in spite of Selbach's pre-empting the plan, whoever
is the main instigator wants the overthrow of my brother to
seem legal,' said Fidelma. 'Only once the princes turn against
Colgú will the Déisi march on Cashel under the pretext of
protecting the decision of the council. It will be seen as an
entirely legal matter rather than a *coup d'état*. If the Déisi
march on Cashel and the princes know they are being manipu-
lated – for, I am sure, the majority are – then war will result.'

'I am not sure I follow.' Her brother was bewildered.

'I find it difficult to think that any of the Eógancht princes
would raise their standards in support of the Déisi,' Enda
commented. 'Anyway,' he smiled, 'this will be the seventh

time Colgú has been acclaimed by the council, and at Beltaine, so I cannot see why the princes will turn on him now.'

'I am not acclaimed yet,' Colgú pointed out despondently. 'You point out that this will be the seventh Beltaine Feast since I was accepted as King, but seven is a bad number in our culture. Were we not told by the ancients that Mide was the great Druid of the Nemedian invaders, who came forward to ignite the very first fire of Beltaine on the great hill of Uisneach? Remember he prophesied it would last seven years before it went out. Therefore each Beltaine fire is extinguished after the seventh year.'

'Who told you that story?' Fidelma asked in a faintly slighting tone.

'I thought it well known, but Congal of Loch Léin reminded me of the story only the other night at dinner. Don't you see the relevance?'

'I see the symbolism but not the relevance,' she said dryly. 'If you see it as symbolism, then it is time that this symbolism is put an end to.' She rose as if a thought suddenly occurred to her. 'Enda, I want the use of a stepladder again. I am afraid I need another look at that sword, brother.'

They made their way into the great hall where the two guards stood near the tapestry with the sword still hanging from its scabbard.

'I told you that the sword is genuine. I have seen it before,' Colgú complained.

Enda entered after them, bearing a ladder across his shoulder.

'I know we have done this before, brother, but I want you to examine that sword one more time.'

Under her direction, the King's carved oak chair of office was pushed out of the way and Enda placed the ladder against the tapestry covering the wall.

'You want me to unhook the sword again and bring it down?' Enda asked nervously. After all, it was the legendary *Frecraid*, The Answerer, the sword of the gods.

'That is precisely what I want,' Fidelma replied solemnly.

He hesitated, then ascended the ladder and unhooked the scabbard in which the sword hung from its strap on a hook so that it dangled over the large banner. Then he carefully descended, turning to hold it out to her. She motioned to her brother.

'Take it and remove it from the scabbard,' she instructed him as, according to the ritual, no one else should draw the sword and she did not want to provoke his anxiety.

Enda carefully handed it hilt first to Colgú, who moved to the small table usually used by the librarian to record the council meetings, which was placed under a window so that it provided the user with some light. He laid the sword on the table.

'Examine it carefully and tell me again whether this is the sword you know as The Answerer. Tell me if it has been changed in any way.'

Colgú peered at it carefully. 'It is the same. This is the sacred sword as I know it.'

'What about the word inscribed there below the guard and down the blade?' she pressed.

'You know the old writing as well as I do. It is just the name of the sword, *Frecraid,* The Answerer.'

'Just *Frecraid*? Nothing else?'

'No.'

'Yet what of the difference between the emerald on one end and the ruby on the other? At the ceremony, the emerald must face towards the rising sun. Towards the east. Why?' Fidelma asked.

'Because the emerald, the *cloch uaine*, is symbolic of royalty and truth and of Beltaine. That is why the sword is used at Beltaine.'

Fidelma peered closely to check and sighed. 'Very well. It can be hung back,' she said to Enda.

It was the work of moments to do so and then Enda took the ladder to carry it outside.

'Well?' asked her brother in a puzzled tone. 'Did you learn anything from that?'

Fidelma paused for a moment before replying. 'I think things are very clear now. Make sure your guards remain watchful, especially now.'

Colgú clearly had to suppress his exasperation. He was about to protest when there came the sound of trumpets from the fortress gates.

'The remaining princes are now arriving,' he muttered unhappily. 'What do you want Gormán to do?'

'Gormán will be aware that the challenge to you will be made in council. But I hope to present the person plotting with Selbach before the council meeting. Gormán must be made aware of the decision at the earliest moment,' Fidelma advised. 'He should be able to march on the Déisi outpost by dawn.'

Colgú looked askance. 'By dawn? But the council doesn't even meet until noon time.'

'I believe the matter will be resolved tonight,' she declared firmly.

Her brother was surprised. 'You mean that you suddenly know who is responsible for all these deaths and whispers of plots?'

Fidelma ignored the question but instead turned to Gormán.

'How many men can you raise tonight?'

'Two *catha* – two battalions. It depends how Prince Cummasach plans this attack.'

'If he is cautious, he will come by way of Árd Fhionáin. If things go well it may be that he won't proceed beyond the river. I should not think that Selbach and those warriors who arrived by ship will move without Cummasach's main force. Selbach's men will probably bivouac by Cluain Meala.'

Colgú and Gormán stared at each other for a moment, perplexed. Fidelma did not enlighten them.

Later that evening, when Eadulf emerged from his *debach*, his evening bath, he found Fidelma seated at a small table with a quill and scraps of papyrus on which she had apparently been drawing designs. They were like crosses, so far as he could see.

'Making patterns?' he asked in surprise.

'Just working out a puzzle,' she replied, hurriedly rising and putting the materials away in her side cupboard.

'Did you solve it?'

She turned with a broad smile. 'Oh, yes; now I know the answer. But hurry and dress for we soon have to meet with Enda. Now we can resolve the entire business.'

*   *   *

It was midnight when Fidelma and Eadulf made their way, at her instruction, to the apothecary. She had told Enda to meet them there and they found the warrior waiting anxiously for them.

'Has there been any movement?' she asked at once, seeing he was agitated.

'It's that young librarian, Brother Dáire,' Enda replied in a low voice. 'I saw him enter the chapel a short time ago. He hasn't come out.'

Fidelma exhaled in annoyance. 'I thought that young man was too clever for his own good.'

'I don't understand,' replied the warrior.

'He overheard what Brother Laig was saying in the library. I think he made the same logical conclusion that I did.'

'I don't follow,' Eadulf frowned, unsure what Fidelma was referring to.

'Fidach was standing behind the altar when he argued with this woman Ernmas. He was pointing down to something behind it. I think he had found that Ernmas had hidden the sacred artefacts stolen from Brother Conchobhar underneath the altar. That is what we came to retrieve tonight.'

'You did not tell me that,' Eadulf protested.

'It was logical. Brother Dáire realised, as I did, that the stolen ritual items were hidden under the altar in the chapel until the moment the council met. Let us hope he has not alerted this woman Ernmas too soon.'

'So, you are certain that she is the killer?'

'Not just the killer but an integral part of the conspiracy.'

'How is that?' gasped Eadulf. 'You know who she is?'

'Enough! There is no time to lose now.'

The chapel was in darkness as they entered and started to cross towards the altar. Then a flickering light appeared as the far door opened. This led to the religious sleeping quarters. Whoever opened it held a glimmering light. Then a woman screamed. Fidelma and her companions immediately went through the door. In the corridor beyond was one of the elderly religieuse lying prone in the corridor. There was still a flickering lantern on the floor by her side, which Eadulf picked up and held high. He raised the lamp and saw there did not seem to be any blood over her robes. Further down the corridor a second religieuse was hysterical. She was pointing along the passage to where the young librarian, Brother Dáire, was slumped in a corner, sitting on the floor holding his hands to his head. He was covered in blood.

'What happened, Brother Dáire?' Fidelma said, bending down to him. The young man had several cuts oozing blood.

'Was it Ernmas?'

'Ernmas,' the librarian muttered painfully. 'She has the strength of a man. It was only the appearance of the two women who distracted her when she attacked me, otherwise I think she would have killed me. Then you arrived. She was carrying the sword.'

'Where is she now?'

'She fled. There is a connecting door to the guest quarters at the far end of this corridor.'

'I know it,' Fidelma confirmed. 'Are you sure she was carrying the sword from behind the altar?'

'I tried to stop her carrying away some of the other items,' Brother Dáire said. 'Several are still there behind the altar. But she has the sword wrapped in sackcloth.'

Fidelma's mouth formed a thin firm line. She turned to the uninjured religieuse.

'Look after him and your companion.' Then she motioned Eadulf and Enda to follow her.

The passage turned at right angles and at the end of one corridor she found the doorway that gave entrance into the main guest quarters. She halted before a door.

'I think this is the one,' she whispered.

However, at that moment there came a faint cry and the sound of running feet came from further along the passage, which ended in a short staircase to the doors that gave entrance to the storerooms.

'Where is she making for?' Eadulf asked breathlessly.

'Hopefully, directly to the person who leads this conspiracy,' Fidelma replied shortly as she continued on. The door into the storage area was still swinging, not being secured. 'This should be the door to the upper storerooms and the entrance to the south-eastern tower; the tower and the battlement where Blinne fell to her death.'

As they emerged, a tall figure in black blocked their path. There was a flash of light glinting on a long-bladed knife in an upraised hand.

Enda pushed forward, his sword already in his hand. There was a scream and the figure fell back as the blade cut across her wrist, causing her knife to fall and bounce on the flagstone floor.

'Give up, Ernmas,' Fidelma commanded coldly. 'There is nowhere else to run to.'

The woman had backed to the edge of the battlements. She stood like an animal at bay, seeking desperately for an avenue of escape. There was none.

'Stay back!' she hissed. 'I know the secret of the sword and now it is too late. You will never have it.'

'It is neither mine nor yours to have, Ernmas,' Fidelma assured her coldly.

'The sword will ensure that my son will rule. I will have my vengeance. My unworthy son is dead but now my true son will ascend to power.'

'I doubt it. The sword has no miracle powers.'

'It has the powers of the Gatekeeper to the House of Death – it will unleash the legions of the Otherworld to destroy false princes. My son is the only righteous prince.'

'The only power the sword has is to turn people's minds to acts of folly.'

'Then learn the power of the symbols and its prophecy.'

'You have nowhere to go, Ernmas. It is you who will answer for the deaths you have caused. Surrender and come with us.'

As they had been speaking, Enda had been slowly moving to the woman's right side while Eadulf had edged towards her left.

'The Gatekeeper to the House of Death approaches!' Her hysterical voice echoed into the night. 'Vengeance is mine. I go to the House of Death so that I may herald my son taking his rightful place. That is the promise of the sacred symbols. That is the promise of the sacred sword!'

The outcome seemed inevitable. It came abruptly. The tall woman threw herself sharply back with one shrill scream as she disappeared into the blackness of the space beyond.

For a moment or two Fidelma and her companions stood staring downwards into the darkness, knowing there was but one outcome as the figure bounced like a rag doll down on to the jagged limestone rocks below.

Fidelma was the first to recover. 'As she was responsible for the death of Blinne, I suppose we could say it was a just end,' she said dryly. 'She has met her Gatekeeper to the House of Death in the same manner as her victim.'

At that moment Luan and some warriors came up through the tower stairs and onto the walkway. They visibly relaxed as they saw Fidelma and her companions.

'Someone fell?' Luan asked, questioning the obvious.

'You will find the body of the woman called Ernmas below,' replied Fidelma. 'Have your men remove her.'

'Sister Ernmas?' Luan gasped. 'That's the woman that everyone has been looking for.'

'Be respectful, for she had been the wife of a prince and the mother of another prince,' Fidelma explained. 'But she was no more a religieuse than you are. Anyway, keep this matter to yourself until I tell you to reveal it. There are a few matters to be finished first.'

Eadulf was shaking his head. 'I am totally confused. I thought the motivation behind all this was a conspiracy to topple your brother from power? Who was she? Where are the things she was said to have stolen? I presume they were hidden behind the altar in the chapel ever since she removed them from Brother Conchobhar's keeping?'

Enda seemed also confused. 'I don't understand who she was. What did she want with the Eóganacht relics? Was she insane?'

Fidelma's expression was grim. 'It is easy to say that she was a deluded creature. Now we should go and meet her son; the person for whom she killed and who she was going to make King. The real leader of the conspiracy against my brother.'

TWENTY

F idelma turned and led the way back across the storeroom and down the few steps into the corridor which led into the guest quarters. She paused before the same door where she had initially halted before Ernmas betrayed her position by moving into the storeroom and up to the main walkway around the walls.

'Be ready,' she whispered to Enda, before bending to quietly turn the handle and, with a swift motion, throwing the door open.

In the chamber, directly facing them, Elódach, Prince of Áine, was seated in a chair, holding a sword across his lap. It was as if he were fondling the weapon. Elódach gazed up at them with an almost peaceful look on his face. Only Fidelma's watchful expression did not change, while Eadulf and Enda's features mirrored their shock and then puzzlement.

'Your mother is dead, Elódach.' Fidelma began without emotion. 'She fell to her death from the same wall where she pushed your mistress, Blinne, to her death.'

Elódach sighed dreamily. 'It's a good way to start one's journey to the Otherworld, for this is the gateway to it.'

'You glorify in the death of your own mother?' Fidelma tried to keep her voice level.

'My mother was aptly named Vengeance,' Elódach replied almost conversationally. 'She was powerful in the Old Faith and was known as a *celamine*, one who knew the prophecies. I was the chosen one of the gods. My brother made a mistake by laying a *geis* on me after the battle of Áine. When I raise this sword of Nuada and rule Muman, her vengeance will be complete.'

Eadulf was shaking his head as he tried to follow the events. 'Ernmas was . . .?'

'Was named Aincride – it means vengeance,' Fidelma reminded him. 'You remember that we were told by Conrí that she was a believer in the Old Faith? She was a *taiscélaid*,

an observer of omens. That is why she came here as "Ernmas",
which means "death by the sword".'

'But how . . .?' Eadulf was trying to follow.

'When Elódach came into the fortress for the council she
came disguised in male clothing as his attendant, Máen,'
Fidelma continued. 'Do you remember that I was puzzled that
we never saw Máen outside of the guest quarters? In fact we
did so but in the person of Ernmas. That was a name from
the Old Faith that she appropriately adopted. As you saw, she
was tall and strong and, once appropriately clad, she could
pass as a male. That is how she passed into the fortress – as
an attendant to her son.'

'She served the gods well.' Elódach nodded approvingly.
'She was a prophetess and servant of Badh, and she realised
my destiny.'

Enda shivered and cast a worried glance at Eadulf. 'Badh,
the female battle demon, inciting warriors to conflict, and
celebrating by dancing on their bloody corpses.'

'Well, it is over now, Elódach,' Fidelma told him coldly.
'Your nightmare has passed.'

The prince chuckled with cold humour. 'Nightmare? It is
the turn of those who have mocked me to begin their night-
mares. Those who led us into battle at Cnoc Áine against the
Uí Fidgente will be punished for betraying the dead and dying
on Áine's Hill. Your brother has made a treaty with the Uí
Fidgente; with those who killed my father in that battle. Your
brother Colgú led us into that battle and then betrayed us by
giving the Uí Fidgente everything they wanted. Others he
betrayed by not seeking retribution for the plotting of Osraige;
of Laigin, and he has even laughed at our dead by his intention to marry a woman of Osraige. Now is the time to call
him to account. He is no longer leader of the Eóganacht princes.
Tomorrow will see him overthrown.'

'So you will claim the kingship?' Fidelma said coldly. 'What
part was Selbach expected to play?'

'I shall appoint him as my *rodamna* – my chief noble and
heir apparent . . . so long as he serves me well. Outside these
walls, the warriors of Cummasach and Selbach stand awaiting
my call. When the council condemns Colgú and his bodyguard

cower in fear behind these walls, those who have not joined
me will be destroyed.'

'And the stories of the pestilence were just a cover for
Cummasach and his warriors to gather ready to attack? We
already realised that the return of the pestilence was a false
story designed to keep us in panic and terror of its spreading,'
Fidelma told him. 'I presume that it was an idea put forward
by your mother?'

'She was inspired by the gods and goddesses to call down
the curse of the plague so that people would walk in fear and
trembling. The memories of the great pestilence would be
enough to cause trepidation at the very thought of its return.'

'And what was Prince Cummasach's reward for his role?
He is a Déisi paying tribute to the Eóganacht. What of him?'

'He would no longer pay tribute to Cashel but be recognised
as one of the senior princes,' the Prince of the Áine replied.
'Every person has his own price.'

'What will their reaction be to someone so without honour
that they shoot a woman in the back?'

Elódach seemed surprised for a moment. 'So you worked
out that it was I who shot at you? I was hoping the blame
would be laid on your Uí Fidgente friend . . . Conrí?'

'I remembered that we were told you commanded an élite
company of archers at the battle of Áine. Also the escape of
Selbach needed an expert archer.'

'It was a difficult shot.' Elódach seemed side-tracked by an
appreciation of his own skill. 'To fire the arrow into the wood
of the window frame so that Selbach could pull the attached
string up with the heavy rope was not easy.'

'I thought it needed a good marksman to bring that arrow
and string into the room so that Selbach could use it to haul
up the rope, secure it, and use it to escape. You went to a lot
of trouble, as did your mother, but do you really think that
you can succeed in persuading the princes to help you overthrow my brother?'

'Of course,' Elódach replied confidently. 'My mother's
prophecy was clear. That is why my mother found the secret
chambers and took the sacred artefacts ready for the council.
It was an inspired idea to hide them under the altar of this

new god. I will use them to make my argument to the princes and they will accept me as the new King.'

'Do you really think so? Why would they accept you?'

'Because I hold the sacred sword. Even those of the New Faith will know that, with it in my hand, I was ordained by the god Nuada, son of The Dagda, to lead the Eóganacht. So the prophecy has been written. This is the seventh of Colgú's Beltaine fires, when it is foretold that his rule will be extinguished. So it is written, so it will be fulfilled.'

'And if he is not overthrown by superstitions?' countered Fidelma.

'I have the sacred sword of Nuada. When the princes of the Eóganacht see this – that Colgú of Cashel cannot even keep the sacred sword safe – they will realise that the gods are not on his side and will turn from him.'

'Do you think they all live in excessive fear of the ancient gods? We no longer live in ignorance but are a rational people.'

Once again Elódach chuckled in genuine humour.

'You have merely exchanged one belief for a new superstition. Why do you think Brother Conchobhar, who claimed to be of the New Faith, fought so hard to protect these sacred artefacts? He knew that thousands of years of a belief in the god cannot be wiped out in a few decades.'

'I presume your mother killed Brother Conchobhar?'

'By striking him with the pommel of this very sword,' Elódach admitted. 'She told me that when the old man turned she brought down the pommel on his head and destroyed the skull of the cynic who claimed to be its keeper. This white quartz stone is the very symbol of the gods. That is poetic retribution: to be killed by what you claim to worship. I hold the sword now. I hold the sacred sword of Nuada. All have to obey me for I am Gatekeeper to the House of Death through which I will compel all who do not obey me.'

Fidelma could see the religious fanaticism burning in the eyes of the man. She gave an inward shiver. Truly, she thought his was the most dangerous form of insanity, for reason and logic no longer existed in his eyes. What made her afraid was the realisation that fanaticism always concealed doubts, and thus doubts had to be destroyed. She had kept him talking for as long as she could in order to wait for the moment when his guard dropped. But his eyes, like the unblinking gaze of a serpent, were watching their every move in spite of the relaxed appearance of his body. Elódach's calm mood was dangerous.

'Tell me one thing,' Fidelma continued, still trying to sound conversational. 'Your mother was considered a scholar, whatever her beliefs or reasons. Did she tell you what made her research so diligently in the library here?'

'She discovered there was a second sword. If the other princes knew then they might demand proof that this was the true sword of Nuada. She wanted to make sure she held the true sword.'

'So she knew a replica existed?'

'She realised that old Conchobhar had hung the replica in the great hall as a distraction. I can expose this with the real one, which I hold.'

'She realised the meaning of the Beltaine ritual?' Fidelma asked. 'The part anciently written where it says that the true sword must be used and not its reflection?'

'Even that stupid priest Fidach found out that there was a replica.'

'But that was not the reason he was killed?'

'He found the relics hidden under the chapel altar before we were ready to present them to the council. I helped my mother get rid of him in the bell tower.' The Prince of Áine was indifferent.

'But your mother did know about the replica?' pressed Fidelma.

'Yes, she knew it. She was not misled.'

'She realised the meaning of the lines in the work of Seanchán Torpéist?'

'She heard from that fatuous woman Moncha that you were asking about that. Yes, my mother knew the clue.'

'That "brother" and "sister" are not the same? That the reflection of the true sword meant that a copy of the sword had been made to mislead people even so far back in the time before time?'

'That is why, when she took the sword, she killed Brother Conchobhar.' The Prince of Áine smiled grimly. 'Perhaps there was a symbolism in the fact that she used the round pommel of that weapon to smash down on the old man's head. She even thought to mislead you by placing a rock by his head when she removed the sword.' The amusement in his voice did not waver. 'She had an idea that if your Saxon companion saw the wound he might guess that the round pommel would be the weapon that had been stolen.'

'Except I was not here to examine the body and the wound,' muttered Eadulf. 'And, by the way, I am an Angle, not a Saxon.'

It seemed that Elódach was locked in his own thoughts and ignored him.

'It was her ultimate jest to hide the sword and the other ritual items beneath the altar of the New Faith. She was bringing me the sword in readiness for tomorrow when that reckless young librarian tried to stop her. So you chased her to her death. But she had already given me the sword . . . And now the sword is in my hand and you must atone for her death.'

Fidelma seemed to take everything he said unmoved. Eadulf and Enda stood nervously glancing at her, wondering what she intended.

'Well, *a* sword is truly in your hands,' she said softly but with emphasis. 'Remember that a brother and sister are not the same.'

An uncertain look entered into the eyes of Elódach. His hand gripped the hilt of the sword more tightly.

'Your point is?'

'*Frecraid*, The Answerer,' she went on thoughtfully. 'To answer can be interpreted in many ways. You can answer in combat; you can answer an attack by retaliation. You would, of course, find that sort of answer in a masculine endeavour. Did your mother ever mention the words in one of Líadan's poems?'

'Not that I recall. Anyway, Nuada was a warrior god. If honour was impugned, it must be answered. He led the gods in battle with this sword from which none could escape.'

'Yet he lost his right arm in the great battle against the Firbolg and the god of healing, Dian Cécht, had to make him an arm and hand of silver. Had he picked up the wrong sword?'

'So he answered in battle and so shall his sword answer for me.'

'Yet there is another method of answering,' she said quickly. 'That is to respond with logic and reason.'

'That is a female attribute,' Elódach sneered.

'Indeed, brother and sister are not the same,' Fidelma agreed cheerfully. 'Did your mother tell you how brother and sister might be recognised?'

The prince did not seem concerned.

'You seek to distract me while that warrior,' he indicated Enda, 'attempts to disarm me. It will not work because I know this is *Frecraid*.'

'But something else is necessary to recognise it.'

The Prince of Áine frowned uncertainly. 'If you are talking about the green emerald and the red ruby being on opposite sides of the sword guard, it does not signify as, however you hold the sword, either in left hand or right, it is still the same.'

'But brother and sister are not the same,' went on Fidelma. 'You might have the replica and not the sacred sword of Nuada. There is a difference. Look closely. Is it brother or sister?'

In spite of himself Elódach glanced down at the hilt. His face went pale. Before Enda could take advantage, he gave a cry of a cornered beast and rose in his chair. In a moment the hilt of the sword was firmly in his hand and he raised the sword aloft to strike at Fidelma.

Enda pushed her out the way; crouching low, he made an upward swift thrust with his own blade. At that angle it entered the man's chest under the ribcage. Elódach, Prince of Áine, was dead even before he fell back into his chair.

Fidelma moved forward and picked up his fallen sword.

'I'll take care of that,' she said crisply.

Enda was looking nervous. 'I have killed an Eóganacht prince,' he muttered, staring down at the body.

'No blame on you,' she replied. 'It was in defence of my life.'

'What did he see that made him believe he held the replica and not the true sword?' Eadulf asked, staring at the weapon. He could see no difference between it and what he remembered of the sword hanging in the great hall.

'It was male vanity,' Fidelma replied softly.

'But your brother claims the one in the great hall is the authentic sword.'

'Doubtless it was, for him. Brother and sister are not the same,' Fidelma reflected. 'It was the line of poetry that gave the clue after the reference to the fact there was a copy of this sword.'

'The words of the ritual as to how the sword should be held – the emerald to the east?'

'Not just that. Think.'

'Nuada was a warrior god, so then The Answerer would surely be male for it is masculine to defend a people by battle,' Eadulf declared with a frown.

Fidelma did not respond for a moment. She turned to Enda. 'Inform my brother of these events and tell him I will explain in the morning, before the council. Then I shall leave you and Luan to take the bodies to the apothecary. But the important task is to send a message to Gormán. He is to move on Árd Fhionáin at first light to meet Prince Cummasach of the Déisi. He can inform Cummasach and Selbach that the Prince of Áine is dead.'

She bent to the body of Elódach, removed his chain of office and gave it to Enda.

'Gormán is to show this to Prince Cummasach as proof that there will be no *coup d'état* tomorrow. The great sword of Nuada still hangs in its rightful place, ready for the Beltaine ritual.'

It was not until Fidelma and Eadulf were in their chamber that Eadulf, staring thoughtfully at the sword, admitted he was still puzzled.

'I just do not understand why Ernmas or Aincride – whatever her name was – and her son believed that this was the genuine sword of Nuada.'

Fidelma smiled sadly. 'It is a matter of interpretation. Each had their own ideas of what The Answerer was.'

'I still don't understand,' Eadulf replied with a shake of his head. 'I remember all the references to brother and sister but I did not really make sense of it until you asked Elódach to examine the sword. His reaction when he saw the sword was like a sword stroke itself. So I presume he had the wrong sword. As you warned Elódach, there are differences between the way a male and a female will answer a threat. As Nuada was a warrior god, when he presented a sword called The Answerer as a sign of sovereignty to a kingly dynasty, to defend their rights, then challenges could only be answered one way.'

Fidelma smiled sadly. 'You are typical of your sex, Eadulf, which I concede is natural as you are a prisoner of it.'

'I don't understand.' Eadulf felt he was being insulted.

'I think our world is sadly turning towards the male concepts, especially those brought in by the New Religion, which are no more than those ideas and philosophies of the old empire of Rome. Our world seems to be becoming a place where male ideology is increasingly dominant. That is a retrogressive step.'

'But Elódach was full of superstition and the old religion.'

'Elódach was also a prisoner of his male sex and attitudes, whatever religion he held. Swords and warriors must both be male. Yet think of the traditions of my people. We claim descent from a mother goddess, Danu. Then we have traditions of sovereign goddesses . . . *goddesses*, not gods. And we agree that the triune goddesses of this land were Éire, Banbha and Fodhla. According to the bards, our people are only safe in this land so long as we call it after one or all of these goddesses. It was said that this island would be given to our people in perpetuity so long as we recognised them.'

'I am even more confused,' Eadulf said, frowning helplessly.

'I wonder if Ernmas herself was confused,' Fidelma suddenly said. 'I would not have thought so, for the triune goddesses of war, the Morrígna – Badb, Macha, the Morrígán herself, were all the daughters of the goddess Ernmas.'

Eadulf was perplexed.

'As I said, it is not what the symbol is, but what people believe it is a symbol of.' Fidelma gave a sigh. 'The symbolism of passing sovereignty is a female attribute because a woman gives birth to the subsequent generation. We all have our traditions and our symbols.'

'Are you saying that not all symbols mean the same thing?'

'Some people follow the raven, others the dove. I have often said that symbols are only what we make of them. They are meaningless until we give them meaning. Just cast your mind over the number of symbols, of objects said to have been brought and given to us by the gods and goddesses from the Otherworld.'

'You mean like that old cauldron that they kept in that village of Cloichín?' Eadulf remembered the recent case, when they rescued the itinerant Celgaire from being hanged by a superstitious priest.

Fidelma made an affirmative gesture. 'It was supposed to be the cauldron of life brought by the gods from their Otherworld city of Murias. It was no more the *Coire ansic* – the magic cauldron of The Dagda – than the cauldron in which Dar Luga prepares soup. And how many sacred stones for the inauguration of kings have you seen? Which is the true Lia Fail, supposedly brought from the Otherworld city of Falias? Which of the many *Gae Assail* is the true magical spear from Findias or, indeed, which is the *Claideb Solair,* the sword of light, from Gorias? All are just symbols and not reality.'

'But, as you say, it is what people think that they are that is important,' said Eadulf, finally seeing what point she was making.

'That is sadly true. Look at the amazing amount of items associated with the New Faith, which the Empress Helen of Byzantine gathered. Do you remember the Venerable Gelasis, whom we met in Rome? He showed us that the New Faith began as a secret society. Symbols had to be used to identify members. But there were many diverse types of symbols, confusing the followers of this faith.'

'But we all use the crucifix,' frowned Eadulf. 'The symbol of the cross.'

'The first symbol of the New Faith was the outline of a fish – the Ichthys as the Greeks called it. There were many other symbols. Some still use the Tau Rho while others the Chi Rho. Symbols are the concept of man, not of gods or goddesses.'

'Well, if the mother of Elódach was so knowledgeable about

the Old Faith she should have known the sacred sword by the feel of it. If it was supposed to be an instrument wrought in the Otherworld, I would have thought there would be something special about it. The legends say that kings and princes have given their lives and souls for it.'

'Things are not always as they seem,' Fidelma replied softly with a shake of her head.

Eadulf frowned, wondering if she was implying something more. 'There's no chance that the sword in the great hall is . . .?' he began, then paused and glanced at the sword she had taken from Elódach. 'If that was made by the god-smith of the Otherworld, then there should be something extra special about it.'

Fidelma pursed her lips reprovingly. 'Wasn't it Juvenal who said, "*fronti nulla fides*"?'

'I know, I know,' Eadulf sighed. '"No reliance can be placed on appearance". But that strange woman was willing to give her life for it . . .'

'But worse, other people's lives. Poor Brother Conchobhar, for one.'

'There is one thing that bothers me,' Eadulf insisted.

'Only one thing?' Fidelma queried with a smile.

'What made Elódach, in that last moment, believe that the sword, no matter which one and whoever made it, was the replica and not the genuine sword passed down through the generations from the time of Eógan Mór?'

'It was a matter of considering the male mind and the ritual instruction of Báetán of Loch Goir, which also occurs in the poem of Líadan. The sword he held had the hands palms outwards towards the attacker. It did not have the fists clenched in aggression. Elódach realised he held the female sword.'

L'ENVOI

The early summer sun was not even above the eastern mountains when Fidelma made her way to the stables. She had left Eadulf asleep as there had been no disturbing him after the late night's adventure. The fortress was mainly asleep also, although there were sounds of a few early risers. Even the household guards were barely awake. She crossed to the stables, carrying an object wrapped in sacking. An alert stable lad roused himself to wait attendance on her and harnessed Aonbhárr, her favourite Gaulish pony. Before mounting, she instructed the lad to get someone to tell Eadulf, if he awoke and was concerned, that she had only gone for a morning ride, as was her custom.

She gave Aonbhárr a slack rein and let the animal make its own way down into the township, which was also bathed in silence, since Gormán and his warriors had departed southwards. She made her way through the silent square, passing Rumann's tavern and stables in total darkness. She rode along the main street and turned up the cow road beyond Della's smallholding. She soon found the way to the forge of Gobán, if by no other means than the sound of the crackling wood fire of the forge.

'You are abroad early, lady,' greeted the smith as Fidelma rode up to the forge and dismounted.

'You must have been up extremely early, to have heated your fire to that temperature,' she replied, as she tied the reins to a rail.

The smith grinned appreciatively. 'Not up early but rather not yet to bed. There are some heavy metals that I needed to smelt by this morning. That has forced me to have the fire going through the night. Also, there was something in the air that told me my forge would be called upon to do a service.'

'It is an important service,' she confirmed.

'Something in the wind indicates it,' agreed the smith. 'But tell me, for that is your privilege.'

Fidelma took the object from the sackcloth that had been attached to her saddle bow and drew from it the sword, handing it to the smith.

'How long would you say that it will take to melt down?'

Gobán took the blade and hilt gingerly from her hands and turned it over in his, examining it carefully.

'An ancient work,' he muttered. 'It seems of an age beyond the ages.'

'Don't worry . . .' she said, watching the expression on his features. 'The brother of this blade hangs in the great hall where the council is meeting shortly.'

'The brother or the sister?' queried the smith with a smile.

'There should be only one Answerer for a King to defend his honour,' she observed with meaningful humour.

'So new generations are now told,' the smith agreed. 'But are we not also told to beware of the one that is *brionnach*?'

'It is a word that means both a dream as well as something false,' Fidelma pointed out.

'And is this the dream?'

'This is the dream, and has been a dream in this age, at least.'

'One has to beware, lady,' the smith observed gravely. 'Many people think they are delivering a dream while they offer only a nightmare.'

'You are so right, my friend. It is often hard to tell the difference between the dream and the nightmare. So often we see things as we want them to be.'

'And you think people have been seeing this symbol as they want it to be and not what it really is?'

'People are often blinded by symbols; lost in the dream and not in the reality. I believe you understand me, my friend, just as you understand the philosophy of the ancients, which is now being lost to us.'

'That brother and sister are not the same?'

Fidelma smiled broadly. 'Does true protection reside in the person who can inflict the most aggression or who can receive it. That is both the dream and the nightmare.'

She returned to the fortress in time to join Eadulf at his breakfast, feeling satisfied with her decision.

It was a long hard day as the remaining princes questioned her, but even Furudrán came to support the decisions of Colgú, albeit reluctantly. That evening, they received details of what had happened after Gormán had left for the territory of the Déisi with two full *catha*, or battalions, of the army of the King of Cashel at his command. There had not even been a skirmish between Prince Cummasach and Gormán's forces. It appeared that Cummasach's decision to surrender had been made once he had been shown the chain of office of the Prince of Áine and the banners of the remaining five Eóganacht princes arrayed together. As soon as the news had been delivered to the Prince of the Déisi, he had agreed to the submission of his forces, a promise of tribute and a renewal of his allegiance to Colgú and his council. To express his good faith, he also agreed to hand over Selbach of Ráithlinn as a prisoner, to be tried by Chief Brehon Fíthel.

The next day was hot, and in other circumstances Fidelma and Eadulf would have preferred to have been out riding in the shaded woods, or sitting by some stream, content to bask in the sound of gushing waters and in the warmth of the early summer air. However, Enda had warned against such freedom until it was confirmed that Prince Cummasach had begun to fulfil the conditions of his submission. Once confirmed, Fidelma and Eadulf intended to ride for the Abbey of Imleach to escort their son, Alchú, and his nurse, Muirgen, back to Cashel and, they hoped, attend the few remaining days in enjoyment at the Beltaine fair and entertainments.

'I could never understand the thinking of Cummasach,' Eadulf said as he stretched idly in his chair, having heard the news concerning Prince Cummasach's capitulation. 'Why would Elódach need the backing of a Déisi army?'

'Elódach still had a suspicion that he couldn't entirely rely on his fellow princes, for all his vaunted belief in symbolism. What he hoped to have done to Colgú they could equally do to him. So Selbach and Cummasach would simply be his insurance.'

'I still cannot get used to your system of kingship,' Eadulf suddenly confessed. 'That everything a king does has to be approved by his – what do you call it – *ceithirfine*?'

'The fourth circle of kingship,' Fidelma agreed with a smile.
'The council of Eóganacht princes have endorsed the major
decisions. But, similarly, I find your system among the Angles
and the Saxons totally strange. Because the father is a king,
it is inevitable that his eldest son must become the king . . .
even though he may be weak in mind, body or otherwise
unworthy to take such office?'

'Yet Elódach was thought worthy of being nominated and
endorsed as Prince of Áine,' Eadulf pointed out cynically.

'But he would have eventually been removed by his peers
as soon as they realised the fault. It would have been done
without bloodshed. I think his mother, Aincride, carried a lot
of influence among the family. Had we captured him, he would
have lived but been sent into exile. Among the Angles and
Saxons, I am told that once a king is king, only his assassination can legally remove him.'

'So what happens to replace the role of the Princes of Áine
and of Ráithlinn? Will the heir apparent take over automatically in both cases?'

'The *derbhfine*, three generations of the family, will meet,
and now, without Aincride's evil influence, will discuss matters
and agree on new heads of their households.'

'So at least there might be arguments among the princes,
as we have recently witnessed in your council?' Eadulf smiled,
warming to his argument. 'I know that your brother has to be
of a certain bloodline, but then generations and relatives of
his family have to meet to approve of him by . . . what is it
. . . the *derbfine* in princely families but *indfine* when a kingly
office is selected?'

'The *indfine* is the generation that traces its lineage from a
great-great-great-great-grandfather. The *derbfine*, which is
from a great grandfather, selects the prince as being one who
is best able and talented to fulfil the task,' Fidelma reminded
him. 'This is our system; we have no primogeniture kingship.
The person who is the most suitable in the eyes of his family
becomes king.'

'Yet there are many who then disagree and seek to overthrow
him,' Eadulf pointed out.

'But have to do it before the wide family circle. The *indfine* council that met here have to publicly explain their reasons. Better that than the system in your land, which, as I recall, means a knife in the back, or murder of the first-born.'

Eadulf ignored her jibe. 'What is going to happen to Selbach? Exile?'

'There will be fines and compensation. He will stand before Brehon Fíthel and the council of his family. He has already lost his honour price and his principality. I suspect he has already lost any support from his lover, Esnad. He will probably be exiled to tend goats on a rocky western island.'

They heard footsteps hurrying along the corridor to their room and a moment later there was a rap on the door.

At Fidelma's call, Enda entered.

'It's too hot a day to be hurrying about,' Fidelma greeted him. 'Sit down and take a drink with us.'

Eadulf rose to pour some cider and motioned the tall warrior to a seat. Enda sank into the chair and took a sip of the cold drink.

'I wanted to tell you that Brehon Fíthel has to go to Árd Fhionáin to oversee the legalities of the submission of Prince Cummasach and the new tributes due to King Colgú.' Enda paused and added meaningfully: 'That should have been your role, lady. Without you—'

Fidelma interrupted with a gesture of her hand. 'I am not Chief Brehon of this kingdom,' she reminded him softly.

'It is not my place to comment, lady, but I am sure that you would deal fairly with this. Personally, I could never understand why a man would nurse such malice all these years. Why a mother would turn one son against the other and unleash their hatred. It is worrying that Ernmas, or whatever her name really was, was such a fanatical believer in the old gods.'

'Men and women are never so completely and enthusiastically evil as when they use a deity to justify the unjustifiable,' Fidelma replied softly. 'It is rare our law demands a life rather than seeking compensation or rehabilitation. For such a person as Selbach, the loss of his title, of all his rights, being downgraded to just a *fuidhir*, a non-freeman, which is closest to being a slave, will be punishment enough. He will have no influence left.'

'In which case,' Eadulf intervened, 'one should always remember that grey embers can often be rekindled into fire. I hope Fíthel will be careful not to be too punitive with Cummasach also. Thinking you have extinguished the fire, you might drive it underground, then find it erupts into a raging inferno that cannot be stopped.'

Fidelma gave him a smile of approval. 'At times, you sound like a philosopher, Eadulf.'

'Just an observer of human nature.'

Then without warning Enda suddenly uttered an expletive. They stared at him as he started to rummage in the leather bag at his waist. He looked at their astonished expressions and apologised.

'Your pardon, lady. There was a reason why I came.' He drew out and handed to her a small vellum packet. 'Abbot Cuán asked me to give this packet to you before he returned to Imleach.'

Wonderingly, she took it and found it fastened with leather thongs. She held it in her hands, examining it with a puzzled expression. It was Eadulf who handed her a small knife to cut the thongs. She drew from the packet a piece of embossed vellum. She examined the writing, staring at it as if reading it several times. Then she burst out laughing. It was a deep and genuine amusement. Eadulf and Enda exchanged puzzled glances.

'Something is wrong, lady?' Enda asked after a few moments.

Fidelma had difficulty overcoming her apparent mirth.

'You remember that I once said that Brother Conchobhar would have nominated his successor as Keeper of the Sword because there had to be continuity of that office? We were surprised when no one came forward?'

They waited for her to continue.

'Apparently Brother Conchobhar had left such an instruction. He had left it with Abbot Cuán in the care of the Abbey of Imleach. Cuán had not realised the importance of handing over the document until now.'

'Why not?' Eadulf queried.

'Don't forget Cuán only became abbot and chief bishop of this kingdom less than a year ago. He has only just caught up

with all the matters of his office. The announcement of the
Keeper of the Sword is one of them.'

She started to chuckle again and shake her head
helplessly.

'Well, who is it?' Eadulf demanded when she paused.

'I am appointed the Keeper of the Sword.'

Eadulf and Enda were puzzled by her apparent mirth at the
news, but it was a humour that she could not fully share with
them.